CAPTURED!

Nate gestured for his family to stop, and drew rein. "Hold it while I see what's going on," he said quietly. He slid off his horse and crept to the opening. Dense vegetation cloaked a narrow trail and prevented him from seeing what lay beyond. Cautiously, he stepped into the open, and as he leveled his rifle he remembered to his dismay that he had forgotten to reload it. He had broken the first law of survival.

Above him, leaves shook. Nate looked up and saw two husky warriors balanced on a stout limb.

They had just dropped a net.

Other *Wilderness* Double Editions:
BLACK POWDER/TRAIL'S END
IRON WARRIOR/WOLF PACK
KING OF THE MOUNTAIN/
  LURE OF THE WILD
SAVAGE RENDEZVOUS/BLOOD FURY
TOMAHAWK REVENGE/
  BLACK POWDER JUSTICE
VENGEANCE TRAIL/DEATH HUNT
MOUNTAIN DEVIL/BLACKFOOT MASSACRE
NORTHWEST PASSAGE/APACHE BLOOD
MOUNTAIN MANHUNT/TENDERFOOT
WINTERKILL/BLOOD TRUCE
TRAPPER'S BLOOD/MOUNTAIN CAT

WILDERNESS

THE LOST VALLEY/
MOUNTAIN MADNESS
DAVID THOMPSON

LEISURE BOOKS NEW YORK CITY

Dedicated to Judy, Joshua, and Shane.

A LEISURE BOOK®

February 2001

Published by

Dorchester Publishing Co., Inc.
276 Fifth Avenue
New York, NY 10001

ISBN 0-8439-4837-X

The name "Leisure Books" and the stylized "L" with design are trademarks of Dorchester Publishing Co., Inc.

Printed in the United States of America.

Visit us on the web at www.dorchesterpub.com.

THE LOST VALLEY

Chapter One

The Rocky Mountains were magnificent in the summer. Emerald hills blended into stark ranges capped by pristine snow. Cottonwoods and willows wound along rivers and streams. Firs, spruce, and aspens adorned the higher regions. The land was green, ripe, lush.

Wildlife thrived. White-tailed deer foraged in the lowlands, while their black-tailed cousins roamed the upper slopes. Elk claimed the high meadows but had to share their domain with small herds of shaggy mountain buffalo. Bears were much in evidence. Smaller creatures—chipmunks, squirrels, rabbits, and the like—were everywhere.

Nate King had lived in the mountains for sixteen years, yet he never tired of Nature's wondrous spectacle. Every day brought something new. Each moment was different from all those that went before it.

Nate never missed the dull sameness of city life, the boring routine, the daily grind that broke a person's spirit and made him feel as if he were no more than cogs in a machine. City dwellers were like cattle cooped up in small pens, with nothing to do and nowhere to go. Day in and day out they suffered in a prison of their own making.

Not Nate. Give him the raw wilderness any day. Give him true freedom: being able to do whatever he wanted, whenever he wanted. Give him a life where he was not beholden to anyone for anything, where he need not account to any man for his actions.

These were the thoughts that occupied the mountaineer as he wound up a game trail to a sawtooth ridge and reined up.

He had no idea of the picture he presented. It had been a coon's age since Nate had last seen his reflection in a mirror. If he had bothered to look, he would have seen a tall, broad-shouldered man with piercing blue eyes, raven-black hair, and a cropped beard. A buckskin hunting shirt and leggings covered his powerful frame; moccasins protected his feet. Slanted across his chest were a powder horn and ammo pouch. A possibles bag hung under his left arm. In a beaded sheath on his right hip nestled a Green River knife; on his left hip was a tomahawk. Wedged under his wide leather belt were two flintlocks; cradled in his elbow, a heavy Hawken.

Behind Nate rode his wife, Winona. A full-blooded Shoshone, she wore a fringed dress she had made herself, just as she had crafted her husband's clothes. Her luxurious dark hair hung in neat braids. A necklace of blue beads lent a splash of color. She was lovely by any standard, but she was not one of those women who took on airs over her own beauty. As Nate had once put it, she was as levelheaded as the day was long.

In Winona's wake rode a miniature version of herself. Evelyn, their seven-and-a-half-year-old daughter, was a bundle of energy. She always had a sparkle to her eyes, a bounce to her step. She was their pride and joy.

That did not mean they loved the last rider any less. Zachary King, their son, held his head high as he rode up over the crest. The confidence of youth was in his gaze. An air of invincibility wreathed him like a crown. He was a few months shy of sixteen, full of life, cocky and adventurous. Experience had not yet taught him humility. Hardship had not yet bred wisdom. Now, bringing his bay to a halt, he asked, "Why'd you stop, Pa? I thought you wanted to reach those twin peaks yonder by sundown."

Nate King did not answer right away. The peaks to which his son referred were a good twenty miles to the southwest. Of more immediate interest to him were wispy gray tendrils wafting skyward less than a mile from the ridge. Nodding at them, he responded, "When are you going to learn to always keep your eyes skinned, son? First things first."

Zach flushed with embarrassment. No warrior worthy of the name would miss spotting that smoke. And above all else, more than anything he had ever yearned for, Zach desired to be a full-fledged Shoshone warrior.

The youth had always been partial to his mother's people. Part of each year was spent living with them. Most accepted him for what he was, unlike many whites who tended to look down their noses at 'breeds.

One day soon, Zach planned to take up with the Shoshones permanently. To have a fine lodge of his own, to be accorded a position of honor at tribal councils, these were his goals, his dream.

At the moment, though, Zach mentally kicked himself and said, "Utes, you reckon?"

Nate King would not hazard a guess. It might be, but he had made a point of fighting shy of Ute country. For more years than he cared to recollect, the Utes had tried their darnedest to oust him from the remote valley his family called home. Recently, a fragile truce had been put into effect. But Nate knew there were plenty of warriors who would like nothing better than to count coup at his expense.

Winona regarded the smoke anxiously. Should they run into anyone unfriendly, it would be partly her fault. After all, she was the one who had insisted the family needed to get away from their cabin after being cooped up most of the winter. She was the one who suggested they venture into new territory, that they go somewhere they had never been before.

Here they were, eleven days out. So far as she knew, no white man had ever set foot there. Nor any Shoshones, for that matter.

"We should avoid them, husband," Winona said in her flawless English. It was a great source of pride to her that she spoke the white man's tongue so well. She had a knack, as Nate would say. "They might be hostile."

"I agree." Nate had no hankering to court trouble. The mountains teemed with savage beasts and even more brutal men, two-legged rabid wolves who would slaughter his loved ones without a moment's hesitation.

Little Evelyn rose on her pony for a better look-see. "What if they're nice folks, Ma?" she asked.

Winona looked at her offspring and smiled. *My sweet, darling Blue Flower*, she thought, using her daughter's Shoshone name. *So young. So innocent.* "We cannot take the chance."

"But how do we ever get to meet new people if we don't take chances?" Evelyn asked.

Nate shifted in the saddle. It was the kind of question only a child would ask, only someone who believed the world was made of sugar and spice and everything nice. "There's a time and a place for meeting new folks. This isn't it."

"Why not?"

Logic was no match for innocence, Nate decided. Rather than go into a long-winded spiel about the nature of the human race, he resorted to the one argument every parent could count on. "Because I say so."

"Shucks. That's no reason, Pa."

No, it wasn't, but Nate was not about to admit as much. Reining westward, he started down a steep slope bordered on the right by talus and on the left by a tangled deadfall. "Be mighty careful," he warned.

Accidents were a constant dread. It wouldn't take much. A single misstep, a careless slip, and one of them could well be crippled for life—or worse. It was the one drawback to wilderness living, Nate mused. There were no doctors just around the corner, no convenient hospitals nearby.

The mountain man was consoled somewhat by the fact that accidents were part and parcel of life everywhere, not just in the mountains. How well he remembered that time back in New York City when he had almost been run down by a wagon. And that incident when he had fallen off a pier and nearly been crushed by a passing boat.

Why the Almighty had seen fit to set up things so that accidents could happen, Nate had no idea. There was a lot about life he did not understand, and probably never would. Sometimes it seemed as if the more he learned, the more mysteries cropped up.

Zach King was the last to descend. He happened to glance one last time toward the smoke, and was startled to spot shadowy figures flit through trees west of it. "Pa!" he said, speaking softly even though the distance to the trees was too great for anyone to overhear. When his father turned, Zach pointed.

Nate caught sight of five or six vague shapes as they vanished into the vegetation. He could not distinguish details, but his impression was that they were Indians. "We need to hunt cover," he cautioned.

A stand of pines offered a haven. Dismounting, Nate moved to a vantage point overlooking the narrow valley. The smoke issued from dense growth that flanked a stream. Hills rimmed the valley to the west, and they, in turn, were dwarfed by a snow-crowned range. It was toward a gap in those hills that the figures had been heading.

Zach slid up close to his father. Eager to be of help, he said, "Anything?" And when Nate shook his head, Zach stepped to a tree, leaned his rifle against the trunk, then leaped straight up. As agile as a monkey, he seized a limb, whipped his lean body upward, and climbed.

Nate did not object. His son had the right notion. From high up, Zach would be able to see better.

Winona admired her son's dexterity. Stalking Coyote, as the Shoshones called him, was one of the best riders, swimmers, and climbers of all the boys in the tribe. His prowess was so exceptional that great feats were expected of him in the years to come. A mighty warrior of promise, her uncle rated him.

Evelyn toyed with the idea of climbing the tree, too. She did not see why her brother should have all the fun. But then again, it was a serious situation, and her parents might not take kindly to her acting the fool. So she stayed put.

Zach was careful to climb on the side of the bole opposite the camp. After going as high as he dared, he scanned the heavily forested terrain. There was no sign of the strangers. He could see the campfire, though, and what appeared to be a man lying next to it. He reported as much to his father.

"Awful peculiar" was Nate's assessment. Indians did not make a habit of sleeping in the middle of the day. "Any horses?"

"Not unless they're real well hid."

"All right. Come on down."

Nate faced a dilemma. It would be foolhardy to cross the valley. But going around would delay them a full day, maybe more. Nor did laying low appeal to him. There was no telling when the makers of that fire would douse it and move on. Maybe that very afternoon, maybe in a few days, maybe longer. "I'm going down there," he announced.

"Count me in, Pa," Zach said.

"And Evelyn and I," Winona threw in. "We will not be left behind," she added when her husband opened his mouth as if to object. "Remember. You made the rule that we should never be separated."

"I meant for more than short spells," Nate hedged. Truth was, he had laid down the rule to ensure that none of them, but especially the children, fell prey to any of the thousand and one perils travelers might confront.

"We are all going."

Nate hid a frown by pretending to be interested in the smoke. Winona had used *that* tone, the one she always did when she put her foot down. It would take forever to persuade her to change her mind, barring a miracle. "Let me check by my lonesome," he proposed. "If the coast is clear, I'll signal."

"Who will cover your backside?" asked Zach, who had clambered to the lowest limb. Looping his legs around it, he dangled upside down, winked his sister, then executed an acrobatic flip that resulted in a perfect upright landing. Reclaiming his rifle, he took his place at his father's elbow.

Sometimes, Nate reflected, being a husband and a father was a lot like being a tree. A man had to learn when to bend with the wind. "We'll walk the horses. Evelyn, stick to your mother like her shadow."

"Too bad we don't have blackberries handy, huh, Pa?"

"Blackberries?"

"Then I could smear myself with the juice and be just like a real shadow."

Where kids came up with comments like that, Nate would never know. His stallion's reins in hand, he led the way to the base of the ridge, sticking to dense timber wherever possible. The valley floor was more open. Scattered boulders, random clusters of trees, and tall brush provided some cover.

Nate's nerves were on edge. When a chipmunk burst out of nowhere and commenced chattering in fury at having its domain invaded, he spun and thumbed back the Hawken's hammer. Another fraction of an instant, and he'd have blown it to bits. Calming himself, he advanced, his rifle level.

Zach King tingled with excitement also, but for a reason completely different from his father's. All he could think about was the likelihood of counting coup. Every Shoshone boy shared his ambition. Proving their courage in war was the key to one day being a great leader like Pah-da-hewak-um-da or his brother Moh-woom-hah.

Winona and Evelyn brought up the rear, leading their horses. Like her husband, Winona was armed with a Hawken and a brace of pistols. Thanks to his patient tutelage, she could shoot as well as most free trappers, a rarity among Indian women. He had insisted she learn, for her own sake as well as that of their children.

Several hundred yards from the campsite, in a copse of deciduous trees, Nate raised an arm to signal a halt At a gesture from him, the rest tied their horses to low limbs or saplings. Nate crept to the edge of the next open space. The smoke had turned almost black, and an odd sickly sweet scent filled the air—a scent he felt certain he should recognize.

"Want me to scout it out?" Zach asked hopefully. As a scout he would make first contact, possibly draw first blood.

"You're to cover me, remember?" Nate said testily. His son's thirst for glory had not escaped his notice, and he could not say in all honestly that he entirely approved. Oh, he realized why Zach was so het up to prove himself. As an adopted Shoshone, Nate had likewise adopted some of their customs. But counting coup was not one he subscribed to. Bloodshed, in his estimation, was never worthy of praise. He had seen too much of it to ever glorify it.

"Not a peep out of anyone," Nate advised as he cat-footed forward. The sweet smell grew stronger, reminding him, strangely enough, of the first buffalo surround he had been on, of the cloying odor that rose from the scores of butchered animals afterward. A disturbing premonition came over him, and his gut formed into a knot.

Among a bunch of willows, Nate motioned for his family to hunker. "Stay here. I'll holler if it's safe."

"But, Pa—" Zach began.

Nate's glare silenced him. Silently, the big mountain man glided closer. He was an arrow's flight from the flickering flames when he heard a low, wavering groan. Someone was in immense agony. A little farther, a horse nickered, a feeble whinny, barely audible. Threading through cottonwoods, Nate came to the clearing where the camp had been set up. An overturned rack of dried elk meat explained why the Indians had been there.

His initial impression was that someone had traipsed around the clearing painting patches of grass and some of the surrounding growth with bright red paint. But of course, it wasn't paint.

It was blood.

Chapter Two

A more ghastly spectacle was hard to imagine. It was one of the most horrible scenes of rampant bloodletting Nate King had ever witnessed, rank butchery of the worst order. Stunned by the sheer magnitude of the slaughter, he surveyed the carnage, piecing together what had happened.

The victims were Utes. A hunting party of ten had been in the valley a couple of days, judging by the number of strips on the giant spilled meat rack. They had slain several elk, carved the carcasses up, and hung the meat to dry.

The attack must have come swiftly, taking them completely by surprise. Nate based his conclusion on the fact that most had fallen without a weapon in hand. A bow lay next to one man, a war club was clutched in the stiff fingers of a second, while a third warrior had gone down swinging a knife. The rest were sprawled in gory displays of violent death, their hands empty even though knives rested in sheaths on their hips or bows and quivers were slung over their backs.

Since the fire had not yet gone out, Nate reckoned that the attack had taken place sometime during the early-morning hours, perhaps at daybreak. Maybe only a few of the Utes had been up, the rest struck down as they leaped to their feet.

But struck down by whom? That was the question. Nate warily emerged from concealment, pivoting to the right and the left, ready to blast anything that moved. His scalp prickled as he stared close up at the grisly handi-work of their attacker. He realized that he had it all wrong. It wasn't so much *who* as it was *what*.

Nothing human could have inflicted the wounds Nate saw on the nearest warrior. His chest had been ripped wide open, the flesh peeled back like the skin of an or-ange, the ribs exposed. Half the bones were shattered, the white spikes jutting obscenely. His left arm had been sev-ered at the shoulder and was nowhere in the vicinity.

As Nate edged closer, he saw that the warrior's innards had been partially devoured. It churned his stomach. Fighting the queasiness, he bent down. On the warrior's thigh were four scarlet furrows. Claw marks they were, but unlike any Nate was familiar with. And he knew every animal that inhabited the wild.

Cats, wolves, bears, they all had five claws. Granted, sometimes the smallest claw would not show. But bear claws left wide gashes, and these were slender. Wolf claws dug shallow, but these were deep. Painter claws were thin and they dug deep, rending flesh neatly, as knives would. In this instance, the claws had ripped rag-ged grooves.

Bewildered, Nate went on. His horror mounted when he discovered that one of the bodies was that of a boy not much older than Zach. The young Ute was on his stomach, blank eyes wide, tongue lolling. Something had torn his back open from the shoulder blades to the hip, tearing out his spine in the process.

Involuntarily, Nate shivered. Cold fingers rubbed across his skin, or seemed to, and he erupted in goose bumps. Just then a burning branch in the fire crackled loudly, causing him to jump.

Angry at himself, Nate firmed his grip on the Hawken and moved to the middle of the clearing. The bodies he passed all bore similar terrible wounds. One man had no head, and the stump of the warrior's neck bore clear teeth marks. Again Nate leaned down.

Grizzly teeth were broad and strong, designed for crunching. Wolves had teeth capped with sharp points, for cutting. Painter teeth were long and razor sharp, perfect for slicing and shredding. Whatever had slain the Utes had teeth that combined all those traits, and more. They were broad at the base, long and slightly curved, with thin points. A vicious combination, ideal for hooking into prey and ripping it to ribbons.

As Nate straightened, he beheld a clear track, an impression left by the creature responsible in a puddle of blood. His breath caught in his throat. "It can't be!" he exclaimed in a whisper. "It just can't!"

The print was twice as long as his own, longer even than that of a grizzly. But where a grizzly's was broad and flat, this was narrow, exceedingly so. He thought that he could make out the faint outline of a fifth claw, but he could not be sure.

Among the trapping fraternity, Nate was regarded as one of the best trackers. That said a lot, considering that the mountaineers, as they were fond of calling themselves, had to be skilled at reading sign in order to make a living at their trade. Even among the Shoshones, Nate's ability was envied.

Nate could identify any animal by its track. From the smallest to the biggest, from chipmunks to buffalo, he had memorized the traits of each. So it was another jolt to discover that the print in front of him had been left by something totally alien, by an animal he had never encountered, by something out of a lunatic's worst nightmare.

A low groan reached Nate's ears. Whirling, he studied the bodies and was surprised when one feebly twitched—surprised because the Ute in question should, by rights, be dead. The man's torso had been rent every which way. Strands of skin were all that was holding him together.

Nate hurried over. The warrior's eyes were open. A spark of life shone in them as Nate sank onto a knee. "I am a friend," he said in the Ute language. He was not as fluent in it as he was in the Shoshone tongue and several others, but he could get by.

The man's mouth moved. His tongue flicked out, wetting his dry lips. "Grizzly Killer?" he gasped.

The Shoshones, the Flatheads, the Crows, the Utes, all knew Nate by that name. It had been bestowed on him years before by a Cheyenne after Nate barely survived a clash with a fierce silvertip. "I am," the trapper confirmed.

The warrior reached up and weakly gripped Nate's sleeve. "You are friend to Two Owls."

"Yes." Two Owls was an Ute chief Nate had befriended many moons before, and was largely responsible for the current truce.

"I am Red Feather. Remember me?"

Nate's brow furrowed. The man's face was somewhat familiar, now that he thought about it. "Did we meet when I visited Two Owls at his village?" he prompted.

"I am his brother."

It came back to Nate in a rush of vivid memory. Two Owls had four brothers, and one night they had been invited to a feast in his honor. Red Feather had been rather aloof, never saying much. Nate had chalked it up

to the abiding mistrust the Utes had for whites in general.
"I remember you."

The warrior's fingers dug into the mountain man's
brawny arm. "Please, Grizzly Killer. Save him."

"Save who?" Nate replied, thinking the man must be
delirious. "I am sorry. The rest of your band are all
dead."

"My son. Find him. Take him to Two Owls."

Nate surveyed the clearing once more. No one else
showed a trace of life. Red Feather was the sole survivor.
"Rest. I will bring water and—"

"No!" the Ute declared, his voice thick with emotion.
"Please." With a monumental effort, he rose onto an
elbow, clinging to Nate for support. "I saw them take
him."

"Who?"

"The others. The People of the Mist."

"I have never heard of a tribe by that name." Nate
tried to pry the man's fingers loose so he could gently
lower the warrior. It was common knowledge that a person's mind played tricks on them at the end. They saw
things that were not there, they heard voices no one else
could.

Red Feather would not let go. "Please," he begged
yet again, passion restoring some of the color to his
cheeks. "Promise me, Grizzly Killer. Promise me you
will save Nevava."

Running Fox, Nate mentally translated as he at last
succeeded in freeing his arm and slowly eased the Ute
to the ground. "Be still, friend. I—"

Desperation lent the distraught father extra strength.
Suddenly clawing at Nate's hunting shirt, he practically
wailed, "Promise me!"

The heartfelt appeal stirred Nate in the depths of his
soul. It was a plea from one warrior to another, from one
father to another. "I promise," he pledged. Hardly were

the words out of his mouth before Red Feather stiffened, exhaled loudly, then sagged, as limp as a wet rag. The spark of life faded from his eyes, and the last word that passed his lips was the name of his son.

"Nevava."

Nate slowly rose. Plainly, Red Feather had loved his son as much as Nate loved Zach. Mightily moved, he coughed to clear a lump in his throat. "I'll do what I can," he vowed to the corpse. Which might be awfully little. He had no idea who the People of the Mist were, or where to find their territory. Remembering the vague figures spotted earlier, he walked toward the west end of the encampment. A low bank marked the boundary of a shallow stream, its surface shimmering in the sunshine.

A nicker brought Nate up short. He had forgotten about the one he had heard a while before. Southwest of the camp lay more than a dozen horses in the same state as their former owners. Bellies had been cut open, spilling intestines and other organs. Legs had been broken like so much kindling. Throats had been torn apart, drenching the animals and the grass, forming red pools linked by trickling rivulets. Already a legion of flies buzzed thick and heavy, drawn to the feast by an unseen force.

A sorrel still lived. Once it had been a splendid mount. Now its coat had been raked repeatedly by iron claws. Huge jaws had taken enormous bites from its haunches. Crimson froth flecked its mouth, and every breath wheezed from its ruptured lungs like a bellows. Yet it clung tenaciously to life, as did all living things. Its eyes swiveled as the trapper walked over.

Nate could not stand to see the poor horse suffer. It was beyond help, so there was only one thing to do. Sliding a pistol from under his belt, he cocked the flint-lock and touched the muzzle to the animal's head.

The horse looked at him. Nate swore that it knew, that

it sensed what he was going to do. It gazed at the blue vault of sky, as if for a last glimpse before the end. When Nate squeezed the trigger, the pistol boomed, spewing smoke and lead. The shot was true.

Sighing, Nate promptly reloaded. It was the first important lesson his mentor, Shakespeare McNair, had taught. Never leave a gun unloaded. To do so invited trouble.

Going to the stream, Nate examined the bank. Fresh footprints were proof that the figures he had glimpsed had indeed crossed and gone to the west. He counted six sets of tracks, five belonging to grown men, one set belonging to a boy of ten or twelve.

"Nevava," Nate said aloud. Evidently Red Feather had not been delirious. The People of the Mist, whoever they were, had taken the Ute's son. Nate pondered, wondering what link, if any, there was between the mysterious new tribe and the calamity that befell the hunting party. The grotesque tracks, the claw and teeth marks, they all pointed to an unknown creature of incredible size and power. Could it be a beast under their control? The notion seemed far-fetched. But another lesson Nate had learned was to never take anything for granted.

A hint of movement brought Nate around in a twinkling. Winona, Evelyn, and Zach were crossing the clearing, the three of them in a collective daze.

Winona could not believe what she was seeing. This was worse than the time the Blackfeet massacred a band of her people, worse than the havoc wrought by a rampaging grizzly. She held Evelyn close to her bosom so the girl could not see the worst of it.

Zach was flabbergasted. In his short life he had tangled with bears, buffalo, and wolverines. He had fought Piegans, Bloods, and murderous whites. He had seen plenty of dead people, but nothing to match this. Coming on a track of the brute responsible, he gawked in mingled awe

22

and dread. What sort of monster could do such a thing? he asked himself.

Evelyn was glad her mother had averted her face. The sickening scene had made her queasy. One warrior in particular. He had been shorn nearly in half, the upper part of his body connected to the lower section by a strip of flesh barely as wide as her hand.

"What are you doing here?" Nate demanded. "I told you to stay put."

"We heard a shot," Winona answered absently, distracted by the slaughter. "What happened to these men, husband?"

"I don't rightly know," Nate admitted. Briefly, he related the sequence of events, concluding with "I've always been a man of my word. Which means I'm obligated to honor my pledge to Red Feather."

"Fine by me, Pa," Zach said, excited at the prospect of counting coup on Nevava's abductors. Equally thrilling was the possibility of killing whatever had wiped out the Utes. His standing among the Shoshones would rise immensely. "When do we start?"

"We?" Nate repeated. "I'm the one going after the boy. You and your mother will return to our cabin."

Winona and Zachary both said "No!" simultaneously. Mother and son swapped glances, then Winona took a step forward, saying, "You would abandon us here? What if more People of the Mist are in this area?"

"Or the critter that tore this bunch to shreds?" Zach interjected, upset that his father would even think of denying them the right to go along. Fate had given them a golden chance to reap untold glory. They would be fools to waste it.

Nate had anticipated objections and was set to stand firm, but he hesitated, bothered by the truth of their assertions. No matter what he did, he was taking a gamble. So what if the tracks of the People of the Mist and those of the creature pointed westward. "I guess the only thing for me to do is to take all of you home, then come back alone."

"It would take over half a moon," Winona said. "The trail would be cold by then." Something else occurred to her. "Afternoon thunderstorms are common this time of year. One might erase the tracks." Shaking her head, she stated, "To save the boy, we must go on now. Together. As a family. As we always do."

"I agree with Ma," Zach said, just to throw in his two bits' worth.

Evelyn did not comment. Being the youngest, she was used to not having her opinion asked, so she seldom gave it. If someone *had* asked, though, she would have told them that she would rather be with both her folks—and, yes, even with her rascally brother—than anywhere else.

Affection and common sense waged a war in Nate King's heart, and affection won. It would always win. For the mountain man was not one of those who could easily turn his back on those he cared for most in the world.

He had known men like that back in New York City and elsewhere. Coldhearted husbands who could go off carousing at cards or frolicking with tavern wenches for days on end, with nary a twinge of regret. Men who would up and cut out whenever the mood was right, not caring one whit how their families fared while they were gone.

"A strong family, a family that endures, is one that sticks together through thick and thin." Those were his very words, expressed on a number of occasions.

So now Nate King swallowed hard, prayed he was not making the worst mistake of his life, and announced, "I know when I'm licked. We'll cut out after the People of the Mist and try to catch them before they get very far."

Only Zach whooped for joy.

Chapter Three

The farther they went, the more mystified Nate King grew.

When it became apparent that the People of the Mist did not have horses hidden near the camp and were traveling on foot, Nate waxed confident that he would overtake them quickly. Two days at the most, he figured. But the mysterious warriors held to a pace few could rival. Not only that, they always stuck to the roughest terrain; picking a route that taxed horses to the limit. Nearly impassable timber, the steepest of slopes, over ravines and through gorges, the People of the Mist did not miss a trick.

It had to be intentional, Nate decided. Either they knew they were being followed, which was highly unlikely, or they had developed the habit of always making it ungodly hard for possible enemies to shadow them.

If they were that wary, it might explain why few tribes had ever heard of them. Nate found it mighty strange that no one had mentioned them before. At one time or another he had visited every friendly tribe within four hundred miles of his homestead, yet not once had anyone alluded to the People of the Mist.

It was all the more strange when he considered that Indians had refined conversation to a fine art. They liked nothing better than to sit around a toasty fire in the evening swapping stories. Accounts of battles, coups earned, heroic deeds, tragedies that befell hapless individuals, anything and everything was ripe to be discussed. Unusual happenings were a favorite topic. So why, then, had no one ever brought up this mysterious new tribe?

The small band was on a beeline to the southwest. Adding to the mystery was the fact that the creature responsible for making worm food of the Utes was *also* heading to the southwest. It could not be mere happenstance.

The tracks of the People of the Mist and the creature often overlapped, and Nate could not determine if the People of the Mist were following the creature or if the creature was following them.

Yet another curious aspect were the footprints of the warriors. As every frontiersman was aware, no two tribes fashioned their moccasins exactly alike. Usually it was possible to peg the makers of any set of tracks by the characteristics of the prints. The Arapahos, for instance, favored broad-soled footwear, while the Sioux went in for soles with narrow toes and heels.

The prints of the People of the Mist showed that they wore moccasins totally different from any other, but oddly so. The soles were narrow their entire length, which told him that the warriors had extremely narrow feet. In addition, the soles left odd circular impressions every few inches along the outer edge, as if they had knobs of some sort on the bottom. Which made no sense.

As for the creature, it held to the same tireless pace as

the People of the Mist. Several times, where it crossed soft earth, Nate discovered a long furrow. At first he thought the creature must be dragging something. Then the truth hit him. The thing had a tail, a *big* tail.

It was conclusive evidence, as if any more were needed, that the beast was a monstrosity, so out of the ordinary, so different from the wildlife Nate was accustomed to, that he could not begin to guess what it might be.

Five days passed. Five days of hard riding, of being in the saddle from sunup to sunset, of spending restless nights and having to make do with pemmican and jerky instead of freshly killed game.

Nate was used to such hardship. Working a trapline year in and year out for over a decade had tempered his muscles into living steel and rendered his will as rock-hard as his whipcord body.

Trapping was not for the weak or the timid. A man had to go off into country rife with hostile Indians and roving predators. He had to contend with the worst of weather. With bitter wind and stinging cold. With water so frigid that standing in it too long induced frostbite, which might end up costing a few toes or part of a foot.

His days were spent slogging through creeks and rivers to set half a dozen traps, or to check on those previously placed. Doing so in itself was a chore. A trapper had to locate a choice spot, then pry the jagged jaws of a trap apart, carefully set them, and just as carefully lower the trap under the surface. The idea was for the beaver to mosey along, catch a whiff of the castorium that the trapper applied to a leaf or twig above the trap, and blunder into it.

Then came the really hard part. The trapper had to lift the heavy beaver out. Considering that most of the critters weighed upward of fifty pounds, that they were waterlogged and mired fast in the steel jaws of the

Newhouse, a day's work often left a trapper so exhausted that he eagerly crawled under the covers as soon as the sun went down, only to wake up at the crack of dawn to repeat the whole ordeal all over again.

No, trapping was not for the puny. Thanks to his years of toil, Nate could endure hardships most men could not. Picture the harshest of conditions, and he had survived them. He could go for days with little food or rest, and often had.

So the pursuit of the People of the Mist did not bother him in the least. But his family was another matter. Winona had demonstrated time and again that she could hold her own under the worst of circumstances, and Zach was willing to endure any hardship to prove he was becoming a man. But Evelyn, tiny Evelyn, had never gone this long with so little rest and nourishment.

Nate fretted about her constantly. He saw the weariness in her face, and he admired how she gamely rode on, mile after mile, day after day, without complaint, although she was so stiff and sore that in the evening she grimaced whenever she stood up or sat down.

After five days, Nate was inclined to call it quits. He had done his best, but the People of the Mist were too crafty. Catching them would take much longer than he had anticipated. His daughter was at the limit of her endurance, and the horses were flagging.

One more day, Nate told himself. He would give it another twenty-four hours, and if fortune did not smile on them, if they did not catch sight of a campfire or the People of the Mist themselves, he would recommend that they turn around and head home.

Promise or no promise, Nate would not put any of his family at risk. Evelyn's health was more important than his word.

Then came the sixth day. It dawned crisp and clear, as had the others. The morning was spent winding down a series of heavily forested slopes, which was no different from their activity on any other day.

But along about noon, as they neared the bottom of a slope, the pines thinned, then abruptly ended. Before their wondering eyes unfolded a startling vista of arid buttes and mesas and canyons. Hardly a tree grew anywhere. The scant grass was dry and withered. A few stunted shrubs had managed to take root here and there. It was a desolate wasteland, normally shunned by whites and Indians alike.

Yet to Nate's amazement, the tracks of the People of the Mist *and* those of the creature had trekked off across it, into the heart of the foreboding unknown. Reining up, he rose in the stirrups. Nothing moved out there, not so much as a bird or a lizard. "I don't like it," he announced.

"We cannot stop," Winona said. "Think of the Ute boy." Unslinging the water skin from her saddle, she opened it and held it out for Evelyn to take a drink.

"I'm thinking of us," Nate responded, grimly surveying the desolation. There was hardly any cover. If they were caught in the open, they could be picked off one by one.

Zach fidgeted and hefted his Hawken. "I don't mind going on if Ma doesn't," he commented, afraid his chance to count coup was slipping away. Each day he grew more and more impatient to catch the other party.

Evelyn grinned at her father. "It's fine by me, Pa," she chimed in.

Always the sunny one, Nate mused. *Always ready to do her part*. "Thank you, princess." He fibbed to spare her feelings. "But it's the horses I'm concerned about. They're tuckered out. And from the look of things, finding water from here on out will be like pulling a hen's teeth."

Giggling, Evelyn said, "Pa, chickens don't have teeth. Even I know that."

Nate faced his wife. "We can rest here until morning, then head back. What do you say?"

"I have already told you. There is the boy to think of. Would you give up if it were Stalking Coyote or Blue Flower? No, of course not. We must go on." Winona held up a hand when Nate opened his mouth to speak. "I know what you will say. You are concerned about us. You do not want us to be harmed. I share your sentiments, husband, but I will not let them stop us from doing what is right. No one else knows the Ute boy was taken captive. Unless we save him, his fate is sealed." She paused. "Is that the right expression?"

Nate nodded, peeved that once again she was relying on pure logic to thwart his wishes. Women were like that. Whether red or white, they always gave the impression of being highly emotional, of wearing their hearts on their sleeves, as it were. But the truth was that they had minds like steel traps. Deep down, they were as logical as men. No, they were more so—as any married man would confirm.

"Then we're pushing on?" Zach asked. In his mind's eye he saw himself riding into the village of his mother's people, new scalps slung across his horse for everyone to admire. Or else with the hide of the strange creature wrapped around his shoulders like a royal robe. Wouldn't that impress the Shoshones no end!

"We are," Winona said, clucking to her mare before Nate could object. Yes, she sincerely appreciated his devotion. But she would not allow him to compromise his ideals for their sakes.

Of all the men she had ever met, Nathaniel King was one of the most noble. No one had been more shocked than she when she realized she was falling in love with him. How ironic, in light of the interest in her by virtually

30

every unattached warrior in her village. She had been the one woman they most wanted, the ''prize catch,'' as Nate once phrased it.

And she picked a white man.

Small wonder hard feelings resulted, and a leading warrior later tried to tear her from Nate against her will.

Winona dispelled the bitter memory with a toss of her head. She had no regrets over her decision. Nate was the one for her, the ''love as deep as a chasm, as wide as the heavens'' her mother had always talked about.

That they were husband and wife was a minor miracle. They had been drawn together over vast gulfs, gulfs they had to surmount in order to be united. A race gulf, a culture gulf, a gulf of many miles.

She was proud of her man. Proud of his love for her, of his love for their children, of the hard work he did to provide for them. She was most proud that he was not like some other husbands she had heard about. Men who treated their women worse than they treated their horse or their dog.

Nate had always treated her with the utmost respect. True, they had spats from time to time, but he never ranted and raved, never tried to ''put her in her proper place,'' as the husband of a cousin always did. He regarded her as an equal partner and valued her insights. What more could any woman ask of a man?

The clatter of hooves alongside the mare brought an end to Winona's reverie. ''Are you mad at me?'' she bluntly asked.

''I just hope you're right,'' Nate answered with a meaningful look at their daughter and son.

''We are doing what we must. Come what may, my love, we will live by our decision and accept the consequences.''

As he had so many times in the past, Nate marveled at her command of English. He could speak Shoshone, but nowhere near as eloquently as she did his language. Part of her mastery, he suspected, stemmed from the small library he had painstakingly collected, books by James Fenimore Cooper and others, each as precious as gold.

Nate had always loved to read. It inspired him, transported his imagination to places he had never been, taught him about aspects of life he otherwise might not have paid attention to. Cooper, Scott, Byron, Shakespeare, they all had something to impart, and impart they did, each and every night. It was a family custom that after the evening meal he would read aloud for half an hour or more.

Naturally, Winona had picked up words even most trappers rarely used. Shakespeare McNair liked to say that listening to her was the next best thing to reading the bard, a high tribute from a man whose fondness for the English playwright had earned him his nickname.

"Pa, what's that up ahead?"

Zach's query made Nate realize that he had let his mind stray, a dangerous practice in a land where death struck fast and furious, without warning. Ahead was a bluff. A hundred yards to the north of it, prone in the dust, was a reddish object. It was not a plant, not a rock. Another twenty yards and Nate recognized outspread limbs and the outline of a human head. "Hold up," he directed.

Spurring the stallion, Nate moved in for a closer look. After the carnage at the clearing, he knew what to expect. The stink of rotting flesh was awful. It unnerved the stallion. The horse balked, and he had to goad it onward.

A halo of dry blood framed the victim's head. Half the flesh was gone from his rib cage. So was most of his right thigh. Something had feasted well at his expense.

The stallion grew more agitated. So much so that Nate drew rein, slid off, and continued on foot.

The Lost Valley

At last he had found one of the People of the Mist. The man was tall and lean in build. A hawkish nose dominated a pear-shaped face with high cheekbones, a firm mouth, and a strong jawbone. The hair hung loose, falling past his shoulders at the back but clipped just below his ears on the sides and just above his eyebrows in front.

His clothes consisted of a long-sleeved shirt, baggy pants, high moccasins with quilled heel straps, and a wide headband similar to those Nate had seen worn by Apaches. Around his neck was a bear-claw necklace. No weapons were on him, but it was evident he had sold his life dearly. His torn shirt and pants were soaked with blood. On his forearms were many bite marks.

Nate inspected the moccasins. Thick leather cord had been used to sew on the soles. Every few inches along the edge the cord had been knotted, which accounted for the unusual impressions Nate had observed in the tracks.

It was no mystery what had slain the man. Dotting the bare earth were more of the gigantic tracks Nate had been following for days. He backtracked, reading the spoor as he might read print in a book.

Apparently the creature had been ahead of the warriors all along. Either it had stopped to rest in the shadows at the base, or it had deliberately lurked there, waiting for them to catch up. The onslaught had been swift, catching them off guard. They had scattered, but the victim had not been quick enough. He had paid with his life.

Nate hunkered beside a perfect set of huge prints. "What in the world are you?" he said uneasily. The Utes, the People of the Mist, no one was able to stop it. He lowered a hand to run a finger over a claw mark.

"Pa! Look out!"

Zach's cry snapped Nate erect. From out of the shadows had hurtled another warrior, a war club upraised to strike.

Chapter Four

Nate King brought up the Hawken just in time to block the blow. The impact jolted him backward, and his right foot snagged on the dead man. He lost his balance and fell, landing on his back. The club arced down again, but Nate rolled to the left and heard it thud into the corpse. Dimly, he was aware of Winona, Zach, and Evelyn flying to his aid. He had to dispatch his attacker before they were close enough to be harmed.

Surging onto his knees, Nate warded off another blow. Briefly, the club and the rifle barrel locked together. He saw that it was a type of club foreign to him, different from those used by the Blackfeet, the Crows, and the Shoshones. This was a curved affair about as long as a man's arm, pale brown except for black ritual markings, with thin edges for hacking rather than bashing.

The warrior holding it had the same size and build as the dead man. His clothes were the same style, only his shirt was red and he did not wear a bear-claw necklace.

His face was not as broad, his eyes aglow with battle lust.

With a wrench the warrior tore the club free. Side-stepping, he sheared it at Nate's neck. Nate countered, but the rifle was jarred from his grasp when the warrior jerked the club to the right. In sheer reflex Nate threw himself at the man's legs, tackling him. Nate brought the warrior crashing down and quickly scrambled onto the man's chest to pin him. But the warrior was as strong as a panther and as slippery as a wet weasel. Bucking upward, he dislodged Nate, then twisted and swung the club.

Nate whipped both arms up, catching hold of the man's wrist a split second before the club could connect. Grappling, they rose onto their knees. Nate was bigger and heavier and more powerful across the shoulders. Gradually, he forced the man back, bending him nearly in half. Sweat broke out on the warrior's forehead and he sputtered from his herculean effort, but he could not tear loose, could not bring the club to bear.

Unexpectedly shifting, Nate shoved the warrior onto his back and flung his body across the man's upper torso and arms. Now the warrior *was* pinned. He heaved and thrashed, but Nate held on fast.

"Give up," the mountain man said. "I don't want to harm you if I can avoid it."

Evidently the warrior did not understand English. He renewed his struggles, and had nearly succeeded in slipping out from underneath when a rifle barrel flashed out of nowhere and jammed against his cheek. The warrior froze.

"Want me to shoot him for you, Pa?" Zach asked eagerly, thinking how great the man's hair would look hanging from a coup stick.

Nate glanced up, appalled by the blood lust his son's expression registered. Something was happening to his

35

son, something he did not like. They needed to sit down and have a long heart-to-heart talk. But this was hardly the right time or place. "No," he said sternly. "He's not our enemy."

Winona stepped into view, her rifle leveled. The warrior saw her and his brow knit. He said a few words in a tongue she did not understand. She shook her head to signify as much, and he frowned in disappointment.

Nate slowly rose, yanking the club from the man's grip. It was surprisingly light in weight. Casting it aside, he drew a flintlock and moved several strides back. "Let's try to communicate with him," he proposed.

The warrior sat up, glanced sadly at his slain companion, then rested his arms on his knees and clamped his mouth in sullen defiance.

"Do you savvy my language?" Nate asked. Eliciting no reaction, he reverted to Shoshone, asking the same question. He tried the Flathead tongue, the Crow. Tucking the pistol under an arm, he employed sign language. It was his last resort, and he was highly hopeful it would work. Nearly every tribe knew sign. At least, those who dwelled on the plains and in the eastern half of the Rockies did. During his trek to the Pacific Ocean he had learned that many in the far northwest woods did not.

The warrior stared blankly as the trapper's fingers weaved patterns in the air.

"He doesn't savvy, Pa," Zach noted the obvious. "Or else he's faking it."

"Why would he?" Nate held the pistol and mulled over what to do next. Squatting, he pointed at the warrior, then drew a crude outline of a human figure in the dirt. Pointing at the dead man, he did the same. Next he drew three more, one for each of the other members of the band. Finally, he drew a small boy and looked expectantly at their captive.

The warrior stared at the drawings, at Nate. He spoke

at length. When Nate shook his head and shrugged, the warrior jabbed a finger westward a few times, said a few words, then drew a rectangular shape in the dirt with what appeared to be a door at the bottom.

Nate gathered that the man had told him the boy was being taken to their village. But the shape of the structure was puzzling. Most Indian lodges were either conical te-pees or domelike wigwams. "How far?" he asked, for-getting himself. To demonstrate, he pointed at the sun and swept his arm across the sky from east to west.

The warrior caught on right away. He made three sweeps, then raised his arm from the eastern horizon to midway in the sky.

"Three and a half days is not much," Winona said. "We have come this far. We should see it through."

"I could go on alone from here," Nate offered, know-ing full well he was wasting his breath. "You can wait back up in the trees by the last stream we passed. It would take a load off my mind knowing you were safe."

"Where you go, my husband, we all go."

There were occasions, Nate reflected, when women were the most exasperating creatures on God's green earth. They were willing to abide by logic only when it was *their* logic that was being followed. And they had the gall to call men stubborn!

Turning to the warrior, Nate touched his own chest and said his name several times. He indicated each member of his family and did likewise. When he was done, he pointed at the man and waited.

"Pahchatka," the warrior declared, smacking his ster-num.

It was a crucial moment. Their captive had grown more at ease once it dawned on him that they were not going to kill him outright. Now Nate picked up the war club and handed it to him.

Pahchatka could not hide his astonishment. Accepting

the weapon, he studied each of them in turn, focusing at last on Nate. His mouth curled upward. He put a finger on his chest and drew the outline of a heart, then closed his fingers around the imaginary organ.

"Lower your guns," Nate directed, doing so himself. Wedging the flintlock under his belt, he extended an arm. Pahchatka looked at his hand a few moments, then gripped it and let himself be hauled erect. Nate reclaimed his rifle, contriving not to turn his back just in case he had misjudged.

Winona did as her husband bid, but she was nervous about arming the warrior when their children were so near. To be safe, she did not let down the hammer, and she made a mental note to never let the man out of her sight.

Zach was fit to be tied. They had wasted an ideal opportunity to count coup. It aggravated him that his father was being so friendly. That did not bode well for the future, when they caught up with those who had stolen the Ute boy. Based on the overtures his pa had made, they would attempt to get the boy back without bloodshed—without counting coup.

"Son, fetch the horses," Nate instructed. As Zach ran off, Nate moved to where prints of the mystery beast had not been trampled in their struggle. Dipping a toe onto one, he said, "What is this critter?" accenting his question with an arch of his eyebrows.

Pahchatka grew somber. "Kachina," he said, and to Nate's amazement, he trembled slightly from head to toe.

Nate sorely desired to learn more, but the language barrier handicapped him. "How big is it?" he inquired. Naturally, the warrior regarded him quizzically, so Nate held his hands at arm's length to suggest size.

Comprehending immediately, Pahchatka walked a few yards and scraped a short furrow with the tip of his club. Pivoting, he took ten precise paces to the north, then scraped another furrow. Swinging around, he held out his arms as Nate had done.

"Impossible," Nate said. Yet he could not deny the evidence of his own eyes. The tracks hinted at immense bulk; now Pahchatka had confirmed it. But *thirty feet*? That was four times the length of a grizzly, three times the size of a bull buffalo. And what was he to make of the long tail? "What kind of monster are we dealing with?" he breathed.

"Maybe it is something from the Old Time," Winona said.

"The what?"

"The time when Coyote and his woman gave birth to the first people. The time when many strange things roamed the land."

Nate was familiar with the Shoshone account of Creation, and their belief in the hereafter. Initially, it had surprised him to learn they had a strong belief in life after death. Most whites branded them as heathens, little better than animals, a prejudice that had tainted his outlook until he learned differently.

According to their legends, the father of their people was called Coyote, the Trickster. But the two branches of the Shoshones could not agree on exactly how Coyote brought them into being.

The Shoshones who lived west of the Rockies, called "Diggers" by the mountain men, believed that in ages past Coyote formed the first man and woman from clay, then breathed life into them.

The Shoshones who lived in the mountains, Winona's people, held that Coyote had married a wild woman who killed and ate anyone who came to her lodge. By the power of the special blue stone Coyote always carried, he tamed this wild girl, and the fruits of their union brought into being the firstborn of all the tribes in the world.

David Thompson

The Shoshones had other tales of those ancient times. Tales no sane man would credit. Tales of beasts with skin as thick as a knight's armor, of birds without feathers that had wingspans wide enough to blot out the sun, of shaggy animals twice as big as buffalo but with shiny tusks instead of black horns and noses like writhing snakes.

There were other things. Horrid things, things the Shoshones talked about only in whispers and never in the presence of children.

Was this one? Nate wondered as Pahchatka walked toward them. Could it be possible that some of the old tales had a basis in fact? He dismissed the notion for the time being and set about learning something else. Pinching his cheek, he said, "White man," over and over. Then, going to his wife, he rubbed her cheek, saying, "Shoshone."

For once Pahchatka was at a loss. Nate had to repeat himself several times, then point at the sun, at the bluff, and at a rock, and say each of their names, before the warrior grinned and declared proudly while pinching his own cheek, "Anasazi."

Nate had never heard of them, but then, he had never heard of the Chinooks, the Spokans, or the Wenatchis before his trek to the Pacific with Shakespeare McNair. McNair claimed there were scores of isolated tribes scattered in regions so remote that no white man had ever visited them. The Anasazis must be one of them.

At that juncture Zach arrived, leading the four horses.

Evelyn mounted without being told to do so. She had not uttered a word since the warrior attacked her father, and she did not feel comfortable around him. Secretly, she wished the man would go away, but she trusted her parents enough to go along with whatever they wanted.

Nate mounted last. He offered a hand to the Anasazi so they could ride double. But Pahchatka recoiled as if

40

he had been slapped. Nate beckoned, smiling to show his peaceful intentions. To no avail. The warrior motioned sharply, refusing. Nate reined the stallion toward him and was stunned when Pahchatka frantically bounded to the west a dozen feet. "What in the world?"

"He is scared of horses," Winona guessed. From her grandfather she had heard of those days long past when her own people first set eyes on them, and the terror horses had inspired. A band of Shoshones had been hunting buffalo far to the south of their usual haunts when they met up with a group of mounted Comanches. While not strictly allies, in the old days the two tribes had traded on occasion. Her grandfather loved to tell of the return of the hunters with two of the wondrous beasts, and the widespread panic it caused. She could remember the wizened oldster laughing uproariously as he related how women screamed and scooped up their bawling children and fled into their lodges, while warriors milled in numb panic.

"How can that be?" Nate was saying. "He must have seen them before. There were horses at the Ute camp."

"But perhaps he does not know what they are."

Nate tried once more. Climbing down, he stroked the stallion to show how tame it was, then smiled and gestured for the Anasazi to do likewise. Pahchatka would have none of it. Muttering, the warrior made repeated signs in the air, as if warding off evil.

Recognizing a lost cause, Nate swung back on and was set to ride off when the reek of the rotting body reminded him of an oversight. Nodding at it, he looked at Pahchatka and gestured as if to say, "What should we do with him?"

The warrior tilted an arm to the heavens. Half a dozen vultures had assembled. Soon more would arrive, and by sunset of the next day the dead man's bones would be virtually stripped bare.

Once Nate would have been incensed by the idea of leaving a man to be consumed by the ugly carrion eaters. That was before he traveled west, before he learned—the hard way—that life in the wild was a never-ending test of wit and brawn, and those who failed the test were seldom given the luxury of a decent burial. As his mentor had once put it, "Dead is dead, young coon. It doesn't make a lick of difference to a lifeless husk if worms and maggots consume it, or if it ends up as what comes out of a buzzard's butt." Crude, yet oh so true.

Pahchatka broke into a steady jog he maintained for hours at a stretch, far longer than Nate could have done. The only other warriors able to duplicate the feat, to his knowledge, were Apaches.

The countryside grew more arid the farther they went. No grass grew, and the stunted bushes vanished. Clouds of dust rose from under the hooves of the horses, clinging to them, getting into their hair, their eyes, even under their clothes.

They never lacked for water. Pahchatka seemed to know where every spring and tank was and arranged it so that each evening they bedded down with a source of refreshing water nearby. For supper they ate roasted lizard or snake, usually caught by the Anasazi.

For four nights and three days they paralleled the tracks of Nevava's abductors. On the fourth morning they were awakened before sunrise by an excited Pahchatka. He insisted they push on right away. It soon became apparent why.

Directly to the west reared a towering mesa. They had first seen it about noon the day before, a reddish stump in the distance that grew and grew and grew. Now, in the pale light of false dawn, Nate was startled to see that the entire lower half of the escarpment was sheathed in a swirling, shimmering mist. "The People of the Mist," he said, understanding what Red Feather had meant at last.

As if in answer, from out of the thick veil wavered a piercing howl.

Chapter Five

The Anasazi drew up short and cocked his head, listening to another howl that rose to a inhuman crescendo, then tapered. Pahchatka hefted his war club and glanced at Nate and Winona. Baring his teeth as would a savage beast, he made slashing movements with his left hand.

His message was clear. Whatever lurked in the mist was dangerous. Nate pointed at the eastern horizon, where a pink tinge heralded a new day. He was content to stay where they were until the sun had risen and burned the mist off. When the Anasazi resumed walking, Nate called his name. Pahchatka watched intently as Nate sought to explain, using hand gestures.

The warrior pointed at the sun, then at the mist. He held his hand at shoulder height and lowered it several times, always stopping at his knees.

Nate was perplexed and looked at Winona. "Do you savvy what he's trying to tell us?"

"No."

The Lost Valley

Again Pahchatka went through his pantomime, only this time he would point at the sun and sweep his arm a bit higher before he held his hand flat and lowered it by degrees until it was at his knees again.

"Beats me all hollow," Nate said.

"Me too, Pa," Zach said. He would never admit as much, but the howls had unnerved him. They were different from those of wolves or coyotes. They were louder, throatier, ripe with menace. Deep inside, they provoked a twinge of unreasoning fear, similar to the fear he'd had of the dark when he was barely old enough to walk. He felt ashamed.

Winona stared thoughtfully at the roiling wall of mist. "I think I have it figured out," she told her husband. "He is telling us that even after the sun rises, the mist never goes completely away."

"Impossible," Nate said. Many a fine morning high in the mountains he had come out of their cabin to see their valley shrouded in mist or fog, but neither ever lasted long. Heat from the rising sun always evaporated them, just as it did the dew that moistened the grass.

Pahchatka said a few words, then moved on, stalking forward like a cat, poised on the balls of his feet, his war club ready to swing.

Nate did not like it one bit. Fighting wild animals he was familiar with was one thing. But the beasts in the mist were as mysterious as the giant creature that had wiped out the Utes. He had no inkling of how big they were, or how strong, or how fierce, and being ignorant of their nature could prove fatal.

A man not only had to know the habits of the wildlife he shared the wilderness with, he had to learn their weaknesses, as well. Many a young would-be trapper, on being charged by a grizzly for the first time, had discovered to his dismay that shooting a grizzly in the head was a waste of lead. So massive were their skulls that bullets invariably glanced off. A grizzly's sole weak spot was behind its humped shoulders, halfway down its body. A ball there stood a good chance of hitting its heart or lungs.

Pahchatka had stopped and was waving them on. Nate hesitated, unwilling to expose his loved ones to unknown peril. If the Anasazi was right about the mist always being there, it made no difference whether they went in now or waited until sunrise. But he could not, in good conscience, lead them farther.

Winona sensed her husband's turmoil. It pleased her that he always thought of their welfare before all else. Unfortunately, sometimes he was too protective. It was wrong of her, she knew, but she could not help feeling that he did not think she was competent enough to deal with whatever situations might arise. And no woman liked for her man to think she could not hold her own. "Keep going," she said. "We have come too far to turn back."

Against his better judgment, Nate clucked to the stallion. No more howls broke the eerie stillness as they neared the shimmering wall, which in itself was profoundly unsettling. A whitish gray, it roiled and writhed as if alive. The Anasazi halted fifteen feet out, squatted, and peered into the veil.

Nate could not see a thing. Up close, the mist was composed of wispy tendrils, always in motion, vaporous snakes that ceaselessly entwined among one another. "Hold on," he said when Pahchatka rose, and the warrior looked back.

Reaching into a parfleche, Nate pulled out a coiled rope. Ordinarily it was for tethering the horses at night. Wheeling the stallion, he moved down the line and gave one end to Zach. "Whatever you do, don't let go,"

"Don't worry, Pa." Zach bent his neck to gaze at the top of the shimmering barrier. It had to be two hundred

The Lost Valley

feet high. Above the mist reared the mesa, a sheer rock wall that gave the illusion of stretching to the clouds. Zach could not say why, but a tremor rippled through his body.

Nate turned the stallion and rode to his daughter, uncoiling the rope as he went along. She smiled at him in her innocent, trusting manner when he came alongside her pony. "Hold up your arms," he said. After she did, he looped the rope once around her waist. "It's so we won't get separated."

"This should be fun," Evelyn said. "It'll be like riding in fog." Sometimes, when her mother took her for morning rides along the shore of the lake near their homestead, they would dash through lingering patches.

"Keep your eyes skinned," Nate advised.

"For what? Those wolves? They don't scare me." Evelyn had seen wolves plenty of times and they had never given her any trouble. Her brother had even raised a wolf cub once. When it grew up, it had gone off to be with its own kind. But she could fondly recall many a winter's evening spent lying on the soft bear rug in front of the fireplace with the wolf snuggled at her side. Blaze, as they called him, had often licked her face and hands, making her giggle. She missed him.

Nate tousled Evelyn's hair and moved to Winona. Bending to lightly kiss her cheek, he whispered, "Watch our little muffin like a hawk."

"Would I do otherwise?" Winona said, taking hold of the rope.

It struck Nate that she was miffed at him, but he did not know why. "We'll keep the horses close together, nose to tail," he stated loudly for the benefit of the rest, and wagged the other end of the rope at the Anasazi.

Pahchatka accepted it, then immediately strode into the mist.

The black stallion pricked its ears. It had heard some-

47

thing in there, something that caused it to prance skittishly. "Steady, big fella," Nate said, patting its neck as he followed the warrior.

Evelyn had been right. Entering the mist was like entering a fog bank. The tendrils were cool, moist, and clinging. Nate swatted a hand at some in front of his face and they parted, only to re-form the very next instant. Swiveling, he could barely see Winona, and absolutely nothing of Evelyn or Zach. "Damn," he swore softly. If something attacked, it would be on them before he could lift a finger.

Nate was at a loss to guess how Pahchatka found his way. The Anasazi traveled unerringly onward, never once faltering or stopping, as sure of himself as would be a person out for a Sunday stroll in a park in New York City.

Winona was equally puzzled, and apprehensive. They had not gone far when a breeze sprang up, faint at first but growing stronger. It was a warm breeze, warm yet oddly dank and strangely sweet, like the smell of a field of flowers on a hot summer's day. She twisted to keep an eye on Blue Flower, whispering, "Are you all right back there?"

"Just fine, Ma."

"And you, Stalking Coyote?"

"Don't worry about me. I can take care of myself," Zach said. Although, truth to tell, he was a bundle of nerves. Being swallowed by the mist was an uncomfortable sensation. He could not see more than an arm's length in any direction, and a warrior could not shoot what he could not see. A soft patter to his left startled him. Was it his imagination, or stealthy footsteps? He opened his mouth to warn his parents, then changed his mind. If it was his imagination, his folks would think he was just plain scared. He couldn't have that.

Nate King became aware of a soft, intermittent sighing

up ahead. He strained his ears to identify the sound but could not. Rustling to his left almost made him rein up. Something was out there, shadowing them. He heard the rasp of claws on stone, heard a low growl that was echoed by another on his right.

"Pahchatka!" Nate whispered. Receiving no response, he twisted to signal his wife. She had her rifle up, pointed into the mist. "See anything?"

Winona shook her head. And even as she did, an indistinct shape materialized, a shadowy specter that was there one moment, gone the next. The glimpse was too fleeting for her to make out what it was.

"Ma?" Evelyn said. She had seen the creature, too. It looked like a wolf to her, a really big wolf. She wished Blaze were there to protect them.

Zach brought his Hawken to his shoulder. His father had taught him never to shoot unless he had a clear target, but he was sorely tempted to fire blindly into the gloom. Twice he had seen a shaggy *thing* flanking them.

Suddenly a bloodcurdling howl rent the mist. Without thinking, Nate reined up. The rope grew taut, then went slack, and he feared that it had slipped from Pahchatka's hand. But in a few seconds the warrior appeared beside the stallion and stabbed a finger at various points in the mist. Each time he did, he said, "Nasci."

Nate reckoned it was the Anasazi name for whatever was stalking them. To defend themselves, they must get out of the mist quickly. To that end, he motioned for the warrior to go on. Pahchatka gripped the end of the rope more securely, then hustled forward.

On both sides snarls broke out, so many that Nate could not count them all, drowning the clomp of the stallion's heavy hooves. The beasts were working themselves into a killing frenzy, girding themselves for a concerted rush.

A rumbling growl from the rear was the signal for hell

to break loose. Zach shifted, saw a squat form streak toward his horse, and fired. Whether he hit the thing or not he could not say. At the booming retort it veered off and was engulfed by the mist.

Winona saw one coming toward her. She noticed a beetling brow and a long snout rimmed at the bottom by wicked teeth. Reddish-brown hair covered its face and neck, and there were longer, darker tufts on its throat and shoulders. Splayed paws capped by curved claws dug at the earth. The beast was almost on her when she stroked the trigger.

Momentum carried the thing forward even though its front legs buckled. Sliding to a stop close to the mare, the creature looked up.

It was like a wolf, and yet not like a wolf. Bigger, brawnier, hairier, it had uncommonly wide ears and exceptionally thin legs. A feral gleam lit its dark eyes as it snarled and heaved upward at the mare's jugular. Winona flung back her arms to club it, but she was much too slow.

Nate's rifle cracked just as the nasci's steely jaws were about to crunch shut. It was smashed to the ground, but it did not stay down. With two balls in its body, the creature scrambled erect and plunged into the mist. In its wake rose a chorus of horrendous howls.

Whipping out a pistol, Nate braced for the second wave. Abruptly, unaccountably, the yowling ceased. Total silence reigned—silence more nerve-racking than the howling had been, because Nate knew the things were still out there, standing just beyond the limits of his vision.

Out of the wispy soup appeared Pahchatka, urgently beckoning.

Winona reloaded as they moved on. Slowing so her mare was abreast of Evelyn's pony, she smiled encouragement. Evelyn returned the favor, remarking, "Don't fret, Ma. We can lick these varmints."

Zach drew a flintlock rather than reload his Hawken. He nudged the bay forward so he was close enough to reach out and touch his mother and sister. Come what may, he would protect both with his life, if need be.

The sighing had grown louder. Nate linked it to the breeze, which was stronger whenever the sound increased. The dank scent filled his nostrils, so potent it was like sniffing a pile of freshly dug dirt.

After another dozen yards, Nate was conscious that a subtle change had taken place. The mist was darker, the air a bit more chill. The thud of their hooves rang hollowly, as they would if walls hemmed them in. Soon he realized his hunch was right. He glimpsed stone surfaces on either side, and when he craned his neck, portions of a low ceiling were visible.

They were passing through a tunnel! Nate was elated beyond measure when he saw the mist begin to thin. Presently he could see the Anasazi. And that was not all. The end of the tunnel was a hundred yards distant, the pale glow that framed it serving as a beacon.

Pahchatka glanced at them, smiled, and rattled on in his birdsong tongue.

Nate checked behind his family. The wolf pack—if that was indeed what it had been—had not entered the tunnel. Once he learned to communicate better with their newfound friend, he would find out why.

"Pa, do you smell water?" Zach asked. His sense of smell had always been above average. Uncle Shakespeare was so impressed that he had the habit of calling Zach the Human Bloodhound.

Nate sniffed but registered only the same dank scent. Since they were nearing their goal and he was not hankering to antagonize the Anasazi, he said, "Remember. All of us must be on our best behavior once we reach the village. Don't say or do anything that would give them cause to lift our scalps.''

"It's not what we'll do that worries me,'' Zach mentioned. "It's whether Pahchatka's people will be as friendly as he is.''

"He'll vouch for us,'' Nate said confidently. He flattered himself that he was a fair judge of character, and the warrior impressed him as being a man of integrity.

"They might refuse to turn over the Ute boy,'' Winona said. "What then?''

"We're not leaving without Nevava.''

The tunnel broadened, the ceiling rose. Nate removed the rope from around Evelyn's waist, coiled it, and placed it in the parfleche. By then they were thirty feet from the entrance, which was wide enough to permit two horses to walk side by side.

Pahchatka could no longer contain his excitement and ran on ahead. The Kings lost sight of him but heard his voice and those of others.

"If we have to,'' Nate said, "we'll trade for the boy. Offer them a knife and a couple of blankets.'' Little else could be spared. They had packed light for their journey, just the bare essentials; they would live off the land as they went.

The voice of Pahchatka climbed to an angry shout, then, in the bat of an eye, the warrior stopped talking. Someone else spoke harshly.

Nate gestured for his family to stop, and drew rein. "Hold it while I see what's going on,'' he said quietly. He slid off his horse and crept to the opening. Dense vegetation cloaked a narrow trail and prevented him from seeing what lay beyond. Cautiously, he stepped into the open, and as he leveled his rifle he remembered to his dismay that he had forgotten to reload it after firing at the thing in the mist. He had broken his mentor's first law of survival.

Above him, leaves shook. Nate looked up and saw two husky warriors balanced on a stout limb.

They had just dropped a net.

Chapter Six

Nate King tried to throw himself into the clear, but the cord web closed around him, entangling his arms and legs. He was brought crashing down. Heaving onto his knees, he frantically tried to break free. It was useless. The net had been ingeniously designed. The harder he struggled, the tighter the coils constricted. In moments he was wrapped as snug as a caterpillar in a cocoon.

The two Indians dropped lightly from the limb. From out of the undergrowth came four more, one of them Pahchatka. He looked glumly at Nate, his demeanor showing he did not approve of what had been done.

A tall warrior whose nose had once been broken and never mended properly walked to the net. Sneering at the mountain man, he drew back a foot to kick him, but at a protest from Pahchatka he desisted.

"Husband! Is anything wrong?"

At Winona's yell, the warriors melted into the vegetation. The pair who had tossed the net dragged Nate

The Lost Valley

under cover with them. Nate opened his mouth wide to shout a warning, but one of the men clamped a hand over his mouth, stifling his outcry.

Inside the tunnel, Winona King grew uneasy. The commotion she had heard did not bode well. "Your father should have answered," she said softly.

"Want me to have a look-see?" Zach volunteered. He was more concerned about missing out on any excitement than he was worried for his pa's safety. His father had proven time and again that he could handle anything that came along, and Zach had unbounded confidence in him.

"No. We stick together," Winona said, hiding the anxiety that welled up within her. As her man would say, they were caught between a rock and a hard place. Her first instinct was to rush to his aid, but she did not know what was out there and refused to expose her children to further peril. Nor could they retrace their steps and try to find another way into the Anasazi sanctuary, not with those terrible wolflike beasts waiting in the mist.

Evelyn squirmed in her saddle. "What are we going to do, Ma?" She was all for riding on out and verifying that her father was all right.

"Nothing, for the moment." Winona dismounted and moved to the left-hand wall. They were safe enough where they were, since no one could get at them from either direction without being spotted.

"You can't be serious," Zach objected. "We can't desert Pa if he's in trouble."

"How dare you!" Winona gave in to a rare burst of anger. "When you have loved someone as I do your father, then you can criticize me. I would never desert him. When his time comes to die, I intend to be at his side and share his fate." Controlling her emotions, she said more calmly, "But it would not do for us to rush out. If something has happened, we are the only hope he has."

"I see your point," Zach said, yet he did not whole-heartedly agree with it. He would rather rush to the rescue with their guns blazing.

In the verdant growth that crowded the entrance, Nate King tried to bite the hand covering his mouth and could not. Thick strands of rope intervened. He was encouraged that his family had not fallen for the Anasazis' ruse. But his elation was short-lived.

The warrior with the crooked nose and two others slunk toward the tunnel. All three were dressed much like Pahchatka, and like him they were armed with curved war clubs. Crooked Nose flattened against the rock outcropping, then edged toward the opening.

Nate redoubled his efforts to warn his loved ones. He had almost succeeded in slipping his mouth free when a heavy blow to the back of his head exploded stars in front of his eyes and he sagged, dazed.

Inside the dark tunnel, Winona King glanced at her children. "Climb down and stay close to the walls," she directed. One thing was in their favor. They would be hard to spot from outside, but they had a clear shot at anyone who might try to enter.

Zach hopped down, then helped his sister off her pony. As he straightened, a face poked into sight, along with part of a war club. His mother was looking at them, not at the entrance, and she did not see the man's cruel features and oddly twisted countenance. Zach reacted without deliberation. Whirling, he aimed his rifle, cocking the hammer as he turned. Thunder pounded his ears when he stroked the trigger.

Outside, Nate saw Crooked Nose jerk back as rock slivers went flying. One raked the warrior's right cheek, digging a furrow and drawing blood.

The Anasazis huddled to confer, except for the one at the mountain man's side.

Pahchatka, Nate noticed, was totally ignored. His family's lone ally, the man Nate had counted on to establish peaceful relations with the tribe, apparently had no say in what the Anasazis did. Presently a warrior broke from the rest to jog off along a narrow trail. Crooked Nose and the others took up positions near the tunnel, and everyone settled down to wait.

Nate glanced at his guard. The man was coiled to bash him with the war club again if he acted up. For the moment his family was safe, so he lay still, testing the net for weak spots on the sly. There were none.

Outwardly, Nate put on a composed front. Inwardly, he churned with apprehension and overwhelming guilt. Should anything happen to Winona and the kids, it would be his fault. He was the one who had insisted on saving the Ute boy against impossible odds.

The minutes crawled by. The pale light grew brighter, but Nate could not yet see the sun over the mesa rim that reared above them. He wondered how his wife was faring, and dreaded her being harmed when the Anasazis made their move.

Winona was likewise thinking of him. She had posted Zach at the right-hand wall and made it plain he was not to shoot again unless she said to, or if their lives were in immediate danger. For all she knew, the warrior who had peeked inside had only wanted to palaver.

Evelyn was hunkered at her mother's knees. She was hungry and tired and scared to death, and she would rather be back in their cabin than anywhere else. It seemed to her that every time they went somewhere, something bad happened. They would be smart to stay home from then on and spare themselves the grief.

Off the top of her head, Evelyn commented, "When I get big, I'm going to live with the Shoshones the year round."

What brought that on? Winona mused. Aloud, she said, "That would be nice. I will come to visit you as

57

often as I can. After you have children of your own, I will stay in your lodge for as long as you need me to help out.''

''I'm not having children, Ma.''

''You think so?''

''I know so. Sorry, but I'm never getting married. Boys are too icky. All they do is tease me and pull my hair. The only nice one is Pa, and he's taken.''

Winona laughed, despite their plight. Why was it almost all little girls and boys felt the same way? She had shared their outlook once. How old had she been? Seven? Eight? On several occasions she had seen older boys and girls sneak caresses, and her sensibilities had been shocked. Once she had accidentally caught an older friend kissing a young warrior. It had nearly made her sick. All that night she had tossed and turned, having nightmares about a boy's mouth touching hers. How silly she had—

The tramp of feet alerted Winona to a new development. Voices murmured, many more than before. She wondered what it meant.

Nate could have told her. Fifteen more warriors had arrived, led by a tall Anasazi in an elaborate outfit. Fringed white moccasins covered his feet. His legs had been painted black as high as his knees, which were adorned with red tassels of some kind. Instead of pants or a breechcloth, he wore what Nate could only describe as a white skirt sprinkled with painted symbols. His shirt was blue and brown. A wide necklace hung from his neck, while on his head rested a high headdress not at all like those worn on special occasions by the Shoshones and the Crows. It was circular, the feathers rising straight up.

The newcomer had great authority. At a gesture, Nate was dragged from the brush. The man examined him with probing dark eyes. Pahchatka spoke up, but Nate could not tell if the newcomer paid any attention.

Crooked Nose brought over Nate's Hawken, which had dropped to the ground when the net snared him. The newcomer inspected it with much interest. As for Nate's pistols, they were still under his belt, but he could not get at them. Nor could he unlimber his Green River knife.

Pahchatka stepped between Crooked Nose and the leader, who listened as Pahchatka talked on and on, frequently pointing at Nate and at the tunnel. Relating what had happened, Nate figured. He watched the leader's face closely and saw no hint of friendliness. His last hope had been dashed.

The chief turned to Crooked Nose. Instructions were given. Half the warriors filed to the right side of the entrance, half to the left. Their intent was transparent. They were going to charge in and overwhelm Winona and the children.

Nate glanced around. For the moment the Anasazis had forgotten about him. Even the guard was riveted to the scene about to unfold. Sucking in a breath, he hollered at the top of his lungs, "Look out! They're getting set to rush you!" He was going to say more, but the war club descended and the grass leaped up to meet his face.

Winona King's heart soared to learn her man was still alive. His warning galvanized her into spinning, grabbing Blue Flower, and practically throwing her daughter onto the pony. "Climb on your bay," she told Zach.

"What are you fixing to do?"

Winona had been thinking while they waited. She remembered how scared Pahchatka had been of their horses. It stood to reason that the rest of the tribe shared his outlook, and she aimed to exploit their fear. Slipping a foot into the mare's stirrup, she pulled herself up and grasped the reins. "When I give the word, you are to ride as if a grizzly is trying to catch us. Don't stop for anything or anyone. I will be right behind you."

"I should go last to cover the two of you," Zach said.

"No. I need you to lead your father's horse while I protect Blue Flower. We are counting on you, son, to fight your way through and clear a path for us."

Zach squared his shoulders. "Don't worry, Ma. I won't let you down."

Winona nudged her mare close to the pony. The Anasazis were bound to be so shocked when the first rider appeared that they would scatter like leaves in a gale. Stalking Coyote and Blue Flower would have the best chance to escape. As for herself, well, she had meant what she said about sharing her husband's fate if need be.

Outside, Nate King forced his sluggish mind to function and raised his head. The man with the headdress lifted an arm to signal the attack.

"Now!" Winona shouted, and as her son goaded the bay into a gallop and hauled on the stallion's reins, she smacked her daughter's pony on the flank with all her might. Lashing the mare into step behind them, she vented a Shoshone war whoop.

Zach King was tingling with the thrill of it all. Shrieking lustily, he reached the opening just as Anasazi warriors filled it. Their amazement was almost comical. The bay slammed into them like a living battering ram, bowling some over, scattering others right and left. He saw his father lying to one side, wrapped in a net, but he could not stop, not when his mother and sister were depending on him to get them to safety.

Evelyn was petrified. She clung to her pony with rigid fingers, scarcely breathing as she flew past stunned warriors. One recovered his wits and lunged at her.

Winona was right there. With a sweep of her rifle, the man was knocked sprawling into several of his companions. Then she was in the clear. She glimpsed her husband, helpless and under guard. For a fleeting instant their eyes locked, and it was as if a dam had broken deep within her, pouring all the love she bore him from her soul. *We will save you!* she mentally vowed.

Yells of outrage rose from the Anasazis. In a pack they sped in pursuit. Nate swung his legs into their path, tripping two. For his cleverness he was grabbed and punched and rolled a few yards away so he could not interfere.

The man in the headdress stood over him, glaring. Nate glared back. A pair of hefty warriors flanked the chief, and if looks could kill, they would have seared him to a cinder. Any likelihood of smoking the pipe of peace with the Anasazis was growing slimmer by the second.

Pahchatka was aloof, over beside a tree. His expression was an open book, revealing his disgust and resentment. He glanced at Nate as if to say, "I am sorry."

The drum of hooves faded fast. Nate listened for telltale outcries that might be a clue that his family had been captured. Fiery shouts blended with the crash of limbs. A horse whinnied stridently, and he feared that it had been brought down.

The chief addressed the guards. One hurried into the woods and returned bearing a long, relatively straight limb. Its purpose became apparent when Nate's wrists and ankles were tied to it. Each of the guards took an end.

Trussed like a deer, enmeshed in the net, Nate could only fume as he was borne along the trail at a brisk clip. In the lead was the chief. Pahchatka hung back, as glum as a rainy day.

The trail wound lower through verdant forest. To call it woodland did not do it justice. "Jungle" was more appropriate. Vines dangled in lush profusion, colorful flowers adorned the lower and middle terraces, gaily plumed birds warbled and chirped and cawed. Butterflies twice the size of those Nate was accustomed to flitted in thick clusters. The sweet scent Nate had caught wind of now and then in the tunnel was thick enough to cut with a knife.

In due course the growth thinned. The chieftain stopped on the lip of a grassy terrace, affording Nate an unobstructed view of the Anasazis' domain. And what a domain it was!

The interior of the mesa was actually an oval valley approximately two miles in length and a mile wide. Towering cliffs encircled it, forming an impassable protective barrier, impassable except for the tunnel that came in under the bottom of the east wall. In the center a tranquil lake was home to ducks, brants, and geese. Goats and sheep grazed along the shore.

In a nearby meadow deer were feeding, deer much taller and broader than those that called the Rockies home, the bucks sporting antlers a moose would envy.

Nate forgot about the rope chafing his wrists and the numbness in his hips and legs. The incredible scene dazzled him. It was a literal paradise, a safe haven where the outside world did not intrude. Small wonder not many had ever heard of the People of the Mist.

A score of questions begged answers. How long had the Anasazis lived there? Where did they come from originally? Why had they set themselves apart from all the other tribes? Were the many unusual varieties of wildlife in the lost valley there before they came?

The leader adjusted his headdress, then started down the slope. A low cry from one of the men carrying Nate drew their attention to a spot on the cliff high to the north, and the Anasazis commenced chattering like agitated chipmunks.

Nate had to twist his neck to see. He caught a tantalizing sight of *something* as it skittered up the sheer surface, something enormous, something that vanished into the inky mouth of what could only be a cave. One of more than a dozen.

The Lost Valley

The Anasazis were visibly shaken, including Pahchatka. Just as in the Garden of Eden, their paradise had a serpent in its midst. Or rather, a reptilian relative. For the creature Nate had seen was more like a lizard than a snake, a gigantic lizard with a blunt head, four legs, and a tail three times as long as its body.

The kachina.

Chapter Seven

Winona King flew down the narrow trail in her daughter's wake, ducking low limbs and dodging branches that spiked at them from either side. The howls of the Anasazis swelled in frustration. She glanced back and saw several of the fleetest doggedly sticking to the chase. One man, in particular, was as swift as an antelope, and almost came within throwing range of his war club.

But no human could ever match a horse. The warrior faltered, his steps flagging, his body caked with sweat. He shook a fist at them and shouted in impotent fury.

Winona smiled at him, which made him shake his fist more violently. Her plan had worked, but only because none of the Anasazis were armed with bows and arrows.

Another low limb materialized directly ahead. Winona bent over the saddle, her chest rubbing against the mare's mane. The limb whisked overhead. She saw Blue Flower look back, so she waved.

Evelyn was close to tears. The more she thought about

leaving her father in the clutches of those bad men, the more upset she became. They might kill him. Until that moment, she had never really imagined that her pa could die. She had always regarded him as the bravest, strongest, smartest man alive. She had always pictured him as invincible. But seeing him in that net, seeing him so helpless, unable to lift a finger to protect himself, made her realize that he was flesh and blood like everyone else.

A cackle made Evelyn look up. Her brother was laughing and shaking his rifle at her. She rode sadly on, unable to see what he was so happy about.

Zach was thrilled by their escape. The heady excitement had his blood racing, his temples pounding. It was moments like these, he reflected, that all true warriors lived for! The next time his family visited his mother's people, he would have a fine tale to tell the other boys.

A sharp bend reminded Zach to concentrate on the matter at hand. He galloped along until an open hilltop appeared. Rather than expose himself, he brought the stallion to a halt and moved to one side. Within seconds his sister and mother had joined him. "What now, Ma?" he asked.

Winona disliked putting more distance between them and her husband, but the Anasazis were bound to try to track them down. Saving Nate would have to wait until after they eluded the trackers. She had her pick of going north or south. On a whim, she spurred the mare northward. "Follow me."

Zach reluctantly obeyed. He would rather wait in hiding and drop the first few Anasazis who showed up, then light a shuck for heavy timber. The screech of a bizarre bird awakened him to how strange their surroundings were. It had a red head, a yellow body, and tail feathers as long as his arm. He had never set eyes on a bird quite like it. Nor could he identify many of the trees and lesser plants.

Zach grew confused. His pa had made it a point to teach him about every wild animal and all the varieties of plant life found in the Rockies. It was essential. To survive, a man had to know all there was to know about everything he came across. He had to know which plants were edible, which were not. Which thrived near water. Which were good for burning. And so on.

The lore his father taught had been expanded on by some of the Shoshones. Certain ones, like the old healer lady, had stored an incredible amount of knowledge they were gladly willing to share.

Zach had assumed he knew all there was worth learning, but now he saw that he had been mistaken. So much here was new, so much was strikingly different. He saw a long, thin green snake with oversized eyes. He spotted a large hawk with feathers on its head that jutted out at an angle instead of lying flat. He saw a small animal that seemed to be a cross between a deer and an antelope. What was this place? he marveled.

Winona had been studying the lay of the land. The stone ramparts not only safeguarded the tribe from outside enemies, they trapped any outsiders caught inside. Even if she rescued Nate, eventually the Anasazi would hunt them down and slay them.

It did not help any that the soil was so fertile, so rich and soft. Their mounts left a trail a four-year-old could follow.

She passed a bush bearing round reddish berries, and her stomach growled. But she left the berries alone, since she had no way of telling if they were safe or poisonous. ''Don't touch these,'' she told her children.

Evelyn was not hungry anyway. She was too sad to be hungry. All she could think of was her father and how very much she loved him.

Zach kept twisting to check their back trail. All he wanted was a clear shot at one of the Anasazis. Just one.

Time passed. Once the sun rose above the mesa's rim, the temperature soared. By the middle of the morning Winona was sweltering. She swatted at a large ugly insect with a thin needlelike nose that alighted on her arm. Farther on she tensed when a spider the size of her hand scuttled up a tree.

Winona decided she would not like to live in this valley. It had an air about it, a feeling of menace that had nothing to do with the unfriendly Anasazis. It was bad medicine. Her people had learned long ago to shun such spots. Certain lakes and streams and mountains were always avoided because they brought disaster down on the shoulders of anyone foolish enough to defy the taboo.

One lake came to mind. It was way up in the mountain range that the whites called the Tetons. Long ago, back when only Indians roamed the land, back when the Shoshones were new to the earth, her people had camped at that lake. The next morning a Shoshone maiden and her suitor had gone rowing in a canoe. Watchers on shore had been horrified when an enormous creature heaved out of the water, shattering the canoe, and took the maiden into its huge jaws. The suitor had pulled his knife and tried to save her, but the doomed girl was pulled under the surface and never seen again.

A water horse, her people called it. One of many in different lakes. Lakes that were bad medicine. Just like the valley.

Presently, Winona noticed that the vegetation was thinning, the ground becoming rockier. They were near the north wall of the escarpment. Midway up were a number of dark openings she judged to be the mouth of caves.

The mare started to act skittish. Every so often it would toss its head and snort for no reason at all.

Winona came to the end of the trees and grinned. A wide belt of solid rock rimmed the base of the cliff, extending for as far as she could see in either direction.

Their horses would leave no tracks on it. "Let the An-asazis try to follow us now," she said, riding out of the shade into the glaring heat. She crossed to the cliff and reined up. "We'll rest here a spell."

Above them were the caves. Up close, the cliff face was pockmarked with holes and cracks and fissures. Winona noted a lot of deep scratch marks she could not account for. Dismounting, she unslung the water skin and opened it. "Anyone thirsty besides me?"

Evelyn drank first. As her mother tilted the water skin, she bent her head partway back. Her gaze drifted to the dark openings high overhead. For a fraction of an instant she thought that she saw something jut out from one of the lowest caves, something big. But then she blinked and it was gone.

Convinced it could not have been real, Evelyn drank with relish. She told herself that she should be glad, not sad. After all, they were safe for the moment, weren't they?

A well-worn series of footpaths led from the terraces toward the lake. Nate King swayed with every stride the warriors took, his wrists and ankles lanced by aching pangs. He was so depressed by the turn of events that he did not take much interest in the landscape until they had descended three levels.

The grassy slopes were not as smooth as they should have been. The grass grew in grooved sections, grooves that Nate recognized for what they had once been: neatly arranged furrows, such as a plow might make. Once, not all that long ago, the terraces had been tilled.

Lower down, Nate's guess was confirmed. The tiers closest to the lake were being worked by near-naked An-asazi farmers, men and women alike, tending crops of corn, squash, pumpkins, and other vegetables. They had a variety of implements: hoes, rakes, short sickles, and

The Lost Valley

more. Most stopped what they were doing to stare.

As yet Nate had not seen the Anasazi village. He scoured the shore and a small plain beyond for their lodges, which he assumed would be made of wood since the Anasazis lived too far from the plains to rely on a steady supply of buffalo hides for tepees.

Then he looked to the south, where a section of the cliff had long ago collapsed and was piled high in deep shadow. As his captors stepped from the last terrace onto a wide dirt avenue, the rubble began to take on definite form, to acquire a symmetrical shape. It was not rubble at all, but an immense city situated at the base of the rampart.

Nate was dumbfounded. As his captors neared their destination, the sun cleared the mesa, bathing the entire valley in a golden glow. The Anasazi city was revealed in all its majestic glory.

It was an architectural wonder, a gigantic structure that resembled a horseshoe in its outline. Hundreds of rooms were stacked one on top of another in ever-higher layers or rings. The innermost was a single story high, the outermost three or four stories. The open end of the horseshoe faced the lake.

The only thing Nate could compare it to was a tremendous honeycomb. People were bustling about on the roofs, which were linked by ladders. A central stairway led from the plaza to the roof of the dwellings that abutted the cliff.

Nate was so entranced by the city that he almost didn't notice a curious aspect to the lake. A broad belt of dried mud ringed it, evidence that the lake was shrinking. He judged it to be only a third the size it once had been. Whether the shrinkage was seasonal, a result of the hot weather, or caused by some other agency, he could not say.

They passed Anasazis going about their daily routines.

Farmers trudging to or from the terraces, hunters heading to or coming from the jungle, warriors on official business. A party of the latter were stopped by the man in the headdress, and at a command from him, they fell into step to the rear, two of them replacing the pair who had carried Nate so far.

One of the warriors was sent ahead at a sprint. When he was within earshot of the city, he began hollering.

The town crier, Nate observed. People moved toward the plaza. Some on the roofs stepped to the edges so they could see better. From a large building set apart from the honeycomb came half a dozen men in stately feathered garb.

Nate's wrists had grown numb. He rubbed them back and forth to restore circulation and felt a wet, sticky sensation trickle toward his left elbow. The skin had broken, and he was bleeding. But it was nothing compared to the agony in his shoulders and the pain in his parched throat. The glistening lake, so near yet so unattainable, only aggravated his thirst.

A sizable crowd had gathered by the time Nate's captors reached the plaza. In the forefront stood the group in feathered outfits. The man in the headdress stopped in front of them and greeted them solemnly.

"Put me down, damn you," Nate groused when it became obvious his bearers were not going to do so.

A tall Anasazi bedecked in yellow and red feathers strode over. He wore an outlandish mask crafted to mimic a bird's head. From between the open beak dark eyes bored into Nate's. A guttural voice rang out.

Crooked Nose appeared at the bird-man's side. They talked at length, and when they were done it was Pahchatka's turn to be quizzed. Hope bloomed in the depths of Nate's being, hope that withered like a blossom in the desert as Pahchatka became more impassioned and the bird-man—or High Chief, as Nate had taken to thinking

70

of him—grew ever more stern. It did not bode well.

Finally Pahchatka bowed his head and walked away, the look he cast at Nate conveying a world of meaning.

At a command from the High Chief, Nate was unceremoniously dumped on the ground. Caught off guard, he grunted and winced as pain shot up his left arm and along his ribs. Fingers pried at the net, loosening it, and before long the Anasazis had unwrapped it and cut the bonds that held his limbs fast to the pole. He was free, but his legs were so deadened that he could not stand on his own. He tried after being kicked several times and prodded by a warrior's club.

The High Chief spoke, and two men seized hold of the mountain man. Roughly jerking him erect, they moved toward the east end of the horseshoe. Three warriors took up positions on either side.

Talking excitedly, the crowd parted to let them pass. Nate saw scores of swarthy faces, but not one he would rate as friendly until he was almost through them. That was when he spotted a face that did not belong, a face that was Mexican, not Anasazi. There could be no doubt, even though the man was dressed in typical Anasazi attire. A prisoner? Nate wondered, and smiled, only to feel his insides turn to ice when he saw that the man was blind. Scarred pits existed where the eyelids should be. *"Hola, amigo!"* he croaked, but received no reply.

The warriors dragged him to a ladder. One shoved him so that he fell against it, and if Nate's arms and legs had not been so stiff that he could barely move, he would have punched the man full in the mouth. "Hold your horses, damn you!" he complained. It was a waste of breath. A war club jabbed him in the ribs, inciting him further.

"I hope the kachina eats every one of you," Nate fumed, with astounding results. The nearest warriors stepped back, and all of them fingered their weapons.

What had he done? Why were they giving him a wide berth? "Is it the kachina?" he said aloud, and was rewarded by having one of the warriors weave a symbol in the air and intone a few words as if to ward off an evil spirit.

Nate laughed bitterly. The Anasazis feared the thing that had slain the Utes. They even feared its name. Or was there something more to it? Whatever the case, he could not resist licking his lips and yelling just as loudly as he could, "Kachina! Kachina! Kachina!"

Every last Anasazi froze. Mothers clutched children. Men muttered, many gazing at the cliffs above their city with what could only be described as barely concealed fear.

No one molested Nate as he slowly scaled the ladder to a flat roof. Six of the warriors followed him, and the one who had pushed him walked to a hole in the center and motioned at the top of a ladder that jutted from the square opening.

"You want me to go down there?" Nate deduced. His legs were working well enough for him to manage it nicely. The interior was musty but cool, refreshingly so. At the bottom he straightened and waited for his eyes to adjust to the murk. He shifted, and as soon as he turned his back to the ladder, it was yanked up.

Nate glanced at the opening, the *only* opening, apparently. The warrior who had pushed him was smirking. And why not? The Anasazis had him right where they wanted him; they could do with him as they pleased.

They could even kill him.

Chapter Eight

The stallion started acting up only a few minutes after Winona had called the halt. She was seated, her back to the cliff, when the big black snorted and pawed the ground, then looked up, way up, bending its neck as far as a horse could.

"What's the matter with him, Ma?" Blue Flower asked. She was so hot she couldn't stand it. The drink from the water skin had barely slaked her thirst.

"I don't know," Winona answered, and glanced up. From that angle it was like gazing over an endless pockmarked expanse of stone dotted by black patches. The cave mouths yawned wide. They would have been an ideal haven for her and the children if they were not so high up.

Zach was pacing and watching the woodland. As yet there had been no sign of the Anasazis, but that was bound to change. He took the responsibility of protecting his mother and sister with the utmost seriousness. If his

David Thompson

pa had told him once, his pa had told him a hundred times that it would be up to him to look after them if the unthinkable happened.

Winona pushed her hair back and leaned her head against the cliff. She closed her eyes to savor a few moments of rest. But she was too agitated to relax. Nate needed her. She must think of a means of saving him, and the Ute boy, as well.

Something brushed her face. Thinking it was a fly or some other insect, Winona idly swatted the air without opening her eyes. Again it brushed her, this time on her forehead. She swung both hands, listening for the buzz of tiny wings. Hearing none, she sighed and sat up and gazed around. Whatever had landed on her was gone.

Winona was pleased at how well her children were holding up. Stalking Coyote had fought enemies before and had exhibited a degree of courage that might one day result in a position of leadership among the Shoshones. Blue Flower, though, had lived a generally sheltered, safe existence. As would most any mother, Winona had done all she could to protect her daughter from the worst life had to offer. Sometimes, Winona would scold herself for being too protective. But how else should she act? Motherly instinct was deeply ingrained. A woman could no more resist it than she could resist basic urges like hunger and the nightly need for sleep.

Once more something lightly touched Winona, this time on the chin. She saw no insect, nothing to account for it. Suddenly a tiny piece of stone fell into her lap with a *plop*. Mystified, she twisted and craned her neck. Specks of dust and motes of dirt were fluttering toward her from on high. She moved away from the wall and stood, an instant before a rock the size of a walnut hit in the exact spot she had been.

The particles were falling from the mouth of the lowest cave. The only explanation Winona could think of was that something was moving about up there and had dislodged debris on the cave floor. A silly notion, since the only creatures able to reach the caves were birds and she had not seen a single one fly anywhere near them.

A feeling came over her, a gut-wrenching feeling that she and the children were in great peril. She tried to tell herself that it was a wild fancy, that her nerves were frayed and her mind was not behaving logically, but the premonition persisted, growing stronger by the moment.

"We're leaving," Winona announced.

"So soon?" Evelyn said. She wouldn't have minded another swig from the water skin and maybe a short nap.

"Now."

Zach mounted without objecting. To stay in the open invited disaster. They needed to find cover and come up with a plan to save his father. Without being bidden, he grasped the stallion's reins.

Winona gave Blue Flower a boost into the saddle. After mounting the mare, she led them along the cliff's base, circling the valley in the direction of a lake that sparkled like a giant jewel.

She was puzzled by the absence of the Anasazis. Swift trackers would have been there by then. Either the warriors were taking their sweet time, or they had given up the chase, which was preposterous.

Or was it? Winona put herself in the Anasazis' moccasins and saw the situation in a whole new light. Why should the warriors wear themselves out chasing quarry on horseback? All the Anasazis had to do was post a sufficient number of men at the tunnel, and Winona and the kids were as good as caught.

They couldn't get out of the valley. They would have to live constantly on the run, never having a moment of real peace, always on the lookout for the Anasazis. It would wear them down, weaken them. Sooner or later they were bound to blunder and the Anasazis would snare them.

Winona resolved then and there that it was not going to happen that way. She would think of something. She had to.

The clatter of hooves on stone was uncomfortably loud. Winona veered to the tree line, where the soft clomp would not carry as far on the wind.

The presence of the breeze was a minor puzzle in itself. Winona would have thought that the towering ramparts would block the wind. Did it come over the top? Through the caves? Or were there other openings she did not know about, openings that might offer a safe route from the valley?

It was midday when the lush vegetation ended on the crest of a grassy terrace. Reining up, Winona crawled to the edge and peeked over. Slope after grassy slope rippled down to the valley floor. In the distance, near the lake, figures moved about. She could not quite make out what they were doing.

A bright shaft of reflected sunlight to the south pinpointed the Anasazi village. But what a village! Enormous beyond belief, it shone in the sunshine. She knew that was where her husband had been taken, so that was where she must go. But how to get there without getting caught?

Winona started to stand when the ground under her feet moved. The horses whinnied, Blue Flower cried out, and Winona flung her arms down to keep from falling. A muffled rumbling filled the valley. Trees swayed, the cliffs to the west seemed to shake violently, and the very air vibrated. The birds in the forest squawked shrilly, and somewhere in the brush a small animal bleated.

The effect did not last long. Within seconds the ground stilled, the rumbling died. Winona pushed upright and surveyed the valley. All appeared normal.

"What was that, Ma?" Evelyn asked. She had never heard of the whole earth quaking like that, and she cast wide eyes at the crags above, terrified that they would topple, crashing down on top of her.

Zach answered first. "I know what it was. An earthquake. Pa told me about them, how one shook him when he was a little boy. They're nothing to be scared of."

Winona did not share her son's outlook. Quakes were infrequent in the region the Shoshones roamed, but they did happen on occasion. Once, many winters past, so the story went, a quake had opened a wide crack that swallowed several warriors whole and then closed again, burying them alive.

"We must find a place to rest until sunset," Winona said, stepping to the mare. As she lifted her leg, a bellow rose from the nearby undergrowth.

Into the open bounded Anazasi warriors.

Nate King was lying on his side when the quake struck. He had made repeated circuits of the room, confirming that the only entrance was the hole in the roof. Grooves in one of the walls hinted that at one time a door to another apartment had existed but been walled over.

The construction fascinated him. The walls were made of stone embedded in mud mortar. Wooden beams braced the ceiling. The craftsmanship was outstanding. Overall, it rivaled a typical New York home.

His estimation of the Anasazis jumped considerably. In all his wide-flung travels, in all his contacts with Indians from the Mississippi to the Pacific, from Canada to the Texas border, he had never met a tribe quite like them. No one else, absolutely no one, built buildings on the scale of the Anasazis. Their city was an engineering masterpiece, as different from the hide tepees and brush wigwams of other tribes as night was from day.

The scope of their expertise was food for thought. Where had they learned such advanced techniques? How was it that none of the other tribes ever duplicated their achievements? What set the Anasazis apart from everyone else?

In a corner Nate found additional proof of their extraordinary talent. Someone had left behind a number of pots and baskets so exquisitely made that Nate could have sold them for many dollars to art collectors in New York City.

One prime example was a wickerwork vessel in the shape of a long cylinder. Bits of turquoise and small shells had been inlaid on the outer surface. It was flawless.

Another work of art was a black-and-red basket. Nate carried it under the rooftop opening so he could study its intricate design. The patterns had been woven from thick fibers with a precision that bespoke a master craftsman or craftswoman.

Nate also found a large striped sack that had seen better days. It was worn and torn but it was softer to lie on than the floor, so he spread it out and lay down. Sparkling shafts of sunlight streaming in through the hole lit up the center of the room but could not brighten the corners. He folded his arms and was mulling his bleak prospects when the whole apartment shimmied and shook.

In a flash Nate was on his feet. He had not experienced an earthquake since he was eight. His father had taken him to an uncle's farm for a week, and while there a rare quake had rattled upper New York. It had not done any damage or killed anyone, but to his young mind it had been a revelation. The planet had fits, just as people did.

Now Nate moved to the middle of the floor in case the ceiling collapsed or the walls buckled. The shaking stopped, and he breathed easier. Outside, the buzz of Anasazi voices had risen in alarm.

The Lost Valley

A shadow fell across the opening. The head and shoulders of a man were silhouetted against the azure sky as he dipped onto his knees and poked his head below the rim. *"Hola, señor. Esta conversacion es sin ambages ni rodeos, asi que escucha astentamente."*

Nate recognized the blind Mexican from the plaza. "I'm sorry, but I don't speak Spanish all that well. Do you savvy English?"

"Sí, señor," the man said. "I speak it some." He lowered an arm. "Can you reach my hand?"

"It's too high."

"I was afraid of that." The man elevated his head to listen. "Pay attention. I do not have much time. When the ground shakes, the Anasazis are scared. But they do not stay scared long. My name is Pedro Valdez, and I am from Sonora."

"What are you doing here?" Nate asked. Sonora was a northern Mexican province hundreds of miles to the south. "You're a long way from home."

The man's scarred eyelids moved as the eyes under them shifted toward the sound of Nate's voice. "How well I know it. Four years ago I was a vaquero on a hacienda. I made a good wage, and I had plans to marry a pretty senorita. One night, as I rode herd, I was captured by Indians."

"The Anasazis?" Nate broke in.

"No. Navajos. They traded me to the Anasazis." Pedro extended two fingers and touched his eyelids. "They saw to it I can never escape."

The full implication jarred Nate with the force of a physical blow. "They blinded you on purpose?"

"Sí. With the flat of a red-hot blade."

"My Lord."

"They will do the same to you. If they do not feed you to the kachinas."

The mention of the creature that had slaughtered the

Utes prompted Nate to ask, "What are those things? I tracked one from the mountains to this mesa and never really had a good look at it."

"The kachinas are spirits made flesh," Pedro said. "Or so the Anasazis believe. Me, I say they are demons." He paused. "They don't often stray from their caves. The one you followed killed two men and went out the tunnel. Warriors hunted it, but they could not catch it. So they say. I think they were afraid." Pedro raised his head. "I must go. Someone comes."

"Wait! One last thing. Do you know of an Ute boy named Nevava?"

"Tokipha brought a new boy, I am told."

"I aim to get him out of here. You, too, if you want to go along."

Pedro grew downcast. "I wish it were so simple. No one ever escapes the Anasazis. Many have tried. None have succeeded." Standing, he shook his head in sorrow. "I am most sorry, *señor*. One way or another, you will end your days here. Accept it and you will be better off."

"Never," Nate declared, but there was no one to hear. Pedro had vanished, moving with surprising speed for someone who was sightless. "Come back when you can!" Nate shouted, the cry echoing hollowly. In the Mexican's absence he felt keenly alone, pathetically vulnerable. The four walls seemed more confining, the room seemed gloomier, matching his spirits.

Nate walked in a circle under the opening, racking his brain for a miracle. Knowing it was useless, he backed up a dozen paces, coiled, then hurtled forward and upward. His spring swept him high in a vaulting arc—but nowhere near high enough. His outflung hand missed the rim by several feet.

Confined spaces had never bothered Nate, yet suddenly he could not stand being in that room. He wanted out. Unbridled panic clawed at his insides and he wildly roved the chamber, seeking salvation. There had to be a way. There just had to be.

He thought of his makeshift blanket, of the striped sack. Examining the weave, he found a loose end, which he pried at with a fingernail. It was painstaking work, but he slowly unraveled it and wound the heavy twine or whatever it was around his left hand. When he had enough for his purposes, he walked to the corner where the baskets and other items had been left. Broken pottery shards sufficed for the next step. Selecting the sharpest, he cut the twine.

There was nothing to use as a hook. He had to settle for the elaborate vessel decorated with turquoise. Wrapping the twine around the middle, he made a knot, then wrapped it from top to bottom and tied another.

It was crude, but it might work. Nate swung the vessel around and around, leaving little slack. At the apex of a swing he launched it at the opening. His insane scheme called for somehow snagging the ladder that must be lying near the entrance.

The vessel soared up and out, and he heard it thud onto the roof. Gingerly, Nate pulled, but it did not catch on anything and soon appeared at the lip. "Consarn it." Nate moved under the opening and tugged. The vessel was supposed to fall into his hands, but it rose instead, the twine giving a hard jerk.

A leering face explained why. Crooked Nose held the vessel for Nate to see, then slashed the twine with a knife. He flipped the vessel, caught it, and strolled off, his mocking laughter boiling the mountain man's blood.

Nate had to face the truth. There was no way out.

No way out at all.

Chapter Nine

Winona King had split seconds in which to make up her mind what to do. Since charging the Anasazis had worked once, she thought it might work again. Consequently, as she sprang onto the mare, she reined the horse around. The turn saved her, for as the animal rotated, a war club flashed past, missing her head by inches.

Other warriors cocked their arms to throw. Zach had his rifle up and extended, and fired at the foremost. The ball cored the man's shoulder, crumpling him in his tracks.

"Down the hill!" Winona bawled. The shot scattered most of the Anasazis, who dived flat or sought cover. She saw Blue Flower flee over the crest and cut the reins to follow. From out of nowhere a bronzed hand streaked, grabbing the mare's bridle. A stocky warrior intended to take her alive.

Winona kicked, striking him in the chest. The Anasazi staggered but held on. Grimly, Winona drove the stock of her rifle at his head. Others were closing in, and if she did not break free quickly it would all be over. The man holding on to the mare lunged, his other hand seeking her leg.

"Ma!"

Zach barreled to his mother's side, wielding his Hawken as if it were a club. It smashed into the warrior's chin as the man shifted to confront him. A shove, and the warrior was prone, holding his broken jaw. "Ride, Ma! Ride!"

Winona did not waste another moment. She galloped on her daughter's heels and glanced back to make sure Stalking Coyote was following her. The air sizzled to war clubs deftly thrown, but only one connected, a glancing blow off her son's shoulder as the bay cleared the rim.

Zach had to grit his teeth to keep from crying out. Excruciating pain spiked through him, and his left arm went numb. Gamely, he sped on down the slope as the Anasazis spilled over it in his wake.

Evelyn slowed at the bottom of the first terrace. Below lay open ground, and her father had always told her to seek cover when bad men were after her. She looked at her mother for guidance, yelling, "Which way?"

Winona saw that the figures on the valley floor were not moving. They had heard the shot, and some might rush up to help the warriors. She and the children would be caught between the two groups, trapped with nowhere to run. To the north lay the rocky belt that bordered the ramparts. To the south the terraces stretched for half a mile, blending into thick forest.

"That way!" Winona said, jabbing southward.

For her age Evelyn was a superb rider. Her parents had placed her on a horse when she was barely old enough to walk, and by the time she was seven she could ride as well as most grown men. Now she proved it by wheeling her pony on the edge of a coin and making for the distant woodland at breakneck speed.

The Anasazis shrieked and yipped like bloodthirsty Blackfeet. They gave chase, but it was the same story as before. They soon fell behind, shrieking all the louder.

Some of the people below were working their way up. Winona was not worried; they couldn't possibly cut the horses off before the animals reached the trees. She should feel relieved, but she wasn't; she was only delaying the inevitable. The lost valley was simply too small for the three of them to elude the Anasazis forever.

She squinted skyward at the sun, which was on its descent but would not set for hours. Night offered the promise of temporary safety. Or did it? The huge tracks of the monster that slew Red Feather's hunting party had led into the valley, so the creature must be there, somewhere. If it was like most meat-eaters, it would be most active after the sun went down.

Why did the Anasazis stay, with a beast like that abroad in their midst? Winona's own people wanted nothing to do with the things that should not be, the creatures left over from the old time, creatures like the water horses, the hairy giants and the snakes that could swallow a horse whole.

The elders of her tribe said that in days long gone the creatures had been much more numerous and had constantly plagued the Shoshones and others.

She was thankful the twilight dwellers were now rare. The hairy giants had been driven from Shoshone territory before she was born. And no one had seen a giant snake in more moons than most could count, although a Crow claimed to have stumbled on one out on the prairie and barely escaped with his life.

The worst had been the red-haired cannibals. For many generations they had hunted people as others hunted game. The cannibals had even taken the dead for food.

This unspeakable state of affairs had gone on until the Paiutes waged bitter war against the cannibal tribe and wiped most of them out. Most, but not all. In remote regions of the mountains a few were said to linger on, devouring anyone unlucky enough to cross their path.

Then there were the NunumBi, or the little ones. They were dwarfs who lived in holes in the ground and went about armed with small but very powerful bows. Expert archers, they could pierce a man's eye at a hundred paces. In the old times the NunumBi had bitterly contested the spread of the red man, wreaking a great slaughter before they were themselves almost wiped out. Now they lurked in shadowy canyons and refuges deep in the mountains, and every so often a lone warrior would be found dead with tiny arrows jutting from his body.

Winona had never seen a red-haired cannibal, or a hairy giant or a NunumBi, but that did not mean they did not exist. She believed all the stories, heart and soul. Just as her parents had believed, and their parents before them.

Nate had laughed when she told him the tales. For a week after she imparted all she knew about the NunumBi, he had made a show of peering under tables and behind boulders to "make sure none of those uppity midgets are out to get us." When he learned of the cannibals, every now and then he would bite himself on the arm and say, "Not bad. A little salt and I'd taste downright delicious."

Men could be so irritating.

A yell from Zach brought an end to Winona's reverie. A lone warrior was scaling the terraces well ahead of the pack. The man was too far off to intercept them, but he held a bow, the first Winona had seen any of the Anasazis use.

Planting himself, the warrior whipped a shaft from a

quiver on his back, notched the arrow to the sinew string, and took deliberate aim.

Hope always sprang eternal. The saying was as old as the proverbial hills, yet as true as life.

Nate King did not give up—not even after Crooked Nose had ruined his attempt to snare the ladder. Nate had gone to the corner, rummaged among a pile of pottery shards until he found the biggest, and walked to the doorway that had been walled off. The mortar was newer, so perhaps, just perhaps, it would be easier to pick apart.

He gouged the sharp end of the shard into a likely spot and soon had a furrow dug. At the rate he was going, he estimated it would take him hours to make an opening large enough for him to crawl through. He kept at it, ignoring the tiny cuts and scrapes on his fingers and the pain in his wrist and knuckles.

So engrossed was Nate in his work that he did not realize he had company until a heavy footstep above snapped him erect. Flinging the shard down, he moved to the center of the room just as several heads appeared.

Crooked Nose was back, this time with friends. The ladder was lowered, and Crooked Nose beckoned.

Nate climbed out, blinking in the glare. Eight Anasazis ringed the opening, among them the High Chief in the bird outfit, the man in the tall headdress, and Pahchatka. Also present was Pedro, standing well back, his head bowed and his hands meekly folded. "What is this?" Nate asked the Mexican. "Are they here to put out my eyes?"

Pedro looked up, but he was clearly afraid to talk without permission. He shook his head once and bowed it again.

The High Chief barked, and Pedro stepped forward. Valdez listened closely as he was given instructions.

"I am to translate, *señor*. They have many questions

about you. You must always tell the truth or they will punish you.''

The threat carried no weight with Nate, not when the Anasazis had no way of knowing if he was lying or not. "Tell them I will cooperate, but only if they agree to answer a few questions of my own.''

Licking his lips, Pedro placed a hand on Nate's sleeve. "Please, my friend. Do not anger them. They do not like outsiders. Some need only a small excuse and they will torture you until you beg for them to end the misery.''

Nate could guess whom Pedro referred to. Crooked Nose was fondling his knife as if Nate were a turkey he could not wait to carve into. "What do they have against outsiders?''

"Outsiders bring them death and sickness. Once, the Anasazis ruled this land. They had many cities. They were peaceful and happy.'' Pedro looked at the High Chief. When the man did not object, he continued. "Then new tribes came. They waged war. Many Anasazis were killed, many cities destroyed.'' Pedro paused. "One day a man came from the south. A Spaniard, from what they tell me. They had never seen anyone like him. They took him in, tried to nurse him. But he was too far gone. Soon many were sick. Hundreds died.''

Nate saw the Anasazis in a whole new light. It was a terrible tale, one that had been repeated recently. Not long ago there had been a friendly tribe on the upper Missouri, the Mandans. Nate had known many of them personally, and had been a guest of honor at the marriage of their leader's daughter to an Englishman.

Next to the Shoshones, the Mandans had been among the staunchest allies of the whites. Trappers were welcome in any of their villages. The Mandans gladly shared whatever they had. They traded pelts for trade goods, receiving guns, powder, blankets, and more. It was an arrangement that benefited both sides, until that awful

David Thompson

day when the whites unwittingly gave the unsuspecting Mandans something that devastated them: smallpox.

"These are the last of the Anasazis," Pedro was saying. "This is their last city. Once they are gone, the tribe is gone."

"Tell them that if they let me go, I won't tell anyone on the outside about them. I'll keep the existence of their city a secret. They have nothing to worry about."

"It would do no good, *señor*. They will not let you leave. They are here now to see if they will kill you or keep you as a slave, like me."

The High Chief smacked Pedro's shoulder, then rambled on for over a minute. When he gestured, Pedro turned back. "Wakonhomin wants to know where you are from. They have never seen a white man before."

"Just tell him I come from the rising sun." Nate had an inspiration. "Also tell him that if they do not let me go, many more white men will come, and many of their warriors will be killed. Their war clubs are no match for our guns."

"You do not want me to say that."

"Tell him."

Nate waited as Valdez relayed his statements. Crooked Nose and most of the others scowled. Wakonhomin's bird mask shook as he wagged a short painted stick and curtly replied.

"He says you lie, *señor*. You would not have found this place if Pahchatka had not brought you. The mist and the red wolves keep the Anasazis safe."

The High Chief was no one's fool. Nate chose his next words much more carefully. "Ask him to be reasonable, Pedro. I'm only here for the Ute boy they took. I promised the boy's dying father I would take him back."

Pedro was going to say something, but Wakonhomin interrupted. "He says that your woman, that your *hijo* and *hija*, your son and your daughter, have not been

88

caught. But they soon will be. If the kachinas do not get them first."

Nate glanced toward the terraces and the jungle beyond. Dread for his family almost spurred him into making a desperate bid for freedom. He could leap from the low roof and hit the ground running. But he restrained himself. Scores of Anasazis were in the plaza, scores more tilling the lower terraces. He wouldn't get five hundred yards.

The High Chief had more to say, and Valdez dutifully translated. "You are not sick like the Spaniard was. So they will not kill you right away."

"Tell him thanks for nothing."

Pedro did no such thing. "He wants to strike a bargain with you, *señor.*"

"What kind of bargain?"

"They are most interested in your horses. They have seen horses before, ridden by Utes and others. But the Anasazis have never had any of their own." Wakonhomin talked awhile. "He wants you to teach his people all you know about them: how to ride, how to breed many more. It will make their tribe strong. And if they must leave here, they can take more belongings with them."

"Why would they abandon the last of their cities?"

"This place was a garden when first they came. But now there is much bad medicine. The ground shakes often. The lake is drying up. The kachinas grow bolder. And their women are not having as many babies as they once did."

Now that Pedro mentioned it, Nate realized there were far fewer inhabitants than there should be. A city that size could accommodate more than a thousand without crowding. Yet he had seen only a few hundred. The Anasazis were in jeopardy of becoming extinct, like the Mandans. "What do I get if I agree to teach them?"

David Thompson

"They will spare your life, and the lives of your *familia*."

"Will they let us go eventually?"

Pedro posed the question. It sparked a heated argument between the High Chief and Pahchatka. While they squabbled, Pedro sidled next to Nate. "If you do make it out, *señor*, I would be in your debt if you would send a letter to Mr. Jonathan Levi in San Antonio, Texas. Have him give my love to my *padre* and *madre*." As an afterthought, Pedro added, "I spent six years on his ranch. It is where I learned English."

"If I make it out, you're coming along," Nate reiterated.

"I would only slow you down." Pedro raised his scarred eyes to the heavens. "Once, I prayed to go home. Now I do not want to. Look at me. What could I do for a living? Be a beggar? Sit on a street corner and plead for pesos? I would rather die."

The argument ended and the High Chief cleared his throat. "Wakonhomin says that you must give up thoughts of leaving. You will spend the rest of your days with his people. So will your family. And if any of you try to escape, all of you will have done to your eyes what was done to mine." Pedro paused. "I am sorry."

So was Nate. The Anasazis were leaving him no choice. With a little outside help the tribe might survive the current crisis. But if they persisted in their hardheaded outlook, if they were so ruled by spite and distrust that they would not accept a helping hand when it was offered, then they were doomed.

And unless he could turn the tables, so were those he loved most.

Chapter Ten

Zach King's right shoulder hurt something fierce. The war club had evidently struck a nerve, because he had lost some of the feeling in his arm. It tingled and throbbed, rendered momentarily useless.

But when he saw the Anasazi with the bow take aim at his mother, when he saw that she could not bring her rifle to bear in time, he grit his teeth and willed his right arm to move whether it wanted to or not.

He could not use his left hand. In it he held the bay's reins and the spent Hawken.

Zach nearly cried out as his right arm screamed in protest. By sheer willpower he wrapped his fingers around one of the big pistols at his waist. The Anasazi had the tip of the barbed shaft fixed on his mother's torso; another instant and the arrow would take wing. Shoving his arm outward, Zach thumbed back the hammer and fired.

In his condition, and with the bouncing of the bay,

Zach could not aim very well. He did the best he could. And while the shot did not have the immediate effect he wanted, it had the desired result.

The .55-caliber smoothbore belched smoke and lead. The warrior's fingers were starting to release the string when the ball, by sheer accident or the design of providence, hit the ash bow several inches above the Anasazi's knuckles. It splintered the wood, and the feathered shaft intended for Winona's breast instead fluttered erratically and embedded itself in the earth midway between them.

The Anasazi shook a fist at Zach and howled in fury.

Winona expressed her gratitude in the look she gave Stalking Coyote. Words were not necessary.

Shoshones by nature were passionate about life and deeply affectionate toward one another. As Nate has taken some time to learn, they expressed their affection more in actions than in words. Which was why, after they escaped the valley, once they were back home, Winona intended to do something special for her son as a token of her thanks. Maybe she would get him a new knife. Maybe a new saddle. Whatever she did, it would come from her heart, and mean more than words ever could.

Evelyn saw more warriors hurrying to cut them off and slapped her legs against her pony's sides. She was scared, awfully scared, but she did as her mother had taught her and did not let it show. "Courage is as important for a woman as for a man," Winona had once told her. "Just as you learn how to cook and sew, you must learn to be brave. Never shame yourself or your man by being a coward."

"But, Ma," Evelyn had said, recalling their run-in with a grizzly. "What if I can't help myself? What if I'm so frightened I can't think straight?"

"Don't let it show. As people grow, they learn to control their tempers, to control their tongues. Learning to control how you act when you are afraid is the same. The difference between a coward and a brave person is that cowards let their fear control them while the brave ones control their fear.''

So now Evelyn pushed her fright to the back of her mind, hunched forward, and rode like the wind.

The Anasazis fell behind. Winona did not feel truly safe until the trees closed around them. Slowing, she veered to the southwest, riding deeper into the woodland in the general direction of the horseshoe city. A glance at the sun showed they had several hours yet before the sun would set.

''What are we going to do next, Ma?'' Zach asked. All the running and hiding they were doing did not fit his image of how a true warrior should act.

''What I have planned to do all along. We must find where the Anasazis are keeping your father. Then one of us will sneak in and get him out.''

''I'll go,'' Zach immediately volunteered. When the other Shoshone boys heard about it, they would be green with envy.

''No. I will.'' Winona raised a hand to stifle her son's protest. ''To pass for an Anasazi, you must dress like one. And we do not have the clothes their men wear.'' She touched her dress. ''In the dark, I think I have a better chance of being mistaken for one of their own women.''

''You don't know that for sure,'' Zach said sulkily. ''We haven't seen any of their women close up. The Anasazis might catch you, too.''

Winona knew why her son was so greatly upset, but she would not relent. Trying to lighten his mood, she grinned and said, ''Then you will have the two of us to rescue.''

Rubbing his sore shoulder, Zach rode on without comment. It was downright unfair, he reflected, that every time he had a chance to count more coup, his folks ruined it. They treated him as if he were Evelyn's age. If they kept it up, one of these days he was going to go off on his own, or maybe with a select group of friends, and prove to everyone beyond a shadow of a doubt that he was a worthy son of Grizzly Killer and a warrior in his own right.

In under an hour they came to the high crown of a long-unused series of terraces that overlooked the Anasazi city. A small herd of strange, deerlike animals was grazing on the high grass, and at their approach, fled into the forest.

Zach yearned to shoot one, but the shot would be heard below. He had some pemmican and jerky in a parfleche, enough to last several days, but neither could rival the taste of freshly roasted meat dripping with fat and grease.

After tethering their mounts, the three of them crawled to the rim and spied on their enemies. "Look for sign of your father," Winona said. "He should be the only one wearing buckskins." Even at that distance, her husband would stand out. But though they watched for hours, though they strained their eyes until the sun was perched on the lip of the western cliffs, they did not spot him.

"They must have Pa inside somewhere," Zach said, stating the obvious. "What if they never bring him outdoors?"

Winona was mulling that very problem. To search the entire city was the same as asking to be captured. They'd have to go from rooftop to door, peering into each and every opening.

Evelyn twisted to relieve a cramp in her arm. At the tree line stood one of the cute deerlike creatures they had seen earlier, a young one, contentedly grazing. It did not appear to be afraid of them or their horses. "Look, Ma," she whispered.

Turning, Winona saw the deer, and smiled. "If it comes closer, try to feed it some grass by hand."

Zach thought the idea was terrific. While his sister distracted it, he could grab the critter around the neck and slash its throat before it could let out a peep. Then he'd go back in the trees and light a small fire. His stomach growled in anticipation.

Just then the creature raised its dainty head and sniffed loudly. Its wide eyes swung toward the undergrowth. Tail flicking, ears erect, it took a few steps to one side, then to the other.

"It's acting scared," Evelyn said. "Why?"

The deer bolted, plunging into the wall of green and vanishing. They could not hear it, so quietly did it move. Winona started to turn back toward the slope when a hideous cry rent the shadowy terrain, a high-pitched bleat that swelled to a strangled shriek. Abruptly, the cry died.

"Something got it!" Evelyn said, and went to run to its aid.

"Be still," Winona said, gripping her daughter's wrist.

From the vegetation rose a loud crunch. There was no mistaking the sound for anything other than what it was: a bone being clamped onto by powerful jaws. More crunching ensued, along with low grunts.

The horses had caught the predator's scent and were prancing and nickering. Worst was the pony, which pulled against its tether in a panic.

"We have to shut them up," Zach said. He ran to do so before the thing that had caught the little deer got wind of the horses. Whatever was in there had to be big, and just might decide that one measly deer was not enough to satisfy its hunger.

Winona rose. "We must help your brother."

The horses were growing more agitated by the moment. The mare whinnied and tugged and stomped its hooves, even after Winona rubbed its neck and spoke soothingly. The loudest crunch yet nearly made the horse uncontrollable.

Mixed with the snap of bones was the rending of flesh and the smack of inhuman lips. Snorts and grunts punctuated the grisly feast. It was like listening to a grizzly eat, only louder, more ghastly.

Suddenly the sound of eating stopped. Winona clamped a hand over the mare's muzzle and Zach did likewise with the bay. Evelyn was a shade slow in covering the pony's, and her tardiness reaped a shrill nicker that was answered by a throaty, questioning growl.

New snapping noises arose. Not the snapping of bones, but the snap of tree limbs and the crackle of brush. Winona's breath caught in her throat. Whatever had devoured the red deer was coming toward them!

Nate King's fingers were unbearably sore. All bore cuts, some deeper than others. His left index finger was the worst, always bleeding and stinging, even after he ripped a strip from the hem of his hunting shirt and bandaged the laceration.

The pain had been worth it. In the hours since the Anasazis had quizzed him, he'd made wonderful progress. His hard toil had resulted in a hole the size of a melon. At his feet were piled the heavy stones he had removed, and a mound of dirt.

The room on the other side was unoccupied, but it might not be so much longer. Thanks to the light spilling in from above, Nate could see the many possessions that belonged to its occupants. Blankets, baskets, pots and other cooking utensils, clothes, and much more were neatly arranged around the quarters.

Nate guessed that whoever lived there would return along about sunset. That was when the tillers would come in from the fields, when warriors would come for their supper, when families would come back to their home. He had to get out of there before then.

Incentive was provided by a ladder bathed in waning

sunlight. If only he could reach it! Under cover of darkness, escaping would be easy. But there was a hitch, a hitch that might result in his prompt recapture. He had given his word to take the Ute boy and Pedro along, and he was not leaving without them.

Nate dug into the wall with renewed vigor. He had excavated two deep horizontal furrows, one a couple of feet above the other, and each a couple of feet long. Applying the sharp pottery shard to the top one, he scraped and pried and dug until he was almost through.

He was running out of time. The light was fading, the sky darkening. Soon, very soon, the sun would go down, and once that happened, once the fiery orb sank below the western rim of the mesa, it would be the same as snuffing out a lantern. The rooms would be plunged into inky gloom, and he would have to grope his way in the dark.

Of course, by then the occupants were bound to return. Nate set down the shard, stepped back, and smashed his right foot against the wall, between the furrows. Again and again he pounded, and he was rewarded by hairline fractures that spread with each blow.

Break, damn you! Nate mentally railed. His right foot grew sore, so he switched to his left. More cracks appeared, but not enough, nowhere near enough. Looping his left arm through the hole, he braced it against the opposite side of the wall, then pulled inward with all his strength. Mortar crumbled. Dirt cascaded in an ever-growing quantity. His muscles bulged, his chest heaved.

Brreak! Break! Break! Stepping back, Nate delivered another kick, throwing all of his weight into it. The mortar gave way completely and rocks clattered into both rooms. Bending, he squeezed into the gap. His shoulders made it through, but his chest snagged on the jagged edges. Wriggling would not free him. He pushed against the wall and gained a few inches, no more. He was caught like a beaver in a trap.

Voices above stilled his exertions. Nate heard footsteps. He glanced at the opening and tensed in dread that the silhouette of a person would appear. But whoever was up there walked on by.

The light was almost gone.

Nate applied himself in a frenzy, wrenching and tearing at the wall like a man gone berserk. His fingers bled profusely and his chest flamed with agony. He was beginning to despair of ever freeing himself when the portion of wall under him buckled. He had to throw both arms over his head to keep from cracking his noggin as he was spilled onto the floor.

Not wasting a second, Nate rose and ran to the ladder. Swiftly, he climbed, but he was only halfway up when more voices sounded and footsteps approached. Jumping down, he scrambled into a corner.

The room was now so dark that Nate could not see the collapsed wall from where he stood. Hopefully, neither would the occupants as they came down the ladder.

A woman laughed lightly and lowered her legs through the entrance. Descending, she chattered gaily, looking up, not at the floor. Behind her came a man. Tillers, to judge by their clothing, or lack of it. They were middle-aged, a married couple, Nate figured. Neither was armed, that he could see.

He needed a weapon. Recalling that there had been a broom propped in the corner, he probed along the wall and found it. The handle was short, thick, and heavy, sturdy enough to serve as a cudgel. He did not want to hurt the couple, but he'd be a fool to let them call out. He'd have every last Anasazi in the city down on his shoulders.

The woman reached the floor and turned. Spying the debris, she put a hand to her throat and spoke excitedly.

Her husband looked at the shattered wall, then jumped. Together they cautiously walked toward the hole.

Nate had a choice to make. They had their backs to him; he could drop them both before either knew he was there. Instead, he darted to the ladder and started up, taking two rungs at a stride. They could not help but hear him, and spun. The man took two bounds and grabbed his ankle.

Nate attempted to jerk his leg loose, but the Anasazi was as strong as a bull. A lifetime of toil had turned the man's sinews into solid iron. Nate swung the broom, slamming it against the Anasazi's temple hard enough to knock out most men. All the tiller did was grunt.

The wife leaped to her husband's side. Crying out, she clawed at Nate's other leg. Her weight, combined with the man's, unbalanced Nate. Since he could not hold on to the rung with both hands and still keep hold of the broom, he dropped it.

Clinging precariously as the ladder swiveled and threatened to dump him, Nate fought to climb higher. The Anasazis were intent on keeping him there, their nails digging into him like talons.

A sharp crack rent the room. The ladder was breaking. With a mighty heave, Nate gained the next rung. The woman lost her grip, but not her husband. Glancing around, Nate brought the sole of his foot crashing down on the man's nose. Cartilage crunched, and the Anasazi's fingers slipped off him.

Nate spurted to the top, vaulting onto the roof just as the ladder buckled and fell. He was out, but there was no cause to celebrate. For at that juncture the woman vented a scream that would do justice to a panther. Almost as if on cue, an Anasazi appeared on the next roof, a war club in hand.

Chapter Eleven

Without thinking, Winona King swung astride her skittish mare and prepared to race over the crown of the uppermost terrace. As she was lifting the reins, she hesitated. The sun had just relinquished the vault of sky above the mesa to a few twinkling stars, but it was not yet dark enough to conceal her and the children on the slopes below. The Anasazis might spot them.

Evelyn mounted her pony with difficulty. The terrified animal would not stand still. It nickered and pranced, never once taking its eyes off the wall of vegetation that separated them from whatever approached.

Zach was last to climb on, in case the thing attacked. He was between the trees and the others, so the creature was bound to focus on him first. The crackle and snap of brush being trampled grew louder and louder, and he could hear the beast's heavy breathing, like the wheezing of a bellows in a blacksmith's shop.

A dark shape materialized, the spectral outline of a

gargantuan bulk, and halted a stone's throw away. A tell-tale gleam among the leaves seemed to be an eye. Zach could feel it studying him, and a chill swept his body. He could not be positive, but he had a hunch it was one of the monsters that had wiped out the Ute hunting party. Maybe it was the very same monster.

Evelyn was too petrified to move a muscle. She had never seen anything so huge. To her, it was unspeakably evil. All the badness in the world, all the wickedness, all the vile things that should not be, were centered in that enormous shape.

Winona was filled with inexplicable loathing. She felt as if she were in the presence of an abomination of all that had ever been, an entity that had no business being alive and yet was, a being from the old times when Coyote first walked the earth. Her rifle was loaded and primed, but she could not bring herself to shoot for fear that she would only wound it and provoke it into attacking. Against a thing that immense, they would fare the same as the hapless Utes.

A rumbling growl warned that the creature might charge anyway. Winona saw it lumber a few yards to the north, saw what must be its head tilt in their direction. The rustle of leaves on alien skin was unnerving, as was the sibilant hissing that ensued. A slender object the length of her arm speared the twilight and was withdrawn. She was jolted to realize it must be the creature's tongue. The beast was testing the air as would a snake.

Zach definitely saw an eye fixed on him, an eye the size of a frying pan. An inky pool of brutish malevolence that tore into the depths of his being and ignited fear so potent he could not help trembling. Was this what the Utes had felt during their last moments? he wondered. The same unreasoning panic that gripped him?

The hissing continued, along with an odd regular swishing, as of something being rubbed back and forth over the forest floor. Its tail, Zach guessed.

Winona did not understand why the thing just stood there, watching them. Was it merely curious? Had the red deer satisfied its appetite? Or was it going to explode from the vegetation and overwhelm them before they got off a shot?

The creature answered her question by turning and moving off into the gathering night, its ponderous tread resembling muted drumbeats. Then the rending of limbs grew fainter and fainter, until at last the only sound was the sigh of the wind and the distant cry of a bird.

"What was it, Ma?" Evelyn breathed. "Is there anything like it where we live?"

"No, of course not," Winona said with confidence she did not feel. No one could say with authority what lurked in the remote vastness of the mountains. There were places so remote that no one had ever visited them, not red men nor whites, mysterious places, places reputed to be bad medicine, places better shunned than visited. In those hidden nooks might dwell creatures long gone from the rest of the world, creatures that clung tenaciously to life as if waiting for the day when the reign of man would end and their kind could spread out over the world again as they had in the dim past.

The thought made Winona uneasy, as if she had stumbled on a truth better left unknown. "Come," she announced, and rode along the summit to the south, to where the trees did not crowd the rim. To where they would have a few second's forewarning if something rushed out at them.

"What now?" Evelyn asked.

"We wait."

And wait they did, for another hour, until the terraces were cloaked in an inky mantle. It was an hour that further frayed their frazzled nerves, thanks to savagery gone amok in the forest.

The Lost Valley

The beasts claimed the night as their own. Again and again the verdant growth was punctured by fierce roars, unearthly howls, and bestial screeches. Night transformed the tranquil valley into a slaughter ground, a constant contest for survival between predators and prey, between hunters and hunted.

Winona did not let on that the din rattled her. The sounds were similar to those she was accustomed to outside the lost valley—similar, yet different. The cries were those of creatures she had never encountered, of animals unlike those that dwelled in the mountains and the plains, of animals probably unlike those found anywhere else.

Once a frenzied bleating broke out close at hand. It was the death cry of another red deer, or something like it. When the bleating died they heard loud thumping, then a roar to end all roars, a roar of triumph that drowned out all the other sounds in the valley. For the longest while after the roar died, not a peep was heard.

Toward the end of the hour a battle broke out between two meat-eaters. Their snarls and roars rose in a feral chorus amplified by the towering cliffs.

Winona was at a loss to explain why the Anasazis had chosen to live there, and why they stayed on. At night it was virtual suicide to be abroad in the woodland. In effect, the Anasazis were prisoners in their own city once the sun went down.

Maybe, Winona mused, the tribe liked it that way. The mist, the red wolves, the high ramparts were all barriers that kept the outside world at bay. Possibly the same was true of the dense forest and its nocturnal bloodletters: They were another barrier, certain death for anyone unwitting enough to roam the woods after dark.

Winona was glad when the moment came to mount and descend the terraces. She reined up halfway down, where Zach and Evelyn had a clear view in all directions and no one could come at them without being seen.

"You will wait here for me," she directed as he gave her reins to Stalking Coyote.

Zach did not like it, but he did not argue. "How long do we cool our heels? What if you're not back by dawn?"

"Then go into the trees and hide. It should be safe enough in the daytime."

Evelyn was not keen on being left alone. "Why can't we go with you?" she asked. "We'd be real quiet."

Winona verified that her rifle was loaded and primed. "There are bound to be sentries, little one. One person can slip in where three would find it hard."

"I want to be with you," Evelyn persisted. She could imagine all kinds of hideous creatures slinking out of the forest to devour them once her mother was gone.

Gently resting a hand on her daughter's shoulder, Winona said, "I know. And if it were safe, I would take you. But now you must be brave. Remember our talk earlier? You must control your fear, not let it control you." She nodded at her son. "Besides, Stalking Coyote will protect you. He is as brave as his father, and a fine shot."

Zach was flattered by the compliment. "Don't worry about us, Ma. Nothing will get her while I'm alive."

Winona kissed her daughter, squeezed her son's arm, and left, working steadily lower until she came to a road. The tilled terraces lay quiet under the starlight. None of the Anasazis were abroad.

On the valley floor the nightmarish sounds of the prowling beasts were faint. Evidently they confined themselves to the woods, perhaps because that was where the game hid to escape.

Her thumb on the Hawken's hammer, Winona jogged toward the city. The walls gleamed dully, in part from the starlight, in part from countless torches kept lit along the outer perimeter. Figures moved on top of the walls and in the plaza.

Winona tried not to dwell on the daunting challenge ahead. Locating her husband would be next to impossible, but she was not leaving the valley without him. To her right the lake glistened. Something splashed loudly. She turned to see what it was, when suddenly the ground shook violently under her feet.

It was a repeat of the afternoon, only this time it was worse. The valley floor convulsed and heaved. Winona could not stay on her feet. The road surged upward, pitching her onto her stomach.

Suddenly, directly in front of her eyes, the earth split, yawning wide. And as she looked on in rising horror, the ground under her fell away.

Nate King whirled and crouched. The Anasazis would not retake him without a fight. In the room below, the woman and the man were yelling loud enough to rouse the dead. Certainly loud enough to bring every Anasazi within earshot on the run.

The man on the next roof raised the war club, but not to throw it. "*Senor* King, is that you?"

A low parapet divided the two apartments. Nate leaped over it and clutched Pedro Valdez's arm. "It's me, hoss. What the devil are you doing here?"

"I came to help you escape," the Mexican said, with a nod at the ladder he had just lowered into the apartment in which the mountain man had been originally imprisoned. "But apparently you do not need my help."

"We're both getting out of here."

Or were they? The hollering had drawn the interest of Anasazis in the plaza below and on the walls above. Patches of torchlight reflected off warriors and others hurrying to investigate.

At the moment, Nate and Pedro were sheathed in

shadow and were safe from detection. But they would not be so for much longer. "Where can we hide?" Nate asked.

"There is nowhere they will not look," the blind vaquero said. "They will search the city from top to bottom."

Shouts on the level below spurred Nate into action. Grabbing Valdez's hand, Nate pulled him to the ladder. "Can you climb down without making any noise?"

"You want to go back into the room where they held you?"

Nate did indeed. It was the last place the Anasazi would think to look. Or so he hoped. "Can you or not?"

"*Sí.* I can be like a tiny mouse when I need to."

"Then follow me."

The apartment was inky black. Nate did not take his eyes off the opening in the north wall as he went down. The couple in the next room had not thought to light a lamp or torch yet. They were still bawling their lungs out.

At the bottom Nate coiled and waited. His new friend was true to his boast and made no noise. Snatching Pedro's wrist, Nate pulled him into a far corner and had him hunker. Then Nate ran to where he had left the frayed sack. As he groped for it, feet drummed overhead.

The tillers yelled louder, and whoever was up there answered. Nate dashed to Valdez, squatted, and draped the sack over their heads. Lifting the edge, he peeked at the collapsed wall. From the sound of things, the couple were telling those on the roof what had happened.

A head poked down from the overhead entrance, made a quick scrutiny, and was withdrawn. Someone barked orders. Footsteps pounded off in various directions.

"The search has begun," Pedro whispered. "Wakonhomin himself is leading it."

Light flared in the room next door. A person bearing

a torch came to the buckled wall and poked the torch past it. The glow cast by the crackling flames illuminated most of the floor but not the far corners, not the corner where the trapper and the vaquero were. Whoever held the torch snorted like an angry bull and turned away.

Soon the whole city thrummed with movement. Anasazis were constantly shouting, reporting, receiving instructions, as they hastened from door to door, apartment to apartment. Nate compared the situation to being caught in a hive of riled bees.

"My congratulations, *señor*," Pedro whispered after half an hour. "You are very sly, like the fox."

"We're still not out of danger," Nate reminded him. Which was the understatement of the century. To reach the jungle they must sneak from the city and cross a lot of open space. In broad daylight it would be impossible. So they must make their bid before sunrise, when the city might still be swarming with Anasazis.

"No matter what happens, my friend, I thank you for trying to save me," Pedro said solemnly. "But I ask you again to change your mind. I will only slow you down."

"It's whole hog or nothing at all."

A racket in the next apartment led Nate to believe that the couple had joined the hunt. The glow faded when they departed, leaving both rooms in total darkness. Nate could not see his fingers when he held them six inches in front of his nose.

Pedro touched his elbow. "I almost forgot, *señor*. I found the Ute boy."

"Nevava?"

"I do not know his name. He does not speak English or Spanish, and I do not speak his tongue. He is being held in the temple. The priests will use him as a helper. When he is older, if he proves he can be trusted, they will adopt him into the tribe."

"The temple? Is that the building by itself at the south-west corner of the plaza?"

"*Sí*. The kiva is there."

"The what?"

"A special place where the Anasazis worship. They pray there every day, and hold rites. There are other kivas in the city, smaller ones, not as important."

Nate would have liked to learn more about the religious aspect of the Anasazis' lives, but it had gotten quiet nearby. Now was as good a time as any to make their break. "Stay close to me," he cautioned, tugging at the blind man's sleeve.

They crept toward the ladder, Nate alert for obstacles his friend might trip over. His foot bumped a basket, and he kicked it aside. "When we reach the top we'll head straight for the temple."

"How will you get across the plaza?"

"I'll cross that bridge when I come to it." Nate had a half-baked plan. If he could get his hands on a blanket, he would throw it over him and trust in—

Suddenly Pedro grabbed his shirt. "*Señor*, do you feel it?" he anxiously asked.

"Feel what?" Nate responded, and the next instant the whole room shook as if it were being buffeted by cyclonic winds. But Nate knew better. He darted to the ladder and steadied it, saying, "Another earthquake! Hurry! We've got to get out of here!"

"Above us! Do you hear?"

Pedro's sensitive ears had registered the cracking and splintering of mortar and beams a second before Nate's had. Glancing up, Nate blinked as dust rained onto his head and into his eyes. A heartbeat later, a section of the roof caved in on them.

Chapter Twelve

Zachary King was honing the blade of his hunting knife when the earthquake hit. For a short while after his mother left them he had paced the rim of the terrace, worry gnawing at him like a beaver through bark. Deciding he needed to do something to take his mind off his folks, he had taken a whetstone from his possibles bag, sat facing the Anasazi city, and proceeded to sharpen his knife.

Evelyn had spread a blanket on the grass and curled into a ball. She was too upset to sleep, so she lay there fretting and wishing the family had never left home. She was not like her brother, who always craved excitement and adventure. Peace and quiet appealed to her more. Fondly, she recalled the many quiet evenings she had spent lying warm and toasty in front of the fireplace, her mother sewing or knitting, her father reading aloud.

She would give anything to be doing that now. No hostile Indians would be trying to kill them. Nothing would be trying to eat them. They would not be trapped in a strange place that reeked of evil. They would be happy, at their ease, content. Which was how life was meant to be.

"I don't think I'm ever going to go on one of these gallivants again," Evelyn announced.

"You will."

Her brother's blunt reply disturbed her. He was always so smug, always acting superior. "What makes you so sure?"

"Because you're glued to Ma. Where she goes, you go. If our folks were to take it into their heads to travel to Canada or the Pacific Ocean, you'd be right at their side."

It was the truth, but Evelyn was not going to openly admit as much. "Maybe I would, maybe I wouldn't," she hedged. *Just because he's older, he thinks he knows everything.*

"Oh, please," Zach said while stroking the edge of his blade at the proper angle across the whetstone. "What else would you do? Stay home by yourself?"

"I could always live with Uncle Spotted Bull and Aunt Morning Dove." Evelyn had him there. Her mother's brother and his wife would be glad to look after her for a spell. They were always delighted when the family came to visit.

Evelyn enjoyed her yearly stays in the Shoshone village, but it was not the same as being at home. She did not much like it that the men got to go off and do all the hunting and such while the women were expected to do all the chores around the lodges. Her aunt was always cooking or mending or skinning or curing hides and never seemed to have much time to relax and enjoy life.

Secretly, Evelyn harbored a desire to venture east of the Mississippi one day and visit a big city. Her father had told her all about them, about the shops where a woman could buy pretty dresses and hats and anything else she needed. He'd told her about the theater and concerts and gay parties where people danced the night away.

Evelyn's fondest possession was a catalogue her pa had picked up somewhere. It showed all sorts of items a person could purchase, everything from clothes to plows. Many an evening she had spent flipping its pages, fascinated by the many strange and wondrous marvels on sale. On many an afternoon she had daydreamed about what it would be like to live in a lodge made of brick or stone, to have servants wait on her hand and foot, to go for strolls wearing the latest in fashion. *Wouldn't that be grand!*

Evelyn had grown drowsy. Closing her eyes, she listened to the wail of an animal in torment. Suddenly she felt the ground shake and she sat bolt upright. "Zach!"

"It's another quake," Zach said, and began to rise. He was on one knee when the whole terrace bucked and heaved like a mustang. His Hawken lay on the grass at his side, and he made a grab for it, afraid it would slide down the slope. To his consternation, a second later his legs were jarred out from under him and *he* tumbled over the brink.

"Zach!" Evelyn yelled, trying to rise. She was thrown onto her back, unhurt but terribly scared. The horses shared her fear, for they were whinnying and rearing. She rolled onto her side and saw her pony bolt, racing pell-mell up the slopes toward the forest.

"No!" Evelyn shoved onto her hands and knees, but that was the best she could do until the upheaval ended a minute later. She did not move right away, afraid it was just a lull.

At the bottom of the terrace, Zach slowly rose, rubbing a sore spot on his ribs. He had dropped his whetstone when he fell and nearly stabbed himself as he tumbled.

Sheathing his knife, he started back up. "Evelyn, are you all right?"

"Yes, but the pony ran off."

"Drat." Zach reached the top and spotted his whetstone. Shoving it into his possibles bag, he picked up his Hawken. "Which way?"

Evelyn pointed at the black fringe of vegetation visible high above them. "We have to go after him."

"We'll do no such thing," Zach responded. "Ma told us to stay put, and that's exactly what we're going to do."

"But what if one of those monsters gets wind of him? He'll be eaten."

"It's his own fault for being so stupid. I always said that critter was too mule-headed for its own good."

Evelyn was shocked her own brother could be so coldhearted. "You don't care if George Washington winds up dead?" She had given the pony that name because she had always been fond of the first president after hearing about his life from her pa. Her favorite part was where young George owned up to chopping down a cherry tree.

"What a dumb name for a horse," Zach said for the umpteenth time as he stepped to the other animals to calm them.

"Is not." Pouting, Evelyn moved to her mother's mare. "Fine. If you won't lend a hand, I'll catch George myself. Give me a boost."

Zach knew how stubborn his sister could be when she set her mind to something. "Look. I'd like to help you. Really and truly. But what if Pa and Ma come back and find us and the horses gone?"

"That's easy. Leave the stallion and the mare here, hobbled. That way they can't wander off. We'll take your bay and be back before you know it."

The suggestion made sense, but Zach balked. His sister

did not seem to realize that if they followed the pony into the forest, the pony wasn't the only thing that might wind up in the belly of one of those huge beasts.

"Please," Evelyn pleaded. "The longer we take, the harder it will be to catch him."

She had another point. Reluctantly, Zach took a pair of hobbles from his pa's parfleche. "Have it your way. But I hope we don't regret this."

"Don't worry. We won't."

Winona King flung herself to the right as the gaping earth yawned wide to swallow her. She landed on her shoulder and rolled, then kept on rolling, over and over and over, until she was confident she was in the clear. Half dizzy, she stood.

The earth had stopped buckling. A chasm as wide as a Shoshone lance had rent the middle of the road. She thought of the children, but figured they would be safe enough. From what she could see, the terraces had not split apart as the valley floor had.

Behind her a peculiar gurgling erupted. Winona pivoted and was startled to behold the surface of the lake foam and bubble like soup in a cauldron. Only, it was not giving off steam or smoke. She moved closer and saw that the water along the shore was moving, swirling parallel with the shoreline.

Puzzled but unwilling to waste more time, Winona turned toward the city. She stopped cold when the lake made a moaning sound like a woman in labor. The water was flowing faster in the same circular pattern, while in the center it roiled and churned.

Again she started to leave, but surprise rooted her in place. The lake was shrinking! Right before her eyes the water level was falling rapidly. But that could not be, she told herself.

Now all the water was in motion, flowing like a river,

in a great circle. In the middle the surface was parted as if by an invisible hand, forming a funnel. A sucking sound replaced the moans, a sound like that made by a foal sucking on its mother's teat, magnified many times.

At last Winona understood. In her cabin she had a sink, courtesy of her considerate husband. At the bottom was a drain that emptied into a bucket. Whenever she let the water out after cleaning dishes, it swirled in the same manner as the lake and sometimes made the same sucking noises.

The earthquake was to blame. It had cracked the lake bed just as it had split the road, and now the water was being drawn into the depths of the earth. Once it was gone, what would the Anasazis do? How would they survive? Without water, their crops would wither. Without water, they would soon die of thirst.

Winona did not linger to witness the outcome. She had Nate to think of. Cradling her rifle, she hurried to the south.

Nate King threw his arms over his head to ward off the falling stones and mortar, but it was like trying to ward off an avalanche. Some of the stones were as big as melons. They pummeled him, gouging flesh, battering bones, and nearly drove him to his knees.

Pedro cried out. Nate tried to go to him, but a chunk of wall more than two feet wide smashed onto his shoulder and the world blinked out.

How long Nate lay unconscious he could not say, although it could not have been more than a few minutes. Dust filled the air, getting into his nose, his mouth. He fought back a sneeze and tried to sit up, but couldn't. His legs were pinned under the chunk that had fallen on him. Sliding his hands underneath, he pushed, straining against the weight. Inch by gradual inch, the slab slid off.

There was no sensation in his right leg. Dreading it

might be broken, Nate rose gingerly, applying his full weight only when he was erect. His thigh hurt abominably, but the feeling returned after he pumped the leg a few times.

The rest of his body had not fared much better. His shirt was ripped, his chest was cut and bruised, his arms bore welts and slash marks, and his left shoulder hurt if he so much as twitched it. But his own welfare did not concern him.

"Pedro?"

The vaquero lay under a pile of debris, his legs and one arm all that could be seen. Bending, Nate tore into the pile, flinging it to the right and the left, heedless of the noise he made.

"Pedro?"

There was no answer. Nate's hands fairly flew. He came to part of a wide beam and gripped it. Bunching his shoulders, he raised one end. It was like trying to raise a ten-ton boulder. He'd expected the beam to be heavy but nowhere near as heavy as it was. As he swung it clear, his left foot almost slipped out from under him. A glance showed why.

Trickling across the floor were rivulets of blood. Nate let the beam fall and knelt. "Pedro?" he said softly. Valdez was on his back, breathing raggedly, a jagged cavity in his chest. Nate touched the men's cheek.

Groaning, the vaquero stirred to life, his sightless eyes fixed on the shadowed ceiling. "*Señor* King? Is that you? What happened?"

"Another quake." Nate leaned low to examine the extent of the wound. Sorrow racked him, and he wanted to beat on the beam with his fists.

"I feel so weak. My head swims." Pedro attempted to sit up but could not. Wincing, he would have collapsed if Nate had not caught him.

"Lie still."

"How bad is it?"

Nate hesitated, unwilling to impart the truth and just as unwilling to lie. "You need to rest," he hedged.

Pedro Valdez was no fool. "That bad," he said forlornly. His Adam's apple bobbed. "I guess I will never see Mexico again, eh? Never see a golden sun rise over the desert of Sonora, or the beauty of the Sierra Madres."

"Maybe the Anasazis can heal you," Nate said. "I'll go fetch them."

The vaquero's hand groped upward and wrapped around Nate's arm. "You will do no such thing, *amigo*. They would only take you captive again, and this time maybe they would bind you." A coughing fit seized him, and his face flushed purple. When it subsided, he gasped for air, rasping, "It is no use anyway. I am fading. I can feel it."

Nate was at a loss to know quite what to say. They had not been friends long enough for a deep bond to have grown, but he liked Valdez immensely and was profoundly sad. "There might be some water in the next room. Hold on. I'll go see."

"No," Pedro said, and coughed violently again. Froth appeared at the corners of his mouth. "There is something more important. Promise me you will get word to Jonathan Levi of San Antonio, as I asked once before. Have him tell my parents what happened."

"I give my word."

"*Bueno, bueno,*" Pedro said, practically whispering. For a while he was still, so still that the mountain man pressed fingers over his wrist to verify he was still alive. Inhaling loudly, Pedro smacked his lips and said, "Who would have thought it? That I would end my days like this?" He laughed bitterly, inducing another spurt of coughs and wheezes.

"You shouldn't talk."

"Why not? In a little bit I will be gone. I cannot move

and I cannot see. All I can do is talk. If 'that is the only joy left to me, then talk I will." His hand tightened on Nate. "It hurts so much. I would scream, but it would bring the Anasazis down on you."

"They should pay for their atrocities."

"No, *señor*. They do only what they must. Once, I hated them more than any man has ever hated anyone. But now I feel only pity. My time is short, but so is theirs. They are the last of their kind, and soon there will come a day when they will be no more." Pedro could barely voice the words, but the simple exertion took its toll in the form of spasms that had him gulping for every breath.

The trapper cradled the vaquero's head in his lap. Presently the convulsions ended and Pedro tilted his head upward.

"Do you smell the night air? How fresh it is, like a garden of flowers. And that music! Where is it coming from?"

Nate sniffed but did not detect a fragrant scent. Nor did he hear music. Outside, the city was in turmoil, the Anasazis hollering all over the place, the bedlam punctuated by screams and the drumming of feet. "I still think I should find you some water."

Pedro did not respond. Nate placed a hand on the blind man's chest, then probed for a pulse. Sighing, he lowered the vaquero to the floor and slowly rose. "You deserved better."

A harsh yell close by sparked Nate into dashing to the buckled wall and over it into the next apartment. The roof was intact. The new ladder that had been lowered so the tillers could join the search was unscathed. Nate scaled it swiftly, springing out onto the roof without looking to make sure that the coast was clear.

It was a mistake.

Not six feet away stood a husky warrior.

Chapter Thirteen

Evelyn King had never been so scared in her life. As she and her brother neared the crest of the uppermost terrace, blind panic swelled and she came close to changing her mind. As much as she cared for George Washington, she was deathly afraid to venture into the forest after him.

The woodlands were still and quiet, but that did not deceive her. The monsters were in there, many of them, waiting and hungry. Swallowing, she bent to see Zach, whose face seemed paler than usual. "Why isn't there any noise?" she whispered.

"The quake must be to blame. It scared them."

The notion that the monsters could be scared was so novel that Evelyn blinked in surprise. It made them less scary, somehow.

Zach reined up at the crest. Every instinct he had screamed at him to turn around and ride like a bat out of Hades, but his sister was counting on him and he did not want to let her down. She loved that stupid pony as much as he loved his pet wolf. Besides, going in after it was what his pa would do.

In that respect Zachary King was no different from youths all over the world. He measured his performance in life by the standard set by his father. He wanted to shoot as well as his father did, ride as well, track as well—in short, do everything exactly the same, or perhaps a shade better.

So now, with a murky maze of benighted vegetation looming before him, Zach held his Hawken close to his chest and kneed the bay. He listened for the sound of the pony going off through the brush but heard nothing, absolutely nothing. Even the breeze had died.

Evelyn had her arms around her brother's waist, and she tightened them as the undergrowth closed around them. Dark shadows hemmed them in, shadows that seemed to flit and leer, although she knew that could not be the case. Her nerves were to blame. She remembered what her mother had said about controlling her fears and steeled herself to be brave.

Zach paid particular attention to the bay. Its sense of hearing and smell were far sharper than his. If anything came near them the horse would know before he did. When its ears suddenly shot erect and its head swung to the right, he halted. In the distance a wolfish howl put an end to the eerie quiet. As the last reverberating notes faded, others took up the refrain. Somewhere to the east a behemoth roared. Somewhere to the north a victim squealed in torment.

Evelyn shivered, even though she was not cold. The forest was a bad place, a wicked place. Clearing her throat, she hollered, "George Washington! Where are you!"

Zach twisted so abruptly that he nearly knocked his sister off. "Hush!" he snapped. "What in the world has gotten into you? Now everything that's out there knows right where we are."

"Sorry," Evelyn said sincerely, mortified by her mistake. She had only intended to lure George Washington back. Sometimes he came when she called, but not always. As her pa once mentioned, the pony was an uppity cuss.

Zach rode on, avoiding inky areas and thickets and anywhere a predator might spring on them from concealment. The crack of a twig caused him to draw rein again. A ghostly shape was threading through the trees. Fear gripped him until he saw that the animal was small, and that it was moving away from them, not toward them. He smiled when he recognized it as one of the red deer so common in the valley.

Evelyn saw the deer too, and sympathy gushed from her like water from a geyser. It was unfair for the poor little things to have to spend their entire lives on the run from creatures that would rend them limb from limb. She never had understood why God saw fit to create animals that ate other animals. To her way of thinking, the world would be a lot better place if there were no suffering, whether for wild things or for people.

The deer dashed off, and Zach goaded the bay onward. The vegetation was so dense, the night so dark, that he began to fully appreciate how hopeless their task was. Finding the pony would be as hard as finding the proverbial needle in a haystack. But he had given his word to his sister, and his pa said that men always kept their word, no matter what.

Farther on, a wide clearing broadened ahead. In the center, grazing, were a number of creatures Zach had never seen before. They were short and squat, with snouts the shape of pie plates and gleaming tusks that jutted from their bottom jaws. Hideous beasts, but he figured they posed no threat. He stopped anyway, wary of the damage those tusks could do to the bay's legs if the things charged.

Suddenly the biggest one lifted its snout and sniffed. It was facing away from Zach. Whatever scent it had caught came from something on the other side of the clearing. The tusked critter grunted, its squiggly tail flapped, and then it let out a piercing screech and whirled. Instantly all nine of them bolted, fleeing in the opposite direction from whatever had spooked them.

Unfortunately, that put the bay directly in their path. Zach tried to rein into the brush, but the tuskers were quicker than he gave them credit for being. Squealing and snorting, they were on the horse in the blink of an eye and the one in the lead, the biggest one, the brute to blame for starting the stampede, slashed at the bay's forelegs.

Winona King was mildly surprised to find no sentries had been posted close to the Anasazi city. Nor did she see any men high on the outer walls, as she had earlier.

To judge by the racket she heard, the city was in chaos. Yells and shouts and screams hinted at utter bedlam.

Tucked at the waist, Winona sprinted to the northeast corner of the horseshoe. Once safe among the shadows, she crept toward the plaza, keeping her back to the wall. Above her it reared some thirty feet, lowering by degrees the closer she grew to the central open area.

She was midway when she noticed a wide crack, almost wide enough for her to slip through. From within wafted a musty odor, and she thought that she could hear someone softly crying.

Going on, Winona came to the end of the wall and peered around it. She did not know what she expected to find, but certainly not a city in smoldering ruins. The earthquake had devastated it. Roofs had buckled, walls collapsed. The central stairway was a shambles. More

wide cracks laced nearly every dwelling, forming a spi-
derweb pattern that covered the city from bottom to top.
Smoke rose from some of the rooftop openings, mostly
tendrils, but in a few places choking black clouds billowed out.

The high building that was set apart from the rest had
suffered the worst. Two-thirds of the north wall was
gone, lying in crumbled piles. The east wall had partially
given way. Flames were shooting from the roof, flaring
bright red and orange and illuminating the tragic spectacle below.

Many Anasazis had been hurt or mortally stricken.
Falling walls and heavy debris had crushed them where
they stood. Bodies were scattered at the base of the wide
stairs and on many of the shattered steps above. The living were doing what they could for the fallen, moving
from body to body to check for signs of life. Some Anasazis, though, were in a state of shock. They drifted
aimlessly, arms limp at their sides, their faces as blank
as the slate Nate had bought for schooling the children.
Wisps of smoke hovered over the scene, writhing and
twisting like vaporous snakes.

Winona was at a loss to know what to do next. How,
in the midst of all that, was she to find her husband?

Suddenly an Anasazi stepped past the end of the wall
and halted right in front of her. She automatically brought
up the Hawken, but she did not fire. The man was staring
through her, not at her. In his arms he held a child of ten
or twelve, a boy whose rib bones stuck out from a
smashed chest. Both the man and the boy were covered
in blood.

The Anasazi mumbled a few words, turned, and shuf-
fled off.

Winona slowly rose. Maybe finding Nate was not as
hopeless as it appeared. She was sorry the Anasazi had
been afflicted so, but the quake had provided her with a

golden opportunity. The Anasazis were too preoccupied to pay much attention to a lone woman wandering among them. Or so she fervently hoped.

Lowering her rifle so it was flush against her leg, Winona boldly strode into the plaza. She moved as the man had been moving, in a slow shuffle, pretending to be in the same stunned state, her head bowed. Peeking out from under her eyebrows, she scanned the honeycomb. Her man was nowhere to be seen.

Winona roved from east to west and back again. More and more smoke was spilling from the high building and spreading out over the city. It helped her in one respect since it cloaked her in an acrid fog, but it hindered her in another since soon she could not see even the lowest level of apartments.

The city reminded her a little of St. Louis. Nate had taken her there once, years ago. The stone buildings had been a source of awe. The whites' penchant for sticking down roots in one spot and never leaving it the rest of their lives had amazed and mystified her.

The Shoshones were always on the go. Villages were routinely packed onto travois and moved to new locations during the course of each year. Staying in one place more than a couple of moons was just not practical. Game was soon depleted, forcing the hunters to range farther and farther afield. Forage for the large horse herds became scarce. And, too, their enemies could strike more often if they stayed at one site for too long.

Winona's musing came to an end, and she looked up. Nearby were several women gathered around a dead man. She had drifted too close to them. Now she veered to give the group a wide berth and saw one of the Anasazi women gaze in her direction. Lowering her head, she walked more briskly, thankful for a column of smoke that drifted between them.

Glancing back, Winona saw the woman following. The

Anasazi's suspicions had been aroused. Increasing her pace a bit, Winona made for the east side of the plaza. She resisted an impulse to break into a run.

Maybe it would have been better if she had. For seconds later the Anasazi jabbed a finger at her and started yelling shrilly.

The warrior saw Nate King at the exact instant that Nate saw him. The man's reflexes were astounding. In three swift strides he closed in, elevating a war club to bash out Nate's brains.

Pivoting, the mountain man drove a brawny fist into the Anasazi's gut, doubling the warrior over. A knee to the jaw lifted him clear off the ground and dumped him on his back. Gamely, the warrior sought to rise while wildly swinging the club to keep Nate at bay.

Worried that more Anasazis would pounce on him at any moment, Nate dodged the club, slipped in under the man's long arm, and delivered a punch to the chin. Coming as it did on the heels of the previous blow, it folded the warrior like a piece of paper. Without a sound the Anasazi dropped onto the roof and was still.

Nate whirled, fists ready, but no other warriors were in his proximity. Taking a few steps toward the plaza, he discovered why. Widespread destruction had left the city a shadow of its former self. Dead and wounded—too many to count—littered the roofs, the stairs, the main plaza.

Recollecting that Pedro had told him the Ute boy was being held in the temple, Nate swatted some smoke aside and saw the demolished building. Sheets of flame had engulfed the upper levels. From the main entrance and side doors spilled refugees, many hacking uncontrollably.

There was a very real chance Nevava was no longer alive, yet that never gave Nate pause. Running to the edge of the roof, he saw the ladder that had been propped against it lying on the ground.

The drop was about twelve feet. Gripping the rim, Nate lowered himself over the side, dangled, and dropped. As he alighted, a cloud of smoke enveloped him. Landing on the balls of his feet, he tucked into a roll that brought him up in a crouch. Before he could straighten, a heavy blow slammed him between the shoulder blades and he was pitched onto his stomach.

Scrabbling onto his knees, Nate twisted just as a lean Anasazi with a knife thrust at his neck. Jerking aside saved his life—but he was safe only for the moment. The warrior waded in, cold steel flashing.

Nate lurched upright and frantically backpedaled. The smoke was so thick that he could barely see his adversary, so thick that his next breath seared his lungs with burning pain. He succumbed to a coughing fit, making it more difficult to keep dodging.

Suddenly the warrior dived, his free arm wrapping around the trapper's legs. With a powerful heave, they both were down, side by side, the warrior spearing his weapon at the mountain man's throat again and again.

Nate blocked, ducked, shifted, doing anything and everything to evade the onslaught. Taking the offensive, he grabbed the Anasazi's wrist and wrenched. His aim was to make the man drop the knife, but the warrior gritted his teeth and held on to it.

The smoke had grown steadily heavier. Since he could not disarm the Anasazi, Nate resorted to another tactic. Pushing the man with all his might, he leaped to his feet and scooted into the thick of the gray veil. He had to hold a hand over his mouth and nose, and breathe shallowly, in order not to cough and give his position away.

Cries, wailing, and screams swirled around the plaza, but in the center of the smoke the only sound Nate could hear was the pounding of his own temples. He turned this way and that, poised to defend himself. For all his diligence, though, the Anasazi caught him off guard; the knife streaked out of the smoke, nearly severing his jugular. That it didn't was through no effort on his part. The warrior misjudged the distance and missed.

Nate lashed out, connecting with a solid right. Recovering immediately, the Anasazi drove the tip of his blade down and in, going for the groin. Nate flung his legs wide, saw the knife pass between them.

All the warrior had to do was twist to either side to slice into Nate's thigh. To prevent that, and to give the Anasazi something else to occupy him, Nate flicked two fingers into his eyes.

Blinking furiously, the warrior retreated. Nate pressed the advantage he had by leaping behind the Anasazi and tripping him. As the man fell, Nate seized the knife arm in both hands and twisted sharply, throwing his entire weight into it. There was an audible crack. The Anasazi cried out and sagged.

Nate made short shrift of him, a flurry of punches finishing the fight. Scooping up the knife, Nate rotated, seeking to get his bearings. The smoke was thinning, and he could see the outline of a building a ways off. Was it the temple?

The mountain man started forward but took only two strides. Another Anasazi was rushing toward him. Unwilling to be delayed any longer, Nate cocked his arm. The smoke briefly thickened again, hiding the warrior, but Nate had gauged the man's speed well, and when a shadowy shape materialized in front of him, he was ready.

Nate's left hand closed on a shirt. His right hiked on high for a killing stroke. In another fraction of a second he struck. It was then, as the knife swooped down, that the smoke parted, and he saw it was not a buckskin shirt he held but a buckskin dress. And the upturned face so close to his was not that of an Anasazi—but his wife's.

Chapter Fourteen

It was the bay, not Zach, that saved them from the tuskers. As the big one bore down on them and slashed at the bay's knee, the horse's hoof flicked out, bowling it over. The rest of the herd slanted to the right or the left to go around. Unhurt, the big tusker leaped up and hastened after its companions, the crackle of brush fading rapidly.

"What was that all about?" Evelyn wondered.

Zach had a hunch he knew, and his gut balled into a knot. The night had grown unusually quiet. Then the bay snorted, its ears swiveling forward. Another couple of seconds and Zach heard it, too, the heavy tread of ponderous steps, the rhythmic *stomp-stomp-stomp* of something coming toward them, something enormous.

Evelyn was terrified to her core. "Get us out of here," she whispered, her nails digging into her brother's sides.

"Hush." Zach felt that staying perfectly still and making no noise was their best bet. The thing might not notice them, especially since the wind had died. Across the clearing, he saw a sapling bend and a massive form rear skyward nine or ten feet. He could not see it clearly, but what he did see was enough to change the blood in his veins to ice. It was almost manlike, with a huge mis-shapen head and sloped shoulders three times as broad as those of a typical man. Rumbling deep in a chest that must be as big around as five barrels, the thing swiveled from side to side, scouring the clearing.

The bay did not twitch a muscle, for which Zach was grateful. His sister was rigid against his back and did not let out a peep. The creature turned to the south and started to walk off, and Zach smiled.

Suddenly the thing halted and swung toward the clearing again. Zach did not understand why until he felt a breeze—against the back of his head. The monstrosity tilted its own head to test the air. In profile, the silhouette revealed a high conical forehead, wide, thick brows, and almost no neck. The protruding jaw sloped directly into its broad shoulders.

The rumbling became an ominous growl.

Zach did not linger another instant. The breeze had betrayed them and the thing knew right where they were. Hauling on the reins, he wheeled the bay and fled, crying, "Hang on tight, sis!"

Evelyn was too petrified to do anything else. A glance showed the creature barreling into the clearing, crossing it in four long leaps, and plowing into the undergrowth in pursuit. "Hurry!" she screeched. "It's after us."

Zach was doing the best he could, but there were so many trees and boulders and dense pockets of brush to be avoided that he could not bring the bay to a full gallop. A trot was as fast as he dared go. And as if that were not bad enough, low limbs lashed at him, branches tried to gouge his eyes or rip his face. He was constantly ducking and dodging and having to divert his gaze from the terrain ahead, which compounded the risk of a mis-step or a collision. Should that occur, the thing would be on them in a twinkling.

It was incredibly fast for its bulk. Smashing through brush and plowing over small trees, the loathsome horror gained swiftly. Soon it was close enough for Evelyn to see its glinting eyes and hear its raspy breaths. The crea-ture had an ungainly, rolling gait, due in part to the fact that its front legs appeared to be considerably longer than its rear ones. Yet despite that physical quirk, it narrowed the gap.

Zach veered sharply to go around a boulder, and the bay had to slacken its speed ever so slightly in order to adjust to the abrupt change.

The monstrosity had been waiting for just such a mo-ment. Evelyn screamed as it hurtled at them and a hairy paw or hand thrust at her face. She felt something brush her hair and closed her eyes, afraid she would be yanked off and devoured. But just then the bay put on a spurt of speed. Anxious seconds went by. Evelyn fanned her courage and opened her eyes again to find that the crea-ture had lost ground and was losing more each second.

"We're getting away!" she cried.

Zach would not believe they were safe until the thing was lost in the night. Goading the bay on, it occurred to him that he had lost all sense of direction. He did not know whether they were heading west, south, or north. No sooner did the question cross his mind than the bay burst from the woodland onto the top terrace.

Evelyn patted him on the back. "You did it," she said, amazed at their hairbreadth escape. She made a mental note to have more confidence in her brother in the future. Sure, he was obnoxious at times, as all boys could be, but he wasn't all bad.

Zach did not stop on the crest. Racing over it, he gal-loped down the slopes and was halfway to where they had left the stallion and the bay when an animal hove out of the darkness on their right. Thinking it was another meat-eater, he shifted to bring his Hawken to bear. His surprise on recognizing the animal was matched only by his anger at the peril it had put them in.

"Damn stupid pony," Zach said, reining up.

Evelyn squealed in delight and vaulted off the bay. Her pony was peacefully munching on grass, unruffled by the din in the forest. "George Washington!" she said as she threw her arms around his neck and kissed him below the ear. "You had us worried to death."

"Speak for yourself," Zach grumbled. "Me, I couldn't care less if the stupid critter wound up as worm food."

Evelyn grasped the pony's reins and turned. "You can be so mean, you know that? After all we went through, you should be happy George is alive."

"That's just it. We wouldn't have gone through what we just did if not for that dumb pet of yours." Zach glanced toward the upper terraces. "Now, quit jawing and climb on. The thing that was after us might follow our scent."

"Ma said those things mainly stay in the woods, remember?"

"Mainly," Zach emphasized. "And doesn't Pa like to say there are exceptions to every rule?"

Her brother had a point there. Evelyn mounted and patted her pony's neck. "By the way," she mentioned as she trailed the bay lower, "don't think I didn't hear that cussword you used. Pa will want to hear of it."

Zach twisted and glared at her. His father was a stickler for never using bad language in mixed company. Most of the mountain men had a flair for colorful speech and could "cuss rings around a tree," as Shakespeare McNair once put it. Some even did so in front of women, but his pa did not approve of the practice.

The Lost Valley

It had only been a year or so ago that Zach made the mistake of swearing in front of his mother. His pa had set him down and said, "When you're with other men, son, having a rollicking good time swapping lies and guzzling liquor, then cussing might be in order. But when you're with a lady, if you're so lazy that you can't say what has to be said without using cusswords, then you might as well keep your mouth shut."

"It was only a 'damn,' " Zach now told his sister in his defense. "You'd tell on me after all I just did for you?"

Evelyn was going to say that he deserved it for all the times he had teased her and played tricks on her, but the hurt in his tone gave her pause. He had saved their lives, after all. And he had gone in search of her pony even though he despised George Washington. "That makes two bad words," she said impishly, and when he puffed out his cheeks like an irate chipmunk, she said quickly, "But no, I won't tell on you. Not this time, anyway."

Zach's anger deflated and he nodded in approval. "For once you're showing some sense, sis. Not bad for a girl."

"Since when do you have something against girls?" Evelyn could not resist saying. "I saw how you were making cow eyes at Yellow Sky the last time we were with the Shoshones."

Yellow Sky was the pretty daughter of a prominent warrior. Zach had given her a small folding knife as a gift. In return, one evening as she returned from the river bearing water, she had let him sneak a kiss. He blushed at the memory and faced front. "You're imagining things again. Girls do that a lot."

Evelyn knew better, but she did not make an issue of it. She had George Washington back and she was content. Or as content as she could be with her mother and father missing. Where were they? she asked herself. Had something happened to them?

*   *   *

The answer to that question lay in the devastated Anasazi city.

Nate King's knife was inches from his wife's heart when he checked its plunge. All else was forgotten as he swept her into his arms and held her close, inwardly quaking at how close he had come to slaying the woman who meant everything to him, the woman he loved more than life itself. "Darling," he breathed. "I didn't know it was you."

"I certainly hope not," Winona quipped, sensing how deeply upset he was. She blamed herself for the incident, since she had recognized him as she was running through the smoke and should have called out instead of rushing to embrace him.

Winona recalled the reason she had been running, and urgently peeled herself from her husband's arms. "Anasazis are after me."

Nate looked up and saw dim figures gliding toward them. Grabbing his wife's wrist, he backed into the thickest of the smoke and ran to the right a dozen yards. Crouching, he pulled her down beside him and impulsively kissed her on the lips. "That will have to do until we get home," he whispered.

His romantic nature was an undying source of wonder for Winona. He was forever bringing her flowers and trinkets and whatnot, and lavishing her with finer things he obtained at one of the frontier forts. Many of her friends had told her it was unusual for a man to be so romantic; their own husbands seemed to lose more and more of that special quality the longer the couples were together.

Winona counted herself fortunate she had married a man who was so attentive and who daily treated her as if she was special.

Babbling voices and the patter of moccasin-shod feet

heralded her pursuers, almost a dozen swarthy warriors and Anasazi women who had come on the run when that first woman started yelling. They plunged into the smoke and spread out, swatting at it in a vain bid to see.

Stooped low to the ground, Nate could see their feet and the lower portion of their legs, but that was all. The smoke had grown thicker, a reminder that the temple was rapidly being consumed and might well burn to the ground—and that the Ute boy, Nevava, might be inside.

Rising partway, Nate drew Winona after him as he stealthily moved in the direction he hoped the temple lay. The babbling voices diminished in their wake, and he was beginning to think they had eluded the searchers when a man appeared out of the wispy fog, a stout Anasazi who wore a short plumed headdress and had a red blanket draped over his shoulders.

The man opened his mouth to cry out. Nate's fist silenced the shout, and the Anasazi tottered. Wading in, Nate rained a flurry of jabs and punches that drove the man to the ground, sprawled senseless.

Winona had covered the Anasazi in case he resorted to a weapon. She scanned the smoke as her husband donned the red blanket, and when he beckoned, she jogged at his side, out into the open.

The bedlam, if anything, was worse. Fires were spreading on all levels. Panicked women and children milled aimlessly. Some of the men were striving their utmost to snuff the flames, but they could not douse them fast enough.

No one paid much attention to the Kings. It helped that patches of smoke were everywhere, providing plenty of cover. They could not go ten feet without encountering one. As Nate barged through yet another swirling cloud, he saw the temple clearly again. Up close, the destruction was ten times as bad as he had imagined.

Wide cracks covered the outer walls. The lintel over

the entrance was split in half and ready to collapse at any moment. Giant flames rimmed the roof and shot from upper windows. Inside, screams and sobs and hysterical raving testified to the pandemonium.

Turning to Winona, Nate said, "I'm going in after the Ute boy. Stay here until I get back."

"No."

That was all there was to it. Nate did not protest or launch into a hundred and one reasons why she should heed him. She wanted to go and she was going to go, and short of tying her up he could not stop her.

Darting in under the lintel, Nate gasped as a wave of blistering heat slammed into him, nearly driving him back against Winona. More wood had been used in the construction of the temple than in the apartments, a lot more wood, and now that wood crackled the temple's death knell. The roar of fire on the higher levels was like the whoosh of wind on a blustery day.

A short passageway led to an expansive chamber. Far overhead beams were ablaze, raining cinders and sparks onto the ornately decorated floor. A section of the opposite wall had fallen, showering a massive amount of stone and mortar and wood onto a group of priests and others. Their crushed, ravaged bodies lay amid the rubble.

Nate counted three passages at the north and south ends of the chamber. The place was a maze of corridors and rooms that would take months to explore fully, and he had mere minutes to find Nevava before the whole roof came crashing down. As he debated which passage to take, it dawned on him that he might not recognize the boy even if he saw him, not if the Anasazis had dressed him in Anasazis garb and cut his hair to match theirs.

Winona saw two women emerge from a hall, coughing and sputtering, their hands over their mouths. Smoke had gotten into their eyes, which were watering profusely, and they stumbled as if drunk, groping toward the passage that would take them to the main entrance.

"Let's try that one!" Nate said, picking a hall on the right at random. Dodging cinders and debris, he sprinted toward it. A hiss overhead alerted him to a falling piece of wood as long as his arm. He leaped out of harm's way with a whisker to spare.

"That was too close for comfort," Nate remarked. Winona did not respond as he threaded a course toward the corridor, passing a prone man who wore a mask that resembled a bird's head, and feathers in imitation of plumage. Nate recognized that mask and drew up short.

Evidently Wakonhomin had been heading for the entrance when a portion of the roof weighing several hundred pounds smashed onto him. The High Priest's torso and hips had been flattened to a grisly pulp. Only his bizarre mask and feathered arms and legs were showing.

Nate was wasting precious moments. "Hurry," he said, vaulting over a beam. The south side of the temple had sustained the most damage from the quake. Mounds of litter were as abundant as sand dunes in a desert. He weaved among them until he came to a clear space.

Ahead was the corridor, mired in shadow. Nate was a few strides from the opening when he saw the giant slab that blocked it, just inside. From under the slab jutted a hand. "Damn!" He bent his shoulder to the obstacle and pushed for all he was worth, but it was like trying to move a mountain.

"Forget this one." Nate turned toward the passageway on their left, when suddenly it hit him that his wife had not said a word since they entered the great chamber. "Winona?" he said, pivoting, and was stunned to his core to find he was alone. "It just can't be!" he blurted, taking a step. But it was.

Winona had disappeared.

Chapter Fifteen

Minutes earlier, when Winona King saw the two women groping blindly for the way out of the temple, she had rushed over and taken the foremost by the hand. From the Anasazi's eyes streamed a torrent of tears. When Winona gripped her and pulled her toward the right passageway, the woman mumbled a few words, possibly in gratitude.

Winona, not responding, hastened the pair along. She was anxious to rejoin her husband, who was heading toward the south end of the huge chamber, unaware of what she had done. Winona would have called out to let him know, but that would announce to all the fleeing Anasazis in the chamber that she was not one of them. No sense in inviting trouble, she mused.

A logjam had formed at the entrance to the corridor that linked the chamber to the plaza. More than a dozen Anasazi men and women were all trying to get through the opening simultaneously, with predictable results.

Most, like the women Winona guided, had been blinded by the stinging smoke and were half out of their minds with fear.

Winona owed the Anasazis nothing. To them she was an enemy to be enslaved or slain. Yet she could not bring herself to run off after Nate knowing that some or all of them would perish if they did not escape the building before the roof came crashing down.

So without hesitation Winona barreled into the thick of the melee and sought to restore some semblance of order. Not being able to communicate handicapped her immensely. She had to resort to pushing and pulling and barring the way of some of the more frantic ones so that others could slip into the corridor without hindrance.

Three or four were able to untangle themselves and do so. Winona pried two women apart who were battling to see who would go next, and held on to the more frantic of the pair so the other one could dart to safety.

The frantic one was outraged by Winona's interference and began to berate her in the Anasazi tongue. Suddenly the woman's eyes widened. She had gotten a good look at Winona and realized Winona was not one of them. Yelling shrilly, she abruptly stopped trying to break free and instead tried to seize Winona.

A number of other Anasazis paused in their headlong flight to turn and stare. They saw an outsider in their midst, an outsider who had no business being there. Worse, an outsider who mysteriously appeared at the very moment their city was stricken by calamity. Some immediately jumped to the conclusion that there must be a connection, that the outsider was bad medicine and had somehow brought the disaster down on them. Others unconsciously channeled the impotent fury they felt because they were unable to do anything about the spreading destruction toward this outsider. Here was someone they could vent their fury on, and vent it they did.

Winona sensed the rising tide of hatred and pivoted to dash into the open. She took but a stride when they were on her, seven, eight, nine of them, men and women alike, yowling like rabid coyotes and battering her with fists and open hands. Under the human deluge she went down to her knees, and lost her rifle.

Raising her arms overhead to ward off the worst of the blows, Winona levered herself erect and fought to get clear. She hit, she pushed, she kicked, but they had her hemmed in now, ten or eleven of them, their faces contorted by hatred so potent that it transformed them from human beings into demons, into a bloodthirsty bestial pack that would not be satisfied with anything short of her death.

Winona opened her mouth to shout for Nate and was struck on the jaw by a heavy fist. Stunned, she sagged onto her left knee. It was the moment the Anasazis awaited. Screaming and raving, they closed in, battering her mercilessly.

She tried to protect herself, but there was only so much she could do. Tucking into a ball, she let her back and shoulders absorb the worst of it. One factor in her favor was that the Anasazis were so tightly packed together they were hampering one another; they actually fought among themselves for the right to beat her to death.

Winona saw an opening between a pair of legs and shot through it like a prairie dog down its burrow. Momentarily free, she scrambled to her feet. Or tried to. A tremendous blow between her shoulder blades drove her to her knees again, and before she could recover the Anasazis were on her, hammering her head and neck and body.

A sob escaped Winona's lips, a sob of frustration. She had only been trying to help the Anasazis, and *this* was how they repaid her! She sobbed, too, at the thought of dying so far from her home and her people, and at the idea of never seeing her husband or her children again.

A jarring kick to the ribs whooshed the air from Winona's lungs and lanced her with mind-searing agony so acute the world around her spun. Dizzy, nauseous, she marshaled her strength and began to fight back.

Shoshones did not go meekly to their deaths. Warriors or maidens, it made no difference. They were not cowards, and they clung tenaciously to life for as long as it animated their limbs.

Winona pushed a woman so hard, the woman went sprawling. Heaving into a crouch, she rammed her shoulder into the big belly of a priest trying to bash in her skull. A warrior gripped her from behind, his arm encircling her waist. As he lifted her, exposing her to the blows of the others, she whipped her head back, into his nose. She heard a loud crunch, and the warrior roared like a wounded bear.

But he did not let her go. Winona stamped her foot onto his instep. His grip slackened, though not enough, so she did it again and again, heedless of the knuckles that thudded into her chest and sides and the ringing slap of a palm on her cheek and the sting of nails raking her neck.

The Anasazis were beside themselves. Screeching, bawling, howling, they shouldered one another aside for the right to strike her next. Gone was any semblance of rational thought. They were a mindless mass bent on murderous intent. They were not people, they were not animals. They were worse than animals. Any shred of intelligence had fled, replaced by raw savagery.

Against that irresistible tide of primitive blood lust, what chance did Winona have? The warrior heaved her into their midst, and they were on her like ravenous wolves on a doe. She landed a punch or two, but for each one of hers that connected she was in turn pummeled a score of times.

Winona's strength was ebbing. In desperation she clawed for her knife and succeeded in grabbing the hilt. She cut into a man about to batter her with both his hands locked together, then slashed a woman trying to claw out her eyes.

The Anasazis gave way. Encouraged, Winona swung wildly to keep the pack at bay. Those in front of her backed off, but those behind her pounced. Iron fingers found her knife arm and clamped it in a vise. She sobbed again as the ones in front renewed their attack. Her knife was torn from her grasp.

The next moment, Winona was on the floor. A ring of distorted snarling visages swooped down on her and the pain became worse than ever, much, much worse. She felt darkness nipping at her mind, and she tenderly voiced the word that meant the most to her in all the world: "Nate!"

"Did you hear something?"

Zach King was seated on the lip of a slope, the Hawken across his thighs. Behind him were the hobbled horses, including the pony. The stupid cayuse had nearly gotten him killed once; it wouldn't get the chance to do so again.

On hearing his sister's question, Zach shifted and surveyed the terraces above. Other than the sigh of the wind, which had picked up in the past fifteen minutes, he heard nothing unusual. "No. Why?"

Evelyn was not entirely sure. She would be the first to admit her nerves were shot. The ordeal in the forest had left her as jumpy as a rabbit that had caught the scent of a fox. Every little noise she could not account for was made by a monster creeping toward them.

She had tried to tell herself that it was all in her head. That maybe the things they had seen were not monsters after all, but animals they mistook for monsters. The brute that had chased them might well have been a bear, its features twisted by the play of starlight and shadows. Those red wolves that roamed the valley were just that— reddish wolves. Nothing peculiar there, since wolves came in a variety of colors. She had personally seen gray wolves and black wolves and even a few white wolves. As for the giant lizard that killed the Utes, sure, it was bigger than any lizard she ever heard of. But by the same token, her own pa had once tangled with a grizzly twice the size of most silvertips. And the Shoshones, among other tribes, believed in the existence of something called the Thunder Bird, a hawklike bird bigger than a horse. So an overgrown lizard was not all that extraordinary.

Still, Evelyn could not help jumping every time she heard a sound from above. A howl, a squeal, they were all the same, all fraught with menace.

Now she stiffened and turned on hearing an odd swishing noise, sort of like the noise she would make walking through a field of tall grass. The slopes above were empty of life, so it had to be her imagination.

Zach saw his sister scan the upper terraces, and did likewise. He knew she was terrified, and he considered scolding her for being so childish. But after their harrowing trial in the woods, he figured he would go easy on her. "You're hearing things, sis," he said, and went to resume his scrutiny of the valley floor and the road leading to the Anasazi city.

A faint swish was his first inkling that maybe Evelyn's ears were not deceiving her. Zach scoured the high terraces a second time, more intently than before, and the short hairs at the nape of his neck prickled when he detected movement where there should be none, movement so startling and horrifying that for a few shocked seconds he gaped, dumbstruck.

A sinuous shadow was winding downward, a shadow so broad and so long that Zach could be forgiven for not recognizing it for what it was right away. The shape was low to the ground, so low that its blunt head cleaved the grass like the prow of a ship cleaving the sea. In sinuous S-shaped movements the colossal thing-that-should-not-be glided slowly toward them.

"It's a snake!" Zach breathed, and was on his feet in a flash. Springing to the horses, he worked frantically to remove their hobbles, saying over a shoulder, "Help me, or we'll be eaten alive!"

Evelyn wanted to help. She honestly and truly did. But her legs were paralyzed by fright so potent it chilled her soul. As she had done with the wolves and the lizard, she tried to convince herself it was just a snake, just an awfully big snake the night made seem even bigger. *Just a snake! Just a snake! Just a snake!* she mentally chanted. But it was useless. She could not deny her own eyes. Yes, it was a snake, but it was much more. It was exactly like the giant serpents her mother had told her about. Maybe it was one of them.

"Sis!" Zach barked harshly when Evelyn did not budge. He could not do it all himself, not in time to get out of there before the snake reached them. Finishing with the bay, he turned to his father's stallion.

George Washington nickered, and the whinny broke the spell that held Evelyn in place. Her pony, her friend, was in danger. She tore at his hobbles, shutting her mind to the thing above them, refusing to think about it for fear she would freeze again.

The swishing grew louder, punctuated by a sibilant hiss. Zach glanced up and beheld a sight that would petrify grown men.

The snake had paused and reared, its triangular head swaying from side to side as it regarded the horses and humans through orbs that gleamed with yellow fire. Still forty yards away, it appeared to be almost on top of them.

A forked tongue flicked in and out, stabbing the air for their scent.

Zach moved to his mother's mare. He never even considered using his rifle. Snakes had few vital organs; at that range, in the dark, with a serpent that size, he would be kidding himself if he thought he could bring it down with one shot. Or two. Or three.

"I'm done!" Evelyn announced, popping erect. Something—the sound of her voice, her movement—caused the snake to flatten and crawl swiftly forward. She clutched at the pony's reins but missed. "Zach!" she wailed, spiked by panic.

Meanwhile, the serpent bore down on them like a living nightmare.

In a berserk rage Nate King plowed into the Anasazis who surrounded his wife. He had seen her go down as he rushed across the chamber to her rescue, and when he reached the Anasazis it was not Nathaniel King, meek New York accountant, who tore into them, or Nate King, hardy free trapper. It was someone else entirely, a throwback to the trace of Nordic blood in his veins. It was a barbarian, a Crusader, a Viking all rolled into one. It was elemental man, savage man, man protecting the woman he held dearest of all.

He did not act according to reason, because reason had fled. He did not think and then act, because conscious thought was gone. Raw instinct thrust him into the thick of the Anasazis. Instinct, and pure ferocity.

Nate had picked up part of a broken beam. A yard long and as thick around as his thigh at one end, it made for a stout club. Flailing it right and left, he rained blows on the Anasazis, felling four of them before the remainder awakened to his presence. The heavy thuds of his club were drowned out by their oaths and cries.

They surged against him like surf pounding on breakers, seeking to overpower him by sheer weight of numbers. For a moment they almost succeeded. Warriors had him by the legs and one arm, and a woman clung to his chest, impeding him. His legs started to buckle under the strain, causing the Anasazis to whoop in triumph.

They were premature. Nate King planted both feet firmly and refused to go down, even if every last one piled on top of him. With a mighty shake of his chest, he dislodged the woman, freeing his arms so he could attack the warriors holding his legs. One collapsed with a split head; the other sustained a broken arm.

Heaving upright, Nate laid about him with a vengeance, his club connecting with each swing. He felled Anasazis right and left, felled them as they hit and stabbed and clawed, felled them as they circled and leaped and dived, felled them as more poured from a side tunnel to join the unequal clash.

Broken women and men littered the floor, groaning, spitting blood, convulsing.

A warrior with a lance appeared and flung it, wooden lightning that impaled a woman who blundered in front of the mountain man at the wrong moment.

A woman holding a knife tried to plunge it into Nate's groin and was rewarded with a broken shoulder.

Nate swung in a frenzy, never picking targets but striking as they presented themselves. He did not know how many Anasazis he had downed, or how many more there were. He swung until he realized his makeshift club beat empty air.

A red haze seemed to lift from Nate's eyes. He saw bodies on all sides, bodies he had shattered, some never to rise again. As he lowered his arms, the huge roof rumbled, a portent of its imminent collapse.

"Winona!" Nate cried, and spun, seeking the love of his life. She lay where she had fallen, pale as a ghost, her dress stained scarlet. "Winona?" he repeated, but she did not respond. She did not even move.

Chapter Sixteen

It would have been so easy for Zachary King to vault onto his bay and race down the terraces well head of the slithering horror that drew nearer every instant. But to do so he must abandon his sister, a notion he never entertained. As many spats as they'd had, as many times as he had wanted to throttle her, he could no more desert her than he could stop breathing. Taking a bound, he forked his hands under her arms, swept her onto the pony, and hollered, "Ride, sis! Ride like the wind!"

Most girls would have done so. Most would have spurred their mounts over the crest without looking back. Evelyn was different. She was much too young to realize it, but she was made of sterner stuff. She had what her pa would call "true grit." "I'm not going without you," she responded.

Zach did not dispute the point. The snake was only twenty yards away, gliding swiftly along, quicksilver with scales. Snatching the reins to the stallion and the

mare, he leaped onto his bay and lit out of there as if his
britches were ablaze. "Dally and we're dead!"

Evelyn was not about to. A jab of her heels sent the
spooked pony over the rim. George Washington seemed
to know what was at stake, for he flew like the winged
horse Pegasus in a tale her father had read to her one
evening before bedtime. It was all she could do to hold
on. Mane and tail flying, George Washington proved that
the size of a horse was no indication of how fast it could
go. Most horses were larger than he was, but few could
have flown faster down those slopes.

The pony went so fast, in fact, that Evelyn feared for
their safety. A misstep was all it would take. In the dark
she could not see ruts and holes. Should George Washington step into one they both would go down, George
Washington with a broken leg, she to fall prey to the
massive reptile that wanted them for supper. Automatically, she slowed a trifle.

"What in the world are you doing?" Zach demanded.
He was right behind her, hauling on the reins to the other
horses. Shifting, he saw the serpent hurtling on their
heels, now fifteen yards off and closing rapidly.

The road was their only hope, Zach reckoned. On a
flat, straight stretch the horses could outrun the snake.
The trick lay in reaching the road alive. It seemed impossibly far away, a pale ribbon in the vast darkness of
the night, so near and yet so distant.

"It's gaining!" Evelyn cried, and imagined being
swallowed whole. A sickening feeling came over her.
Her stomach churned. She imagined what it would be
like to slide down the snake's gullet, to have its digestive
juices get into her nose, her eyes, her mouth. To have
her skin eaten away and the breath stolen from her body.

"Go! Go!" Zach hollered when the pony began to
flag. He was prepared to let go of the stallion and the
mare and pluck her from her saddle, if the need arose.

She was more important than any old horse. Heck, she was more important than all the horses put together.

The pale ribbon widened. It was so tantalizingly close that Zach had the illusion he could reach out and touch it, but the truth was that several terraces stood between them and their salvation. He urged the bay to greater speed and pulled alongside George Washington. His sister was clinging to the pony like a drowning woman would cling to a log. She smiled gamely at him, and he had never loved her more than that exact moment.

"We're almost there!"

The thunder of hoofs was as nothing compared to the earlier thunder of the earthquake, but it was sufficiently loud to echo off the high cliffs and make it seem as if a herd of buffalo were stampeding.

Ahead lay the last terrace. Zach spurred the bay into putting on an extra burst of speed. Evelyn was only a few feet behind him as they clattered onto the dirt road and reined toward the city. "Don't stop for nothing!"

Evelyn was not about to. She didn't care if a horde of Anasazi warriors were to rise up in front of them; she would not slow down. Let them deal with the snake. If they dared.

Zach looked back to see how much of a lead they had. It should be about ten yards, but it wasn't. Stupefied, he scanned the lowest terrace, then the one above it, concentrating on the areas deepest in shadow. The serpent had to be there, somewhere, yet for the life of him he couldn't find it.

Galloping another hundred feet, Zach drew rein and called out for his sister to do the same. As the bay came to a halt he turned his mount broadside so he could plainly see the road and the benighted slopes.

Evelyn thought he was loco, but she did as he bid her. On studying the tilled terraces she exclaimed in consternation, "Where did it get to? It was there a moment ago."

Corn rattled in the breeze. Row after row of carefully cultivated vegetables stretched to the north and the south in undisturbed ranks. On the upper terraces not a living creature was visible. The giant snake had disappeared off the face of the earth.

Zach checked the other side of the road in case the serpent had crossed when they weren't looking. As startled as he was by the absence of the reptile, he was even more shocked to see the lake had also vanished. For a body of water that size to simply blink out of existence defied belief. Yet he knew he had seen it earlier. As for the snake, could it be they had imagined the whole thing?

Evelyn did not like sitting there. The scaly horror had to be nearby, probably slinking toward them unseen, ready to rear and strike when their guard was down. "What are we waiting for?" she asked impatiently.

"Nothing," Zach admitted, and trotted on. Now that they were safe, he had another problem to deal with. Namely, what should they do next? Anasazis were bound to be abroad, and who knew what else? They needed a hiding place, a place where they could watch the road for their mother and father. But precious few trees grew on the valley floor, and fewer tracts of undergrowth.

"Look yonder," Evelyn said. "Their city is burning."

That it was. Flames leaped from many a rooftop, licked at many a wall. Zach recollected his pa reading to him about a place called Pompeii and idly wondered if the scene he beheld was similar to the fabled city's last moments.

Evelyn bit her lower lip in heartfelt dismay. Her folks were in that terrible place, beset by the heat and the smoke. Screams wafted to her, screams and the hubbub of hurting, scared people. The Anasazis must be beside themselves, and in that state they might do anything to her mother and father.

Zach was likewise glued to the spectacle. He did not pay particular attention to the road ahead. A snort by the bay remedied his mistake, but too late. Directly under its front legs yawned a chasm where none should be.

Flinging the beam to the floor, Nate King ran to his wife and knelt. "Winona?" he cried, his voice quavering from the emotion that clawed at his insides like the razor talons of a bird of prey. He could not bear to think of losing her, not her, not the kindest, most loving woman he had ever met, not the woman who cherished him with all her heart, the woman who had given him the greatest gift any woman could ever give a man: her undying love.

More and more smoke cascaded from on high as Nate gently lifted his wife's head onto his lap. He felt her neck for a pulse and did not find one. Despair swamped him. He went dead inside, as if someone had thrown a switch and all sensation had fled his body. Sagging over her, his finger moved a quarter of an inch. Suddenly a bolt of lightning jolted him. He had probed the wrong spot! She did have a pulse, a strong steady heartbeat, and as tears of supreme joy moistened his eyes, she opened hers.

"You saved me."

It was a simple statement, yet the tone she used expressed the depth of her love as eloquently as a poem.

"The next time you take it into that pretty head of yours to go up against an entire tribe by yourself, remember what I always do when I'm outnumbered."

"Which is?"

"I run."

Winona smiled, and regretted it when her puffy lower lip flared with torment. Casting her arms around him, she held him close and would not let go. Not even when the roof rumbled and burning embers showered around them.

It was when the floor rumbled and shook that Nate lifted his head and saw the walls sway and the burning beams above them jiggle dangerously. "Another quake," he warned Winona, pulling her upright. "An aftershock, they call it." As he said it, the rumbling ceased.

Winona had to lean against him for support. Her legs were weak, her muscles were like mush, a delayed reaction to the punishment she had suffered. She felt sore all over, from the crown of her head to the tips of her toes. Her back and shoulders had borne the brunt of the blows and hurt viciously when she moved.

"Can you walk?" Nate asked. The roof was perilously close to collapse, and he did not want to be under it when the tons of fiery debris fell.

"I can if you need me to." Gritting her teeth, Winona straightened unaided and moved stiffly to her rifle. As she bent, her lower back knotted in a spasm and she inadvertently uttered a low cry.

"Let me," Nate said, retrieving the Hawken himself. Looking at her tore his heart. Her left eye was swollen half shut, both cheeks had been raked and clawed, her neck was bloody, her mouth would take weeks to heal. And those were just the visible wounds. He shuddered to think how many welts and bruises must cover her body.

"Where to, husband?" Winona asked, full well knowing his answer.

"We still have to find the boy."

"I will be right behind you." Winona mustered a wan grin. "And this time, I will stay behind you."

Nate clasped her wrist and steered her to a passage on the left. It was dark, narrow, foreboding, as still as a crypt. Most of the Anasazis who had been inside when the destruction occurred were either gone or had perished. Quite probably the Ute boy had also fled or was lying dead somewhere in the temple. But Nate could not just up and leave, not without trying to find out.

A large crack had split the right-hand wall. Another, farther on, ran the width of the ceiling. Thinner ones were more common the farther they went, and around a wide bend they came on a partially crumbled section.

Nate began to worry that another aftershock might bring the whole passageway toppling down. They passed doorways, some to small rooms, others to spacious chambers. Here and there they came on lifeless Anasazis, most crushed by falling slabs.

The smoke grew steadily thicker, to the point that Nate found it difficult to breathe. He had about made up his mind that he had done all he could and it would be better to seek an avenue of escape when yet another room appeared on the left. In it were war clubs, lances, and knives, enough to outfit an army. Since these were of no special interest to him, he was almost past it when he glanced into a far corner.

"My guns!"

Not only his rifle and flintlocks, but his knife and tomahawk, his possibles bag, and his ammo pouch were all there. In short order he was armed to the teeth and feeling fit to tussle with a ravening griz.

"I have not seen you this happy since you traded for your stallion," Winona mentioned lightheartedly. Her husband was grinning like a Shoshone boy just given his very first bow. Men were like that, though. At heart they were all oversized boys.

"We must hurry," Nate said, taking her hand once more.

The corridor wound upward to a flight of stairs. A gust of air gave Nate hope they were near one of the side entrances, but the stairs brought them to a balcony of sorts on the north side of the temple. Steps led down to the plaza, where mass confusion continued to reign.

Pausing, Nate faced the passage. Dared he risk another try at finding Nevava? As if in answer, from the bowels of the temple came a thunderous boom and seconds later a gusting cloud of dust and heat spewed over them, compelling Nate to cover his face with a hand.

Far down the corridor a pinpoint of light sparkled, a pinpoint that expanded and swelled until it filled the entire passageway even as it spurted toward the balcony at twice the speed a man could run. "Look out!" Nate hollered, throwing himself against Winona and sweeping her to the side.

From out of the corridor belched searing flames that lapped at the dark like so many tongues. Briefly, a good portion of the plaza was lit up as bright as day, revealing scores of dead and dying, countless dazed and wounded, and the few who were trying in vain to stem the tide of disaster.

Intense heat ballooned around the Kings, transforming the balcony into a furnace. Heat so hot it threatened to incinerate their clothes and sear them to the bone. Nate shielded Winona, feeling as if he were being fried alive. His back, the back of his legs, the nape of his neck, they were as hot as molten lava. Or so it seemed.

As quickly as the flames flared, they died. With an arm around Winona's waist, Nate hustled down the steps, relishing the cool breeze that had sprung up. At the bottom he nearly tripped over a priest whose head resembled a squashed pumpkin thanks to a bloody chunk of roof.

"Where to now? Winona asked.

Nate's first inclination was to keep on searching, but the pain in her voice, the misery etched on her face, stirred him into saying, "We're getting the hell out of here."

"Are you sure that is best?"

"I'm sure."

Holding her close, Nate moved away from the steps. Enough smoke blanketed the plaza that they should be able to make it across if they avoided clusters of Anasazis. "Ready to do some running?"

"Whatever must be done, I will do."

Nate could never say what made him glance back. He had no intimation that anyone was behind them. No noise or movement demanded investigation. He just looked over his shoulder and there, under the steps, deep in shadow, was a small huddled form. Something inside of him spurred him to go see what it was.

Winona raised her head when her man turned. She saw a child of ten or so, a boy clad in buckskin leggings with his thin arms around his bent knees, a terrified child whose wide eyes were damp with tears. "Nevava?"

The Ute boy blinked, then wiped at his eyes. "Who are you? I have never seen you before."

Nate had learned enough of the Ute tongue to get by, enough to reply, "We are friends of Red Feather. We are here to take you back to your people."

Nevava shot to his feet, his fear forgotten. "You knew my father?"

"I met him—" Nate began, and was cut short by nearly having his legs jarred out from under him by another quake. An aftershock, he thought. But unlike the last one, it grew more and more violent until it rivaled the quake that had destroyed the city, then surpassed it. The ground bucked and shook and pitched him to his knees. He heard Nevava cry out, and raised his head.

The upper third of the north wall had split nearly in half and was teetering outward, poised to snuff out their lives.

Chapter Seventeen

Zach King hauled on the bay's reins harder than he had ever pulled on a pair of reins in his whole life, harder than any rider ever should, so hard that the animal's mouth would be sore for a week. And as he did, he slammed his legs against its sides.

Horses were unpredictable at times. In moments of stress they did not always do as their riders desired. The bay was a case in point.

Zach intended to wheel it to the right to avoid the yawning crevice, but instead the bay bounded to the left, hopping stiff-legged like a giant rabbit. It cleared the edge of the crevice with barely a hand's width to spare, while the stallion and the mare cleared it by a wider margin. Zach trotted a dozen yards before he brought them to a halt.

As for Evelyn, her pony shied wide of the cavity, allowing her to avoid it with no problem. But now she was on one side of the rift, her brother on the other.

Annoyed that the bay had not done as he wanted, Zach raised a hand to give it a smack, then changed his mind. Now that he thought about it, he realized the horse had been smarter than he was. If it had veered to the right as he wanted, it would have collided with George Washington and maybe sent him over the brink into the fissure. While Zach would not miss the pony one little bit, his sister was another story.

"Zach, how do we get back together?" she called out.

The crevice was only six feet across at the widest, but Zach did not have a hankering to jump it, not in the dark, not when he could not see the bottom even when he rose in the stirrups and leaned way out over the chasm. "Keep going. It might narrow farther along."

It did, another forty yards on. Evelyn was glad to be reunited, even though she did not admit as much. Her brother had a habit of poking fun at her when she showed too much affection. Why that should be had puzzled her for the longest while. Her mother always showed tremendous affection for her father and her pa did not mind. But she had to take into account that her pa was a man, and boys were different from men. They had worse table manners, for one thing.

She was reminded of what her uncle Shakespeare had once said when a boy at a rendezvous had taken to pulling her hair. "Always try to remember, princess, that a little girl is a little lady waiting to sprout, while a little boy is a pint-sized hellion." She had understood that part, but then Shakespeare added, "And may never the twain meet until they're old enough to know better." Whatever that meant.

"So now what?" Evelyn asked after they had ridden a spell in nervous silence.

Zach was glad she could not read the indecision in his eyes. She was relying on him to pull them through, to keep them safe until they rejoined their parents. The trouble was, he was at a loss. They needed to hide. But where? There was no cover within a quarter of a mile—or was there?

Ahead lay a terrace seeded with corn. The stalks were not fully grown, but they were high enough to suit him.

"Follow me," Zach said.

They had to climb a short tract of open slope to reach the crop. Zach was in the lead, tugging on the reins to the mare and the stallion, when without warning both horses whinnied and tried to break loose. His own bay snorted, then plunged, almost throwing him.

"Zach!" Evelyn shouted, goading her pony forward to help. Suddenly George Washington began to twist and fight the bit, and she had her hands full keeping him under control.

A low rumbling resounded in all directions, swelling in volume, steadily swelling until the entire valley reverberated like one gigantic drum. And as the sound swelled, the ground under them shook with more and more force until the horses were slipping and tilting and stayed upright only by a monumental effort.

This time Evelyn was not afraid. She knew what she was dealing with, and that she was safe as long as George Washington did not fall on her. Then she recalled the wide fissure in the road, a fissure where she was sure there had not been one before the sun went down. She put two and two together and leaped to the conclusion that the earthquake was to blame, that it could split the earth as easily as she split a loaf of bread. And if it should do that underneath her, she would be gobbled whole like a ripe berry.

The quake did not last long. Zach managed to hold on to the extra horses, and once assured his sister was all right, he made his way to the rows of corn. They dismounted, used a rope taken from one of his father's parfleches to tether the four mounts, and sat side by side, their elbows nearly touching.

"I plumb forgot those hobbles," Zach remarked. "Hope Pa doesn't bend my ear for being forgetful again."

"I'll stick up for you," Evelyn said. "But I wouldn't worry. If you'd taken the time to grab them, that snake would have grabbed you. Pa would rather have you than a bunch of hobbles any old day."

"We're pretty lucky to have them for parents, aren't we?" Zach said. He had never really given it much thought before, tending to take his ma and pa for granted. But they were always there for his sister and him, always looking out for their welfare.

"I'd say so." Evelyn had always rated her mother as the best mother in all creation. When she came down sick, her mother mended her. When she wanted a new dress or some such, her mother always made it or helped her get it. When she had wanted a horse of her own, it had been her mother who talked her father into going to Bent's Fort and bartering for George Washington. Yes, a mother was a girl's best friend.

Time passed, anxious time spent worrying. Evelyn grew drowsy and had to shake her head often to stay awake. Her lids had closed for the fiftieth time when she was startled to feel the grass under her rise up as if to pitch her headlong down the slope.

"Another quake," Zach cried, leaping to the horses. "Grab that mangy critter of yours."

Scrambling to her feet, Evelyn lurched toward her pony. The unstable footing threw her off stride, and she tottered as some of the trappers did when they had too much liquor. Snatching George Washington's reins, she sought to calm him, but he pranced wildly and it was all she could do to hold on.

Zach figured this latest quake would be like the

last, short and mild, but he was woefully mistaken. It was the most violent yet, and it seemed to go on and on and on. How he held on to the three horses he would never know. Presently the shaking tapered to mild tremors, and he congratulated himself on having lived through it without anything going wrong.

At that very instant the stallion reared, tearing from his grasp. Still holding on to the mare and the bay, he ran after the big black as it cantered onto the road and stopped, its ears pricked.

"Dang it," Zach complained, sliding on the slick grass. He spread his legs to brace himself, but his left foot snagged on a bump and down he went, sprawling onto the road on his hands and knees. His only consolation was that the stallion had not gone any farther.

"I always reckoned Pa trained you better," Zach told it as he placed the stock of his rifle on the ground and used it to pump himself up out of the dirt.

"Say! What's that?" Evelyn hollered.

Zach looked where she was pointing. To the south inky figures moved, flowing toward them. Or rather, toward him, for the figures were coming down the center of the road. He did not need the starlight to identify the onrushing forms. Apprehension seized him by the throat as his mind screamed, *Anasazis!*

Some men and women are gifted with superior reflexes. They can run faster, throw farther, jump higher. They are the physical cream of the crop, the ones who make exceptional athletes. In ancient times it was such as these who gained immortal fame in the Olympic Games.

Nate King had never participated in a sporting event in his life, but if he had it was likely he'd have won a few. For even among the mountain men, who were as tough a breed as ever lived, he was one of the fastest, the strongest, the most agile.

He gave the wilderness the credit. The constant grueling fight for survival had tempered the soft sinews of a New York accountant into muscles of virtual steel.

Everyday tasks around the cabin likewise hardened a man. There was wood to be chopped, horses to be shod, game for the supper pot to hunt, and a thousand and one other jobs that kept a man busy from dawn until well past dusk.

As a result, Nate King was in his physical prime. He had an iron frame, lightning reflexes, and they were both put to the ultimate test by what happened next.

With a rending roar the massive section of all three floors above them plummeted groundward. Nate bent, wrapped his left arm around the Ute boy, whirled, and ran. His wife had turned to flee, but she was in no condition to sprint. The brutal beating had taken a fearful toll. She was slow, much too slow.

Nate scooped Winona into his right arm, lifting her clear off her feet. He pumped his legs, barely feeling the strain of bearing both his wife and the boy and both rifles. A quick tilt of his head showed the wall swooping down on them. It loomed blackly against the backdrop of flames consuming the temple, blotting out the sky.

Streaking toward the plaza, Nate heard Nevava gasp in fear and the boy went as rigid as a board. A shadow fell across them, a shadow that grew larger and larger and darker and darker. Nate could sense how close the falling wall was. Intuition told him that in the next several heartbeats it would smash onto them with pulverizing force.

Winona held herself limp to make it easier for Nate. She did not look up; she did not want to know how close the end was. Her confidence in her husband was unbounded, but she was a practical person and she knew the odds were against them. For Nate to be able to out-race the slab while carrying both of them was next to impossible.

She thought of Evelyn and Zach, her precious children, the two who had given her so much joy, who had made her laugh and on occasion brought tears to her eyes. She would have liked to see them grow up, to see Evelyn wed and Zach grow into a respected warrior. She would have liked to bounce their children on her knee, to be called "grandmother" and to see a whole new generation blossom.

Winona blinked, and saw the dark shadow blot out all the light. The slab was almost upon them. The remainder of her life could be measured in fractions of a moment.

Nate King realized the same thing. Taking one more mighty bound, he flung himself outward, his steel-spring legs hurtling the three of them through the air as if they had been hurled from a catapult. Six, eight feet he leaped, and as he came down he twisted so his shoulder bore the impact. At the instant of contact Nate rolled, not once but over and over in a whirlwind of motion.

Behind them a thunderous blast rocked the plaza. Under them the ground shook as if from another quake. Around them and on top of them rained stones and mortar, some pieces small but others large, pelting them, stinging them, bruising them.

Their momentum expended, they came to a stop. Nate was on the bottom, on his back, and raising his head, he saw a mountain of debris where the slab had hit. It had missed them by six inches, if that much.

"You did it," Winona said softly. Tenderly, she pressed her sore lips to his cheek.

Nevava was trembling like an aspen leaf in a strong wind. Nate set the boy down and stiffly sat up. Somehow he had managed to hold on to the rifles, and he gave Winona hers. "As much as I'd like to sit here awhile, we can't,'' he said. In the Ute tongue, he asked the boy, "Can you stand?''

Nevava rose unsteadily. He was scared and shaken, but like a true warrior's son he was doing his best to hide it.

Half of the temple had been devoured by the fire. In its flickering glow much of the plaza and the surrounding apartments were starkly revealed, showing the extensive damage wrought by the latest quake. Weakened by the earlier tremors, the walls and roofs had folded like a house of cards, collapsing in on top one another in a domino effect, starting with the highest levels and proceeding down to the lowest.

More dwellings had been destroyed than were left standing. Jagged remnants of walls and isolated beams thrust skyward like tombstones in a graveyard. From out of the rubble poked random arms and legs and broken shapes that had once been men, women, or children.

Nate had never been the superstitious kind. He was not one of those who carried a rabbit's foot for luck or believed that finding a four-leaf clover was a good omen. He did not read portents in the stars or signs in ordinary random events. They were so much nonsense as far as he was concerned. But even so, he could not help thinking that the terrible devastation that had befallen the Anasazi city was more than mere happenstance. What they could have done to deserve the destruction, though, was beyond him.

"Come,'' Nate said in Ute, and hurried to the south. Not as many Anasazis were in the plaza as before, and most of those he saw were so severely hurt they were beyond human help. One older man he would never forget. It was a tiller, a wizened oldster whose left leg had been crushed and whose right arm dangled by a strip of flesh. Yet the man was weakly scrabbling across the ground like a wounded crab, smearing a wide red swatch in his wake.

"Where did they all go?" Winona wondered. She had girded herself for another clash, but the few Anasazis still alive were either in no shape to oppose them or were intent on saving their own hides.

The wind was blowing the smoke to the southeast. A gust parted a swirling gray cloud ahead, revealing a long line of refugees who streamed around the northwest corner of the city, fleeing on the road that crossed the valley.

"There's your answer," Nate said. He noticed she was limping and put an arm around her waist, but she pushed his hand away.

"I can hold my own, husband."

"You and your darned pride."

"Pride has nothing to do with it. You must keep your hands free in case we are attacked. We are not safe yet."

Not by a long shot, Nate mentally agreed. He prayed their kids were all right, that they had stayed where they were supposed to. As he approached the apartment where the Anasazis had imprisoned him, he looked up, thinking of Pedro Valdez and the promise he had made. What would Winona say when she learned they were bound for Texas after they took Nevava to his people? Maybe it would be best if he went himself.

A shriek snapped Nate out of his musing.

Rushing toward them was a bloody apparition, an Anasazi warrior whose right side bore a shallow wound and whose muscular physique was caked with grime and soot. It was Crooked Nose, war club overhead, a knife in his other hand, the gleam of blood lust in his dark eyes.

Winona started to level her rifle, but Nate stepped in front of her. "No. There might be others nearby. Protect the boy. I'll deal with him." And with that, Nate shoved his Hawken into her hand, drew his tomahawk and his knife, and closed on his nemesis.

Chapter Eighteen

There were times when Winona King did not understand her husband at all.

More than sixteen years of marriage had given her keen insight into why he did the things he did. She knew all of his habits and quirks, his likes and dislikes. She knew he liked to sleep on his right side, that he was partial to blackberries above all other foods. She knew his favorite color, which books he liked best, how he felt about the Great Mystery and life in the higher realms.

In short, she knew everything there was to know about the man. So nine times out of ten she could predict how he would react in any given situation. But there was always that tenth time when he behaved exactly the opposite as he should. Such as now.

When the enraged Anasazi charged, Winona fully expected her husband to shoot him. That is what she would have done, what any Shoshone warrior would have done. The Anasazi wanted to kill them, so they should kill him.

163

Swiftly, efficiently, showing as much mercy as the Anasazi planned to show them.

But not Nate. No, he gave her his rifle and never bothered to draw either flintlock. Instead, he met the Anasazi head-on, using only a knife and tomahawk—in effect meeting the warrior on equal terms.

He was making a mistake. Combat was not a game. Warriors did not play at killing. As her father once instructed her, "There might come a time when our village will be raided, when enemies might try to kill you. Should that happen, remember it is your life or theirs. Do not try to reason with them. They will not listen. Do not try to wound them to spare their lives. You must kill them before they kill you. It is that simple."

It upset Winona no end that her husband had never learned the same lesson. He was forever trying to be "fair," forever striving to do "what was right." He could never bring himself to shoot a foe in the back, or to take undue advantage. Noble sentiments, but exactly the kind of thinking that got a person killed.

So now, as her man and the Anasazi flew at each other, Winona had half a mind to disobey him and shoot the warrior dead. She started to take aim, but she had delayed too long. The moment to act had passed. They were locked in a duel to the death.

Nate countered a swing of the war club with his tomahawk. Shifting, he parried a thrust of Crooked Nose's knife speared at his chest. They circled, trading blows, cold steel ringing on cold steel, war club and tomahawk weaving intricate patterns of skill and trickery.

Crooked Nose feinted, pivoted, snapped his blade at Nate's neck. Deflecting it with his own knife, Nate drove his tomahawk at the Anasazi's midsection, but Crooked Nose was too quick for him.

Borderline madness animated the warrior's features. Crooked Nose fought like someone possessed, with maniacal fury and inhuman strength. Evidently the loss of all he held dear had been more than he could endure.

Nate countered a high slash at his throat, a low cut at his thigh. The swish of their weapons, the crunch of dirt under their feet, their heavy breathing were the only sounds they made. Grim determination compressed their lips, locked their jaws.

From the moment they had set eyes on each other they had been bitter adversaries, and now they vented their shared dislike in a blinding flurry, swinging and spinning and stabbing and hacking too fast for the eye to follow.

They were evenly matched, Nate and the Anasazi. Neither was able to gain the upper hand in the first few moments. Their clash became an endurance test. Which one of them had more stamina? Which one would make the first mistake?

In the ebb and flow of their conflict, it was as if they were joined at the hip. But not in a mutual bond of devotion, as in a marriage. Theirs was a bond of mutual spite. Crooked Nose was the type who hated any who were different from his own kin, and Nate King despised bigots.

Suddenly the Anasazi tucked his knees and flicked the tip of his blade at the mountain man's stomach. Only by a whisker did the trapper deflect the knife.

In retaliation Nate jacked his left knee up, into Crooked Nose's mouth, connecting with an audible crack. Crooked Nose fell backward and Nate warily skipped in to open the other's jugular, but the warrior elevated the war club, foiling him, then sliced the knife at his shin. Nate had to jerk his leg back to spare himself from harm, and in doing so he slipped. His leg was propelled backward while he stumbled forward, directly at the Anasazi.

Crooked Nose flung his arm outward to impale Nate on his blade, but Nate swatted it aside and then brought the tomahawk sizzling downward in a tight arc. Since he was falling as he swung, he could not put all of his weight into the swing and he did not anticipate it being effective.

Fickle fate took a hand. Crooked Nose pumped his war club up to block the tomahawk as he had done a dozen times already. In each instance the club had proven the tomahawk's equal. But this time the short sharp edge of the tomahawk must have caught the club at just the right angle, for it sheared through the wooden club as if it were a piece of kindling, sheared through and thudded into the Anasazi's forehead.

Crooked Nose stiffened and grunted. That was all. His hate-filled eyes locked on Nate, and as he crumbled to the ground he spent the waning seconds of his earthly existence glaring at the object of his hatred.

Nate was breathing hard and caked with sweat. Placing a foot on the warrior's chest, he wrenched the tomahawk out, wiped it clean on the Anasazi's shirt, and slid the handle under his belt. "You had grit, I'll give you that," he said in eulogy.

The smooth feel of a rifle barrel brushing his palm reminded Nate of where he was, and their plight. Accepting the Hawken from his wife, he gestured. "Let's light a shuck while we can."

It was fine by Winona. As no other Anasazis had rushed to aid the warrior, she deduced few were left in the city. The Ute boy hung close to her, like a second shadow, perhaps afraid they would become separated.

Nate jogged from the plaza, pacing himself in order not to tire Winona any more than she already was. They passed more rubble, more bodies. The road was deserted, but to the north spotty wisps of dust confirmed that the general Anasazi population, or, rather, the meager remnants, had forsaken the last of their grand city.

The Kings and Nevava hastened into the night. Winona, recalling her experiences in the forest, remarked, "We must stay alert, husband. There are . . . things . . . in this valley."

"Things? Like the creature that killed this boy's father?"

"That and more."

Just what I need, Nate reflected. Something else to worry about. Zach and Evelyn would be no match for a beast that could slay ten grown men. "Where did you leave the children?"

"It is a ways yet." Winona sensed and shared his anxiety, and hiked faster. Soon the roar of flames dwindled, the infrequent groans and cries faded. She scoured the middle terraces, seeking the exact spot where her son and daughter should be waiting for them. Because she was concentrating on the upper slopes, she was startled when a feminine squeal gushed from a row of corn at the side of the road.

"Ma! Pa!"

Out of the corn darted Evelyn, grinning from ear to ear. She had been fighting sleep, her eyelids drooping, when footfalls stirred her to wakefulness. Now she threw herself into her mother's arms and hugged her mother close, saying repeatedly, "You're alive! You're alive! You're alive!"

Zach emerged, leading all four horses. He was ashamed to admit that he had dozed off, and to cover his embarrassment he said, "For a second there I figured you were more Anasazis. They've been drifting by for the past half an hour."

"Did they give you any trouble?" Nate asked. He had an urge to embrace his son, but did not out of respect for the boy's wishes. A while back Zach had made it plain that he did not like to be fawned over in front of others. "Childish," Zach had called it. The boy would learn better, someday.

"None at all, Pa. We were on the road when the first bunch showed up. But they treated us as if we weren't even here. Most were in shock, it looked like."

Nate turned and gazed out over the lost valley of the Anasazis, wondering what the few survivors would do now that the last stronghold of their once flourishing empire had been destroyed. He thought about Pahchatka and hoped the man was one of those who made it out alive. About to suggest they mount and ride, he froze when the ground under them shook just enough to be felt, and immediately stopped.

"There will be more quakes," Winona predicted.

"On your horses, everyone," Nate directed. Another major tremor might tumble the high cliffs onto the valley floor. Or—he had a sudden, awful stab of fear—it might collapse the tunnel, severing the sole link to the outside world. Provided the tunnel had not already caved in.

At a gallop Nate led his family up the terraces. At the tree line he had no difficulty finding the trail his captors had used, and he moved along it at a reckless pace.

Winona rode double with Nevava. She was the only one with whom the boy was comfortable, and he clung to her as if she were his own mother. Patting his arm, she said, "You are safe now. No one will harm you." He did not respond.

No sounds broke the unnatural stillness. Nate rode with both hands on his Hawken, his wife's warning about the strange creatures fresh in his mind. But none appeared. Not a single animal stirred anywhere. The upheaval, he reflected, had cowed them into taking refuge in their dens and burrows.

At length Nate came to where the trail widened. In front of them reared the towering cliff. At its base was the dark rectangle that marked the entrance to the tunnel. Eagerly, Nate went to ride into it. Then he saw the opening clearly and an oath escaped his lips.

The Lost Valley

They were too late. The roof had buckled. A giant slab blocked the entrance, a slab so heavy it would take a hundred men to budge it.

Vaulting from the saddle, Nate conducted a closer inspection. He was elated to find a gap on the right side of the slab, a gap barely wide enough for a horse to squeeze through. Poking his head in, he tried to see how far back the gap extended, but it was pitch black. "We need torches," he announced.

With Zach's help, Nate constructed three. First they broke short limbs and trimmed them. Next they uprooted tall dry weeds, which they wound tight around one end of each limb, using whangs from Nate's hunting shirt to tie the weeds fast.

As he took out his fire steel and flint, Nate commented, "Maybe it would be better if I went in by my lonesome, just to make sure it's safe."

"We will stick together," Winona said. She would rather share his fate than be trapped in that horrible valley without him.

"What if another quake hits and the whole cliff comes crashing down?" Nate asked. If any of them had to die, he would gladly sacrifice himself to spare them.

"What will be, will be."

"We're with Ma on this one, Pa," Zach chimed in, and his sister nodded in agreement.

To try to talk them out of it would waste precious time. Every minute they squandered increased the likelihood of another severe earthquake erupting. Nate lit the torches, passing one to his wife and one to Zach.

Grasping the third, the mountain man entered the tunnel. He had to tug on the reins when the big black balked, and reluctantly it followed him. Three-fourths of the tunnel was gone, jumbled rubble all that remained. Some had spilled into the gap.

Nate stepped over a small boulder and advanced

169

briskly, holding the torch well in front. He did not like the feeling of being hemmed in, of having untold tons of solid rock and earth above and around him, ready to enfold him in its stony grip.

Winona gave the mare's reins to Zach, clasped her daughter's hand, and filed in. Nevava dogged their heels, following so closely that he bumped into her now and then. "Stay calm," she said in Ute. In English, she called back, "Can you handle those three by yourself, son?"

"I'll do just dandy, Ma," Zach replied. But the truth was that he could not lead his bay, the mare, and the pony in single file; their reins were not long enough. So he resorted to a rope, linking them by their necks. Pulling roughly, he hurried to catch up with his folks.

Nate King was beginning to think he had made a grave mistake. The gap had narrowed a couple of inches and the roof lowered a few, besides. What if there was no way through? How would he get the horses back out when they couldn't turn around?

Navigating the gloomy tunnel was like winding through the bowels of the earth. From time to time Nate heard dirt rattle down from above. More nerve-racking were the creaks and groans that testified to the tremendous pressure being exerted on the tunnel from all sides. It would not take much to bring the whole mess crashing down.

Around the next bend Nate beheld a ghastly spectacle. Some of the fleeing Anasazis had not made it out. Dozens had been partially buried, their smashed figures sprawled amid gore and blood. Shattered bones gleamed palely. Already the reek of death hung heavy. Bitter bile rose into Nate's mouth, and he spat it out.

Revulsion seized Evelyn. Averting her eyes, she dug her nails into her mother's palm and wished they were out in the open. If they ever made it home she was never going to leave again.

The passage of time became like the tunnel itself, dragging endlessly by. Nate's torch had about burned itself out when the stallion nickered loudly. The next moment the walls jiggled and the solid rock over his head sagged and split with hairline cracks. With nowhere to run, all Nate could do was fling an arm over his head.

The tremor lasted only a few moments. "Hurry," Winona urged after the trembling stopped. They had lived through that one, but they might not live through the next.

Nate did not need any encouragement. Soon his torch flickered its last and he flipped it onto the rubble. From then on he had to grope along in near-total darkness. Twice he stubbed a finger. Once he banged his shin.

There was no describing the delicious sensation that coursed through the trapper when a puff of wind caressed his face. It galvanized him into doubling his stride. He broke into a grin when at long, long last the tunnel ended and stars shone overhead. "We're out!" he exclaimed.

The air was wonderfully fresh, delightfully clean, unlike the air in the valley, which had been so thick and humid and tainted with a faint sweetish scent. As Nate turned to make sure his loved ones were safe, a bat flitted close above them.

Fleeting dizziness assailed him. For several bizarre seconds, Nate had the impression that the bat was ten times its normal size, and that its mouth was ringed with teeth as long as his Green River knife. Then the dizziness faded, the illusion vanished. Not knowing what to make of it, he shrugged and inhaled deeply, again and again.

Winona and the children were imitating him. "Where is the mist?" she asked. "And those red wolves?"

"Gone with the wind, like the Anasazis" was Nate's answer. "The same as we should be."

Off into the wilderness they trotted, into the wilderness they knew and loved, the wilderness they called home.

MOUNTAIN MADNESS

Chapter One

They were gong to die. They just knew it.

Isaiah Tompkins and Rufus Stern staggered westward under the hot summer sun. On all sides a sea of grass rustled dryly, fanned by a sluggish breeze. The two men walked with their heads bowed, their shoulders slumped. Neither noticed when a pair of coyotes rose from hiding to study them and then padded noiselessly away.

"We were fools," Isaiah declared bitterly. "We never should have left New York." He did not bring up the fact that the idea to get rich quick had been his. Which made him to blame if they died there in the middle of nowhere. He did not say it, but he thought it, and felt twice as bitter.

Rufus licked his dry lips. His mouth and throat were painfully sore. He did not want to talk, but he knew if he did not say something, his friend would sink deeper into the depths of despair. "Others have done it and succeeded."

"I don't see how."

They had both heard the stories of how scores of bold young

David Thompson

men had ventured beyond the frontier. Across the wide Mississippi to the vast prairie some called the Great American Desert, then beyond, to the fabled Rocky Mountains. Where peaks that glistened white with snow the year round towered miles into the sky. Where humpbacked bears bigger than horses prowled in constant hunger. Where painted savages lurked, waiting to slit the throats of the unwary.

What had most interested Isaiah and Rufus, though, were the tales about the trappers. Hardy souls who braved daily perils to reap thousands of dollars in bounty for beaver skins. It was said that beaver were as abundant as rabbits. All a man had to do was walk along a stream and pluck them out of the water as a child might pluck daisies.

Why, in a single trapping season, or so the accounts went, a man could earn upward of two thousand dollars. This, in a day when the average laborer was lucky if he earned four hundred a year. All it would take, Isaiah and Rufus had calculated, were five or six successful seasons and they could return to New York City with their pockets bulging with money.

Their loved ones argued against it. ''Think of the dangers!'' many had said. Parents, sisters, brothers, and others had all pointed out that there were plenty of good jobs to be had at home. Rufus's father had even offered to take them into his clothing business.

But Isaiah and Rufus would not be denied. Their heads swimming with visions of more money than either had ever seen in their entire lives, they combined their meager savings and bought what they felt they would need.

''Westward! To the Rockies!'' Isaiah had cried on that fateful day they left. Now here they were many weeks later, stumbling wearily along, exhausted, starving, on the verge of collapse.

Gone were their mounts, their packhorses. All their supplies. Everything except the clothes on their backs, the heavy rifles

GET YOUR 4
FREE* BOOKS NOW—
A VALUE BETWEEN
$16 AND $20

Mail the Free* Book Certificate Today!

FREE* BOOKS
CERTIFICATE!

YES! I want to subscribe to the Leisure Western Book Club. Please send me my 4 FREE* BOOKS. Then, each month, I'll receive the four newest Leisure Western Selections to preview FREE* for 10 days. If I decide to keep them, I will pay the Special Member's Only discounted price of just $3.36 each, a total of $13.44 ($14.50 US in Canada). This saves me between $3 and $6 off the bookstore price. There are no shipping, handling or other charges.* There is no minimum number of books I must buy and I may cancel the program at any time. In any case, the 4 FREE* BOOKS are mine to keep—at a value of between $17 and $20!

*In Canada, add $5.00 Canadian shipping and handling per order for first shipment. For all subsequent shipments to Canada the cost of membership in the Book Club is $14.50 US, which includes $7.50 shipping and handling per month. All payments must be made in US currency.

Name _____

Address _____

City_____ State_____ Country_____

Zip_____ Telephone_____

Tear here and mail your FREE* book card today!

Get Four Books Totally F R E E* — A Value between $16 and $20

Tear here and mail your FREE* book card today!

PLEASE RUSH
MY FOUR FREE*
BOOKS TO ME
RIGHT AWAY!

LeisureWestern Book Club
P.O. Box 6613
Edison, NJ 08818-6613

AFFIX
STAMP
HERE

in their hands, and their ammo pouches and powder horns.

Isaiah did not like to dwell on dying. He had to admit, though, that barring a miracle neither of them would live to see another sunset. It had been five days since they ate last. Almost three since they had a sip of water.

"I'll miss Agnes," Rufus commented sadly.

A twinge of conscience spiked Isaiah. Agnes Weatherby had been Rufus's betrothed. Of all their loved ones she had most resented their leaving. As well she should. Rufus had postponed the wedding in order to go along.

"I'll miss the theater, the nightlife," Isaiah said. *And the women.* A rake and a lady's man, he could never get enough of the opposite sex. His friends liked to joke he was addicted to them. And there were a bevy of beauties who could attest to his carnal cravings.

One of his fondest memories was the night he took Claire Beaumont to the Bowery Theater to see Madame Francisquay Hutin, a famed French dancer. Madame Hutin had bounded onto the stage wearing a short, semitransparent garment that had scandalized half the women in the audience into walking out. Claire, though, had stayed, and for some reason later had thrown herself at him in wild abandon. *How sweet that night had been!*

And how ironic, Isaiah mused, he should now regret his decision to leave New York when only a few short months ago he had craved to escape the bustling city, to strike out on a "grand adventure," to leave the past behind in order to finance the future.

"I am a dolt," Isaiah criticized himself, and did not realize he had spoken aloud until Rufus responded.

"Makes two of us. I could have backed out, but I didn't." Rufus paused to try to swallow. "I'm as much at fault as you."

They fell silent, too spent to waste energy talking. Isaiah willed his feet to keep shuffling, even though his legs protested every step. He tried not to dwell on how hopeless their situation was.

Lacking food and water was bad enough. But they had no idea where they were. Yes, they were somewhere in the vast prairie, but exactly *where* eluded them. They had no inkling of how far off the mountains lay, and the mountains were their only hope of survival. There they'd find game in abundance, find streams and rivers where they could quench their thirst to their heart's content.

Squinting up at the afternoon sun, Isaiah wiped a sleeve across the sweat beading his brow. The hat he had purchased in New York—"guaranteed to hold up for years under the most adverse weather conditions"—hung limply down around his ears. The first rainstorm they encountered had about ruined the thing.

It had been the same with the rest of their provisions. Nothing held up as it should have. Clothes supposed to last a lifetime had frayed in no time. Their boots—"the most rugged and durable ever constructed"—were cracked and split and would soon fall apart.

It's this damnable wilderness, Isaiah thought. Blistering hot during the day, bone-chilling at night. Harsh winds that swept out of nowhere. Storms that pounded man and beast into the ground. And the lightning! How did one describe the vivid bolts raining out of the heavens? One after the other, so many they lit up the sky as brightly as midday, crackling and booming in a deafening din. One, in fact, had killed their best packhorse, charring the poor brute in its tracks.

Movement roused Isaiah out of his daze. At the limits of his vision animals moved.

More of those slender antelope he had seen before. Automatically he started to raise his rifle, then decided not to waste the effort. They never came within range, and whenever Rufus and he tried to sneak close enough for a shot, the antelope always streaked away in magnificent leaps.

Deer were no easier to slay. Again and again the two of them tried to shoot one; again and again the wily creatures had fled unscathed.

Small wonder Isaiah and Rufus were starving. Neither had done much hunting before they trekked westward. Until they reached the Mississippi it hadn't posed much of a problem, since there were taverns and inns galore to stop at each night. And once beyond the river, they had counted on their carefully hoarded supplies to see them through.

But the supplies were gone, along with the rest of their horses—which in itself was a major mystery. Isaiah was sure he had tethered the animals securely, as an innkeeper had advised. Yet one morning all six had been gone, with no clue to what happened. Even the tether rope had vanished.

Rufus was of the opinion the horses had somehow tugged free and wandered off. Isaiah was inclined to blame sinister forces. He was sure a smudged print he had found was part of a track left by a red heathen.

"I don't want to die," Rufus suddenly announced.

"No one in their right mind does," Isaiah replied.

"No, you misunderstand. I *really* want to live. I want to see my mother and father again. I want to hold Agnes in my arms and tell her how sorry I am for being such a fool."

Agnes again. "I owe her an apology too," Isaiah said. "If we ever make it back, I'll get down on bended knee and beg her forgiveness."

Rufus doubted it would do any good, but he held his tongue. He had never told Isaiah that Agnes despised him. She would never forgive Isaiah for luring him away. Rufus had lost count of how many times she broke into tears during the final weeks of preparation.

"I just can't understand you," she had sobbed on more than one occasion. "Leaving me alone. Going off to God-knows-where. And for what? Isaiah's silly dream. So what if you come back five thousands dollars richer? I would rather have

11

you than any amount of money in the world.''

Always, she had clutched him, pleading, ''Please don't go. For my sake. I'm begging you to stay. We'll marry and be together the rest of our lives. As it ought to be. Please say you won't go. Please!''

And always, Rufus sorrowfully recalled, he had pried her fingers loose, kissed her, and smugly told her not to worry. ''Everything will be fine. You'll see. A year from now we'll have enough to buy our own house. Think how wonderful that will be.''

Agnes would only sob louder.

Now Rufus forlornly gazed out over the unending plain. *I should have listened to you, sweet Agnes*, he reflected. *I am sorry for being such a dunderhead, for always thinking I knew best.*

An unexpected rumbling grunt brought Rufus and Isaiah to a stop. From out of the high grass on their left rose an ominous dark shape. A massive form, dense and shaggy, with a great wedge-shaped head crowned by wicked curved horns. It grunted again and swung toward them, its short tail twitching.

''A buffalo!'' Isaiah blurted.

They had come on their first herd a few days west of the Mississippi, a small bunch that fled at their approach. Later, of course, they encountered much larger herds, some so immense it took a full day for the ungainly brutes to file by. Having heard lurid reports of men being fatally gored and trampled, they wisely stayed clear.

Still later, while in search of game, Rufus had stumbled on a cow and a calf. The mother had charged without warning. Rufus, safely mounted, easily escaped.

But now they were on foot. And the enormous bull glaring at them was less than ten yards away. It had risen from a wallow, a broad circular depression worn by constant rubbing and rolling.

''Do we shoot?'' Rufus breathlessly asked.

"No." Isaiah had been told buffalo skulls were so thick, bullets bounced off. Striking a vital organ would be hard for a marksman, and they were fair shots at best. "Be still," he whispered, "and maybe it will let us be."

Rufus prayed his friend was right. Images of lovely Agnes paraded through his mind. If the time had come to meet his Maker, he wanted his last thoughts to be of her. "Yea, though I walk through the valley of the shadow of death," he intoned, "I will fear no evil."

"Hush," Isaiah warned. The bull had snorted and taken a step forward. It would not take much to provoke the monster.

Rufus wouldn't heed. "For Thou art with me. Thy rod and Thy staff, they comfort me. Thou preparest a table before me in the presence of mine enemies. Thou anointest my head with oil. My cup runneth—"

"Shush, in the name of all that's holy," Isaiah demanded, but the harm had been done.

Uttering an irate bellow, the gigantic bull lowered its head and attacked. It did not paw at the ground or toss its head. It did not give them an instant's forewarning of its intention, as a wayfarer at a tavern had assured Isaiah was always the case. No, it simply charged, exploding out of the wallow like a cannonball out of a cannon. Close to two thousand pounds of corded sinew propelled it with dazzling speed. In the blink of an eye it was on them.

Isaiah threw himself to the right. He fully expected to be smashed by that awful head. To be plowed under by heavy, hammering hooves. So he was pleasantly relieved when he hit on his shoulder and rolled up into a crouch, unhurt.

Rufus was not so quick—or so fortunate. He tried to dive to the right, but in his weakened state his unsteady legs would not cooperate. In midair he was jolted by an impact that whooshed the breath from his lungs. Sky and grass changed positions. He tumbled, wincing when he crashed onto the hard ground. Exquisite pain flared up his right leg, nearly swamping his consciousness.

The world spun. A murky veil sought to shroud Rufus, but he cast it off with a vigorous shake. He was flat on his back, pillowy clouds floating above. Muted drumming reminded him of the buffalo.

Thinking he was about to be attacked again, Rufus rolled onto his left side to push erect. A wave of pain struck, and once more the world danced crazily. Nausea afflicted him. Swallowing sour bile, he tried to gain his knees, but his left leg was racked by torment so overwhelming he nearly cried out.

Isaiah rushed over, his rifle extended, prepared to preserve his friend's life at the expense of his own if need be. But the bull was through with them. It had paid them back for daring to disturb it and was trotting toward the southern horizon.

Where there was one, though, there might be more. Isaiah looped an arm around Rufus's shoulders and lifted. "Come on. Let's keep going."

Rufus would have liked nothing better, but when he tried to stand, his left leg would not bear his weight. Raw agony doubled him over. If not for Isaiah he would have pitched onto his face. "My leg," he said. "I think it's broken."

Isaiah gamely braced Rufus against his side and hastened westward, casting repeated glances at the grass, fearful of another huge shape materializing. He tried not to think of the consequences. On foot—and healthy—they barely stood a prayer. With Rufus stricken, they would never reach the mountains. They would weaken further and die. As simple as that.

Rufus noticed that his ribs were sore to the touch. When he took deep breaths, several lower down hurt tremendously. He suspected one was cracked or broken, but he did not say so. A busted limb was enough to worry about. Head bent, he gritted his teeth and struggled to hold his own.

Isaiah was so worried about being set upon from the rear

or the sides that he did not pay much attention to what was in front of them. Another step, and the earth abruptly fell away. Too late, he saw that he had blundered onto another wallow. Gravity seized him, and he fell. He flung an arm out, but it was no use.

An outcry was torn from Rufus. Ribs and leg combined in an onslaught of sheer torture. Again he wound up on his back, dazed. And in no hurry to stand. He hurt too much. Propping himself on his elbows, he scrunched his nose in disgust at the awful reek of urine.

Isaiah reclaimed his rifle, then Rufus's. Except for the buzz of flies the prairie was quiet. "I don't think there are any other buffalo close by."

"Lucky for us," Rufus commented. Their first bit of luck in a blue moon. "Although I wouldn't mind a thick, juicy slab of roasted meat right about now."

Isaiah's stomach growled. "Don't remind me." Thinking about food only aggravated their plight. "Let's take a look at that leg." As he sank down, he heard a distant sound, one he assumed had been made by the buffalo.

Rufus levered high enough to sit up. His left side throbbed. His leg was infinitely worse. "Without a splint I won't be able to go half a mile."

"First things first. Roll up your pant leg." Isaiah did not point out they had not seen a tree in days. A splint was out of the question.

The brown pants Rufus had bought in New York were grimy, faded, and frayed at the bottom. Fabric guaranteed to last ten years had not lasted ten weeks. Gingerly, he pried at the hem, rolling it upward, afraid of what he would find. He did not understand when Isaiah suddenly gripped his wrist. "What's wrong?"

"Listen."

Rufus did, and heard nothing out of the ordinary. About to continue hiking the hem, he froze at the unmistakable faint

15

nicker of a horse. To the southwest. "We're saved!" he exclaimed. "Maybe it's one of ours."

"Unlikely." Isaiah half rose, then thought better of exposing himself.

"White men, I'll bet. Let's give a shout to attract them."

"Hold on. What if it's not?" Isaiah's skin prickled as if from a heat rash. "Remember what that old fellow in St. Louis told us? Indians like to hunt buffalo." He paused. "What if it's a savage? Or an entire hunting party?"

Rufus's short-lived elation shattered on the jagged rocks of cruel reality. So far Fate had spared them from hostiles. They were long overdue to run into some. "Take a gander and tell me what you see."

Isaiah crept to the top. Flattening, he parted some grass. A pair of riders were heading in the wallow's general direction. As yet they were not close enough for him to note much detail other than the buckskins they wore and the white feather jutting from the head of the tallest. *A feather!* Isaiah slid down to Rufus and seized him by the arm. "I was right. Indians. We have to get out of here."

Rufus balked. If they had to make a stand, the wallow was the best spot they were likely to find. About nine feet in diameter and a foot or so deep, it offered more protection than the open prairie. He explained as much.

Reluctantly, Isaiah agreed. His foremost impulse was to run and keep on running until they were safe. But he would never desert Rufus, no matter what. "I'll help you to the top. Shoot anything that moves."

"What if they're peaceful?"

"Can we afford to take the chance?" Isaiah strained to keep his boyhood chum upright. "If they're friendly, they'll let us be. If they're not, they'll try to get in close to use their bows and lances. Be ready for anything."

Rufus felt there was a flaw in his partner's logic, but in his befuddled state he could not quite say what it was. Racked by pangs in his torso and his leg, he was grateful when they came to the crest so he could lie down.

Isaiah peered out. Dismay beset him on discovering the horses were in plain sight but the riders were nowhere to be seen. The men had dismounted, leaving the reins to dangle. "They're sneaking up on us," he whispered.

"How do you know?"

"Why else did they leave their animals out there and come on afoot?" Isaiah fingered the trigger of his rifle. "Don't fire until you have a sure shot. We can't afford to waste lead."

Rufus agreed. All their spare ammunition and powder had disappeared when the horses did. For which Isaiah couldn't blame him. Not when he had strongly suggested his friend remove the packs from the packhorses before turning in that night. He couldn't help it if he had been too tired to do the chore himself.

Each of them had about twenty balls left in his ammo pouch. Once that was gone they must resort to their long butcher knives. Hardly an appealing prospect.

A haze made the grass shimmer as if it were a reflection in a warped mirror. Rufus scoured the area without spotting the warriors. Apprehension tingled his spine as he imagined them snaking toward the wallow. He'd never fought an Indian before. He'd never fought anyone, in fact. So he couldn't honestly say if he had the courage to confront one in mortal combat, let alone actually take the life of another human being.

Judging by the lurid stories he'd heard during their travels, Rufus was glad he'd never had to find out. Harrowing tavern tales of captured whites skinned alive, of mountaineers who were scalped and lived to tell of it, of frontiersmen like Colter and others who had been made to run vicious gauntlets in order to save their skins.

Indians committed brutal acts. Everyone knew that. Many claimed it was because the red race was barely a notch above wild beasts in the overall scheme of things. While Rufus wasn't sure he would go that far, he was nonetheless petrified at the prospect of clashing with the warriors.

He glanced at Isaiah, who was scanning the prairie. Rufus wondered what his friend was thinking, if maybe Isaiah shared his sentiments.

At that exact instant, the other New Yorker was cursing himself for being stupid enough to think reaping a bonanza in beaver furs would be as easy as picking ripe cherries from a tree. Absently, he brushed a hand against his shirt. Under it was his dog-eared copy of *The Trapper's Guide* by Sewell Newhouse. It, more than anything else, was responsible for firing his imagination with dreams of being a trapper.

To those who were "looking out for pleasant work and ways of making" a lot of money, the *Guide* claimed to contain all the essential information anyone needed. Crucial provisions were listed in detail, along with tips on how to trap.

What the manual had *not* fully detailed, however, were the countless hardships. No mention of the unending trek across the Great American Desert, of the horrible storms, the lack of food and water. Isaiah wondered what else the manual didn't include.

Stirring grass brought Isaiah's musing to an end. Stems had rustled as if to the passage of a slinking form. Isaiah sighted down his rifle and applied his thumb to the hammer. Tense seconds expanded into a minute of anxious anticipation. When no one appeared, Isaiah relaxed a smidgen. Maybe he was jumping to conclusions, he tried to assure himself. Maybe the Indians were merely curious.

Rufus was gnawing on his upper lip, on a mustache that had sprouted over the past fortnight. Initially he had shaved every morning, just as he had done at the start of each day in New York. The scarcity of water put a stop to the habit. Now he had the mustache plus stubbly growth on his chin. Dear Agnes would hardly recognize him.

He also had hair well down past his ears. Since hostiles

were partial to lifting the hair of enemies, Rufus could not help but shudder at a gruesome mental image of his blood-stained scalp hanging from a peg in an Indian hovel. He couldn't let that happen. For Agnes's sake as well as his own.

"See anything?" Rufus whispered, and received a curt gesture in return.

Isaiah was annoyed his friend had been so careless. The hearing and eyesight of heathens were extraordinary, conditioned as they were by a lifetime of competing with wild creatures. Isaiah fretted the warriors had heard and pinpointed exactly where the wallow was, if they did not already know.

Rufus was upset. His friend could be rough on him on occasion, and it always stung. He would be the first to admit he wasn't necessarily the brightest individual who ever lived, but he always had their mutual best interests at heart. Hadn't he tagged along on Isaiah's grand adventure? What more proof could he offer of his undying friendship?

He became interested in the two horses. One was a splendid black stallion, the other an older white horse. The former grazed, the latter dozed. Rufus calculated the odds of reaching them before the Indians, but dismissed it as hopeless with his leg severely hurt.

Suddenly Rufus stiffened. A shadowy shape low to the ground had flitted briefly from west to east a dozen yards out. Elevating his rifle, he aligned the rear sight with the front sight as he had been taught, but by then the shape had melted into the earth. "Damn," he said to himself.

Isaiah heard, and frowned. Didn't his partner have a lick of common sense? Shifting to warn Rufus not to make the same mistake again, he ducked lower when something moved out among the thick stems. It had to be one of the Indians.

Just then, on the west side of the wallow, a loud thud sounded. Isaiah and Rufus both spun, bringing their weapons to bear. No one was there; they exchanged puzzled looks. It was Isaiah who spotted a rock lying on the wallow's slope, a

19

rock that had not been present earlier. Its significance wasn't lost on him.

"Rufus! Look out!" Isaiah bawled, but the distraction had served its purpose.

Over the rim from opposite sides rushed two figures in buckskins, one springing at Isaiah, the other at Rufus.

Chapter Two

Isaiah Tompkins tried to bring his rifle to bear. Before he could, a pair of brawny arms encircled his chest and he was borne backward. For a brief instant he saw his assailant clearly and he was startled to his core. It was a white man, not an Indian. A tall, barrel-chested man with long black hair and a black beard. He also glimpsed a powder horn, ammo pouch, and large leather pouch slung crosswise, as well as a pair of pistols wedged under a wide brown leather belt.

Isaiah was so startled that when he struck the ground he made no move to defend himself. Which was just as well. Because in the time it would take a heart to beat, a pistol was pressed against the tip of his nose and a deep, resonant voice said, "Don't get your shackles up, hoss. This beaver feels like chawing, not making wolf meat of you." Isaiah wasn't quite sure he understood, but he made no attempt to resist.

Across the wallow, Rufus Stern had fared no better. He had not even begun to lift his rifle when the second attacker caught him across the shoulders in a tackle that left him flat on his

21

back, rendered limp by anguish. It shocked Rufus to see the man was old enough to be his father. No, make that his *grandfather*. White hair and a bristly white beard framed a face crinkled by leathery wrinkles. Laughing blue eyes regarded him closely. "Pleased to make your acquaintance, young coon," the oldster said. "Don't be afraid." He leaned down and, incredibly, winked. "Remember what old William S. said."

"Huh?" was all Rufus could muster.

"Cowards die many times before their deaths. The valiant never taste of death but once. Of all the wonders that I yet have heard, it seems to me most strange that men should fear. Seeing that death, a necessary end, will come when it will come."

"Huh?" Rufus said again.

"The bard, son. Surely you've heard of Shakespeare?"

Rufus was not illiterate. He could read and write and knew a little about literature. Yes, he had heard of William Shakespeare, the English playwright. But to hear the bard being quoted by this white-haired apparition was bizarre beyond measure.

Isaiah Tompkins was no less astounded when the tall man who had pounced on him reached down and boosted him to his feet.

"No harm done, I reckon," said the giant, breaking into a smile. "The handle is Nate King. My pard and I were out hunting buffler when we spotted you. Sorry about sneaking up like we did, but we're not partial to lead between the eyes. And we know how skittish *mangeur de lards* can be."

"*Mangeur de* who?" Isaiah said in bewilderment.

"Greenhorns, pilgrim. Fresh from civilization. Like you and your friend, yonder." Nate King lowered the pistol and tucked it under his belt to the right of the big buckle. He was satisfied neither young man posed a threat.

Isaiah recovered his wits enough to ask, "Where did you

22

come from? Are you heading for the mountains to trap beaver?'' Something inside him seemed to snap, and his tongue wagged of its own accord. ''We're so glad to see you. We thought you were Indians. We've lost our horses and our supplies and my friend is hurt and we're just about on our last legs and—''

Nate King chuckled and raised a callused hand to quell the torrent. ''It's all right now. You're safe. We'll take you to my cabin. My family will love having company.''

''Cabin?'' Isaiah surveyed the plain. ''You live around here?''

Pointing westward, Nate said, ''Just a little ways off. Up in the mountains.''

Shakespeare McNair leaned closer to Rufus. ''Did I hear correctly, child? You've been hurt?''

Rufus was insulted. ''Just because I'm younger than you doesn't give you the right to call me that. I'm a grown man, damn it.''

''In the reproof of chance lies the true proof of men.''

''What?''

''The sea being smooth, how many shallow bauble boats dare sail upon her patient breast, making their way with those of nobler bulk! But let the ruffian Boreas once enrage the gentle Thetis, and anon behold the strong-ribb'd bark through liquid mountains cut, bounding between the two moist elements, like Perseus' horse. Where's then the saucy boat, whose weak untimber'd sides but even now co-rivall'd greatness?''

''Huh?''

Shakespeare peered intently at the younger man's hair. ''Were you knocked on the head? Is that why you're so addlepated?''

''I can't understand half of what you say, old man.''

Nate King roared with laughter as he came over. ''You're not the only one, stranger. I've been telling him that for years.

23

But what can you expect from a gent who totes around *The Complete Works of William Shakespeare* everywhere he goes?'' He lowered his voice as if confiding a secret. ''I'm partial to James Fenimore Cooper, myself.''

Isaiah shook his head. It was too ridiculous for words. He was half-tempted to pinch himself to verify he wasn't dreaming. Here, apparently, were two honest-to-goodness mountain men, the kind he had read about, men who lived in the wilderness year in and year out, who fought bears and Indians daily, who were supposed to be the hardiest souls alive. And what were they doing? Joshing about their favorite authors! ''I didn't think trappers liked to read,'' he lamely said.

Nate started up the wallow, saying over a shoulder, ''There's nothing like a good book during those long winter spells when the snow is higher than the cabin door.''

''In the old days us mountaineers would swap books all winter long,'' Shakespeare elaborated. ''We'd sit up past midnight discussing all the greats. Byron, Scott, Clark's Commentary, you name it.'' He brightened at the memory. ''The Rocky Mountain College, we called it. A man could get quite an education thataway.''

Rufus knew next to nothing about the others McNair had mentioned. Reading had always seemed like a waste of time to him. Why spend hours with his nose in a book when he could spend those same hours living life to the fullest? Not having anything to contribute, he said instead, ''I was attacked by a bull buffalo.''

Shakespeare turned serious. ''You don't say? Let's have a look.''

Rufus was going to say the man did not have to bother, but the oldster squatted and probed him from head to toe with the precision of a New York physician. He answered ''Yes!'' when McNair lightly pressed against his ribs, and again when the mountain man examined his left leg.

Isaiah, watching, did not realize Nate King had left until

the tall trapper returned bearing two rifles unlike any he had ever beheld. Shorter than his own, both were thicker and had elaborately decorated stocks. "Nice guns," he commented.

Nate wagged the pair. "Made by the brothers, themselves," he said, and proudly held one for Isaiah to read the capital letters engraved on the lockplate: J & S HAWKEN—ST. LOUIS.

Shakespeare rose, scratching his beard. "Well, our young friend here has a busted rib and a badly bruised leg, but he can ride."

"My leg isn't broken?" Rufus asked in some surprise.

"No way but gentleness. Gently, gently. The fiend is rough, and will not be roughly used."

"Pardon?"

"Go easy on that leg, Horatio. It's not busted, but you won't be playing hopscotch for a week or so." Shakespeare accepted his Hawken from Nate. "I'll fetch the horses. Won't Winona be surprised when we show up? What with her kin visiting and all." Chortling, he scampered off.

Nate King did not share his friend's glee. Studying the two greenhorns, he wondered if he was making a mistake in taking them to his home. How would they react once they arrived? Were they decent at heart? So many whites harbored mindless hate born of ignorance.

"Who is Winona?" Isaiah asked.

"My wife." Nate changed the subject. "I don't recollect hearing who you are, mister. Or what brings you to this corner of the world."

Isaiah corrected his oversight. Briefly, he explained about his dream to be a beaver trapper and was puzzled when King gave him a peculiar look. "Now, of course, our dream is ruined," he concluded. "Without horses and provisions, we have no choice but to somehow make our way back to St. Louis." He hesitated, reluctant to ask someone he did not know for aid. For Rufus's sake, he added, "Any help you can give us will be greatly appreciated."

"You'll be taken care of, don't fret." Nate walked to the rim to await Shakespeare and to ponder. Tompkins and Stern had no notion of how fortunate they were. Countless well-meaning but foolish men just like them had paid a fatal price for their folly. It was just dumb luck that McNair and he had happened on the pair when they did.

Nate sighed and reached up to adjust the eagle feather adorning his hair. Not more than three moons ago he had been out on the prairie hunting and stumbled on a collection of bones and moldy store-bought clothes.

A yellowed journal, warped and discolored but still partly legible, had recorded the final thoughts of a would-be trapper from Ohio. A youth who had struck out on his own and suffered a fate similar to that of the New Yorkers.

Indians, most likely Pawnees or Lakotas, had stolen the youth's horses and his possibles. He had pressed on in the forlorn hope of reaching the Rockies, but died of starvation. The last journal entry had been a plea. A request scribbled to anyone who might find his remains. Would they please find a way of getting the journal to his kin? he had begged. To his ma and pa and sister.

Nate had mulled it over and finally sent the journal back with a party of mountain men bound for St. Louis. It might lessen the family's torment. Knowing the youth's fate was better than not knowing. Wasn't it?

Shakespeare trotted up, leading Nate's big black stallion. Glancing at the would-be trappers, he said so only Nate could hear, "Are you sure about this, hoss? I can take them to my cabin instead."

"In the shape they're in? No, you live a lot farther away."

"Suit yourself." McNair grinned. "Weigh what convenience both of time and means may fit us to our shape. If this should fail, and that our drift look through our bad performance, 'Twere better not assay'd. Therefore, this project should have a back or second, that might hold if this did blast in proof.''

"Translation?"

"If the worst comes to pass I'll take them on to my cabin anyway. Blue Water Woman won't mind. Too much.'' Shakespeare dismounted and said to the greenhorns, "Let's light a shuck. You boys get to ride double on Pegasus. Nate's horse tends to act up if someone it doesn't know tries to climb on.''

Isaiah snickered. "You named your horse after that Greek myth?''

Shakespeare gave his animal an affectionate rub. "All he's missing are the wings. And when he was younger, you'd have sworn he had a pair. He flew like the wind. Wasn't a horse alive could catch him. Why, once Nate and me were over the Divide when a band of Utes swept down, chasing us for plumb near fifty miles—''

"It was more like five,'' Nate amended, and nudged his mentor. "Help me lift Rufus on Pegasus, then you can jabber us to death.''

"Jabber?'' Shakespeare drew himself up to his full height. "Say what you will, my sweet Hamlet, but one thing I never do is *jabber*.'' Jaw jutting, he made for Rufus and Isaiah. As he squatted to assist Rufus in standing, he thrust a thumb at Nate and whispered, "Here's Agamemnon. An honest fellow enough, and one that loves quails. But he has not so much brain as earwax.''

Isaiah burst into peals of mirth. He couldn't help himself. Not after the nightmare he had been through, after believing he was doomed, believing his time among the living could be measured in days rather than years. That awful certainty had gnawed at his soul for hours on end. Then—to be abruptly saved by so comical a character triggered a flood of laughter he couldn't stop if he wanted. All the emotions he had pent up, all the frustration and heartbreak and fear, gushed from him in rowdy, joyous laughs.

Shakespeare joined in, thinking his jest was responsible. Soon it was obvious something else was. Stopping, he scrutinized the New Yorker to determine if maybe, just maybe, the man suffered from too much sun.

Nate King was glad when they were finally under way. After sharing water from a water skin and a handful of pemmican apiece, they climbed into the saddle. Nate rode double with McNair, the big stallion showing no strain at having to bear their combined weight.

Isaiah had been under the impression the mountain man's cabin was close by. Yet the prairie extended to the west for as far as the eye could see. "Didn't you say you live in the high country?"

"In the prettiest little valley in all Creation," Nate confirmed.

"Will it take long to reach it?"

"It's just a short piece. You'll see. We'll be there before you know it," Nate assured him.

Mile after mile fell behind them. Presently a bloodred sun perched on the brink of the world, banding the heavens with bright pink, orange, and yellow hues. "Lord, I never tire of the sunsets out here," Isaiah mentioned.

Neither had Nate. Not even after living in the wild a good fifteen winters. Sunsets, sunrises, each and every day was precious. No two were ever alike. Unlike the days during his fledgling career as an accountant, when drudgery had been the norm and boredom had been routine.

Slavery, pure and simple. That was what city life amounted to. Getting up every morning at the crack of dawn to eat a bland breakfast and then trek off to work, filing along the same narrow streets, passing the same tightly packed buildings, to sit at a small desk in a crowded room and spend ten to twelve hectic hours scrawling tiny figures in thinly spaced ledgers.

And for what? A pittance. For barely enough money to scrape by. Adding insult to injury, he'd had to abide the abuse of a cranky employer, a boss who delighted in nitpicking. A skinflint who was not above carping about every flaw his workers had but could never condescend to compliment those who did their jobs well.

How many untold thousands had to put up with the same daily drudgery? How many millions? Nate had heard tell that some of the bigger cities, bustling places like New York and Philadelphia and Boston, were now so crammed that people couldn't walk down a street without bumping elbows. Even worse, sections were unfit for decent folks to be in at any time of the day or night. Fallen women, footpads, charlatans, and murderers were as common as fleas on a coonhound.

Nate never regretted leaving the city for the wilderness. He had traded slavery for freedom. From being totally dependent on others, he had come full circle and was now dependent on no one except himself. And his wife, naturally. She was as much a part of him as the air he breathed, as the blood coursing through his veins.

Winona. Nate never stopped marveling at the depth of their love. Or at how their love had grown over the years, mushrooming from the first heady rush of raw lust lovers always experienced into the mature love adults shared.

It was downright strange how men and women were so different yet so alike. Strange how they spatted like cats and dogs, yet couldn't live without one another. Strange how each complemented the other. How even their bodies had been designed by a Higher Hand to match perfectly, to fit snugly, as it were.

At a rendezvous Nate had listened to a blowhard say that females were the bane of existence, that no man worthy of the name would shackle himself to one. The simpleton had deserved a rap on the noggin with a rock, but Nate had refrained.

Some men were too vain or selfish or stupid to see the point.

Being in love wasn't the same as being in bondage. True love was not forged from chains but from the furnace of passion and desire mixed with a deep sense of need. Need that surpassed all human understanding.

His need for Winona was a prime example. He could no more live without her than he could without his own heart. Years ago, shortly after they were joined as husband and wife, she had confided her belief that the Great Mystery had brought them together. That their meeting was foreordained. That they had been destined to be together from the day they were born. Possibly before.

He had laughed, dismissing it as a flight of female fancy. But as time went by, as their affection grew into an unbreakable bond, as he saw how perfect a match they were, he had come to think that maybe, just maybe, she was right.

Their bond had seen them through many a hardship. It was his hope, his prayer, that it would see them through many more. Including the major inconvenience he was about to inflict on her.

As if to remind the trapper of the gamble he was taking, Isaiah Tompkins picked that moment to declare, "That feather you wear almost got your head shot off, King. I mistook you for an Indian."

Rufus was leaning against his partner, his jaw muscles clenched. "Why do you wear that silly thing, anyhow?" he wanted to know.

Nate held in check a fleeting surge of resentment. "It was a gift long ago from a Cheyenne warrior. A token of friendship. I value it highly."

Isaiah's interest was piqued. Rumor had it that some of the wilder mountaineers, those more animal in nature, mingled with various heathens from time to time. "Have you ever lived with the Cheyennes?"

"No. With the Shoshones, my adopted people. And with the Flatheads, who took Shakespeare into their tribe. A few times I've stayed overnight with the Crows. And once or twice with the Utes.''

Isaiah was flabbergasted. "Am I to understand that a tribe of heathens actually *adopted* you? Made you one of their own?''

Nate looked squarely into the New Yorker's eyes. "Do yourself a favor. Don't call Indians heathens and I won't call you a bigoted son of a bitch. Fair enough?''

"Now, see here. Everyone knows Indians don't believe in the Bible. What else does that make them, if not heathens?''

Shakespeare came to Nate's defense. "There are more things in heaven and earth, Horatio, than are dreamt of in your philosophy.''

"Meaning what, old man?''

"Meaning it's not wise to judge another's bushel by your own peck." Shakespeare clucked in disapproval. "Didn't it ever occur to you that the God you worship is the same Great Mystery or Great Spirit or whatever you want to call it revered by most Indians?''

"Even if that's true, they're still not Christians. They know nothing of our Master, who is our salvation and our glory. He is the way, the truth, and the light, and without Him none of us will taste eternal life.''

"Bible-thumper, huh?" Shakespeare pursed his lips. "Even so, you can't blame the Indians for not being something they know nothing about. Until the first pilgrim set foot at Plymouth Rock, they had never even heard of the carpenter from Nazareth.''

Isaiah was about to say that was no excuse but changed his mind. The old-timer had a valid point.

Shakespeare pressed his advantage. "Instead of branding all Indians as worthless trash or hopeless sinners, maybe you should keep in mind what Jesus himself said. 'The harvest truly is plentiful, but the laborers are few. Therefore pray the Lord of the harvest to send out laborers into His harvest.' ''

Isaiah was impressed. "You certainly know your Scripture."

"I've read the Bible from Genesis to Revelation, from 'In the beginning' to the final 'Amen.' "

"Yet you seem more partial to the works of Shakespeare."

"Old William S. makes me laugh. And Jesus himself said to always be of good cheer."

"Something tells me you're mixing apples and oranges, but I won't quibble. Nor will I think so harshly of Indians from now on. You've helped me to see them in a whole new light."

"Good. There's hope for you yet."

Nate was not so easily appeased. Too many whites and red men alike hated the other race for no other reason than the color of their skin. Often they pretended to be the best of friends but nursed their hatred in secret. He made a mental note to keep an eye on the pair the whole time they stayed at his homestead.

Rufus had another question to pose. "Did you say your wife's name was Winona? Never heard it before. Is she by any chance a squaw?"

The young man had no idea how close he came to being bashed in the face. If not for his weakened state, he would have paid, and paid dearly, for his brash insult. Nate faced due west and answered more gruffly than he intended, "Yes. She's Shoshone. What of it?"

"Nothing, nothing," Rufus said quickly. A bit too quickly. The big trapper's tone hinted he had somehow given offense, but he did not see how. Was it his use of the word *squaw*? he wondered. How could that be, when everyone did it?

Isaiah contentedly took another bite of the food Nate had given them and munched loudly, savoring the taste. "What is this stuff? It's delicious."

"Pemmican. My wife made it."

"What from?"

"Dry buffalo meat, ground up and mixed with berries and

32

fat. It's a favorite of the Shoshones and others. Lasts a long time. And it's nutritious.''

"Why have we never heard of this back in the States? A man could make a small fortune selling it.''

Shakespeare McNair replied, "Haven't you noticed, youngster? Most of what is written about Indians has to do with their so-called bad qualities. How savage they are. How they delight in raping and maiming. How they torture their enemies. Nothing is ever said of their good traits.''

"They have some?''

Shakespeare had to remind himself youth and stupidity went hand in hand. "The evil that men do lives after them. The good is oft interred with their bones.'' He gave his beard a tug in mild exasperation. "Let's take the Flatheads, since I know them best. They're always even-tempered, always friendly. Men and women alike are devoted parents. They frown on drunkenness. Murder is unknown. If you were to show up at one of their villages in the same state we found you in, the Flatheads would feed you and give you a lodge all to yourself. No strings attached.''

"Don't get me wrong,'' Isaiah said. "I'm not saying all Indians are evil. I know my history. I know how the first Pilgrims were treated.''

The drone of voices was having an effect on Rufus. Lulled by a sense of security, with the trappers there to protect them, he was unable to keep his eyes open. Several times he dozed, losing track of the talk.

Nate King rested his Hawken across his thighs and took note of the western horizon. Before long the Rockies would hove into view, and the emerald-green foothills bordering them. Focused as he was to the west, he did not catch sight of the riders to the north until the stallion swung its head and pricked its ears. Instantly he slowed.

Shakespeare and Isaiah were still debating the good and bad traits of the red race. "So we're agreed?'' the young man was saying. "There are some Indians it's best to avoid if you want to stay healthy."

"That there are," McNair conceded. "The Blackfeet and their allies, for starters. They'd as soon slit a white man's throat as look at him."

"Speak of the devil," Nate said, pointing. "Here come some now."

Chapter Three

Isaiah Tompkins was sure Nate King had to be joking. Hostile Indians would not ride right up to them in broad daylight. It was preposterous. Then Shakespeare McNair slid off Pegasus and stepped a few yards to the left, holding his Hawken with the barrel almost level. And Nate King loosened both pistols. then slanted his own Hawken so all he had to do was raise it an inch or so to shoot. Isaiah took his cue from them and tucked the stock of his long gun to his side, ready for use.

Rufus snored lightly. Isaiah twisted to wake him, but Shakespeare said, "Leave him be. The shape he's in, he wouldn't be of much help anyway."

"But an extra gun would come in handy," Isaiah said. He counted seven Indians, strung out in a row, riding with their mounts shoulder to shoulder. Since these were the first Indians he had encountered, with the exception of a few tame ones in St. Louis, he noted every little detail about them.

Their clothing was scanty. Breechcloths or loincloths for the most part, made from soft deer hide, Isaiah guessed. A few had on buckskins. Their bodies were dark from long exposure to the sun. Isaiah was relieved to see that only one warrior possessed a rifle. The rest held bows. Not one had an arrow notched to a string, which was odd.

"Piegans," Nate King said. Along with the Bloods, they were part of the widely feared Blackfoot Confederacy, a loose association of three powerful tribes who controlled the northern plains and the lower part of Canada. "Usually we don't see them this far south."

"Are they really very dangerous?" Isaiah asked. "I mean, they don't look as if they want to cause trouble."

Shakespeare McNair snorted. "Don't let them fool you, youngster. They'll nock an arrow and let it fly before you can blink. Watch their hands, not their eyes. Their eyes won't give anything away. They lie through their teeth and never show it."

"Why are they riding up to us like this? Why don't they just attack?"

"They haven't quite made up their minds whether they want to jump us yet," Shakespeare speculated. "All we have are two horses. Not worth the bother if it costs them a life. So they're coming for a closer look. Everything will depend on whether they think they can lick us without losing one of their own."

The Piegans slowed when they were forty yards out and walked their mounts the rest of the way. Isaiah was surprised to find that overall, they had handsome, finely chiseled features. They weren't the ugly brutes he had been led to believe most savages were. Their black hair was long. A couple wore it loose over the shoulders. Others had braids. In the center rode a lean warrior from whose head rose porcupinelike quills. This man also had rings in his ears and a fine beaded necklace. Over his right shoulder was a short red blanket. Dark, crafty eyes gleamed with vitality. Something told Isaiah this was the one to watch, the one who would decide whether to fight or part in peace.

Nate King had reached the same conclusion. Focusing on the dandy, he waited until they were fifteen feet out, then declared, "That's close enough, Little Robe. What do you want?"

The Piegan's mouth creased in a sly smile. "Grizzly Killer. I hear maybe you dead. I very happy." His English was atrocious and badly accented, but understandable.

"Only believe half of what you see and a third of what you hear," Nate quipped.

Isaiah couldn't believe his own ears. "You know this barbarian personally?"

Little Robe's dark eyes narrowed with thinly veiled disgust. "Who this white dog be, Grizzly Killer?"

"Dog!" Isaiah bristled. "How dare you! I don't take kindly to insults, especially from crude clods like you." He shifted, his arms rising, then turned to marble when several of the warriors flashed hands to their quivers.

Shakespeare McNair advanced a few feet. "Hold your tongue, youngster," he cautioned. "Trading insults is a time-honored tradition out here. Little Robe hates us so much, he couldn't resist trading a few." He plastered a huge smile on his craggy face. "Isn't that right, you fish-eating bastard?"

Little Robe laughed, a brittle tinkle as icy as an arctic gale. "Funny, Carcajou. Like always, eh?" He made a show of inspecting McNair. "How you still live, old one? My father's father knew you when you no bigger my dog."

Shakespeare laughed. "Good one. I see you've been working on your sense of humor. First I ever knew you had any."

Isaiah was utterly confounded. It was as plain as the nose on his face that the mountain men and the Piegans were bitter enemies, yet they sat there trading barbs as nonchalant as you please.

It was Little Robe's turn to laugh. "Tell you, Carcajou. Day

David Thompson

I hang your hair my lodge, day I dance and sing.''

''Glad I'll be dead,'' Shakespeare bantered. ''You can't hold a note worth spit.''

Nate King kept his eyes on the others. They were tense, but not quite as tense as they should be. And each and every one of them was grinning, as if at some private joke. It couldn't be the exchange between McNair and Little Robe, because none of the other Piegans spoke a lick of English. Puzzled, Nate mulled the possible explanations and came to the only logical conclusion.

''Oh, you be dead, Carcajou,'' Little Robe said. ''Be dead soon.''

McNair hefted his Hawken. ''Cuts both ways, hoss.''

An itchy sensation erupted between Nate's shoulder blades. ''Say, Shakespeare,'' he said casually. ''What was the name of that play old William S. wrote about the Greeks?''

''Huh?'' Genuinely taken aback, Shakespeare looked up at the man he considered more as a son than a friend. ''Well, now. That's a real pertinent question, given the situation. Since when have you shown any interest in his masterpieces?''

''The Greek one,'' Nate emphasized. ''Remember it?''

''William S. had Greeks in several. How should I know which one you're talking about?''

''Oh, you'll recall this one. About Troy, remember?''

''*Troilus and Cressida*. What about it?''

The itching grew worse. Nate resisted an impulse to turn and maintained a calm manner. ''Remember the part where that Trojan warrior was in his tent? And what that Greek did?''

''Hector, you mean?'' Shakespeare said, and suddenly insight seared him like a red-hot knife. Yes, he recollected it well. How the Greek Achilles had refused to meet Hector in mortal combat, then later snuck into Hector's tent when the Trojan was unarmed and had his men fall on Hector and hack him to death. ''Though this be madness, yet there be method to it.''

38

Little Robe was displeased. "What you talk about? Who these be?"

"Achilles was distant kin of yours," Shakespeare rejoined. "He had as much honor as you do. Which is to say, none whatsoever."

"Honor?" the Piegan repeated.

"Mine honor keeps the weather of my fate. Life every man holds dear, but the dear man hold honor far more precious-dear than life."

"Fah!" Little Robe spat. "You talk crazy talk. Like always."

Shakespeare edged toward the black stallion without being obvious. "No more crazy talk, enemy mine. From this moment on, the strand between us is severed. What happens next is on your shoulders, not mine. I'd have been content to let bygones be bygones."

"What is bygones?"

"Parting is such sweet sorrow," Shakespeare quoted, and cackled as if he truly were insane. As he cackled, he thrust his rifle up and out. Thumbing the hammer back, he sent a lead ball smack into the middle of Little Robe's forehead.

Simultaneously, Nate King whirled in the saddle. Four more Piegans were within bow range, creeping along doubled close to the ground, making no more noise than would four ethereal specters. The foremost was a husky warrior who had a barbed shaft nocked to a sinew string. Nate's shot cored the man's sternum.

It all happened so fast that Isaiah Tompkins was wreathed in swirling tendrils of acrid smoke before he quite understood what was happening. He saw Nate snatch out a pistol and fire again, even as Shakespeare unlimbered a flintlock and brought down a Piegan sighting down an arrow.

"Ride!" Nate bawled, and leaned down to smack Pegasus on the flank. The white horse bolted, nearly throwing Isaiah, who had to clutch the saddle in order to stay on.

Behind him, Rufus Stern was jolted awake by the blasts. Snapping upright, he blinked in confusion. "What's happening? What's going on?" The violent jerk Pegasus gave breaking into motion threw him backward, and in befuddled desperation he clawed at his friend, almost unhorsing Isaiah along with himself.

Shakespeare was in motion, too, moving remarkably spryly for someone his age. A bound took him to the stallion. Nate's free arm descended and hauled him up while at the same moment Nate applied his heels, goading the big black into pell-mell flight.

Arrows cleaved the air from both directions, buzzing like enraged bees. A shaft meant for the mountain men passed through the space Nate had just occupied, into the chest of the Piegan who had been on Little Robe's left. Confusion reigned. Milling, the warriors hollered at one another.

It bought Nate and Shakespeare the precious seconds they needed to gain a narrow lead. Swiftly, they overtook the New Yorkers, whose legs were flapping like those of disjointed rag dolls.

"Keep going due west!" Nate cried. "No matter what, don't stop!"

Isaiah had no intention of stopping. Not when five Indians were in full pursuit, yipping and howling like a pack of rabid dogs. The others were gathering around the bodies of the slain. From the southeast hastened two more on horseback, leading four other animals.

Isaiah put two and two together and realized the second group had been sneaking up on them the whole time, that Little Robe had intended to keep them talking until it was too late. How on earth Nate King had guessed, he was at a loss to say.

The stallion and the white horse were holding their own. But appearances were deceiving. Horses bearing double weight could never outdistance horses bearing one person.

Eventually both would tire and the Piegans would catch up.

Nate scoured the prairie, seeking a break in the flat terrain. There was none. No gullies, no washes, not a single coulee. To the southwest, though, rose what appeared to be a small bump. Distance and the heat haze were responsible for the illusion.

"Head there!" Nate said, and cut to the left.

Isaiah was a shade slow in reacting. A glittering shaft, whizzing out of the blue within an inch of his head, provided incentive to be more alert. Bending low, he galloped madly toward that far-off bump. What good it would do was beyond him. But if he had learned anything during his short association with the two mountaineers, it was to trust their judgment. Implicitly.

It soothed Isaiah somewhat that neither trapper betrayed so much as a hint of panic or fright. McNair even smiled as if he were enjoying himself immensely. But then, Isaiah had begun to suspect the oldster was a few marbles shy of a full bag. Why else would the old man go around quoting William Shakespeare every chance he got?

Unknown to the New Yorker, McNair *was* enjoying himself. The skirmish reminded him of his younger days, when seldom a week had gone by without a hair-raising escapade. In those days only a few whites roamed the mountains, mostly intrepid Frenchmen known as *voyageurs*. Some of the bravest men Shakespeare ever met. To call them fearless did not begin to do them justice. The *voyageurs* had gone where no white men before them had ever gone, exploring uncharted, untamed country that stretched from Canada to Mexico.

Then came the trappers. Beaver fur had become all the rage among the rich back east, and the rich always set fashion trends for everyone else. The price for beaver peltries shot up like a geyser, luring hundreds of dreamy-eyed men to the Rockies in pursuit of the dream at the end of their personal rainbows. Only a handful ever emerged with the riches they sought.

Their coming forever changed the wilderness. Scattered trading posts and forts were erected. Indians learned to crave trade goods, luxuries they could never obtain otherwise. Rifles, pistols, steel knives and hatchets, Hudson's Bay blankets, tin pots and pans and so much more, became part and parcel of the Indian way of life.

As a result, the Indian way of life was forever transformed. Just as the horse, introduced by the Spanish, enabled Indians to rove far and wide and become lords of their domain, so the trade goods of the whites elevated their standard of living. But where before most Indians had been content to have enough buffalo meat to feed their families and a fine warhorse to use on raids, now they had to have all those wonderful things the whites did.

Indians weren't as self-sufficient as they had been in Shakespeare's younger days. Each year their addiction to simple luxuries made them more and more dependent on white men. And that saddened him. For there was bound to come a day when Indians wanted *everything* the whites had, and that would be the end of their culture and their freedom.

A war whoop prompted Shakespeare to save his musing for later. The Piegans were gaining. One in particular, astride a superb sorrel, had pulled well ahead and was within easy bow range. The man clamped his legs to the sorrel so his hands were free, then pulled his bow string back.

Shakespeare's Hawken was empty. It was impossible to re-load bouncing on the back of the stallion. But the Piegan didn't know that. Snapping the rifle up, Shakespeare pretended to fix a bead.

The warrior had no hankering to die. Guiding the sorrel by his knees alone, he veered sharply to the right and dropped back a piece.

"Called your bluff!" Shakespeare yelled in impish glee.

The same trick might work once or twice, but soon the Piegans would guess the truth and spur their animals to greater speed.

Nate lashed the stallion to stay even with Pegasus. The small bump had grown in size, swelling to a height of ten to twelve feet and a width of twenty. An isolated knoll, the only cover to be had within miles. It would have to do. "How are you two holding up?" he shouted at the greenhorns.

"Just dandy!" Isaiah replied. Although he was scared to death and his heart was hammering as if on the verge of exploding, a perverse thrill animated him. A feeling of keen excitement, a feeling he enjoyed.

Rufus did not share his friend's outlook. His ribs were aflame and his left leg protested every loping stride the white horse took. In addition, his stomach was queasy, so queasy he was afraid he would be ill. He sagged against Isaiah, too weak to lift his rifle.

The war whoops rose in volume when the Piegans divined where the white men were headed. Two slanted to either side.

Shakespeare swiveled when a warrior to the north tried to cut them off. Again he raised his Hawken. Again the ruse worked. Another minute and they would be at the knoll. Then it would be root hog or die.

The Piegans were converging. They had lost the race, so their only hope to avoid a standoff was to overwhelm the whites in a concerted rush. Screeching like banshees, they bore down on their quarry.

Nate still had one pistol loaded and primed. He snatched it as he rounded the knoll and reined up in a spray of dust. Vaulting off, he ran toward the top, halting midway to train the flintlock on the Piegan on the sorrel. Immediately the warrior slanted wide and dropped from sight on the opposite side of his animal, displaying only a heel and an elbow.

Shakespeare had jumped down and was running to the right. A pair of warriors were closing in, arrows notched. Yanking out his second pistol, he fired as the shafts zinged clear of the bows. Then he flung himself sideways. He heard a thud at his feet and a searing twinge in his shoulder. With all three guns empty, he had no recourse but to grab his butcher knife and rise to meet the Piegans head-on. There was no time to reload.

Isaiah had clambered from Pegasus. He rotated on the balls of his feet, then dashed several yards up the incline and saw McNair's predicament. Hastily lining up his barrel on one of the warriors, he fired.

By a sheer fluke the ball struck the man's temple, lifted him clean off his horse, and pitched him into the second Piegan, who tried to rein clear. Both the dead warrior and his companion were unhorsed, pitching roughly to the soil some forty feet out.

Shakespeare dropped onto his knees, uncapped his powder horn, and set to reloading.

Rufus Stern was still on the white gelding. Overcome by dizziness, he plopped onto its back, his arms dangling, his rifle slowly slipping from fingers going limp. He craved nothing more than lots and lots of uninterrupted sleep. Twenty hours or more and he would feel like a new person.

Suddenly Pegasus shied. Rufus sluggishly raised his head and was amazed to see that a Piegan had picked him as a likely victim. The Indian was going to ride right into the gelding. Rufus sat up quickly, lost his grip on the rifle, and listened to it clatter. Feral triumph lit the bronzed features of the warrior.

The Piegan made no attempt to employ his bow. He had no need. Clutched in his right hand was a wicked weapon known as an "eyedagg," a short club boasting a tapered spike at the end. It could shear into an eye socket clear to the brainpan.

On the knoll, Nate King saw what was happening and banged off a hasty shot that missed. Casting the pistol and his rifle down, he rushed to intercept the Piegan. The warrior was almost on top of Stern when Nate palmed his knife and leaped.

The trapper's shoulder slammed into the Piegan's, and both

men fell. Nate tried to twist to wind up on top, but his leg caught on the man's warhorse. Both of them landed on their sides. Heaving erect, Nate parried a blow aimed at his head. The heavy club jarred his forearm to the bone.

Circling, the Piegan swung again and again. Nate dodged, ducked, pivoted, all the while retreating. The club gave the warrior a greater reach, and it was all Nate could do to ward the flurry off.

Around them guns boomed, someone cursed, warriors screeched. Yet Nate dared not take his eyes off his adversary, not for a second, or that eyedagg would find a fatal spot. Once more he blocked a powerful swing to the head, the tip of the spike digging a tiny furrow in his cheek.

In all the confusion Nate bumped into a horse. He could not say which. It brought him up short. The warrior exploited the moment by sidestepping, then driving the eyedagg at Nate's midsection. Nate lowered his empty hand, seizing the eyedagg's shaft. He tried to thrust his knife into the man's groin, but the Piegan grasped his wrist.

Locked together, they strained. The mountain man was larger, but the warrior was as strong as a bull. Neither could gain an advantage. The Piegan flung out a foot, then jerked around, seeking to trip his foe.

Nate imitated a jackrabbit evading a coyote's slashing jaws and jumped straight up into the air. The warrior's foot passed under him. Uncoiling both legs, Nate brought his soles crashing down on the Piegan's shin. The man let out a yelp, wrenched free, and staggered rearward.

Nate speared his knife out. It streaked beyond the eyedagg, the steel biting deep into the warrior's chest, but not deep enough to end their struggle. Springing out of reach, the Piegan grunted as scarlet drops sprayed from the jagged wound.

Among the trapping fraternity there was a common saying to the effect that a wounded bear was ten times more dangerous than usual. The same could be applied to humans. For now, venting a roar worthy of a grizzly, the warrior flailed the eyedagg without cease, seeking to batter the mountain man down by brute force.

Nate had to give ground or lose his life. His shirt was ripped, his leg suffered a hard bash, but so far he had saved himself from serious harm. A backhand swipe almost took him off guard. If he hadn't been holding the knife at chin level, his neck would have been ruptured from jaw to jugular.

The spike rang on cold steel. Nate was rocked onto his heels. Growling, the warrior pumped forward, the eyedagg sweeping lower. It was meant to tear into Nate's crotch but stroked between his legs instead. For a second the Piegan was off balance, overextended, unable to protect himself.

Their gazes met. Met and locked. The warrior's eyes mirrored the knowledge that he was going to die. He did not scream or howl. He did not go berserk in a futile paroxysm of defiance. Acceptance of the inevitable registered a fraction of an instant before the long knife sliced into his neck, cutting upward like a saber through butter.

Nate stood stock still except for his labored breathing. The Piegan was dead on his feet. The inner light faded, leaving a blank expression. Tugging the knife out, Nate stepped aside to avoid a scarlet torrent.

An unnerving silence claimed the prairie. Nate whirled, fearing the worst. Nearby sat Rufus Stern, dazed but otherwise unhurt. Over on the knoll was Isaiah Tompkins, hands on his knees, looking shocked to still be alive. Of McNair there was no sign.

"Shakespeare?" Nate bellowed, raw dread churning his innards. "Shakespeare?" He dashed to the slope and up it for a clear view, halting dead when the white-maned visage of his mentor appeared above the crest.

"What's all the hollering? A body would reckon you cared. I'm plumb flattered." McNair chortled. "More health and

46

happiness betide my liege than can my care-tuned tongue deliver him.''

''The Piegans . . . ?''

Shakespeare gestured at two dead warriors at the north edge of the knoll and another on the south slope. To the east a lone horseman fled for his life. ''That one valued his guts more than grit. The others gave as good as they got.''

Nate hunkered to wipe his knife clean on the grass. ''The rest might show up before too long. We'd best head for the foothills while we still can.''

''Sage advice, I suppose, but I doubt the Piegans will plague us a second time. They've lost too many as it is. When they get back to their village there will be wailing and gnashing of teeth for days on end. Everyone will indirectly blame them.''

''And directly blame us. I wouldn't put it past them to have a war party pay us a visit in a few moons.''

''Maybe. Maybe not. I wouldn't lose any sleep fretting. Piegans generally don't venture too close to Ute country. And they'd have to get past the Shoshones first.'' Shakespeare shrugged. ''What will be, will be, I always say.''

Isaiah Tompkins stared at his rifle in undisguised stupefaction. ''I killed another human being,'' he marveled. ''I took another's life.''

''Don't let it ulcerate your stomach,'' Shakespeare said. ''If you hadn't, he'd have merrily dispatched you to the Hereafter and not missed a wink of sleep tonight. It was them or us, son. That's the short and sour of it.''

''Thou shalt not kill,'' Isaiah reminded him.

''Oh, that. Then what do you make of Ecclesiastes?'' Shakespeare envisioned the page in his mind's eye. ''To every thing there is a season, and a time to every purpose under the heaven. A time to be born, and a time to die. A time to plant, and a time to pluck up that which is planted. A time to kill, and a time to heal.'' He paused. ''Sort of contradicts the Commandment, don't you think?''

47

Isaiah had to ask, "How is it you can remember everything you've ever read?"

"It's a knack, is all. I was born with it."

"Remarkable."

Nate moved toward the other New Yorker, who had not budged. "Are you hurt?"

"No, I fell off the horse," Rufus confessed. The gelding had been spooked when King and the Piegan tangled, and he had been too weak to hold on. "I'm fine otherwise. Just so tired I could keel over."

"Don't fall asleep yet," Nate advised. Beyond Stern, to the northwest, roiling black clouds were billowing out over the prairie. "We're not quite out of the fire yet."

"What do you mean?"

The mountain man motioned. Rufus swiveled and saw vivid bolts of lightning lance the heavens.

"Ever seen a man charred to a crisp?" Nate King asked.

Chapter Four

Nature had gone mad. Half an hour later the raging tempest roared in upon them, and to Rufus Stern it seemed as if the Almighty had gone stark, raving berserk. He had seen storms before, but nothing to rival the terrifying fury of this one.

It began deceptively enough. First the wind picked up in gusts that grew in frequency and strength. In due course it shrieked and screamed like a raving harpy, buffeting them like an invisible battering ram.

Overhead, the sky darkened. Those great roiling clouds swallowed the sky, devouring it with remarkable rapidity. Never had Rufus beheld clouds like these. Gigantic beyond all measure, they billowed and heaved as if alive, as if they were living creatures endowed with all the ferocity Nature could conceive.

It was childish, Rufus knew, but he became scared. It brought back vague memories of his childhood, and how for a time he had been deathly afraid of thunderstorms. Many children were. And just like them, he had outgrown his fear. Or so he thought.

Now the fright returned, more potent than ever. Especially when Rufus saw flashes of elemental energy and heard the rumbling boom of distant thunder. Rumbling that came closer and closer as the flashes grew brighter and brighter. So many flashes, it gave the illusion someone had stockpiled kegs of block powder and was setting them off one after the other in a continuous chain.

The rain proved deceptive, too. Initially a few drops fell. Cold, hard drops that stung the skin. But the drops became larger as they descended in greater number. A steady rain fell for a while, a simple downpour. And just when Rufus believed that was as bad as it would get, the heavens opened, unleashing a titanic tempest the likes of which no human being would believe possible unless they experienced it themselves.

Rufus flinched and tucked his chin to his chest. It felt as if a thousand hard nails were poking his head and face, stinging unmercifully. He heard Isaiah curse. A glance at the mountain men showed them unaffected, sitting the big black stallion in impassive silence. They might as well be sculpted from granite for all the effect the storm had on them.

Suddenly, startling Rufus silly, horrendous bolts of crackling lightning and deafening crashes of thunder swept the prairie. The rain was a steady, solid wall of water, smashing against them in a wave. As weak as he was, Rufus feared being knocked off the gelding. So he clung to Isaiah and prayed to a God gone mad for deliverance.

But that was not the worst of it. Oh, no. Not at all.

The wind intensified. Howling as would a million wolves in raving chorus, it slammed into them as if seeking to bowl over their mounts. Rufus swore he could feel the white horse tense as it lowered its head and plunged on into the cataclysm.

By now the streaks of lightning rent the firmament without cease, one after the other after the other, some far off, but many very close, too close, so close Rufus saw them strike the ground, saw blasts of showery light and was rocked by thunder that threatened to shatter his eardrums. It dawned on him that a random bolt might well strike *them*. He remembered being told lightning usually hit the tallest objects in its vicinity. And on the flat plain, practically barren of trees or even high brush, *they* were the tallest objects to be found.

That was what Nate King had meant about being charred to a crisp. A lump formed in Rufus's throat, and he wished to hell he had never left New York City, wished to hell he had never let friendship impair his common sense. Sweet, wonderful Agnes had been right. He should have listened to her.

The next instant the sky was rent yet again. A bolt smashed into the earth not twenty feet away. Whinnying, the gelding veered. Rufus flinched, cowering as he had once cowered under his bed, his ears blistered, his nose tingling to an acrid odor. His hair tingled, too, some of it standing on end, and his skin was pricked all over as if by tiny pins. Isaiah cursed even more loudly. The mountain men, though, rode grimly on, unbent, uncowed, Nate King tall and straight in the saddle, Shakespeare McNair grinning up at the onslaught as if he were enjoying himself, a child at a fireworks display. The man truly was touched in the head.

How long they forged on, Rufus couldn't say. He only knew he was soaked and freezing and petrified and in abject misery. He only knew he wanted the storm to end. And he never wanted to experience another like it for as long as he lived.

Shakespeare McNair yelled something. Rufus looked, and saw the lunatic pointing to the northwest. Rufus gazed in that direction but saw nothing out of the ordinary. At first. How could he, with the sheet of rain and the pitch-black clouds? Then the rain slackened a little and the lightning revealed a sight that took his breath away.

The sky was alive. Part of it swirled around and around in the form of a giant funnel, the lower end whipping back and forth like an airborne snake. A new sort of piercing howl climbed to a fever pitch. To Rufus's astonishment, the funnel ripped into a small isolated stand of trees, tearing them asunder like so much kindling. Trunks and limbs and leaves were sucked upward and flung every which way. "Sweet Jesus!" he said under his breath.

Shakespeare McNair shouted again. Rufus caught the word "twister." Then Nate King leaned out, grabbed the gelding's reins from Isaiah, and cut to the southwest, riding as if their very lives depended on it. And they did. For Rufus now saw that the twister, as McNair called the funnel, was bearing down on them like a steam engine gone amok, ripping out whole sections of sod. The funnel was expanding rapidly. Already it was forty to fifty yards wide and growing by ten yards every ten seconds.

"We're going to die!" Rufus yelled.

Isaiah Tompkins agreed. He had heard of tornadoes, but he had never thought he would see one. The thing mesmerized him. He clung to the saddle for dear life and watched it approach. It was so high, he had to tilt his head back to see the top. So powerful, it sheared into the earth itself. It was a Titan of old, one of the dawn creatures of antiquity, a living behemoth that would consume them whole. Isaiah didn't see why Nate King bothered to try to get away. There was no escape.

Nate King would have disagreed. As he was fond of saying, "Where there's life, there's hope." And so long as life remained, he would never go meekly to the other side. He would never give up. Especially not when he had a wife and children who loved him and depended on him. He would fight with all his might for the right to go on living for as long as the Good Lord allowed.

He didn't look at the tornado. He didn't have to. The earsplitting roar it made told him exactly how close it was. And how close he was to meeting his Maker whether he wanted to or not.

Nate rode for all he was worth, goading the stallion to its limit and beyond. The gelding's reins were tight in his left hand, the white horse doing its best to hold to the same frantic pace. Both animals sensed impending doom. Both preferred to live. Although drenched and cold and tired, they put all they had into a herculean effort to fend off the seeming inevitable.

Shakespeare McNair stared at the twister, stared into its churning depths, and grinned. Fearsome as it was—and few things in life were more so—there was no denying the tornado was also magnificent. A thing of beauty. Perverse beauty, Nature at her worst, but beautiful nonetheless. He stared, and he marveled.

The leading edge was now sixty yards distant. Shakespeare could see grass being sucked out by the roots. Soon the funnel would do the same to them and they would be drawn up into its whirling heart. He wondered what that would be like, wondered whether they would live long enough to see what was inside.

Shakespeare remembered the time a twister had nearly killed Nate, the only man ever taken up by one and set down again later unharmed. Whenever he raised the subject, Nate clammed up. Would not talk about it, period. Which for Nate was downright strange. He was the most fearless person Shakespeare had ever known. So why wouldn't Nate say what it was like inside? Maybe, Shakespeare mused, Nate couldn't. Maybe there was no way to describe what it had been like in the belly of the beast.

More lightning illuminated the behemoth in all its brain-numbing glory. Shakespeare detected the churning silhouette of its southern side, nearly lost amid the background darkness. It would be a close shave. Very close.

Nate sensed the same. His every instinct shrieked to go faster, faster, but the stallion was already going as fast as it could go, faster than it had ever gone, faster then he had ever thought it could go. Pegasus was winded but keeping up. As for the two greenhorns, their faces were pale specters, their eyes as wide as saucers, the blood in their veins apparently frozen stiff. Rufus Stern's mouth worked as if he were going to scream, but to his credit the young New Yorker did not.

The tornado towered above them, a legendary maelstrom made real. The wind tugged at Nate, threatening to snatch him bodily and whirl him up and away as it had done once before, years ago. Many a night he had awakened in a cold sweat from harrowing dreams in which he relived the ordeal.

A miracle had spared him. What else could it have been? How else could anyone explain a man being snatched up into a whirlwind's inner core and living to tell the tale? And how could he ever describe that awful feeling of being suspended hundreds of feet in the air? That sickening sensation of swirling around and around and around until he was dizzy enough to wretch? Or the total, nerve-numbing, soul-wrenching horror of being completely and utterly helpless?

Nate hunched his shoulders against the twister's pull and slapped his legs against the black. The stallion's mane flew, its nostrils were flared.

Rufus Stern voiced a prayer. He was going to die, and he wanted to set himself right with God. He asked forgiveness for all the bad things he had done and apologized for not making more of his wretched life. From out of nowhere invisible fingers wrapped around his back and tried to pluck him loose, but he clasped Isaiah all the harder. "No! No! No!"

Shakespeare McNair laughed. Of all the ways he had envisioned meeting his end, this had not been one of them. What were the odds? He had no real regrets, other than not seeing Blue Water Woman again. Why should he, when he had lived a long, full life? Against the odds, he had lived to a ripe old age, outlasting by many years most of those who ventured to the Rockies decades ago when he did.

It had been a fine life, all told. Shakespeare had traveled more widely than any man alive. Young upstarts like Joseph

Walker and Jedediah Smith might one day surpass him, but he doubted it.

He had explored whole regions yet to be mapped. He had lived among tribes most whites had never heard of. He'd seen sights no one east of the Mississippi would believe. Huge geysers that spouted hissing steam. Pools of foul sulfur. Enormous clefts in the earth. A canyon so grand it was indescribable. And more creatures than he could shake a stick at. Bears that dwarfed Pegasus. Elk with racks that took two men to carry. Black mountain lions. Majestic eagles, devilish wolverines, white otters, and fish bigger than a buffalo. And then there were the hideous things, the creatures in the high lakes and those hairy two-legged giants who dwelled deep in ancient forests.

Yes, Shakespeare had lived a full life. He'd loved wonderful women, sired children. He had gorged on roasted buffalo, tasted fish eggs, eaten raw rattlesnake. He had laughed until he cried and cried until he laughed. He had done everything there was to do, and then some.

He had no complaints. But if he had his druthers, he would rather live on to savor more of life's rich harvest. For if there was one thing he had learned in his many years of existence, it was to live each day as if there would be no tomorrow. And above all, to be happy. Without happiness, nothing else counted for much. Without happiness, life was barely bearable.

A tug on his buckskin shirt snapped Shakespeare out of his reverie. The tornado was right on top of them. Another few moments and it would all be over. Then he saw the bottom of the funnel bounce upward, high overhead, and skip off to the north. Like the tapered end of a whip being flicked, it skipped hundreds of feet, alighted, and promptly bore to the northeast.

Shakespeare turned his face up into the pelting rain. "Not our time, huh?" he hollered. "Ay me, what act, that roars so loud and thunders in the index?"

The only answer was the yowling wind.

"There is a cliff whose high and bending head looks fearfully in the confined deep. Bring me but to the very brim of it, and I'll repair the misery thou dost bear with something rich about me. From that place I shall no leading need." Shakespeare chuckled gaily.

Nate heard his mentor speak, but the wind blasted the words into garble. He galloped madly on until McNair slapped him on the shoulder and leaned forward to be heard above the rain and the gusts.

"To be, Hamlet. That's the rub. To be." Shakespeare paused. "We're safe. It's gone, son, gone."

Nate had to see for himself. Even then he did not slow, not when lightning continued to pulverize the air and ground in a ceaseless bombardment. Unexpectedly, a broad gully yawned before them, a dark slash in the ground. He went down the slope without slowing. Reining up, he sprang off and held on to the bridle. "Hold Pegasus!" he shouted to Isaiah and Rufus.

Rufus was too dazed to do any such thing. He was numb from head to toe. Numb inwardly as well as outwardly. The merciless chilling rain had rendered his skin insensitive. The close call with the whirlwind had blunted his mind. Coherent thought eluded him.

Isaiah was wet to the bone. He was cold and hungry and stiff. But he was still in control of his faculties. So when the trapper yelled, he obeyed, sliding off and seizing the white mount's bridle and reins.

Rufus did not move. Mouth agape, he gawked heavenward. Rain deluged his tongue, seeping into his throat and making him sputter.

"Get down!" Shakespeare commanded. When the New Yorker did not do so quickly enough to suit him, he reached up and hauled Rufus off. Stern collapsed onto his hands and knees, quaking like a terror-stricken rabbit.

"Some folks never outgrow their diapers," Shakespeare commented, but it was lost in the gale.

A hint of gray to the west signified to Nate that they were about out of the woods. Presently the wind tapered, the rain slackened to a light shower. Lightning stopped rupturing the atmosphere, while the rumble of thunder drifted eastward.

Isaiah had been resting with his forehead pressed to Pegasus's neck. Rousing, he observed the aerial display dwindle. "It's over?" he breathed. "Really and truly over? We lived through it?"

"Unless we're dead and this is heaven," Shakespeare quipped. "I don't see any flames, so it can't be the other place."

"We survived!" Isaiah hiked his arms aloft. He started to titter, then tried to stop. But he could no more hold it back than he could stop the deluge. Hopping in exultation, he flapped his arms like an ungainly bird. "Oh, Lord! We survived!"

Shakespeare faced Nate. "Think how excited he would be if we had really been in danger."

Isaiah didn't care if the oldster poked fun at his expense. He was too supremely happy. So happy he danced a jig, laughing and clapping a hand against his rifle. "We did it! We did it!"

Shakespeare claimed Pegasus and loosened the saddle. "Do we move on?" he asked Nate. By his reckoning it was early yet, no later than nine or ten.

"Why bother? We're not going to find any place drier than here. And we're out of the wind."

Isaiah overheard. "You can't mean that. There's nothing to burn. How will we make a fire?"

"We won't."

"Then how will we dry out? Surely you can't intend for us to spend the whole night in wet clothes."

"They'll be mostly dry by morning," Nate predicted.

"But we'll catch our death."

Shakespeare had untied his parfleches and hunkered. Rummaging in one of the beaded pouches for some pemmican, he snickered. "Mister, after what we just went through, a few sniffles won't hurt you none."

Isaiah indicated Rufus, who had curled into a fetal position. "What about my friend? We can't leave him lying there on the ground. He's liable to come down with pneumonia."

"If he's that feeble, let him," Shakespeare said. Finding what he sought, he hungrily took a bite.

"That's harsh. Even for a man like you."

"*Life* is harsh, son. It doesn't have favorites. It never goes easy on anyone. Either we take what it throws at us and grow stronger, or we buckle and give in and give up the ghost. It's that simple."

"I hope to God I am never as callous as you are, sir."

"Callous, or honest?" Shakespeare bit off more. "Ay, sir. To be honest, as this world goes, is to be one man picked out of ten thousand."

Nate removed his saddle and blanket. Unfolding the latter, he gently draped it over Rufus Stern, who was sound asleep. "It's not much, but it should keep him warm."

Isaiah squatted, his rifle across his knees. What he wouldn't give for a crackling fire and a bowl of piping hot soup! Goose bumps covered him, his hair was plastered slick, and he had water in his right ear. Bending to the right, he smacked his head to force it out. "I swear. If I make it back to New York, I am never leaving again."

Curiosity impelled Shakespeare to ask, "What brought you to the wilderness, anyway? Did you think you'd be the next John Jacob Astor?"

"Not quite," Isaiah hedged. Everyone had heard of Astor, the richest man in America, thanks to wealth earned in the fur trade. Unbuttoning his shirt, he probed and latched on to his copy of *The Trapper's Guide*. The cover was soaked, some of the pages warped. "This is to blame." He tossed it to McNair.

"I should have known."

"You've seen it before?"

"Youngster, I've seen enough of these to pile to the moon. You're not the only poor fool to dream of making a lot of money without much effort."

Isaiah smiled. "Ahh. Then it is as easy as I thought it would be?"

It was Nate who responded. "Thomas, trapping is the hardest work you'll ever do. Let me tell you what a typical day is like."

"I already know," Isaiah crowed, tapping the manual. "A trapper gets up kind of early, fixes breakfast, then goes out to check his traps. He skins the beaver, carries their pelts back to camp, and sets them in a rack to dry. After a noonday rest—"

Shakespeare could not help himself. Cackling lustily, he clamped a hand over his mouth to stifle the noise.

Isaiah glared. "Is something wrong? I'll have you know this information comes on the best of authority. Sewell Newhouse, who wrote the manual, is the inventor of the Newhouse steel-jaw trap. It's used by trappers everywhere." Opening the *Guide* to a favorite page, he held it so the mountain men could see an artist's rendition of a stately trapper attired in a white shirt and dinner pants in front of a white tent. Beside the trapper a trusty dog was nobly poised. A canoe and a small mountain of neatly stacked supplies were prominent.

"Go on," Nate coaxed.

"Well, the *Guide* says that afternoons should be devoted to correspondence, cleaning guns if necessary, and whatnot. In the evening a leisurely supper is in order. After a good night's sleep, it's back to work the next morning." Closing the *Guide*, Isaiah replaced it under his shirt. "Not a bad life, if I do say so myself."

"Not at all," Shakespeare agreed, choking off more hilarity. "Makes me want to run up into the mountains and collect a ton of furs."

Isaiah fidgeted. "You're being sarcastic. All right. What is a trapper's day really like, then?"

Nate bent at the knees, balancing on the balls of his feet. "You wake up before first light and head out. There's no time for breakfast. You have to check the traps and get the beaver before they stiffen up on you. When you find one, you skin it on the spot, then move on to the next. It can take half the day. And most of that time you're up to your waist or higher in icy water. You're half frozen before the sun even rises."

"What's a little cold? That doesn't sound too awfully difficult," Isaiah said.

"Have you ever *seen* a real beaver?"

Isaiah coughed. "No, not really. But I've seen drawings of them. In here." He started to flip through the pages of the *Guide*.

Nate patiently explained, "A beaver can be up to four feet long and weigh upwards of sixty pounds. When it's wet, it is as slippery as an eel. And you have to reach down into that icy water, haul it high enough to open the trap, then lug it onto the bank so you can take off the hide. Sometimes your fingers are so cold, you can't hold the knife. When you're finally done, you reset the trap or move it to another spot. That means you have to go back into the water. By noon you're so stiff and cold you can hardly walk. Most trappers come down with rheumatism sooner or later."

"That's just the beginning," Shakespeare said, warming to the topic. "The hides have to be scraped clean. I like to smear the insides with the brains to keep them soft. And you can't forget to stretch them on a hoop for a couple of days. All that takes a lot of work."

Isaiah was beginning to appreciate exactly how exaggerated the *Guide* really was. "But you must have some time to yourself? Time to relax, to warm yourself at the fire? To write letters home?"

Shakespeare and Nate regarded each other. "No," both men

said simultaneously, and McNair resumed. "The horses need tending, traps must be cleaned and oiled. If you want to eat, you have to hunt. After a while, beaver meat gets mighty tiresome."

"You eat the beavers?"

"What else would you do, boy? Let all that meat go to waste?" Shakespeare shook his head. "Don't make that face. It's as tasty as can be. The tails are the best part. Charred, then boiled, they'll make your mouth water."

Somehow, Isaiah doubted it. "So you're saying there's never a spare moment?"

McNair nodded. "That's not all. If the cold water doesn't do you in, a sinkhole or an avalanche or a flood might. And you have to keep your eyes skinned for silvertips and Indians every second. I won't even mention the stomach complaints, or the fever." Shakespeare recalled the many men who had gone into the high country, never to return. "If you make it through your first year, you earn the right to be called a *hiverman*. Make it through three winters and you've done what not three men in a hundred have done."

"You give the impression trapping is next to impossible," Isaiah protested. "Fit for idiots and simpletons."

"That pretty much sums it up, yes."

"Then why are *you* a trapper? If it's everything you say, yet you keep at it, what does that make you?"

"The biggest damn idiot of all." Laughing, Shakespeare slapped his thigh.

Nate King was listening to the faint growl of thunder. "There's something else you should know, friend. When was that *Guide* of yours published?"

Isaiah had never thought to check. "Two years ago," he said after consulting the copyright. "Why? What difference does that make?"

"All the difference in the world." Nate would have gone on, but at that moment the growls acquired a new note.

Springing erect, he swung toward the east rim of the gully where a massive bulk loomed. He trained his Hawken on it but didn't shoot. "We have company," he announced.

"What?" Isaiah idly inquired. He had not looked up.

"A grizzly."

Chapter Five

At that instant a distant streak of lightning cast the bear in brief stark relief. Isaiah Tompkins saw the grizzly in profile, and the short hairs at the nape of his neck stood on end. It was enormous, seemingly as big as the bull buffalo. A trick of the light imbued its eyes with a spectral eerie glow. Tapered teeth flashed white, teeth as long as Isaiah's fingers, teeth capable of shattering bone with the same ease Isaiah would have biting into a soft piece of bread.

"Kill it!" Isaiah hollered. Leaping upright, he elevated his rifle.

Shakespeare McNair had been expecting some such foolishness. He was ready. Springing, he grabbed the barrel of the New Yorker's gun and snarled in Tompkins's ear, "Do that and we're all worm food! I've seen griz take eight to ten balls or better and not bat an eye. Just stand still and pray it's not hungry."

Stand still? Isaiah wanted to run, not stand there. Then he glanced at Rufus, sleeping soundly in blissful ignorance. The beast would make short shrift of him. Isaiah gulped, quelled his fright, and prayed he was not making the biggest and last mistake of his life.

Nate King waited for the bear to make up its mind. That it had not attacked already was encouraging. But bears were so utterly unpredictable, it was impossible to predict what they would do next. This one might shuffle elsewhere or it might tear into them, huge paws churning.

Nate's main worry were the horses. Both stared hard at the grizzly, their ears pricked. Should either whinny or attempt to flee, it could set the bear off. Running from predators was a surefire invitation for trouble; it triggered a deeply ingrained instinct to chase and slay.

The silvertip moved a few feet along the rim with great, ponderous steps. Its bony slab of a head swung from side to side. Nate heard it sniff loudly, seeking to identify them by their scent.

An old mountaineer had once told him a grizzly was a "walkin' nose," and the frontiersman had hit the nail on the head. Grizzlies lived by their noses, drawn from one tantalizing scent to another. Whether rooting out rodents, ferreting a fawn hidden in high grass, or tracking down other prey, grizzlies relied mainly on their sense of smell.

Suddenly the lord of the wilderness reared onto its hind legs, rising and rising until it loomed a good eleven feet, large even by grizzly standards. The head craned upward as it continued to sniff.

Isaiah bit his lower lip to keep from yelling. He had a well-nigh irresistible impulse to shout at the creature to go away. to leave them alone, to find its supper elsewhere. His legs quivered, his stomach flipped and flopped.

Shakespeare was watching Pegasus. The gelding had a long-standing hatred for bears, ever since a grizzly tore open its flank when it was much younger. He wouldn't put it past Pegasus to go after the bruin.

Nate pivoted, never taking his Hawken off the bear. One shot hardly ever brought a griz down. But he had slain enough of them to know where they were most vulnerable. Not the head, where a thick cranium rendered them virtually bullet proof. Nor the lungs, which were so large that it took several balls to prove fatal.

The best place to shoot a grizzly—the only place, in Nate's estimation—was in the heart. Their sheer bulk, though, made a heart shot difficult. The slug must pass through a couple of feet of solid sinew and various organs. And even when it hit home, such was the ferocious vitality of the brutes that they could live another couple of minutes before they succumbed. More than enough time to rip a man to literal shreds.

Nate braced himself when the bear stopped and looked at him. He could not see the eyes, but he could *feel* them bore into him. This was the moment of truth. The goliath was making up its mind. If it was going to do something, the next thirty seconds would tell.

Nate had no hankering to tangle with it, not after all the close shaves he'd had in previous years. Grizzly Killer, the Indian name bestowed on him, was fitting, for no one, no other trapper or Indian alive, had fought more of the monsters. At one time it had seemed to him that every time he turned around, another griz was there, jaws agape, slavering with ravenous hunger. As if he had been a magnet, drawing them to him from far and wide.

The bear halted. Nate fixed the barrel on where he believed the heart would be, but it was impossible to be sure in the inky darkness. He held his breath to steady his arm. Beside him, the stallion stirred, and he hoped to high heaven it wasn't about to do something that would ignite the bear's blood lust.

Then, grunting, the grizzly turned and lumbered off into the night, its huge pads going *splish-splish-splish* on the drenched ground. The sound soon faded.

Nate knew grizzlies were devious devils. They frequently

circled around to come at their prey from behind. But not this time. To the east the storm still raged, lightning still spewed from the heavens. Backlit against the faint glow was the bear's broad form, retreating off across the plain. "We're safe," he announced.

Shakespeare let go of the New Yorker's rifle and sank onto his haunches. The incident was forgotten before he stopped moving. As incidents went, it was another routine event in an adventurous life crammed with hair-raising escapades. As perils went, this one had been decidedly tame. To someone who'd had more hairsbreadth escapes than he had hairs on his chin, the bear's inquisitive examination did not rate a second thought.

Isaiah Tompkins, however, swore he would never forget it for as long as he lived. He had stared Death in its hairy face and lived. Should he make it safely back to New York, he would regale family and friends with the account. And perhaps no one would blame him if he embellished for dramatic effect.

Sitting, Isaiah held out both hands. They shook like leaves in a breeze. "Look at me!" he marveled. "Another minute of that and I don't know what I would have done."

Nate slid down to the stallion. "I reckon we've all had enough excitement for one day. Let's turn in. Dawn will be here before we know it."

"How can you sleep?" Isaiah responded. "I doubt I'll close my eyes all night."

Shakespeare curled onto his side. "Good. You can have first watch, then. Wake us if you hear anything. Or if the horses act like they do." Removing his beaver hat, he placed it under his head as a pillow. "Wake me in about three hours. Nate will spell me later."

Isaiah shook his head, astounded. He would never understand these mountain men if he lived to be a hundred. "How will I know when three hours is up? I don't have a watch."

Shakespeare surveyed the firmament. Scattered stars were

visible through breaks in the clouds. As luck would have it, one was the North Star. "See that star yonder?" he asked, pointing. When the younger man nodded, he moved his finger a couple of inches. "When it's about there, three hours will be up."

Isaiah watched Nate King stretch out on the cold, wet earth, cradle the Hawken, and close his eyes. How anyone could sleep under such trying conditions was beyond him. Isaiah certainly couldn't. His clothes were soaked, his body was chilled. He stood a very real risk of catching his death of cold.

Nearby, Rufus sawed logs. Isaiah envied him. Clasping his arms to his chest, he rubbed himself to try to warm up. He was hungry again, but he did not want to impose on the mountain men by asking for more pemmican. Between Rufus and him, over half of what the trappers had brought was gone.

The trappers. Isaiah studied them, the giant and the oldster. They were a peculiar breed, these mountain men. Evidently the tavern gossip was true. Tough as iron, fearless as panthers, able to live off the land, handy with a gun or knife, they were an independent bunch, as different from run-of-the mill folks as that grizzly had been from a common black bear.

Isaiah wondered what it was that turned ordinary men into mountaineers. Once upon a time Nate King was probably no different than Isaiah was. By what magic alchemy of circumstance and design had King been transformed? And why, once transformed, did so few mountain men return to the lives they had known? Why did King prefer the Rockies to New York City? What did he know that Isaiah did not?

A wavering howl pierced the gloom. Now that the storm had moved on, the prairie's nocturnal denizens were on the prowl again. Isaiah envisioned an army of red-eyed wolves slinking close to the gully and gripped his rifle firmly.

A yip to the south was answered by another to the northeast. Coyotes, Isaiah knew. A fluttering screech he could not identify. Most likely a doe or something else had fallen to a carnivore's slashing fangs and claws.

Isaiah could never get over how dangerous the wilderness was. A man never knew from one day to the next if he would be alive to greet the next dawn. Savages, wild animals, heat, cold, thirst, any one of them spelled doom if he wasn't careful.

Which added to the mystery of Nate King and McNair and others of their rugged ilk. What sane person would choose living in the wild over the comforts and culture places like New York City offered? Who in their right mind would pick survival of the fittest over a life of ease and pleasure?

Isaiah certainly wouldn't. He had learned his lesson. The hard way. City life was the only life for him. When he needed new clothes, all he had to do was visit his tailor. Not shoot a deer, skin it, treat the hide, cut it, then spend hours sewing it. When he needed food, all had to do was visit a tavern or the latest rage in fine eateries, a restaurant. Not kill something, butcher it, plop the meat in a pot, and wait for half an hour for the morsels to stew.

Isaiah had never truly appreciated how much a life of ease had going for it. Rather than spend most of his time attending to basic needs, in the city he had time to spare, time for the theater or concerts or socials. Time for women. Time for what mattered most in life.

Yet, in order to enjoy city life, a man needed money. Lots and lots of money. Which brought him back to what had brought him to the wilderness in the first place—namely, acquiring enough money to get a head start, enough to last him a good long while, enough to permit him to live in the lavish style to which he aspired.

Being a beaver trapper had seemed the ideal way. A year or two of easy, glamorous work and he would have had enough to launch him on the road to prosperity. But now the dream had been dashed on the cruel rocks of reality.

Or had it? Isaiah stared at the mountain men again. Maybe

he could persuade them to help. They must know every prime trapping site in the mountains. Places where the beaver were plentiful. If they could be persuaded to share a dozen traps, Rufus and he could salvage triumph from the dregs of disaster.

Deep in reflection, Isaiah did not think to check the star for a good long while. When he did, he was surprised to find it had gone past the spot indicated by McNair. Going over, he knelt and lightly placed a hand on the oldster's shoulder.

A knife flashed up and out and pressed against Isaiah's throat. Petrified, he gasped, "It's me! Tompkins! What are you doing?"

"By the Almighty," Shakespeare fumed. "Don't you know better than to wake a man like that? Give him a good swift kick, or smack him." Sliding the knife into its beaded sheath, he sat up.

"What did I do wrong?" Isaiah asked, gingerly rubbing his neck.

"Being so quiet. It's enough to make a coon think an Indian is about to lift his hair. Next time, make more noise so I'll know it's you."

Isaiah selected a flat spot and eased onto his back. Convinced he was too overwrought to rest, he pondered the strange quirks of fate that ruled a man's life. He did not realize his eyes had closed until he opened them and beheld a band of pink framing the horizon. A new day was dawning. "I'll be damned," he said aloud.

"So will nine-tenths of the human race." Shakespeare had been up for half an hour. He had wiped down Pegasus, thrown on his saddle, and was ready to depart.

Isaiah stiffly rose. His back felt as if he had spent six hours on a medieval torture rack. Rufus, incredibly, had not moved all night and was sound asleep yet. With a start, Isaiah discovered that the last member of their party was missing. "Where's King?"

"Checking on those ornery Piegans."

Nate had left an hour before. He had walked the stallion out of the gully so as not awaken the greenhorns, then swung up and trotted to the northeast. What with the storm and having lost half its members, the war party was unlikely to have gone very far.

Just so they don't come after us, Nate mused. Revenge was a dish best served steaming hot, and the Piegans were bound to be out for blood. "An eye for an eye" was a given west of the Mississippi. Turning the other cheek was unheard of—especially since to do so was considered cowardly.

Among the Shoshones a man always avenged the slaying of a loved one. If, say, the Pawnees raided a Shoshone village, a prominent warrior was bound to propose paying the Pawnees a visit to retaliate. Then the Pawnees would need their revenge. And so on and so on. A vicious cycle, with no one the clear winner and everyone poorer for the loss of life and property.

There were exceptions, as there were to every rule. The Cheyennes and the Arapahos had become the best of friends. The Shoshones and the Flatheads were on amicable terms after many years of strife. And even the dreaded Lakotas had recently agreed to a truce with their longtime enemies, the Crows.

But the exceptions were few. By and large, Indians were their own worst enemy. The red race had been at war with itself for so long, whole tribes were devoted to the pursuit of war to the exclusion of all else. Each boasted several warrior societies. Men sought to outdo one another by counting the highest number of coup. For with coup came prestige, respect, influence. With coup came the prettiest women, the biggest lodges, the most horses.

Indian men who wanted no part of warfare were treated as women. They were made to do the work women did, made to perform endless drudgery, made to associate with the women all day, every day. Made to look like complete and total asses. A few short moons of this treatment and practically any man was ready to take up his bow and lance, paint his face, and go off to kill.

Nate occasionally liked to ponder how different history would be if Indians had learned to band together against common foes. It was doubtful, for instance, that the early French and English forces could have taken over so much land so swiftly if the Iroquois and the Hurons had been allies instead of bitter enemies whose hatred was so cleverly exploited.

To the north several large animals grazed. Nate absently looked at them, turned away, then looked again. They were horses. Indian warhorses, paint and all. He was willing to wager they belonged to the Piegans. But what were they doing by themselves? Had they broken loose during the storm? He veered to catch two for the New Yorkers to use, but the war mounts sped off with tails high.

Rather than tire the stallion so early in the day, Nate let them go. Farther on he spotted another four to the southeast. For a few to stray was within the bounds of reason. For most to have done so was unthinkable. The Piegans would never let that happen.

Nate had a hunch where he would find their camp. When the knoll came into view, he slowed and circled. On the other side lay the war party's camp. The Piegans were still there, scattered willy-nilly, some near the knoll, others out in the grass. Dark splotches dotted many of the prone figures. Some were rimmed by reddish pools.

Nate kept circling until he found clear prints heading to the east. Enormous tracks, fourteen inches from the heel to the tips of the middle claws. So fresh that Nate rose in the stirrups and was rewarded with a glimpse of the grizzly in the distance.

Dismounting, Nate led the stallion into the camp—or what was left of the camp. Shredded blankets, busted bows, and broken lances were scattered all over. Bodies were everywhere. One Piegan had been torn open from sternum to crotch. Another had half a face. Still another had been rent limb from limb, the torso cut to ribbons. But the man's head had not been touched and his features were set in quiet repose.

Nate had to avoid scores of body parts. Legs, arms, chunks of stomachs and chests, even entire heads. Several Piegans had been partially eaten.

As best Nate could reconstruct what occurred, it went like this. The war party had made camp at the base of the knoll. Shortly afterward, the storm had struck and the Piegans had huddled against its onslaught. When the tempest subsided, they'd lain down to sleep.

The grizzly had come on them in the middle of the night. It was among them before they knew it was there, ripping and rending, dispatching a third or more as they lurched erect, sleepy-eyed and dull-witted.

A slaughter had taken place. Bows and arrows and knives were useless against a living mountain. The bear had mowed the Piegans down as a scythe mowed grain. They fought valiantly, running close to sink their shafts, but in the end the bear's stamina was too much for them. It slew every one.

At the end a few wounded warriors had tried to escape, but the grizzly chased each down. To the bear it must have been grand sport. Like snatching fish one after the other from a river. Only in this case it had been ripping Piegans into oblivion.

There were too many to bury even if Nate were of a mind to, which he wasn't. They were his enemies. They had tried to ambush him. Their grisly fate was richly deserved.

He salvaged what he could. A steel knife with a bone handle. A parfleche decorated with elaborate beadwork. A rawhide rope. A few other things. He was making a last sweep when the stallion nickered.

Several hundred yards out, the grizzly loped toward them. In a lithe bound Nate gained the saddle, wheeled the big black, and fled up and over the knoll. Why it had come back he would never know. For a quarter of a mile he held the stallion to a gallop, relenting only when the bear gave up. Rising onto its hind legs, it stayed erect until he was out of sight.

By then the sun had risen. They would get a late start. Nate pushed on until he spied the same four horses to the south. They were resting. Procuring the rawhide rope, he fashioned a noose. The quartet observed his approach anxiously. When he was close enough to chuck a stone and hit them, a dusky warhorse snorted and raced away. The others followed suit.

Nate slapped his heels against the stallion. Rather than try to catch the swiftest, he picked the slowest, a tan animal on which a vivid red hand had been painted. The noose at his side, he rapidly overtook it. Sluggish from lack of sleep and having grazed until it was fit to burst, the warhorse was no match for the big black. It slowed to a walk within half a mile.

Wary of being bitten, Nate rode in as close as he dared and flicked the noose. The Piegan animal ducked, skipped to the left, and was off again like a shot. But Nate kept pace, coiling the rope for another try. The next time the warhorse slowed, the rope licked out and slipped over its head.

Expecting resistance, Nate turned the stallion broadside and hauled on the rawhide. But the warhorse stopped and stood docile, as meek as a lamb. Like a dog on a leash, it didn't act up when he headed for the gully.

The questioning screech of a hawk drew Nate's attention to a pair soaring high overhead. A high-pitched squeal alerted him to a prairie dog colony, which he wisely avoided. Bees buzzed by in search of nectar. Small birds flitted among colorful flowers.

Nate inhaled the fragrant morning air, relishing the moment. Life thrived on the prairie and in the mountains. Raw life. Often savage life, often harsh. Yet life that radiated zest and vitality, life the likes of which most city dwellers never experienced.

The wilderness possessed a special quality, an elusive quality that imbued those who had the grit to live in the wild with
a keen relish for living. With the same zest and zeal exhibited
by life itself.

Nate would never go back. Not if someone were to offer
him a million dollars. Once an uncle had done something similar. Had offered him a substantial sum if only he would for-
sake Winona and return to civilization, "where he belonged."

It went without saying that Nate declined. He hadn't bothered to explain why. For it was impossible for those who had
tasted the delicious fruit of pure freedom to describe the ster-
ling taste to those who were used to the dull, drab table scraps
society claimed made a person free.

A lot had changed since Nate left. From newcomers he
learned about the state of the Union, how each year cities grew
more and more crowded, how each year Congress passed more
and more laws, how each year the precious freedom Ameri-
cans secured during the Revolution was being chipped away
bit by bit. Nate doubted whether the average citizen a few
short generations hence would know what true freedom truly
was.

What had Scott Kendall once told him? The feisty trapper
had once wintered in Nate's valley, and in the evenings they
had sat around the fire jawing about books and politics and
religion. All those things trappers were supposed to be too
dumb to understand.

Once, Scott had mentioned a quote from Epictetus, a quote
that stuck in Nate's skull ever since. "No man is free who is
not master of himself." Truer words had never been written.

Nate took stock of the multitude of life flourishing on the
plain, and beamed. All those creatures—as free as the wind.
Humankind could be equally free if only it would shake off
the shackles imposed by those who thought they had the right
to impose their ideas of how everyone should live whether
everyone wanted to live that way or not.

Suddenly a shadow passed in front of him. Snapping erect, Nate raised the Hawken. It was only a raven, the rhythmic beat of its wings as clear as crystal.

Breaking into a trot, the mountain man presently saw a white-maned figure materialize as if out of nowhere and wave.

"Here comes Hamlet," Shakespeare said for the benefit of the New Yorkers. Rufus Stern was finally up and stuffing himself with pemmican. Isaiah, oddly quiet since Nate left, at the moment was cleaning his rifle.

"About time," the latter declared. "Half the morning is gone."

"In a hurry, are you?"

Isaiah paused in the act of shoving a patch of cloth down the barrel with his ramrod. "Yes, I am. Which reminds me. How soon before we reach the damn Rockies? I am so sick of grass, I could vomit."

"Do tell. You're in luck, then, hoss."

"In what respect?"

"Those mountains you have such a powerful hankering to see are a lot closer than you reckon."

Something in the frontiersman's tone brought Isaiah to his feet. He had not left the gully since they arrived the night before, and his legs were wooden as he awkwardly climbed to the west rim. Intent on not losing his footing, he did not lift his head until he was at the top. The sight that met his gaze jolted him.

"God in heaven! Where did *they* come from?"

Chapter Six

Shakespeare McNair chuckled. "They weren't there yesterday. Do you suppose they sprouted overnight like that beanstalk did?"

Isaiah Tompkins didn't hear. He was in shock, riveted to the vista spread out before his wondering gaze.

The mountain man had seen the same reaction before. Most who set eyes on the majestic Rockies for the first time were overwhelmed. And who could blame them?

As it turned out, the gully was located some five hundred yards from the leading edge of emerald foothills high enough to qualify as mountains east of the Mississippi. But here the foothills were no more than footstools, very small footstools, compared to the titans they fringed.

Magnificent. It was the one word that came anywhere close to describing the Rocky Mountains in all their supreme glory. And even that didn't do them complete justice. The Rockies had to be seen to be fully appreciated.

Rising thousands of feet above sea level, they formed a

gigantic wall stretching from Canada almost clear down to Mexico. Over three thousand miles, some claimed. Near the center of the chain, where Nate had his homestead, reared some of the highest. One was Long's Peak, a spectacular summit crowned practically year-round by a mantle of pristine snow. Not quite three miles high, it was breathtaking to behold, especially for first-timers like Tompkins and Stern.

Shakespeare chortled when Rufus joined his friend and the pair surveyed the spectacle in dumbfounded silence. It had taken his breath away, too, lo, those many years ago when he first crossed the plains. Somehow he had known on that very day he would never go home again, never again taste the tainted fruits of civilization. Those glittering gigantic spikes thrusting skyward held an allure impossible to resist.

He had no regrets about his decision. In all the years he had lived in the wild, it was safe to say he'd never had a dull moment. Each and every day was a sparkling new adventure unto itself, which would not have been the case had he gone home. Maybe he'd have farmed, or tried his hand at being a blacksmith, or at running a mercantile. Decent enough work, but it paled against the luster of the untamed wilderness.

A nicker from the black stallion heralded Nate's arrival. He descended into the gully and rode up the other side. The astonishment etching the faces of the greenhorns amused him. "Didn't Newhouse mention the Rockies in that *Guide* you're so fond of?"

Isaiah numbly nodded. "No words can do them justice, though. They're beyond belief."

"They're beautiful," Rufus said. Which struck him as funny. He had never thought things could be beautiful, only people. Yet the fantastic array of rugged peaks, some glistening white as ivory, were as lovely as his beloved Agnes.

"Got a present for you," Nate said, tossing the reins to the Piegan horse at Tompkins. "You'll have to ride double. But we'll make a lot better time with three animals."

Isaiah tore his eyes from the Rockies. "Isn't this an Indian's? Where did you get it?"

"From a Piegan who has no further use for it." Nate
stretched to relieve a kink in his lower back, then glanced at
his mentor. "Are you planning on wasting the day away? Or
can we light a shuck?"

"Thither shall it, then. And happily may your sweet self
put on the lineal state and glory of the land!" Shakespeare
answered.

Rufus blinked. "What did he just say?"

"He can't wait to get back and cram his mouth with food
until he bursts," Nate joked.

Shakespeare feigned indignance. "I said no such thing,
Hamlet, my prince, and you damn well know it." Placing a
hand to his forehead as if he were in torment, he quoted,
"Why, look you, I am whipped and scourged with rods, net-
tled and stung with pismires."

"Huh?" Rufus said.

Nate bent down. "Want some free advice, friend? Ignore
him if you want to keep your sanity." He glanced at McNair.
"As for you . . ." It took a few seconds for him to remember
the right quote. "I know thee not, old man. Fall to thy prayers.
How ill white hairs become a fool and a jester."

Cackling lustily, Shakespeare slapped his thigh. "I'll be!
You *have* been paying attention all these years! And here I
figured all my recitals went in one ear and out the other."
Tremendously pleased, he swung onto Pegasus. "Tell you
what. With a little coaxing, I could be persuaded to read *Julius
Ceasar* as we go along."

"No, thanks," Nate said. Once McNair started reading from
old William S., there was no stopping him.

"Very well, then. With no coaxing at all." Fishing in a
parfleche, Shakespeare produced his well-worn copy of *The
Complete Works of Shakespeare*. The cover was battered,
many of the pages dog-eared, but otherwise it was in fine

condition. His wife liked to joke that he took better care of the book than he did of her.

Opening it to the correct page, Shakespeare cleared his throat. "Act One, Scene One. Rome. A street. Enter Flavius, Marullus and certain Commoners. Flavius speaks—"

Rufus turned to the younger mountain man. "He's not really going to read the whole play, is he? Not the *whole* thing?"

"I hope you brought wax to plug your ears with." Nate prodded the stallion into motion. "It's going to be a long ride."

Isaiah and Rufus hastily mounted. They did not know what to say when McNair brought Pegasus alongside their mount.

"Are you ready for a real treat?"

"If you say so," Isaiah responded. He'd been to a Shakespearean play once and hated every minute. Boring did not begin to describe the flowery language and the silly antics of the actors.

"Hence!" Shakespeare began, gesturing grandly and booming loud enough to be heard in St. Louis. "Home, you idle creatures, get you home. Is this a holiday? What! Know you not—"

Rufus put his mouth to Isaiah's ear. "King is right. This *is* going to be a long ride."

"Maybe not. Maybe he'll get so carried away, he'll fall off his horse and break his neck."

"We should be so lucky."

They weren't. Over the next several hours the New Yorkers were treated to recitals of *Julius Ceasar, Measure For Measure,* and *Pericles.*

"So, on your patience evermore attending," Shakespeare concluded, "New joy wait on you! Here our play has ending."

"Thank God," Isaiah muttered.

Shakespeare closed the big book with a crisp snap. "What was that, hoss? Didn't catch it?"

"I said thanks for entertaining us."

"Think nothing of it. Tonight I'll read *King Henry VI*, Parts One, Two, and Three. And if there's time, I'll throw in *Titus Andronicus* for good measure."

"Good God."

"I know, I know. Sounds too good to be true. At the rendezvous there are usually twenty to thirty coons gathered around each night just to hear me. I reckon you could say I've become a legend in my own time." Shakespeare snickered while sliding the volume back into the parfleche.

"You're something, that's for sure," Isaiah conceded. "But what was that you just mentioned? The rendezvous?"

"The annual get-together for the trapping fraternity. Free or company men, it doesn't matter. Takes place each summer. Mostly up on the Green River." Shakespeare paused. "Or rather, it used to take place. Word is that this year's will be the last."

"How's that?"

McNair sighed. "It's what Nate started to tell you yesterday when he asked how long you'd owned Newhouse's manual. All that business about trappers earning a lot of money. It's no longer true."

A new kind of fear speared through Isaiah. "What are you dithering about? Beaver hats are still popular. So are capes and cloaks with beaver trim."

"Not as popular as they used to be," Shakespeare said. "The market for peltries bottomed out a couple of years ago and never recovered. Once, the fur companies were offering up to nine dollars a hide. Now you're lucky if you can sell prime pelts for three or four."

Isaiah was not to be deterred. "That's still a lot—"

"Think so? Not when black powder costs close to three dollars a pound, and a new blanket will set you back fifteen." Shakespeare ran a hand through his beard. "I'm right sorry to be the bearer of bad tidings, boys, but you've set your compass by a star that just ain't there. The trapping business has gone to hell. With only one rendezvous left, you'd be lucky to break even.''

Dismay ate at Rufus like an acid. "Please. There has to be a way. There just has to be. We've come so far. Been through so much. And we invested over two hundred dollars of our own money to buy the supplies and horses we lost."

Isaiah was thinking of the ridicule that would be heaped on their heads if they went back to New York as failures. Everyone would say, "We told you so!" They would never hear the end of it. "There must be a way," he echoed.

Shakespeare felt sorry for the pair. As greenhorns went, they weren't too obnoxious. Just misguided. A common enough shortcoming. He would like to help, but he couldn't imagine how. The small nest egg he had socked away wouldn't do them much good. "I can't think of one," he admitted.

Crestfallen, Isaiah lowered his chin to his chest. So much for his vaunted dream! So much for buying a house of his very own! He could forget the small country estate that had taken his fancy. He could forget the fine carriage he wanted, and courting the daughters of wealthy men so he could marry into even more money.

"What will Agnes say?" Rufus wondered aloud. Would she laugh at him? Call him dull-witted, as others sometimes did? No, not sweet Agnes. She would hug him and tell him to listen to her advice next time. And he would. From then on, whatever she wanted, he would do. Wasn't that what made the perfect husband?

Nate King heard the exchange but offered no comment. The New Yorkers had made a mistake. They must live with the consequences. At least they were alive, which was more than could be said about three-fourths of those who braved the wilds to obtain a poke of jingling coins.

Isaiah wanted to throw back his head and scream in impotent fury. Once again life had treated him unfairly. Once again the Fates had flung his hopes and aspirations back into his face. Distraught, he glanced up. They were high in the foothills by now, following a narrow winding trail he could never have found on his own. The vegetation consisted mostly of pines and scrub brush. Mountains towered above, reaching to the clouds.

Ahead, Nate King rounded a bend onto a wide shelf, his head bent as he inspected his Hawken. McNair was staring to the south. Only Isaiah saw the lone rider waiting on the shelf. He saw beaded buckskins, a bow and quiver, long black hair worn in a loose mane, and a dark, angular visage. "Nate, look out!" he bawled. "A savage!"

Isaiah drew rein and started to lift his rifle. He thought he was fast, but the figure was liquid quicksilver. The bow elevated, the string was pulled smoothly back, and a barbed tip was lined up with Isaiah's chest, all in the bat of an eyelash.

"No!" Nate hollered, cutting the stallion so he was between the greenhorn and the horseman. "Lower your weapons, the both of you!"

Isaiah was incredulous. The mountain man had put himself in the arrow's line of flight and was bound to take the shaft in the side. The Indian had the string next to his cheek, below the eye. "In heaven's name, get out of the way!"

Nate gestured. "I meant it! Keep that rifle down." To the savage Nate said, "What are you waiting for? Winter to set in?"

"Ahhhh, Pa. He was fixing to shoot me. What else was I to do?"

Had Isaiah heard correctly? The Indian just called King *"Pa"*?

"This man is our guest, Zach. He's to be treated with the same hospitality you'd show Touch the Clouds or Drags the Rope." Nate kneed the stallion over next to his son's roan and placed his hand on the boy's shoulder. "Don't fault him if he's a mite wolfish. We tangled with some Piegans yesterday. Barely got away."

Zachary King lowered his ash bow while rising on his horse to see past the pair of silly whites in their grungy store-bought clothes. "Are they still after you?" he asked eagerly. "Want me to slow them down?"

Nate King smiled, but a small shadow clouded his heart. His son had grown into a strapping young man. Barely seventeen, Zach appeared to be two to three years older. The boy had Nate's broad shoulders and square chin, his powerful frame and supple grace. But Zach still had a lot of growing up to do inside, where it counted most. "No need. A grizzly rubbed the whole bunch out."

"Oh." Zach made no attempt to hide his disappointment. "I was hoping to count some coup. Piegan scalps are as good as any other."

Nate's smile evaporated. Sometimes he found it hard to accept that this was the same carefree boy Winona and he had raised, the same innocent soul who once refused to kill a spider because he couldn't bear to hurt a living thing. Now all his son cared about was earning glory in battle. "Piegans are people, just like us."

"What's that mean?" Zach responded.

"If I need to explain, you wouldn't understand." Nate clapped his son's back, then moved on, toward the high defile that would take them to the secluded valley he had claimed as his own.

Confused, Zach focused on the one man whose insights he valued as highly as his father's. "What did I say, Uncle Shakespeare?"

"He's probably tired, is all, Stalking Coyote," McNair hedged, using the boy's Shoshone name. "Think of it no more. For nature crescent does not grow alone in thews and bulk. But, as this temple waxes, the inward serve of the mind and soul grows wide withal."

"That's nice, but he's upset with me and I'd like to know why." Zach turned the roan to catch up with his father, pausing long enough to scrutinize the greenhorns. They were typical whites, he suspected—unwashed, ignorant of the ways of the wilderness, and headstrong. "Nice hair," he told the one who had tried to shoot him.

"Thanks," Isaiah replied, perplexed by the peculiar compliment. Up close he could see how young the son really was. A combination of traits, both white and Indian, branded him a half-breed.

"I bet it would look great hanging from a peg in our cabin." Laughing, Zach hurried his horse along, yelling, "Pa! Pa! Wait up."

Isaiah felt a flush of resentment. "What's the matter with that boy? Why did he treat me so rudely?"

"He's at that age," Shakespeare said.

"What age?"

"Where he thinks he knows all there is to know. And, for a Shoshone, where coup means everything. He's already counted enough to rank as a warrior, but he's not satisfied. One day he aims to be a leader, a war chief maybe."

Rufus perked up. "Good heavens. Are you saying that child has killed people? And scalped them?"

Shakespeare wagged a finger. "I wouldn't go calling him a child to his face, were I you. You saw how adept he is with a bow? Well, with a knife he's a regular hellion." Shakespeare resumed riding. "Besides, he's not all that younger than either of you. Four or five years would be my guess. Out here that practically makes him a grown-up."

Rufus could not get over the idea of the son of a white man lifting scalps. "I don't care how old he is. How can he cut off someone else's hair? It's inhuman. Indecent."

"He must take after his mother, not his father," Isaiah opined.

Shakespeare's head snapped around so abruptly, he nearly lost his hat. "Let me give you another word of advice, pilgrim. If you ever insult Nate's wife like that in his presence, you'll find out the father and the son have a lot more in common than you think.''

Twenty yards up the trail, Zachary King overtook his father. "Ma sent me, Pa. She was worried when you didn't show up last night like you should have."

"She sent you? Or you pestered her to come look for us so you could get away on your own for a spell?"

Zach grinned. "A little of both, I guess. But I did ask Drags the Rope and Touch the Clouds to go with me. They couldn't be bothered. Tomorrow they leave, and they were busy helping their wives pack." He fluttered his lips. "It ain't right. Great warriors like them doing women's work."

"Don't criticize what you don't understand. Once you have a wife of your own, then you can talk." Nate softened his voice. "I do my share of work around our cabin, don't I? And no one has ever accused me of being puny."

Zach had to admit his father had a point. His pa was widely regarded as a fearless foe, as someone to be reckoned with. The Shoshones, the Crows, the Flatheads, the Cheyennes, even the Utes held him in high regard. Zach felt no small amount of pride at being the mighty Grizzly Killer's son.

Yet, strangely enough, his pa also liked to help his ma around the cabin. Cleaning, doing dishes, even folding clothes, his father was not above lending a hand. It mystified Zach no end. A warrior should never stoop to do menial work.

Zach would do none of that stuff when *he* was married. Warriors should devote themselves to war. To practicing with various weapons for hours on end. To fashioning arrows and bows, to cleaning guns, to sharpening knives, to taking care of prized warhorses. Those kinds of things.

"We'll have to go hunting at first light," Nate mentioned. The family's larder was lower than normal. He had gone to the prairie after fresh buffalo meat, but now they must make do with an elk or a deer. In another week or so he would go again, after the greenhorns had been sent on their way.

"What happened to the packhorse you left with?" Zach inquired.

"Painter got it our first night out."

"Darn. I liked that critter. Hardly ever bit me. It's not as mean as that piebald we got from the Crows. Never can trust those pesky coyotes to deal fair and square." Zach brightened at an inspiration. "I know. Instead of going hunting, why don't we butcher the piebald and eat it?"

Nate looked at his son. The notions he came up with! "We wouldn't eat horse meat unless we were starving."

"Why not? Spotted Bull told me the Apaches eat horse meat. And everyone says the Apaches are the best fighters alive."

Nate did not need to be reminded. Years ago, when Zach was half the age he was now, the family had ventured to Santa Fe, more as a lark than anything else. Shakespeare and Blue Water Woman had tagged along, and the trip had gone well until they reached the Mexican province of New Mexico.

There, one night, Apaches raided a *rancho* they were staying at. Winona had been kidnapped. Nate had set out in pursuit, and after an ordeal worthy of Daniel Boone he again held her in his arms. But it had been close; he'd nearly lost her forever.

So Nate had all the firsthand experience with the dreaded and deadly Apaches he wanted, thank you. And if he never went up against them again, it would be none too soon.

"Spotted Bull says the Apaches are tougher than the Comanches and the Blackfeet combined," Zach divulged. The former were the scourge of the southern plains, while the Blackfeet had long held sway over the northern sections.

"They might just be," Nate said. "But remember what I told you about being tough. There's always someone somewhere a little tougher. One day the Apaches will meet their match."

Zach could not conceive of such an event, but if his pa said it, it must be true. "How long will those greenhorns be staying with us? More than a couple of days?"

"Probably. Why?" Another disturbing issue for Nate was his son's thinly disguised contempt for most whites. A recent development, neither Nate nor Winona could explain it. "They were lost. Indians stole their horses and their provisions."

"Right out from under their noses, I'll bet." Zach laughed. In the wild most whites were as helpless as newborn babes. His father and Uncle Shakespeare and a few others were truly at home, but even most seasoned trappers couldn't hold a candle to the Shoshones. And it was his mother's people Zach admired more than any other.

Each year since his birth the family had spent the summer months among them. His first riding lesson had been courtesy of Spotted Bull, his mother's uncle. His first archery lesson had been given by Drags the Rope, whose skill with a bow was renowned in the tribe.

Each year Zach had been drawn more and more to the Shoshone way of living, and less and less toward the beliefs of his father's people. He never came right out and said so for fear of hurting his father's feelings.

"Don't be so hard on them, Stalking Coyote," Nate advised. "In a big city you would be just as helpless as they are here."

"I doubt that," Zach declared. He had every confidence in his ability to survive any situation. Hadn't he bested bears, cougars, and Blackfeet? "From what you've told me, a city has everything a person needs. Food, clothes, weapons. And I speak the white tongue fluently."

"There's more to surviving among white men than knowing English or where to find a hot meal." Nate did not go into detail. One day—soon, possibly—he intended to take his loved ones east to a city. Perhaps St. Louis. So the children could experience the white man's world for themselves and

87

see that, overall, it had more good elements than bad.

The irony wasn't lost on him. He wanted nothing to do with civilization, he had forsaken his heritage to live in the wilderness, yet it upset him when his flesh and blood showed disdain for the very things *he* disliked.

Zach was talking. "... had that same cat pay us a visit. Leastwise, we think it was the same one. It came down close to the cabin last night and made a ruckus. Screeching and growling something awful. The horses nearly broke out of the corral."

Nate's lips compressed. A mountain lion had plagued their valley since early spring, defying all his attempts to trap or shoot it.

"Touch the Clouds and Drags the Rope went after it, but the painter vanished like a ghost, just like it always does."

"Sooner or later it will make a mistake," Nate predicted. In that respect animals were similar to humans. No matter how savvy they were, eventually they were careless, and in the mountains being careless usually carried a fatal price.

The trail steepened. On either side rose unscalable rock cliffs. Funneled steadily higher toward a gap at the summit, Nate roved the ground for sign of game. Deer and elk tracks were abundant. A black bear had passed by within the past day. And he saw more chipmunks than he could shake a stick at.

The air grew cooler. They negotiated a switchback, coming out on a rounded barren spur. Nate was halfway across when a clear set of tracks in soft dirt caught his eye. Reining up, he noted their size and depth.

Zach whistled, then chuckled. "This cat's a big one, sure enough. Any bigger and I'd swear it must be part grizzly."

Nate was not amused. Not one little bit.

"Do you reckon it followed you down and killed your pack-horse?"

Nate had never even considered that. But the tracks did

point toward the prairie, and they had been made three days before. A chill swept through him, a chill not caused by the high altitude. So far the painter had killed two of his horses. Next it might be one of his family.

Chapter Seven

Winona King considered herself fortunate.

She was the mate of a man who was everything she had ever hoped to find in a husband. A man she loved as passionately now as she had during the heady rush when they courted—as whites would say. They had a fine lodge, or cabin, and were situated in a pristine valley close to an azure lake. Game was abundant, so they never lacked for food. Two fine children lent luster to their marriage.

As far as belongings went, she was much better off than many of her Shoshone sisters. Plenty of clothes, many fine cooking utensils, enough blankets to last a lifetime all were hers. Nine horses were another example of the riches she enjoyed. Or eight, rather, since one had been devoured by a cat. Yes, when Winona thought about her status in life, as she was doing this sunny day while on her way to the lake to fetch a bucket of water, she rated herself extremely fortunate.

She was no misty-eyed dreamer, though. She would be the first to admit her husband had a few flaws. Some, such as being as stubborn as a bull buffalo, and much too protective, were traits common to all males. Men could not help being men. Red or white, it made no difference. They loved to puff themselves up like grouse and strut in front of their women. They thumped their chests and boasted of battles won, glories gained. They always had to have the fastest horse, the best gun, strongest bow, or longest lance.

Even Nate was susceptible. He never formally counted coup as Shoshone warriors did, yet secretly he took pride in having counted more than most. And his accomplishments as a hunter and grizzly fighter had spread the name of Grizzly Killer far and wide.

In fact, Winona was more proud of his reputation than he was. Among her people the bravest men were always held in the highest esteem. And her husband had proven his courage time and again by facing the mightiest beasts in all the wilderness and besting them in vicious claw-against-steel combat.

So now, as she came to the lakeshore and paused to revel in the marvelous beauty of the tranquil scene, Winona smiled and said softly, ''I am truly happy.''

The setting alone was enough to induce good cheer. The lake shimmered blue in the bright sunlight, while above her white fluffy clouds sailed tranquilly along. Ducks paddled merrily, geese sailed majestically. Regal peaks reached to the ether, a ring of mountains that sheltered the valley on all sides.

It was a special place, imbued with good medicine. Her intuition had told her so the first time she set foot there. A sense of peace had permeated her being. Peace and belonging. As if she had come home to a home she had never known but somehow knew. Though that made no rational sense.

Bending to dip the bucket into the water, Winona saw her reflection. Her waist-length raven hair, her oval face, the features Nate swore were the loveliest of any woman who ever lived. The red lips he loved to kiss. The smooth brow he loved to stroke.

She froze on seeing tracks in the soft mud at the water's edge. Not human tracks. *Cat* tracks. Huge ones, the biggest she'd ever seen. Tracks made within the past few minutes, judging by beads of water in the toes.

The mountain lion had just slaked its thirst.

Uncoiling, Winona spun. The pines that bordered the lake were quiet. Much *too* quiet. If she had not been so preoccupied, she would have noticed sooner. Automatically, her hand strayed to the knife on her hip. She wished she had brought a pistol or a rifle, but she hadn't anticipated trouble. That's what happened when someone grew complacent. When someone assumed they were safe when they were not.

Winona scanned the shore to the north and south. No small animals were to be found. No deer, either, and usually a few does boldly ventured from the brush at that time of day to drink.

It could only mean one thing. She had been inexcusably careless, inexcusably stupid.

Winona started toward the trail that linked the lake to the cabin. Hardly had she taken four steps when high grass off to the right parted and a great tawny head appeared. Winona froze again, her breath catching in her throat.

Feral eyes studied her with hungry intent. Slinking low to the ground, the panther commenced the telltale stalk of a cat that had selected its next meal. A black-tipped tail flicked above its hindquarters.

Winona slowly drew her knife. It was no match for the feline's razor-edged claws. But if she could wound it, if she could hold it at bay and yell her head off for help while retreating into the lake, she stood a chance. *If, if, if.*

Soundlessly, the cougar slunk forward another few feet. Its white muzzle framed by jutting whiskers, its devilish green eyes burning with hunger, the cat parted its mouth enough to expose fangs as wicked as any man-made weapon.

Winona backed up a step. Slowly, ever so slowly. To make

a sudden move invited a fierce onslaught. She opened her mouth to yell for those at the cabin when suddenly a gleeful girlish voice called out from a short distance up the trail.

"Ma! Ma! Are you down here?"

Pure fear clutched at Winona's heart. "Evelyn!" she cried. "Go back! Go back! Whatever you do, don't come any closer!"

The warning was too late. Out of the woods bounded a lithe antelope in mortal guise, a girl of nine, the spitting image of her mother attired in a similar buckskin dress. Her innocent face was creased in a warm smile. "What was that, Ma?"

"Please, no!" Winona breathed.

The cat had swiveled toward her child.

Evelyn King saw the stark horror on her mother's face, and turned. She didn't scream. Her mother had told her that to do so was a sign of cowardice, and a Shoshone must never be guilty of that. She didn't bolt, either, because her father had cautioned her against fleeing from a predator. In addition, they were Kings, and as her pest of a brother was so fond of saying, the King family never ran from anything.

Even so, Evelyn felt fright rip into her insides, and she wanted to run headlong back up the path. Clamping her teeth, she glanced at her feet for something she could use to protect herself. A fist-size rock lay to her left. Inching downward, she slowly reached for it.

The panther growled, low and ominous.

"Do not move!" Winona declared. All fear for her own safety was gone. She cared only about her daughter, only about the child she loved more than life itself. Blade leveled, she sidestepped, moving at a snail's pace, pausing between each step to gauge the mountain lion's reaction.

"Shouldn't we holler for help?" Evelyn asked.

"No." Winona had changed her mind. She was too afraid it might provoke the cougar into charging.

Evelyn didn't agree, but she trusted her mother's judgment.

Her mother always knew what was best. Well, almost always. And on those rare occasions when her mother didn't, her father did. Once, she had thought her parents knew everything. Both had since assured her there was much neither had ever learned.

That had been hard to grasp. If her folks, who were as near to perfect as it was humanly possible to be, did not know all there was worth knowing, then no one did, had, or ever would.

Winona watched the panther's tail. Should it stop twitching, should it suddenly go straight and stiff, it would signal an attack. The creature was glancing from her to Evelyn and back again as if it could not quite make up its mind which of them it wanted to eat. "Attack me," she said, gesturing.

Spitting, the mountain lion retreated a pace, then crouched lower.

It would not be long. And Winona had six feet to cover. Remembering the bucket, she swung it gently, the handle squeaking as would a mouse. It attracted the cat's attention. Continuing to swing, she warily sidestepped.

Evelyn heard a commotion up near the cabin. One loud outcry was all it would take to bring her uncle and the others rushing to the rescue. But her mother had said no, so that was that. She saw the big cat stare at her and shivered despite herself. Its eyes were cold, inhumanly cold. Yet at the same time they blazed with an inner fire. How that could be, she didn't know. They filled her with fear, fear that nearly made her head spin when the panther fixed its glare on her mother and took a half-step. "Ma?" she squeaked.

"Hush." Winona did not want to do anything that would invite a rush. But she was only fooling herself. When the cougar was ready, it would attack, and nothing she could do would forestall it.

The cat didn't like the squeaking. It slunk another few inches, then stopped and watched the bucket swing back and forth, growling ominously.

Winona swung faster, wider. If she could hold it at bay long enough to gain the footpath, Evelyn could race for the cabin. Extending her other arm, she looped it around her daughter's shoulders, careful not to poke Evelyn with the knife. "When I say so," she instructed, "run as you have never run before."

"You can count on me, Ma." Evelyn had smothered her fear by reminding herself that her mother would do whatever it took to spare her from harm. Then she had another thought, and the fear returned stronger than ever: Yes, her mother would protect her, but who would protect her mother?

The mountain lion didn't like being thwarted. Suddenly surging forward, it lashed out, a forepaw connecting with the bucket.

Winona nearly lost her hold. Had a claw snagged in the wood, she would have. As it was, her shoulder was horribly wrenched. She went on swinging, though, while steering her daughter closer to the trail.

As if it divined her intent, the painter bounded high into the air and alighted between the vegetation and them. Its tail swishing angrily, the cat vented a feral screech.

So much for that, Winona thought. "Into the lake!" she bawled, and gave her precious pride and joy a shove.

Caught flat-footed, Evelyn stumbled. She had to fling both arms out to keep from landing on her stomach. Her knees stung something awful. She raised her head—and there was the cougar, five feet away, steely legs coiling to spring.

Winona saw, too. "Nooooo!" she cried, aiming a swipe at the cat's face. Lightning reflexes saved it, and in retaliation the painter lashed out. This time those wicked curved claws bit deep into the bucket. Winona tugged—in vain. "Into the water! Hurry!"

The shout galvanized Evelyn into scrambling upright. The mountain lion released the bucket to dash at her. For an instant she figured she was dead. She imagined being torn open and feeling long fangs sink into her neck. But another swing of the bucket clipped the painter on the brow as it was rearing to pounce, and the predator recoiled

Too close, Winona's mind screamed. *Much too close!* She put herself in front of her offspring so the cat would have to get through her first. Not once did she stop swinging, for if she did so it would be on them in a heartbeat.

Evelyn barreled into the lake. A chill, damp sensation spread rapidly up her legs as she churned and flailed. All the splashing seemed to incite the mountain lion even more. It made a beeline for her, water or no.

Winona had both hands on the handle. She slammed the bucket against the cat's side, sparking another screech. Retreating to the water's edge, Winona aimed a terrific blow at the top of the cougar's skull, but it was too smart for her. It leaped to the left, well out of reach, and crouched in baffled frustration.

Water lapped at Winona's legs. She took another step and it rose above her ankles. Any farther in and she risked slipping. Planting both feet, she braced for the savage rush sure to come. She was not disappointed.

The panther had had enough. Snarling horribly, it came in fast and low. Water splashed up around its face and shoulders just as it cocked a forepaw. Spitting, it unexpectedly danced back onto shore.

A flicker of hope animated Winona. The cat didn't like to get wet! Grinning, she kicked out, sending a thick spray at the mountain lion's head. It hissed and backpedaled. Encouraged, she kicked again and again, harder and harder, driving it farther and farther back.

Evelyn laughed for joy. Just when she believed they did not stand a prayer, the cougar turned out to be scared of something as silly as water! Clapping, she hollered, "Go away! You mean coward!"

The cat growled menacingly. Beads of moisture dotted its whiskers, its jaw. In a molten streak it darted to the right as if to flee along the shoreline. Instead, in a twinkling, it turned and came at them, hips churning, tail straight.

Winona had barely set herself before the thing was on them. She did not waste more energy kicking water. The painter would not let anything short of death deter it again. She swung the bucket again. But in her haste she swung too soon. She missed, and before she could adjust, the cat was right there in front of her, a paw slashing at her midriff.

Winona threw herself backward. Her left foot slipped and down she went, onto her left knee. She wound up at eye level with the cougar, the bucket half in the lake, half out. The creature knew she was helpless. She could have sworn it smiled. Then it surged toward her.

"Ma!" Evelyn screamed. The cougar's tapered teeth were about to shear into her mother's neck, and in desperation Evelyn tried to get around past her mother to help.

Gleaming fangs filled Winona's line of vision. They seemed to fill the whole world, the whole firmament. Frantically, she shoved the bucket at its face—and connected. The bottom smashed into the cat's nose. In mindless fury it bit the bucket, its teeth lancing into the wood like spikes into tallow. The bucket was torn from her grasp.

Winona raised the knife, then paused. The cougar was backing away once more, tossing its head, and the bucket, from side to side. It took a moment for the reason to become apparent. The bucket was stuck! Somehow it had bitten so deep it couldn't get the bucket off! Under any other circumstances the comical outcome would have tickled her. But now she pivoted, grabbed her daughter's wrist, and made for solid ground.

Evelyn giggled hysterically. Never in all her life had she seen such a stupid cat. She couldn't believe she had been afraid of any animal so dumb! Struggling to keep up with her mother, she sprinted from the lake.

Winona angled toward the trail. Off through the pines lay

the cabin and salvation. Her rifles and her pistols were there. Nate had insisted she learn how to shoot years before. Subsequent events had proven the wisdom of his persistence, for she had lost track of the number of times it had saved her life.

The cat was in a berserk frenzy, leaping and snarling and tearing at the bucket. Landing on its back, it rolled against a boulder, the bucket smacking with a resounding *crack*. To Winona's consternation, the bucket tumbled loose. Immediately, the panther was erect and spinning.

They were so close! The trail mouth was a dozen steps away. Yet it might as well have been on the moon, since in two incredible bounds the cougar cut them off. Body crouched, tail whipping nonstop, it growled long and loud.

From the vicinity of the cabin yells arose in the Shoshone tongue. Someone had heard the commotion. Soon warriors would arrive. But would it be soon enough? Winona wondered as she speared the butcher knife at the beast's neck.

The mountain lion ducked, then sprang. Iron sinews that could propel it twenty feet in one jump now carried it up and over her arm, up and over the knife. Winona attempted to counter by twisting and impaling it in the stomach, but it was too swift.

Over two hundred and fifty pounds of tawny terror rammed into her. Raking forepaws caught her on the shoulders. She heard Evelyn screech as she was knocked flat on her back. Pain seared her arms, her chest. As well it should. For astride her was the cougar. It had her pinned.

Winona stared up into a contorted mask of icy-hearted blood lust. The cat had her at its mercy. Teeth glistened white. Saliva rimmed its lips. Its eyes swiveled to her exposed throat, to her jugular, and its mouth parted wider.

"Leave her be!"

Evelyn could never say why she did what she did. Most any other girl her age would have been too paralyzed. Small fists bunched, she went at the cat like a tiny bird protecting another. She punched its back, its side, and although she was much too young to inflict serious harm, she did cause it to turn and fix her with those baleful orbs.

"Leave my ma be!"

The cat was going to attack Evelyn! Winona pushed upward, the butcher knife cleaving in an overhand arc. Steel bit into flesh, rent sinew. In a flash, teeth sank into her right shoulder. Agony racked her from head to toe. She felt moisture on her skin and knew it was her own blood, oozing from the wound. The cougar had bit hard and was gnawing at her as it might on a large bone.

"Maaaaaa!" Evelyn pushed the cat, but it would not let go. Mind awhirl, she did the only thing she could think of. She dashed behind it and seized hold of its tail.

Winona felt strangely numb. She should be resisting tooth and nail, but a most peculiar lassitude afflicted her. When she felt the mountain lion's mouth release her shoulder, she attempted to rise, but her limbs refused to obey her will. As if in a haze, she saw the cat rise up and bend.

Resisting the numbness, Winona lifted her head a few inches. Dread without limit welled up within her. "Evelyn!" she breathed. "Run!"

Evelyn was not disposed to do any such thing. She yanked and yanked to force the cougar to get off, but the stubborn cat stood there regarding her more as a petty nuisance than anything else. "I won't let you hurt my ma again!"

The mountain lion uttered a high-pitched shriek, then reared with its front legs wide. Claws that could shred the thick hide of a shaggy buffalo were poised to do the same to the defenseless child.

Despite herself, Evelyn screamed and let go.

Winona screamed also. From the depths of her soul was wrung the anguished cry of a mother about to lose a child. No more heartrending sound is known, unless it's the wail of someone who has lost a sibling. She wailed and fought to scrabble upright. Traitor limbs hampered her, crumbling when she was only inches off the ground. ''No! Please, no!'' she railed.

For unendurable seconds the tableau was frozen. The mountain lion seemed suspended in midair. Evelyn was rigid, tiny fingers splayed to ward off the inevitable. Winona valiantly battled her lethargy, but her blood had the consistency of mud. Dully glittering claws began their descent.

A distinct thud brought the moment to an end. The cat's head jerked and its body was swatted as if by an invisible hand. It did an ungainly partial somersault, upending as it toppled so that it crashed to the earth facing her, mouth agape, tongue protruding. Confounded, Winona saw blood gush out over its tongue. She noted a hole on the side of its head, a neat hole rimmed by crimson.

Voices clamored. Forms materialized.

An elderly warrior whose hair and clothing marked him as a Shoshone had swept Evelyn into his arms and was examining her. Another warrior, younger and leaner, was sighting down an arrow at the prone painter. Yet a third Shoshone, a veritable giant seven feet tall, bent to help Winona stand. In his enormous grasp she was like an infant.

''Touch the Clouds! Thank you for saving us.''

The renowned warrior grunted. ''It was not I who shot.''

She realized the giant didn't have a gun. Nor did either of the others. Yet she was positive a lead ball had brought the mountain lion down. ''Then who—?''

Hammering hooves announced the arrival of someone else. A big black stallion was brought to a sliding halt and from the saddle flew a handsome, bearded white man whose skin had been so bronzed by the sun he could pass for an Indian himself. A smoking Hawken was in his right hand. Features aglow with love, he took her into his comforting arms.

''Husband!'' Winona exclaimed.

Nate King had seldom been so petrified as when he emerged

from the forest across the lake and spotted his wife and daughter in fierce combat with the painter. He had bellowed for Zach and Shakespeare, who were bringing up the rear behind the greenhorns, then brought the stallion to a gallop and sped on around the lake as if outracing a prairie fire.

Nate had yelled himself hoarse trying to entice the cat to pay attention to him and not those who meant more to him than all the wealth the world had to offer, but neither the painter nor his wife or daughter heard.

He had taken a bead. But he was still out of range when the mountain lion bowled Winona over and bit her. Fuming in helpless rage, he had goaded the stallion to go faster when it was already going as fast as it could.

The Hawken swayed and bounced no matter how tightly he tucked it to his shoulder. Allowing the reins to fall, he guided the stallion by leg pressure alone. Simultaneously, he rose as high as he could for a clearer shot. His heart swelled with pride when he saw his daughter grip the panther's tail. And it just as instantaneously quaked with apprehension when the painter turned on her.

He had been too far away, even then. Too far, and unable to hold a steady bead, thanks to the stallion's rolling gait. Yet if he didn't shoot, if he didn't at least *try*, his daughter's life was forfeit.

So Nate had jammed the rifle hard against his arm, held his breath, lightly applied his finger to the trigger, then stroked it when the mountain lion reared. For unending moments he had watched in tense anticipation. Had he missed? Had he misjudged the angle and distance? Had he struck his wife or little girl by mistake? Would he spend the rest of his days in torment, racked by guilt?

The shot, though, had scored! Now Nate embraced his wife, holding her close. The scent of her hair was in his nostrils, the feel of her warm body the next best thing to heaven on earth. Thin arms wrapped around his leg and he looked down into the upturned face of a perfect cherub.

"Pa! You're back! Was that you who saved us?"

Nate could only smile and swallow the lump in his throat. Raising Evelyn to his shoulder, he gave her the same treatment while thanking his Maker for their deliverance.

"Can't you speak?" Evelyn asked, and giggled. "Cat got your tongue?"

Winona gave voice to a partial laugh, partial soul-tearing sob. Of all the many perils they had faced, this one had come closest to doing her in. Which reminded her. She drew back to inspect her wound, but Nate misconstrued and planted his hungry lips on her mouth.

Evelyn looked at Spotted Bull, who winked playfully. One of the oldest living Shoshones, he was a special favorite of hers. He liked to tell stories and spoil her with gifts. A doll she adored more than any other had been a present from him and his wife, Morning Dove, the sister of her mother's mother.

At that juncture another of Evelyn's favorites galloped up. "Uncle Shakespeare!" she squealed.

The mountain man radiated relief. "Thank God!" Dismounting, he took her from her father. "Bring me the fairest creature northward born that I might shower her with affection!"

Nate straightened and saw a dark stain on his wife's dress. "Damn," he said, seeing the bite and claw marks clearly. Some were deep. He bent to examine them, but her stern expression and a restraining hand on his wrist stopped him. She was scrutinizing the New Yorkers.

"What have we here, husband?" Winona asked, reproach in her tone. Almost to herself, she repeated, "What have we here?"

Chapter Eight

"They're Indians."

"Shoshones, to be exact."

Isaiah Tompkins blinked at the veritable giant who regarded him inscrutably. Touch the Clouds, his host had called him. "They're *savages*."

Nate King controlled his temper with an effort. "They are my family and friends. And I won't abide having them insulted. Remember that."

Verbal flint grated on cold steel. Isaiah saw fingers of fire blaze in the mountain man's simmering eyes and recalled Shakespeare McNair's warning. "I didn't mean to offend you. It's just that, well, they *are* Indians. So I can't help but feel a little nervous."

Nate sighed. Relatively few whites had ever actually met an Indian, yet most were scared to death of them. Lurid horror tales of gruesome atrocities supposedly perpetrated by the red race were to blame. That, and the U.S. government's own unofficial but widely publicized policy to the effect that the only really good Indians were those who had been forcibly removed from white lands. Or were dead.

Rufus Stern had an urge to slap his partner silly. What was Isaiah thinking? They desperately needed the trapper's aid if they were to ever see wonderful civilization again. The last thing they should do was antagonize him. "Yes. Please forgive Isaiah," he interjected. "I'm sure we'll get along just fine with your—er—acquaintances."

Shakespeare McNair could not help but overhear, and sighed. "Young gentlemen," he commented, "your spirits are too bold for your years. You have seen cruel proof of this man's strength. If you saw yourself with your eyes, or knew yourself with your judgment, the fear of your adventure would counsel you to a more equal enterprise."

Rufus deemed it sage advice. "Please. Honest. We'll be on our best behavior the whole time we're here. You can trust us."

Nate wanted to, he truly did, but he had his family to think of. Mixing the greenhorns and the Shoshones was like mixing axle grease and water. The two would never blend perfectly. He looked at his wife, who had not uttered a word the whole trek up the trail to their cabin, and who now stood regarding the newcomers much as she might a roving silvertip griz. "They were stranded," he explained. "Either I helped them or they died."

"No need to explain, husband," Winona responded. There was no denying her man had a kind heart. It was one of the traits that first attracted her to him. But kindness extended blindly sometimes reaped more heartbreak than happiness. A few years ago Nate had brought home another lost pair, a treacherous couple who had tried to slay their whole family.

Isaiah sensed the outcome hinged on the woman's decision. Her beauty shocked him. She was the most exquisite female he had ever set eyes on. And as a rake and a rogue, he should know, having wooed more than his fair share. So lovely was she, he had to be careful not to ogle her in front of her husband. Adopting a suave smile, he said earnestly, "We beseech you, madam. Take pity on us. All of this is so new, so exceptional, we're having a hard time adjusting. But I give you my solemn word that Rufus and I will never deliberately do anything to hurt you or yours."

Winona hesitated. Her natural impulse to protect her loved ones warred with her compassion for those in need. "Very well," she said reluctantly. "You may stay. But only until you are ready to travel again."

Isaiah was so elated, he almost hugged her. "You won't regret your decision, I assure you," he pledged while admiring the silken sheen to Winona's luxurious raven tresses.

Rufus was equally delighted. The sturdy cabin in which the Kings lived reminded him of an uncle's in upstate New York. He couldn't wait to sleep indoors again! To have a roof over his head to ward off the elements and four stout walls to keep out predators and whatnot. He took a step toward the doorway.

"You can set up a lean-to yonder," Nate King said, pointing to the north. The lodges of his Shoshone visitors were to the south. He felt it best to keep them separated.

"Lean-to?" Rufus said, crestfallen.

Shakespeare chuckled. "I'll show you how to make one. It'll keep you as dry and snug as two peas in a pod. Used one myself many a time." Clapping Stern on the shoulders, he said, "Come hither, man. I see that thou art poor."

Rufus did not see what his lack of funds had to do with anything. Yes, he was poor, or he wouldn't have agreed to Isaiah's silly quest to reap a fortune in beaver hides. He allowed the grizzled mountain man to steer him toward a stand of pines.

Isaiah tore his gaze from Winona King and followed. Finding her so attractive bothered him. She was an Indian, and everyone knew Indians were little better than animals. The clergy called them heathens. The government branded them as vermin worthy of extermination. Why, even his own father liked to refer to them as "red scum." So how in the name of all that was holy could he find himself attracted to one?

Nate King turned to his other visitors. Spotted Bull was his wife's uncle. Touch the Clouds and Drags the Rope were two of his best friends. Beyond reared their three lodges. Their wives were off gathering roots, he had been told. "I thank you for coming to Winona's assistance," he said soberly in the Shoshone tongue.

Spotted Bull's wrinkled visage acquired more creases. "What else would we do? Let the cat kill her? I do not want to lose my favorite niece any more than you want to lose the heart you treasure more than your own."

Nate smiled. The ancient one had a flair for colorful speech rivaling Shakespeare's.

Drags the Rope nodded at the horses. "Your hunt was unsuccessful?"

"Not through any fault of ours," Nate responded, then proceeded to relate details. Everyone had been counting on some fresh buffalo meat after weeks of venison. The panther would be a nice change of pace, but there wasn't enough to last very long. "Looks as if I'll have to head out in the morning after elk or bear."

"We will do the hunting," Touch the Clouds said. "You must stay to keep watch over the whites."

Ever since the Shoshones had adopted Nate into his tribe, they always referred to him as one of their own. He was no longer a white man in their eyes. And, truth to tell, at times he *felt* more Indian than white. "I would be grateful."

Unnoticed at the corner of the cabin, Zachary King stared after the would-be trappers and scowled in disapproval. His parents were much more considerate than he would be. Were it up to him, he'd have left the pair on the prairie to perish or survive on their own. He owed them nothing. They were strangers. Worse, they were *white*, and hard experience had taught him the majority of his father's people weren't to be trusted. Most looked down their noses at him. He was a *'breed,* the offshoot of a white father and a red mother. Somehow, that made him inferior, made him the butt of contempt and scorn. When he was younger he had tolerated the hatred, but no more. He was on the threshold of manhood. And as a man, he would suffer no abuse.

Zach was about to turn and take his horse to the corral when he saw Isaiah Tompkins glance over a shoulder. At his mother. For a fleeting instant Zach registered something peculiar in the New Yorker's eyes. Something he could not quite identify. Then Thomas spied him and quickly faced front.

What was that all about? Zach asked himself as he grasped the roan's reins and walked off. He could not say exactly why, but it troubled him. He made a mental note to keep a close eye on the pair. Let his father treat them as brothers. They weren't *his*.

Nate held the cabin door open for his wife and daughter. "Let's tend those wounds," he suggested.

Winona let him have his way. She made no comment as he tenderly cleaned the claw marks and the deeper punctures made by the cougar's sharp teeth. Not once did she flinch or so much as bat an eyelid.

His wife's silence troubled Nate. She was upset but trying not to show it. So was he, at how closely she had come to being slain. The bite on her shoulder had seared into the flesh as if it were so much soft wax. Any deeper and she would have been crippled for life. Using a soft cloth soaked in tincture, he carefully applied a wide bandage. "I'll change this every eight hours or so until the danger is passed."

Winona nodded. Festering infection must be scrupulously avoided. Once it set in, it was next to impossible to curb. Many a Shoshone had lived through a fierce battle or brutal animal attack only to fall prey to putrid poison in the blood.

Finishing, Nate bent lower and kissed her on the forehead.

"I'm sorry. Honest to goodness. I didn't know what else to do with them."

"I forgive you." Winona observed her daughter playing with a doll over by the stone fireplace. "I just wish it had not happened now, of all times."

"Shakespeare and I won't let them out of our sight. There won't be any trouble. I give you my word."

Evelyn approached bearing her doll. A gift from a missionary's wife, it was a fine miniature of a white woman in a long dress and bonnet. Her favorite. She liked it even more than the one Spotted Bull's wife had given her, a perfect likeness of a Shoshone woman complete with a cradleboard and tiny infant on its back. "Can we invite Mr. Tompkins and Mr. Stern for supper, Ma?"

"If you want," Winona answered.

"I do," Evelyn said, grinning. "They can tell us all about life in the place they come from. In a big city."

Winona's lips pinched together. Her daughter's growing fondness for the white way of life was mildly unsettling. She had always taken it for granted Evelyn would one day wed a prominent Shoshone warrior, not a white man. It shouldn't make a difference, though, since *she* had taken a white man as a mate. But deep down, it did. "We will invite them, then."

"Good!" Evelyn clapped her slender hands. "I can ask what all the ladies do." She never tired of hearing the latest about white women. At the last rendezvous she had talked her mother into visiting a party of what her uncle Shakespeare called "Bible-thumpers" to badger the minister's wife with questions.

"Just so you do not make a pest of yourself."

"Never, Ma. I'll be real polite."

Nate was at a counter, washing his hands in a basin. He reckoned it was all right for the New Yorkers to come. The sooner they made plans to send the pair on their way, the better off for everyone.

Isaiah Tompkins dreamed. He was alone in a pristine field of golden flowers. Out of a shimmering rosy haze appeared a silhouette, a figure that ran toward him with outstretched arms. A figure that resolved itself into the spitting image of Winona King. Her long hair flew in the wind and she had a warm smile of greeting on her red lips. Isaiah flung his arms wide to receive her. But she ran right on past him, past him and into the arms of her husband, Nate.

Isaiah swore under his breath as they passionately kissed. He yearned to be sharing her embrace and imagined sweet sensations rippling through him. A rocking motion broke the spell, a motion he couldn't account for until he suddenly opened his eyes and found Rufus's hand on his shoulder.

"Nap time is over, partner. We're due at the Kings' shortly."

Yawning, Isaiah sat up. His head nearly brushed the top of the lean-to they had erected under Shakespeare McNair's guidance.

"What were you dreaming about?" Rufus asked.

"I can't recall," Isaiah lied. "Why?"

"You were groaning and moaning as if you were in seventh heaven." Rufus laughed. "Remembering one of your many lusty wenches, were you? Maybe that one who was partial to dressing all in red?" His friend's fondness for women—*all* women—had always amused him. "Or was it that one who liked to suck on your tongue?"

Isaiah vented brittle mirth. Inexplicably, the jest angered him. Even more so since he immediately thought of Winona King. "Must have been one I'm quite fond of, but I can't remember which."

"You? Fond of any one woman?" Rufus laughed louder. "No female in her right mind would tie her apron strings to you unless she was a glutton for punishment."

"What the hell does that mean?" Isaiah snapped before he

could stop himself. "I'd make as fine a husband as you would, I'll have you know. Better, since I'm not half as naive or a third as gullible."

The venom his friend oozed startled Rufus. Isaiah's lack of interest in marriage had long been a private joke between them. "Don't work yourself into a dither. One day some poor gal will come along and let you sweep her off her feet. More's the pity." Rufus playfully nudged Isaiah to show he was poking fun.

"Let's get ready."

Isaiah dismissed the incident from his mind. He also tried to forget about his dream. But the sight of Winona King, radiant in a resplendent buckskin dress adorned with bright blue beads, literally took his breath away. Entranced, he barely heard her greeting, or the remarks Nate made as they were invited to sit at a table fitted with a genuine tablecloth.

It got worse. Isaiah could tear his eyes from her only with a struggle. Her every movement was grace personified. Her laughter was exquisite music. He feasted on her beauty rather than the food, casting secret glances when no one was apt to catch on—which was not nearly often enough to suit him. He had to exercise supreme caution, with Zach King and Shakespeare also present.

McNair was in a spirited frame of mind. He entertained them by quoting from *As You Like It*. Isaiah, enrapt, barely heard four words until a quote perked his interest.

"... when Nature hath made a fair creature, may she not by Fortune fall into the fire? Though nature hath given us wit to flout at Fortune, hath not Fortune sent in this fool to cut off the argument?" Changing his voice to mimic a woman's, Shakespeare assumed the part of Rosalind. "Indeed, there is Fortune too hard for Nature, when Fortune makes Nature's natural the cutter-off of Nature's wit."

Rufus chortled, more at the mountain man's excellent mimicry than the quote, which he would be the first to admit he didn't fully comprehend.

"Peradventure this is not Fortune's work neither, but Nature's. Who perceiveth our natural wits too dull to reason of such goddesses, and hath sent this natural for our whetstone. For always the dullness of the fool is the whetstone of the wits. How now, wit! Whither wander you?"

Rufus reached for his tin cup, then froze. He had witnessed a stolen glance thrown by his friend at their host's wife. A glance that could not be mistaken for anything other than what it was. It could not be! It simply could not be!

Overlooked by the adults, Zachary King sat in the rocking chair by the fireplace, as outwardly impassive as the stones behind him. Inwardly he seethed, for he had not taken his eyes off of Isaiah Tompkins once all evening, although he had *appeared* to. Young he might be, but not so young that the significance of the white man's secretive antics were lost on him. If not for the conviction his ma and pa would deem it bad manners, he'd have pulled out his butcher knife and buried the blade in the white man's back with no qualms whatsoever.

"The more pity," Shakespeare was saying, "that fools may not speak wisely what wise men do foolishly."

A bell reverberated in Isaiah's skull. He was being a fool himself, to think romantically of a heathen. That she was another man's wife was of little consequence. Since she was a heathen, the legality of her marital status was questionable at best.

For the longest while Isaiah daydreamed about taking her with him back to New York. He flattered himself that with a change of clothes and some lessons in etiquette, he could make a new woman out of her. A white woman, as it were. Another quote brought his reverie to an end.

"Is it possible that on so little acquaintance you should like her? That but seeing you should love her? And loving, woo?

111

And, wooing, she should grant? And will you persevere to enjoy her?''

The seed of an idea sprouted in Isaiah's brain. An idea at once fantastical and ridiculous. An idea so riveting, his breath caught in his throat and his pulse quickened. He would have to be insane to carry it out. Yet when he stared anew at Winona's ravishing features, at her sensational bronzed complexion and the shapely fit of her dress, a stirring in his loins echoed a stirring in his core. Impossibly enough, he wanted this woman as he had never wanted any woman, ever. And— dared he even think it?—*he meant to have her.*

Nate King was listening to his mentor, enjoying the recital. Brawny arms folded, he resisted a temptation to doze now and then. A full belly, the presence of his loved ones, being safe at home, all these factors conspired to fill him with pleasant contentment.

Nate's chin was on his chest when a small hand slipped into his. Rousing, he hoisted his daughter onto his lap. She snuggled warmly against his chest and whispered, ''When will Uncle Shakespeare be done so I can ask about the ladies?''

McNair was about to launch into an appropriate part. Winking at Nate, he quoted, ''I will weary you then no longer with idle talking. Know of me then, for now I speak to some purpose, that I know you are a gentleman of good conceit.'' Leaning back, he clasped his hands. ''Ask away, sprite. Far be it from me to stand in the way of acquiring knowledge.''

''Are you talking to me, Uncle?'' Evelyn asked.

''If there be truth in sight, you are my daughter.''

''Huh?''

Evelyn adored her uncle dearly, but he had a knack for confusing her terribly. Rather than attempt to sort it out, she beamed at their guests and gushed, ''Please tell us about New York City. What are the ladies there wearing? What do they like to do?''

Isaiah waved a hand. ''Ask my friend, child. He would

know better than I, since he was engaged to be married."

"Oh, you were?" Evelyn addressed Rufus. "What is she like? Tell us all about her."

"I don't know . . ." Rufus balked. Discussing his beloved in front of anyone was taxing enough; some matters were too personal. But he could and did describe the type of dresses worn by Agnes and her friends, and the entertainments they enjoyed.

Evelyn listened with vibrant interest. Based on the stories she had heard, she pictured white women as living lives of magnificent splendor. Instead of simple hide lodges, they lived in stately homes. Instead of dirt floors, they had polished wood or plush carpet underfoot. Instead of buckskins they wore fancy dresses made of fantastic materials. They rode around in fine carriages pulled by sleek horses. Days were spent in carefree chats, nights were devoted to the theater and social get-togethers.

To Evelyn's way of thinking, white women had a much better life than the women of her mother's tribe. She would rather spend her days sipping tea and her evenings out on the town than spend her days skinning buffalo hides and her evenings slaving over a steaming cook pot.

But Evelyn had never admitted how she felt to anyone. She sensed it would upset her mother greatly, and Evelyn loved her mother too dearly to ever want to hurt her.

Unknown to the girl, Winona already knew. The persistent questions, the obvious excitement when the subject was raised, persuaded Winona her pride and joy had more interest in the white world than the red. It saddened her, but she didn't make an issue of it. Shoshones raised children to think for themselves. So whatever course Evelyn's life took must be Evelyn's to decide.

The candle on the table suddenly flickered when a gusty breeze swept in through the opened door. Drags the Rope was framed in the doorway. "Touch the Clouds and I hunt elk at sunrise," he announced.

"Spotted Bull does not want to go along?" Nate quipped. For someone who had seen over seventy winters, the venerable warrior was as spry as a youth in the prime of life.

Drags the Rope smiled. "He does. But Touch the Clouds says he must stay and protect our families."

Protect them from whom? Nate was going to ask, and saw his friend's eyes dart to the greenhorns.

"Will you join us, Grizzly Killer? Or you, Carcajou?"

Shakespeare chortled. *Some choice.* He could spend long hours in the saddle tracking wary elk into dense thickets where sharp limbs poked and prodded without mercy. Or he could stay at the cabin and while away the day not doing much of anything except playing with Evelyn and treating himself to Winona's sweet cakes. "Reckon you can manage without me," he said with a straight face.

For Nate the decision was not so easy. As the one who had invited the Shoshones to his valley, he was obligated to ensure they were well fed during their stay. On the other hand, leaving his family while the New Yorkers were there did not appeal to him. Torn by indecision, he gnawed on his lower lip.

Shakespeare had not acquired so many white hairs by dipping his head in bleach. Winking at Nate, he commented, "Fret not, Horatio. I'll watch over things here while you're gone."

"I don't want to impose . . ." Nate began.

"Oh, please." Shakespeare gestured. "Why, right. You are in the right. And so, without more circumstance at all, I hold it fit that we shake hands and part. You, as your business and desire shall point you. For every man hath business and desire, such as it is. For my own, poor part, look you, I'll go pray." Rising, he exited the cabin, his merry mirth wafting on the wind.

"What an eccentric character," Rufus remarked.

"Eccentric? Or mad?" Isaiah said. "Seems to me there's a fine line between the two, and your friend, King, has crossed over it."

Nate would have risen in resentment had Evelyn not been perched on his knee. "That madman, as you call him, has been more like a father to me than my real father. You would be better off, friend, if some of his madness rubbed off on you."

Isaiah casually looked at Winona, then just as casually looked away. "I beg your pardon. I do believe you have a point."

Rufus stood and tugged on his companion's sleeve. "I believe we've imposed on these kind people enough. My thanks, Mrs. King, for the delicious meal. I haven't eaten so good since we left St. Louis."

Evelyn hopped off her father. "You're welcome to join us tomorrow, too," she cheerfully offered. "Aren't they, Ma?"

Winona had no desire to invite them again, but she couldn't deny her daughter. "Yes. By all means. Tomorrow night."

Rufus was about to decline. Once was enough of an imposition. But Isaiah surprised him by venturing, "We'll be delighted, Mrs. King. Wouldn't miss it for the world." Pushing his chair back, he smiled at each of the Kings as he rose. Only the girl returned it. Nate merely nodded. Winona showed no emotion. As for the boy—Zachary gave Isaiah such a spiteful look that it slapped Isaiah with the force of a physical blow.

The moment passed so quickly that Isaiah half doubted it had happened. Puzzled, he opened the door for his friend and strolled out into the brisk night air. The scent of burning wood tingled his nose. From the vent holes at the peaks of the three tepees rose spiraling smoke. In one of them a woman hummed loudly.

Rufus fell into step beside Isaiah. "What was that all about back there?"

"Can you elaborate?"

"Don't play me for a fool. I know you too well. And I saw

the look you gave Winona King. What are you up to?''

"Not a thing," Isaiah said innocently.

Much too innocently, Rufus reflected. "I hope for your sake that you're telling the truth. This isn't New York. Trifle with Winona and Nate will gut you like a fish."

Isaiah didn't respond, which only worried Rufus more.

Chapter Nine

Touch the Clouds and Drags the Rope were waiting when Nate King quietly slipped from the still cabin shortly before daybreak. Both Shoshones wore buckskins, and each had brought a bow and a quiver full of arrows.

It took only a few minutes for Nate to throw his saddle and bridle on the stallion and secure a parfleche filled with his possibles. After looping a lead rope around a trio of packhorses, he was ready to depart.

His friends let him lead the way. It was his valley, his domain. He knew it better than they, knew the haunts of the elk and deer and other creatures that shared his home. Nate rode to the northwest, toward emerald slopes thick with firs and aspens.

No one spoke. Such carelessness would be unforgivable. Nate had cleared the valley of predators, but others, like the mountain lion, often passed through, and always there was the danger of stumbling on a hostile war party.

Not that the woods were quiet. Quite the contrary. Birds

broke into a full-throated avian chorus to herald the rising of the sun. Squirrels awoke to chatter irritably at the intruders below, or to scamper playfully through the upper terrace. Chipmunks chittered and flitted among boulders. Occasional deer either bolted for cover or stood watching the riders in perfect natural innocence.

Nate King breathed deep of the pine-scented chill air and thanked his Maker for his own private slice of Eden. Nate *loved* the wilderness.

A grunt from Touch the Clouds drew Nate's attention. To the west a bobcat was bounding into cover. A rare treat, since by nature bobcats were extremely reclusive.

Drags the Rope pointed to the north where a lone bald eagle soared majestically on the currents high above pristine peaks. A good omen, he thought. Eagles were always good omens. It hinted their hunt would be successful. He took the liberty of mentioning as much.

''Hope you're right,'' Nate said.

Touch the Clouds had nothing to say. Everyone was aware of his outlook on omens. To believe in them was silly. That eagle, for instance, was simply hunting for food. There was no hidden meaning.

Touch the Clouds had always been unique among his people. Even as a child, when he had been twice as big and three times as strong as boys his age.

Inside, he had been different, too. Unlike his brothers and sisters, he had questioned everything. When an elder told him something, he always had to prove it was true before he would believe it himself.

His outlook on omens was typical. His people were always looking for sign and portents, always seeking guidance, always striving to unravel the secrets of the Great Mystery. To him it was a monumental waste.

Life happened. The majestic flight of an eagle was just that, nothing more. When a prairie wolf crossed your path, it was a coincidence. It did not mean someone you knew was going to fall ill.

Touch the Clouds often wondered why he was so unlike his brethren. He concluded his size was the main factor. Early on in life he had learned to rely on himself to the exclusion of all else, to depend on his rippling sinews to spare him from diverse dangers.

An eagle soaring on high would not save a man from a hungry grizzly. But that man's limbs could—with the help of a gun or a bow.

The howl of a wolf would not save someone from roving enemies. But strong arms and a brave heart could.

Omens were for those who had not learned to accept the world for the way it really was. For those who preferred to have their steps directed by unseen forces. For those who had never outgrown the need to constantly look up to a parent for guidance.

Touch the Clouds stared at the eagle, wishing it would venture lower. He needed a new supply of feathers for his arrows.

Presently the hunters reached the lower edge of the green slopes, slopes that would eventually bring them to a particular meadow. A meadow where elk congregated to graze. If they could reach it before the heat of the day drove the herd into shaded timber, they could bring one down, carve it up, and be back at the cabin only a few hours after nightfall.

Nate felt guilty about leaving his family alone with the New Yorkers. He would never have done so except for his unbounded confidence in his mentor. Shakespeare would look after them as competently as he would; better, even.

He had nothing to worry about.

Isaiah Tompkins had hardly slept a wink all night. Try as he might—and he didn't try very hard—he could not stop thinking about Winona King.

He told himself he was being silly. The only reason he gave

119

the squaw any notice at all were the long weeks spent on the prairie. The long, lonely weeks without female companionship.

Isaiah had always liked the fairer sex. Rufus teased him no end about the steady stream of beauties he dated, but Rufus was envious. Could Isaiah help it if he'd been blessed with good looks and an abundance of charm and wit?

It had not been hard for Isaiah to leave his family. It hadn't been difficult for him to bid adieu to his friends. But giving up the nightlife of New York City, and the dazzling women who made that nightlife so richly enjoyable, had been a true test of his mettle.

Isaiah had never gone so long without tasting feminine delights. He sorely missed their laughter, their wit, their buxom bodies pulsing for his hungry touch. They had been practically all he thought about while crossing the damnable plain. Until the horses were stolen.

So his infatuation with the Shoshone woman had to be the result of his yearning. That, and nothing more. Yet knowing the truth did not dispel his craving. If anything, he craved her *more*.

Talk about stupid. While Isaiah had trifled with married women on occasion, one look at Nate King was enough to give any rake second thoughts.

Some husbands meekly accepted being put upon. They might rant at their wives if their spouses were caught being unfaithful, but they were too cowardly to confront their rivals. Other husbands, the ones Isaiah avoided, were just as liable to wring a rogue's neck.

Nate King was in a class all by himself. Isaiah could easily picture the mountain man whipping out that long butcher knife and gutting anyone who dared look crosswise at Winona. Without batting an eye.

But Isaiah couldn't help himself. He couldn't stop dreaming about her, about her supple movements, her white even teeth, her red rosy lips. About the halo of vibrant beauty she radiated.

What was happening to him?

Childish mirth intruded on Isaiah's troubled musing. Over by the cabin Shakespeare McNair was swinging little Evelyn, and she was giddy with glee. Close by, Winona and an older Shoshone looked on, smiling. Isaiah was enticed by how amply Winona filled out the top of her buckskin dress, how the dress jiggled when she laughed. A lump formed in his throat. His skin prickled as if from a heat rash.

"Stop it, damn you."

Rufus had come from the bushes. Isaiah's expression was all too familiar, a look of raw lust Rufus had seen on innumerable occasions.

"I don't know what you're talking about," Isaiah said sullenly.

"Liar." Rufus took a seat under the lean-to, crossing his legs as he sank down. He had almost forgotten about the incident the night before. All morning he had been roving the area, enjoying the splendor, the invigorating crisp mountain air. "I won't warn you again. You're playing with fire. It's bad enough you carry on with married women the same as you do with single women. But *now? Here?* Do you have a death wish? If Nate King doesn't slit your throat, any one of those savages gladly would."

Isaiah resented being lectured. "There's no harm in a man admiring a fine figure of a woman."

"There is when the woman has given herself to someone else and your admiration is plain for anyone to see." Rufus thought of his sweet, loyal Agnes. She'd box his ears if he ever ogled another female.

"I can do what I want. Keep your nose out of it."

"Now you sound like a ten-year-old," Rufus said. "Sure, any of us can do what we please. But we had better be willing to pay the price. Are you?" When Isaiah didn't reply, Rufus continued. "Need I remind you that if not for Nate King, we wouldn't ever see New York again?'' Still his partner sat stubbornly silent. ''Damn, Isaiah. King has been good enough to take us in, feed us, protect us. And this is how you repay him?''

''I haven't done anything.''

''Not yet. But I know you. I know how you think. You're trying to figure out how to have your way with Winona without losing your life.''

''I am not,'' Isaiah responded testily. Though, the truth be known, he had been contemplating that very thing.

''I'm telling you here and now, I want no part of it. Whatever you do, you're on your own. I won't back you up.''

''Did I ask you to?''

Rufus had more to say, but just then he thought that he heard something to his left, off in the pines. No animals were evident, not so much as a chirping bird. Yet he was positive he had heard the faintest of noises. He started to swivel his head when a shadowy shape flitted across a shaded patch, a brief flicker of movement that brought Rufus to his feet, his nerves on edge.

Isaiah stirred. ''What is it?''

''I don't know. An animal, I guess. A big one.''

Standing, Isaiah retrieved his rifle. Their host claimed the valley was the safest spot in the Rockies. But King's own wife had nearly been ripped to shreds by that cougar. ''I don't see anything.''

For tense moments the two of them waited for a creature to appear.

''Rosencrantz! Gildenstern! What bodes you ill? You have the aspect of men about to be consumed by their own fears.'' Shakespeare McNair sauntered to the lean-to. ''Angels and ministers of grace defend us! Be thou a spirit of health or goblin damned, bring with thee airs from heaven or blasts from hell, be thy intents wicked or charitable, thou comest in such a questionable shape that I will speak to thee.''

Isaiah had had just about enough of the old man's relentless raving. "You fool. There's something in the trees."

"You don't say?" Shakespeare rested a hand on one of his pistols and moved to the tree line. A fly buzzed by him. A bee droned among flowers.

Rufus moved forward. "Honestly. I saw it myself."

"To be honest, as this world goes, is to be one man picked out of ten thousand." Shakespeare quoted again one of his favorite lines.

"Huh?" Rufus did not see what that had to do with the situation. "I wouldn't go in there, were I you. Not until we know what it is."

"My fate cries out, and makes each petty artery in this body as hardy as the Nemean lion's nerve." So declaring, Shakespeare jerked his pistol and marched into the cool murk of the heavy growth. Here the trees grew so close together and were so tall, they blocked out most of the sunlight.

Rufus was loath to follow, but his conscience would not let him let the oldster face the creature alone. "Contrary joker," he muttered, sidling into the growth as if into a wall of crackling flames.

"A fellow of infinite jest, of most excellent fancy," Shakespeare quipped. His razor-honed instincts gave assurance all was tranquil. As he'd suspected. Greenhorns had a tendency to imagine monsters where none existed. "So where, exactly, did you see whatever it was?"

Pointing, Rufus said, "Right about there. I didn't get much of a look. Sorry."

"We should never apologize for our shortcomings," Shakespeare said. "We should correct them." Stepping to the side of a regal tree, he gazed upward the length of the towering trunk, then down at the ground.

"What is it?" Rufus asked. The mountain man's brow had knit.

"Just some rabbit tracks," Shakespeare fibbed. For there

123

was only one print, the partial scuff mark of a moccasin, so indistinct that Stern would be blind to its presence. Its size gave Shakespeare a clue to the maker's identity. Puzzlement grew.

"That's all? What I saw was no rabbit. It was big, I tell you."

"Could have been anything," Shakespeare said, turning. "A deer. A trick of the wind and sunlight." Shoving the pistol under his belt, he chuckled. "Many a time I've been scared half out of my paltry wits by a wayward shadow."

"You? I didn't think you knew the meaning of fear."

"Ah. Fright and I are old acquaintances. But I've learned to slam the door in his face when he shows up. Denial is the best antidote for a yellow backbone."

Rufus was glad they were safe. He pivoted to rejoin Isaiah—but Isaiah was gone. Rufus surveyed the clearing and the woodland. "Now, where the devil did that fool get to?" he commented.

Shakespeare was on his way to the cabin. He detoured when Zachary King emerged from the forest a stone's throw away. "Young Troilus, a word with you, if you please." Zach slowed and Shakespeare paced him, clasping his hands behind his back. "I realize it's none of my business, Stalking Coyote. But I'm curious as to why you've been spying on our guests."

Zach feigned interest at Long's Peak. "Why would I bother? I have better things to do with my time."

Shakespeare was sincerely shocked. They had always been the best of friends. Many an evening he had read from the bard for the boy's enjoyment, or recounted tales of his own exploits. To his knowledge, Zach had never lied to him—or been so blatantly evasive as the boy was being now.

"If I knew why, I wouldn't need to ask."

"Do you like them, Uncle?"

The blunt question was typical of youth. Direct and to the point. Shakespeare picked his words with as much care as he would pick berries from a thorny stem. "I don't *dislike* them, son, if that's what you're getting at. They're green as grass and have mud for brains, but they haven't done anything to earn my hatred. I'll be glad when we're shed of them, though."

Zachary studied the man who was more like a grandfather to him than a family friend. "You taught me never to judge a man by the color of his skin or the clothes he wears. Remember?"

Shakespeare smirked. "I seem to recollect spouting off about a great many things. Yes."

"So I was willing to give them the benefit of the doubt. Even after the dark one tried to shoot me just because he thought I was an Indian."

"Stupidity is a common affliction," Shakespeare joked.

"Now I *hate* him."

The intensity of the statement disturbed McNair. "Lord, son. If being stupid was cause for hating, the human race would have wiped itself out ages ago."

"I hate him," Zach repeated.

"Mind telling me why?"

Zach wanted to. But no one else had seen the glance Thomas gave his mother. They would say he was making a mountain out of a molehill, as the saying went. But he knew what he had seen, he knew what it meant.

"I'll keep it a secret just between the two of us," Shakespeare coaxed. He figured it had something to do with the boy's resentment toward all whites for how they generally treated half-breeds. 'Breeds were widely despised, their only "crime" being their mixed ancestry. Highly unfair, but then, life was often unfair. Even cruel.

Zach was inclined to open up. He halted and turned. Then he saw Isaiah Tompkins in the brush, staring toward the cabin. In front of it his mother chatted with Morning Dove. A cold chill blew through him and his stomach balled into a knot.

"Yes?"

"You're imagining things, Uncle. I wasn't spying on them."

"Tell that to your tracks. I saw where you eavesdropped from behind that big fir. But you were sloppy. Stern spotted you."

Anger was to blame. Zach had been so mad on hearing Tompkins accused of "wanting to have his way" with his mother that he had spun and left before he did a rash and violent act. Numbed by rage, he had almost given himself away.

"What's it all about, son?" Shakespeare rested a hand on the youth's bony shoulder. "You can confide in me. Haven't we always been the best of friends? Who kept it a secret when you lost your pa's folding knife? And who kept his mouth shut about that duck you bashed by mistake when you were chucking rocks?"

"I—" Zach began, still observing Isaiah Tompkins. The man licked his lips as might someone about to partake of a delicious feast. Fire burned through Zach's veins, and for a few seconds the world spun.

"What?"

"Never mind. It's nothing."

Abruptly, Zach wheeled and stalked westward, past the cabin, well beyond it and into another belt of pines. He had to put some distance between him and the greenhorns. He had get away or one of them would not live out the day.

"Zach?" Shakespeare called, to no avail.

Winona heard the shout and pivoted.

"You should see what that is about," Morning Dove advised. Having raised five children of her own, she was experienced at recognizing trouble.

The forest swallowed Zach. Shakespeare hurried to overtake him, but the hot-tempered youth was nowhere to be found when Shakespeare reached the vegetation. "Damn," he said under his breath.

"What is wrong with Stalking Coyote?"

Shakespeare averted Winona's probing gaze as he raked the greenery. "Not a thing." Revealing the truth might get the boy into hot water. "Why?"

Winona jabbed him with a finger. "Carcajou. Please. Blue Water Woman is right about you."

"Uh-oh." Shakespeare's wife had an uncanny flair for always being right. "What did she say now?"

"That you could not tell a lie if your life depended on it." Winona traced her finger along his jawline. "Your face always gives you away."

"A pox on my face, then, and on me for being as easy to read as an open book. Provided one knows how to make sense of chicken scrawlings scribbled in smeared ink."

Winona gripped his wrist with more strength than was her custom. "You are avoiding my question."

Conceding defeat, Shakespeare disclosed, "He's upset about your visitors. Other than that he won't say."

"Have they insulted him?"

"With other than their presence? Not that I know. But he won't talk to me."

"He'll talk to me," Winona predicted, and hastened in her son's wake. Hiking her buckskin dress, she broke into a run, moving as lithely as a panther, making scant more noise than would the cat she had clashed with on the lakeshore.

Her shoulder pained her, her cuts were sore, but Winona shut them from her mind. She was more concerned about her eldest. Of late he had become unduly irritable, so peckish that on several occasions his anger resulted in sharp exchanges with members of her tribe.

It had nearly brought her to tears. Stalking Coyote had always been the mildest of boys, the most obedient of sons. Now he was as prickly as a wolverine, as volcanic as a geyser.

So drastic a change must have a cause. Winona had tried to pin it down and failed. In her motherly fashion she had sought to cleverly wrest the truth out, but Stalking Coyote foiled her by being unusually closemouthed.

Winona poured on the speed, running with the unconscious grace of an antelope. She vaulted a log, skirted a thicket. In front of her, high weeds shook. "Son?" she called out. "Come here, please."

There was no answer, and Winona suddenly realized the grave mistake she had made. She had plunged into the woods unarmed and alone. Nate would take her to task for being so foolish.

"Stalking Coyote?"

The weeds parted, revealing a dark figure in grimy store-bought clothes. "Afraid not. It's just me," Isaiah said.

"Oh." Winona was surprised. She had moved too swiftly for most men to overtake her, yet somehow Tompkins had gotten ahead. Unless he had been in the woods the whole time, in pursuit of her son himself. But why would Tompkins chase Zach? "Have you seen my boy?"

"I thought I saw him go this way, yes," Isaiah admitted. He did not add that he had been after the brat himself to learn why the youth kept staring at him as if Zach wanted to slice him from navel to neck.

Isaiah had paused to get his bearings when Winona King hollered. Now he tore his eyes from her supple body to prevent his carnal desire from being apparent and said more gruffly than he intended, "I don't know why, but that son of yours doesn't like Rufus and me much."

To deny it would be silly. So Winona didn't. "I am sure it is nothing personal, Mr. Tompkins—"

"Call me Isaiah."

"—Stalking Coyote is just uncomfortable around white men, Mr. Tompkins." Winona deliberately stressed his last name to show their relationship was strictly formal. Nate had taught her all about white customs. What to do and say. What not to do and say. "Several have mistreated him, and I am afraid he bears a grudge."

The lump was back in Isaiah's throat. Coughing, he looked down at the ground and instead wound up gazing at her long, lovely legs, hugged by the soft buckskin. His mouth watered.

Winona did not understand why the New Yorker flushed scarlet. The day was warm, but not *that* warm.

Isaiah coughed more loudly. "Well, he has no right to be spiteful to Rufus and me. We've never done anything to him."

"I am sure—" Winona said, but got no further. For from the weeds behind the white man had materialized a spectral apparition she barely recognized as her own flesh and blood. Features twisted into a mask of hatred, eyes ablaze, Zach crept up close to Isaiah Tompkins and elevated a gleaming butcher knife.

Chapter Ten

The aspens quivered in the breeze as if they shivered from being cold. But the sun was warm on Nate King's bearded face as he prowled among them, the heavy Hawken clutched in his big hands.

Below lay the meadow. The meadow rich with lush grass, staked out by the elk as their very own. Their special grazing ground. Where cows nursed calves. Where, during rutting season, bulls fought fantastic battles for the privilege of siring those calves.

Nate had never shot an elk here before. The meadow was their sanctuary, their home, and he was loath to violate it. But this time he could not afford to spend precious time searching the timber for lone bulls. He had to get back to the cabin as quickly as possible.

Something was bothering him. He could not say exactly what. A vague feeling that had grown during the day. A feeling all was not well. A troubling sense that he *must* return swiftly.

It was all the more unsettling because Nate was not an intuitive person. He wasn't one of those who acted more on feelings than levelheaded thinking.

He tried to chalk it up to needless fretting. Guilt over leaving his loved ones alone with the strangers played heavily on his nerves. That had to be it, he told himself over and over. But a tiny voice deep inside replied, *No, that is not it, and if you do not hurry home you will deeply regret leaving them.*

Perhaps that explained why he blundered. As upset as he was, he did not keep his mind on what he was doing. He did not pay attention to where he was walking, where he placed his feet. When he was close enough to the meadow to see every individual stem of grass, he stepped on a dry twig that cracked like a pistol shot.

Eleven elk were grazing. At the retort, every last one raised its head toward Nate. A bull near the aspens bugled an alarm, and the rest promptly scattered.

Muttering an oath at his own stupidity, Nate barreled on down the slope and out into the open to get a clear shot. Problem was, half the elk had already gained cover and the rest were in full flight. Bringing one down would take skillful shooting.

Nate dropped onto a knee. Wedging the Hawken against his right shoulder, he fixed a hasty bead on a likely target. He held his breath to steady his aim. Lining up the two sights with the elk, he centered them squarely behind the front shoulders. A lung shot was the most reliable. The animal might run on a short distance, but tracking the scarlet spray would be child's play.

His thumb curled back the hammer. His finger curved lightly around the trigger. He pressed his cheek to the stock. Another instant, and he would shoot.

Then the bull stumbled as if it had set a leg into a rut or hole. It staggered to one side, its momentum propelling it headlong to the earth. The great head came up and it bellowed as it struck the ground. From its nostrils spewed crimson. From its side jutted the feathered end of an arrow. Down on its knees, it looked toward the trees.

From out of the aspens strode a giant.

Touch the Clouds had another shaft notched to the sinew string of his ash bow, but he did not raise the bow. Drawing his long knife with the bone handle, he stepped up to the thrashing elk to cut its throat. Without warning the elk lunged, thrusting its antlers at his broad chest.

Touch the Clouds dropped the bow and knife and seized hold of the antlers before they could impale him. Muscles bulging, he held them at bay while the elk grunted and struggled to drive the spikes into him. It surged upward, legs flailing, the desire to live so potent it lent strength to its massive body.

Touch the Clouds dug in his heels and strained his utmost. His people had a saying: Trees are made of wood and bend in the wind; Touch the Clouds is made of rock and does not bend. He proved that now. Sinews rippling, he held the elk down. It snorted and puffed and scrambled at the blood-slick grass but could not stand. Heaving wildly, it wrenched to both sides.

Touch the Clouds changed tactics. Setting himself, he twisted the rack to the right. The bull resisted mightily. Speckled nostrils flared, eyes wide, it fought back with every shred of its being. But Touch the Clouds would not be denied. He continued to slowly twist, slowly turn that thick neck, slowly bend it until the head was at right angles to the body, and still Touch the Clouds twisted. His shoulders swelled, his neck muscles bulged, the veins on his temples were outlined in stark relief.

Animals can sense their doom. This one did. At the very last, the bull went into a frenzy of bellowing and thrashing and pumping legs that would not function.

Touch the Clouds paused, gathering himself, tightening his

granite frame for the final exertion. Then, throwing his full weight and power into the motion, he levered sharply around.

Twenty yards away, Nate King heard the distinct *crack* of vertebrae being shattered. The elk sagged, the huge form limp.

Touch the Clouds let the head fall. From the bull's lips protruded its tongue—a delicacy by Shoshone standards. Picking up his knife, Touch the Clouds sliced off the tip and plopped it into his mouth.

Nate came over, awed. It had been the most incredible exhibition of raw might he had ever witnessed. "The keeper of the past will paint this for posterity."

Split Nose was the oldest Shoshone alive, older even than Spotted Bull, so old that no one living had been alive when he was born. A skilled artist, for more winters than anyone could remember he had taken it on himself to keep a record of important events in the history of his people. He painted the events on buffalo hides kept rolled and stored against wear and tear. Unraveled only on special occasions, the hides were a source of pride to the whole tribe.

Touch the Clouds shrugged. Being remembered for his deeds was unimportant. He chewed on the tongue as Drags the Rope emerged from the aspens.

"Let's get to butchering," Nate proposed, thinking of those who were the whole world to him. "I'll fetch the horses."

"Then you will go," Touch the Clouds said.

"What?"

"Go to your family. Drags the Rope and I will take care of this bull. We will be back tomorrow afternoon at the latest."

Flying to his family on Mercury's flashing wings would not suit Nate as fast enough, but he balked. "It's not fair to the two of you. I should stay."

Drags the Rope motioned. "We have already talked it over. Does a bear leave its cubs alone when wolves are nearby? Go. We do not mind."

Nate's legs pumped toward the aspens. Over his shoulder

he said, "I am grateful. I will always be in your debt."

"You are Shoshone. You are family," said Touch the Clouds.

A warm, fuzzy sensation filled the mountain man as he jogged into the trees. In under three hours, if he pushed the stallion, he would reach the cabin. All would be well.

He could stop fretting.

Shock rooted Winona King in place. Shock that her son would think to stab someone in the *back*. Shock at the mask of unbridled hatred he wore. Shock that the sweet, innocent boy she always envisioned him as could be capable of cold-blooded murder.

"Noooo!" Winona found her vocal chords and sprang forward at the same moment. Arms outflung, she pushed the white man aside just as the knife swept in a tight arc. The glittering steel meant for him now streaked at her.

Isaiah Tompkins was taken aback. Caught flat-footed, he stumbled. He saw the boy, the knife, and comprehended.

Zachary King was livid. He had seen the white man stalking him, and hidden. As much as he wanted to make the man suffer, he would have stayed hidden and let the man blunder about if not for the untimely arrival of his mother. He saw how Tompkins looked at her. And when the white man stepped from the weeds, Zach rose and padded forward. For his mother's own good he was going to end it, then and there.

Rage pounded at him like a hammer on an anvil. Through a swirling mist composed of shimmering reddish pinwheels he saw the New Yorker, and nothing else. It was as if they were the only two people in all Creation. He focused on a spot between the vermin's shoulder blades and hiked his knife for a fatal stroke.

Tensing, Zach drove the tip at Isaiah Tompkins back. Faintly, as if from a great distance, he heard someone yell. Then the greenhorn was in motion, was being shoved out of harm's way, and his own mother was there instead, her face filling his vision and stabbing dismay clear through him.

He was halfway through his swing. He couldn't stop, not in time, not and prevent the blade from shearing into Winona. But he could, and did, shift on the balls of his feet just enough for the knife to miss her by the width of a whisker. He stood quaking with fear at the close shave, then remembered the cause and turned.

Isaiah Tompkins could not believe that someone who was not even old enough to shave had just tried to kill him. He gawked at the glittering steel, stupefied. Anger welled up, animating his limbs. Anger that changed to fear when the boy pivoted toward him and coiled to attack again. Seething blood lust lit the youth's features, reminding Isaiah of some savage beast of prey. "Now, hold on—" he blurted.

Winona sprang between them. Zach took a half-step, starting to go around her, but she shoved a hand against his chest. "Stalking Coyote! What is the meaning of this? What has gotten into you?"

His mother's voice sheared through the reddish mist shrouding Zach's brain. Straightening, he blinked and recovered his wits. "Mother—" he said, his tongue freezing up. How could he tell her the truth?

Horror clutched at Winona's soul. The boy she had given birth to had grown into a bigot, into someone who would kill out of sheer hatred. "How could you? Just because this man is white?"

"What?" Zach said. It took a few moments for the truth to register. His mother believed he had done what he did simply because of the color of the man's skin. How could she think that of him? Hurt, indignant, he opened his mouth to set her straight—and saw Isaiah Tompkins over her shoulder, staring at the back of her body as if she were the rising sun.

A knot formed in Zach's throat and in his stomach. He came

close to pushing his mother out of the way and finishing what he had started. So very, dangerously close.

"I want you to apologize to Mr. Tompkins," Winona demanded. She did not want the New Yorker to think ill of her family, to go back to New York and tell everyone that people who lived on the frontier were rank savages, as so many already assumed.

The words could not get past the knot in Zach's throat, even if he were inclined to obey, which he was not.

"Did you hear me, Stalking Coyote?" Winona said, more sternly than she had addressed her son in her whole life. "I want you to tell him you are sorry."

Zach would rather rip out his tongue.

"Right this instant, if you please."

Uttering a strangled cry of baffled misery, Zach spun and bolted into the trees. Tears moistened his eyes, and he stifled a series of racking sobs. Fleeing blindly, he ran and ran, stopping only when he was too exhausted to go any farther. His emotions in turmoil, he fell to his knees and rocked back and forth, groaning.

Winona started to go after him, then thought better of the notion. He needed time alone to ponder his misdeed. To think about what he had done, how wrong it was. Her cheeks flushing with embarrassment, she faced their guest. "I am afraid I must do the apologizing, Mr. Tompkins. Please forgive him. He can be a bit spirited at times, just like any boy."

"Spirited?" Isaiah said, and laughed coldly. "Playing pranks is spirited. Sneaking liquor when the parents are away is spirited. Doing things behind their backs is spirited. But what your son just tried to do was rank *murder*. If you hadn't intervened, your son would have buried that knife in my back. You know he would have. So don't stand there and tell me it was something any boy would do."

Winona could feel her cheeks grow a darker shade of red. She felt so awkward, so at a loss. "What you say is true. I assure you, though, it will not happen again. My husband and I will take steps to guarantee your safety for the remainder of your stay.''

It was then, like a bolt out of the blue, that a bright burst of inspiration hit Isaiah. An idea so fantastic, so titillating, so devious, he was amazed at his own brilliance. "I don't know . . ." he stalled, buying time to form his thoughts.

Winona gazed into the undergrowth, wishing she had gone after Zach. Maybe she had made a mistake in not talking to him, in getting him to explain.

"Your husband will be gone for a day or two, I understand," Isaiah said. "Are you going to watch over me every minute of every hour until he returns?"

"Well, I—"

Isaiah did not let her finish. "Of course you can't. Sooner or later that boy will get his chance. And then what? I bear him no malice, Winona. I don't want to hurt him. I would rather he kill me than lift a finger against someone his age." Inwardly, Isaiah chuckled at his supposedly noble sentiments.

Winona was torn. Tompkins had a point. She couldn't be at his side every minute. She could, though, ask Shakespeare to help, and she said so.

Isaiah had to think fast. "I'm grateful, but I don't want to impose any more than I already have. Besides, what if your son tries to shoot me from ambush? McNair might take the ball or arrow meant for me."

Zach would never! Winona was going to respond, but she stilled her tongue. After what he had just done, maybe he would. Maybe she did not know her son as well as she had always taken for granted she did.

"I have a better idea," Isaiah quickly went on, taking advantage of her sorrow and confusion. "My friend and I are eager to head on home. All we would need are three or four horses and a sack of food. And some ammunition."

Winona pursed her lips. The horses could be spared. Nate

had plenty of ammunition. And she had enough jerked venison on hand to last the greenhorns a couple of weeks if they rationed it wisely.

"We could leave first thing in the morning," Isaiah suggested. "We'd be out of your hair. Safe from your son."

The more Winona considered it, the more she liked the idea. Nate had been planning to send them on their way soon, anyway. "I could help you," she offered.

Pure delight coursed through Isaiah. He had her right where he wanted her. "There are a couple of conditions, though."

"Conditions?"

"Yes. It would be best if no one else knew. Not even McNair. If word somehow leaked to Zachary, he might take it into his head to ambush us on our way out."

"Yes, he just might," Winona had to concede.

"One other thing," Isaiah said, and paused. Everything depended on how persuasive he could now be. "Rufus and I aren't woodsmen. We don't know how to track. Or to follow a trail very well. We're rather helpless in that regard. So I was wondering . . ." He lowered his voice. "I was wondering if you'd consent to guide us down to the prairie. I'm worried about straying off the trail and winding up God-knows-where."

Winona mulled the request.

"I know it's silly. Two grown men getting lost in broad daylight. But that trail twists and turns a lot, and the going is steep in spots. I'm sorry we're so helpless. If you'd consent to lead us, I'm sure we wouldn't have a problem."

His humility touched her. And yes, Winona had known other whites whose wilderness savvy was, to put it mildly, downright pathetic.

"We'd be greatly in your debt," Isaiah said. Forgetting himself, he impulsively clasped her hand. "Please. I don't want your son to go through life with the burden of my death on his conscience."

Winona pulled her hand free. His own had been cold and clammy, like the scales of a fish. She overlooked his forwardness, blaming it on his anxiety.

"Please," Isaiah begged one last time.

"Very well."

Triumph made Isaiah want to whoop for joy. Instead, he beamed and gushed, "Thank you, thank you, thank you. I'll break the good news to Rufus. We'll be ready to go at the crack of dawn."

"No, before it," Winona said. "We must leave while it is still dark. I will wake you at the proper time, and have everything in readiness. We will sneak off with no one being the wiser."

"You're an angel, Winona."

"It is Mrs. King to you," Winona reminded him.

"Oh. I'm sorry. Of course. It's just that I'm so excited at the prospect of going back, I can hardly contain myself." Isaiah envisioned the two of them entwined on a grassy glade, and had to avert his face once again so she wouldn't notice his hunger.

Winona misconstrued. Thinking he was overcome with joy, she politely put a hand on his shoulder. "Trust me, Mr. Tompkins. I will lead you safely to the prairie. Before you know it, you will be back with your family and friends."

"I can hardly wait."

Smiling, Winona departed. Once the white men were gone, she would sit down with Stalking Coyote. Have a long mother-to-son talk. Save him from himself. All would be well again. As it had been before the white men came, only better.

Isaiah watched the Shoshone woman leave, his loins twitching at the seductive sway to her hips. God, it had been so long since he had a woman. Since he savored the taste of a luscious female. He had almost forgotten how sweetly delirious it made him. He had been a fool to think he could go without.

Chuckling at his clever deceit, Isaiah hefted his rifle and

trudged after her. A rustling sound to his right reminded him of the sole hitch to his scheme. Whirling, he trained the muzzle on the spot. No one appeared, so after a minute he hurried in a roundabout route to the lean-to. He didn't want anyone to see him anywhere near Winona King. No one must suspect what he was up to. That included his best friend.

Rufus Stern squatted beside a small fire he had kindled to boil coffee graciously given to them by their host. He jumped when a shadow fell across the interior, automatically reaching for his rifle. "Oh! It's you!"

"Miss me?"

"Where the hell have you been? I've been on pins and needles."

"I went for a stroll. Needed to stretch my legs," Isaiah lied, sinking down. "What's wrong with that? You traipsed around earlier, if you'll recall, and I didn't raise a fuss."

"I just worried, is all." Rufus didn't mention his worry was for Winona King. As much as he liked Isaiah, he had to be honest. Where women were concerned, Isaiah was a regular fanatic. Any beautiful woman who caught his eye was ripe for conquest.

A particular instance came to mind. A couple of years before they had been ambling along a city street when Isaiah spotted a ravishing redhead in a passing carriage. He had chased the carriage for four blocks, seeking to learn the woman's identity.

At the time Rufus had thought it comical. There was his silly friend, frantically trying to keep pace while declaring his devotion to a woman he had never met. But damned if she didn't order the driver to stop so she could give Isaiah a slip of paper bearing her name and address. As it turned out, she was married. Yet that did not keep her from dallying.

Rufus hadn't approved. New York swarmed with eligible single women, many as lovely as fabled Cleopatra. Married ones should be left alone. Isaiah had laughed when he made his opinion known, and flatly told Rufus that "married wenches add thrill to the chase, zest to the lovemaking. As far as I'm concerned, any woman is fair game, wed or not."

And now Isaiah had his eyes set on their host's wife. Rufus had seen her emerge from the forest a short while ago. "Were you off with Mrs. King, by any chance? What were the two of you doing?"

"I have no idea where she was. I'll thank you to cease thinking ill of me. Honestly, Rufus. You act as if I'm the worst lecher who ever lived."

Rufus grew defensive. "I never said that!" he complained. And let it drop. His fears were probably groundless. Even Isaiah had limits. To change the subject, he asked, "Did you see anything of the King boy?"

"Nary a hair," Isaiah added to his string of deceptions. It would be nice if he knew where the youth had gotten to, though. Just so he could keep an eye on the firebrand. Zach was the one person who might thwart him.

At that exact second, a quarter of a mile to the southwest, the object of the New Yorker's interest was hunched over, beating the earth with his fists, venting his fury the only way he could think to do so.

Zach was madder than he had ever been. If Isaiah Tompkins had appeared at that moment, Zach would have torn the man apart with his bare hands.

He pounded the ground again and again, pounded until his hands ached and his knuckles were raw. Seething in torment, he slumped forward, resting his forehead on the grass. A groan escaped him.

What was he to do? Going back to the cabin would reap a tongue-lashing from his mother. She simply did not understand. And he could not bring himself to come right out and say that Tompkins had been undressing her with his eyes. She was his *mother*.

Some things were never discussed in the King household. Intimate relations was one of them. His father had taken him aside when he was eleven and imparted the information he would one day need to "carry on the King line." But that was the extent of it.

Gentlemen did not talk about such things in front of ladies. His pa had ingrained the teaching into his skull from early childhood. Women were to be treated with respect. Always. Without exception.

His time spent among the Shoshones reinforced the teaching. Some tribes allowed their women to mix freely with whites, to sell their bodies for baubles. The Shoshones frowned on the practice. Womanhood was held in high esteem. Not quite as strictly as among the Cheyennes, who were known to compel their maidens to wear leather chastity belts. But exalted nonetheless.

It was unthinkable, what Isaiah Tompkins was doing. Zach knew his father would throttle the man within an inch of his life. He contemplated sneaking back, saddling his horse, and going to find his pa. He had a fair idea of where the hunters had gone. But that might take the better part of a day—leaving his mother with no one to protect her other than Shakespeare and old Spotted Bull.

Zach thought of telling his uncle. They had always been close. Yet knowing Shakespeare as he did, Zach suspected the mountain man would "go have a little talk" with the New Yorker rather than do what really needed doing.

No, Zach was strictly on his own. The responsibility for safeguarding his ma was his and his alone. He would stay aloof but close by, ready to leap to her defense.

Holding his knife aloft so the blade shone with mirrored sunlight, Zach King solemnly, silently vowed to take the white man's life if Isaiah Tompkins overstepped the bounds of decency. His rage had subsided. In its place a chilling resolve spread. He would never let down his guard. For as sure as he lived and breathed, the white man was going to reveal his vile nature, and when that happened, Zach would be there.

He could always use another scalp.

Chapter Eleven

The mishap took place an hour after Nate King left Touch the Clouds and Drags the Rope at the high country meadow.

In his eagerness to get back to the cabin, in his anxiety over his family, Nate had been spurring the black stallion at a reckless pace. The big horse was showing signs of fatigue, and by rights Nate should have stopped for a while to let it rest. The forested slopes were thick with impassable deadfalls and crisscrossed by deep ruts and defiles worn by erosion.

No mountaineer or Indian with a lick of common sense would have done what Nate was doing. Part of him kept saying *Slow down!* He was fully aware of the great risk he was taking.

Nate counted on luck, and Providence, to safeguard him. Having survived countless scrapes and close shaves over the years, he felt confident the Almighty would watch over him now.

It didn't help, though, that the sun had dipped behind a high jagged peak to the west, plunging the treacherous slope into premature twilight. Nor did it help that the high firs tended to blot out much of the remaining light.

Nate was vigilant every second. He constantly had to avoid obstacles. A log here, boulders there, elsewhere a rift or an extremely dense thicket.

Lesser horsemen would have been too intimidated to hold to the pace he did. Only someone completely at home in the saddle, someone who had spent the greater portion of their adult life with their feet in stirrups, could fly down that slope as he did.

Ironic, since at one time Nate had harbored a secret fear of horses. When he was small, just a sprout, his father had sent him to a relative's farm in upstate New York for a week. "Just for the experience," his father had said.

The farmer had been a boisterous sort, loud and rough but as sincere as a parson. Nate had been in awe, both of him and the many animals that called the farm home. Cows, chickens, roosters, hogs, goats, geese, turkeys, pigeons, Nate encountered them all.

The cows amazed him. How they could convert grass into milk was a mystery too incredible to fathom. The farmer had taught him how to squeeze the teats, and he had delighted in filling a pail even though much of the milk wound up everywhere except in the bucket.

One of his jobs was to collect eggs every morning. He learned that some chickens did not want their eggs taken, and his hands were pecked sore.

The hogs disgusted him. All they did was eat and sleep and wallow in revolting filth. He had decided never to eat ham again, but the taste proved too irresistible.

Then there were the draft horses. Enormous, thick-limbed animals, they'd scared Nate half to death. To his childish mind, they were like creatures out of deepest Africa. Giants that could crush him with a single misstep. He'd helped harness them, terrified every second that one would turn and bite an arm off.

Later, Nate had ridden a pony. A small, cute little pony he had petted and stroked before being lifted on, bareback. His father's cousin had said not to worry, that the pony was the "tamest animal ever born." Nate had giggled while riding in a small circle, proud of himself. Wishing his father could see.

Then a bee buzzed the pony's head. The next thing, Nate was being bounced wildly, every bone jarred, and the farmer was hollering for him to hold on tight. It had been easy for the man to say, but there had been precious little to grab. The reins were no use. The mane was short and stringy. Nate had tried to wrap his arms around the neck, but he was bucked off before he could get a grip.

Miraculously, he'd been spared serious harm. The farmer had laughed and clapped him on the back, joking that he'd looked like a drunk crow as he flew through the air. Nate failed to see the humor. And for many years his stomach had balled into a knot whenever he was near a horse.

Now those childhood memories washed over him. Nate re-lived again that awful moment when the bee swooped in close to the pony's face. He could feel himself being thrown, feel the air rush past his face.

Almost simultaneously, the big black stumbled on a steep, gravel-strewn incline.

Nate clutched at the saddle horn and pressed his legs against its sides. The stallion dipped violently, pitching him forward. He was flung over its neck. His Hawken went flying. Tucking, he hit on his shoulder and rolled, relieved he had escaped unscathed and praying the stallion had done the same.

He tumbled, unable to arrest his descent. A glancing blow to the side lanced him with pain. Then he seemed to be float-ing—or, rather, falling through empty space. The next impact was enough to stun him.

Dazed, Nate grunted and slowly sat up. He had lost his hat

and one of his pistols. His right shoulder ached terribly. It was much darker, and he discovered why when he craned his neck.

The fall had pitched him into a cleft. A narrow defile, two feet wide, maybe eight feet long, the walls a good ten to twelve feet in height. Sheer walls, as smooth as glass. Frowning, Nate braced his back against a side and straightened. His left ankle protested.

Rising to his full height, Nate stretched an arm as high as he could. His fingers were well shy of the rim. Seeking handholds and finding none, he attempted to climb anyway, digging his fingers into the hard-packed earth. Only, it wasn't as hard-packed as he assumed. It came apart, dissolved in his grip, raining dirt and dust and denying him freedom.

"Son of a—" Nate fumed.

The other side was no better. Nate clawed and scratched, showering more debris to the bottom, gouging furrows in the walls.

He was trapped.

It was every mountain man's worst nightmare made real. No one was around to lend a hand. Shouting would be a waste of energy. Brute strength would not suffice. He must rely on his wits.

Resisting the prick of panic, Nate bent his knees as far as they would bend. Girding himself, he hurtled upward, jumping high—but not high enough. In a shower of loose dirt and pebbles, he fell back.

I have to think! Nate told himself. There had to be a way out. There just had to be. Sidling to the left, he roved the length of the ravine. He found no gaps, no breaks, nothing he could capitalize on.

Nate swallowed hard. He recollected the time Shakespeare and he had come on a skeleton along a remote creek, the wrist bones still caught in the grip of a rusty saw-toothed beaver trap. As best they could reconstruct what had happened, the man had been setting the trap and somehow triggered it on his own arm. Shakespeare guessed a vein or artery had been severed. Weakening fast from loss of blood, the man had been unable to free himself. And there had been no one around to save him.

Scrape marks on the bone hinted at the despair the poor trapper had felt. With his strength waning, he had torn and tugged at the unrelenting steel. Death, Shakespeare reckoned, had been a good long while in coming. Nate had shuddered as they rode away after giving the bones a decent burial.

The secret fear of practically every frontiersman was to die alone, in misery, unmourned, forlorn—it was the ultimate horror.

Lending urgency to Nate's predicament was his growing sense that something was wrong at home. He must get there, quickly. Again he clawed at the side, gaining brief purchase and rising maybe half a foot. It wasn't enough. Gravity pulled him back down. Frustrated, mad, he smashed a fist against the opposite wall.

A noise above drew his gaze. The stallion was moving around. He heard the saddle creak, the plod of hooves. "Here, big fella!" he called, but the horse did not heed. It didn't matter. The stallion couldn't throw him a rope or haul him out. He was totally on his own. "There has to be a way," he declared.

Nate roved the cleft twice more, seeking footholds. There were none. Overhead, what little light existed slowly faded. It was so dark at the bottom that he could barely see his hand when he held it at arm's length.

Worry gnawed at his innards like a wolf gnawing a bone. Nate drew his knife and commenced digging a hole at shoulder height. When it was deep enough, he stretched up onto his toes and dug another. Then, replacing the knife, he inserted his left hand in the lowest, his right in the highest, and levered himself upward.

It should have worked. It should have propelled him high

enough to make a grab for the top. But no sooner did he apply pressure than both holes gave way, the dirt crumbling like so much rotted wood, crumbling to pieces and dumping him back down.

Nate bit his lower lip so as not to swear a blue streak. He must keep his head. He would get out of there! He would! It was just a question of time.

The cleft grew steadily darker.

Rufus Stern was awake but had no idea what had awakened him. Inky pitch clung to his eyes. He blinked but could see no better. Annoyed that he had been roused from a deep sleep so early, he started to roll back over when a hand gripped his shoulders.

"Rise and shine, layabout."

"What?" Rufus squinted and distinguished a silhouette. "Isaiah? What are you doing up this soon? You, of all people. Let me sleep, will you?"

"Get ready."

"Quit babbling and get some more rest." Rufus closed his eyes and smacked his lips. He would deal with the idiot later.

"We're leaving."

"What?" Rufus said sleepily. He couldn't have heard what he thought he heard. They weren't going to depart until after Nate returned. Another two days, at least, according to McNair. Plenty of opportunity for him to catch up on his sleep and recuperate from their ordeal.

"We're leaving," Isaiah repeated.

"Quit it. You're not funny."

Isaiah smacked Stern on the chest. "You dunderhead! Gather up your stuff. Unless you'd rather be left behind." A minute before, Winona had shaken him awake and pressed a finger to his mouth to warn him to keep silent. After whispering instructions, she had melted away without a sound.

149

It struck Rufus that his childhood chum was serious. "What?"

"Do I have to spell it out for you? We're going. Mounts and pack animals are waiting for us in the pines. So get your lazy backside out of those blankets and collect your gear. Me, I'm not staying a second longer than I have to."

"What?" Astounded, Rufus sat up.

"Quit saying that. You sound like a silly parrot." Isaiah had made sure his rifle was loaded and his meager possessions in order the evening before. He had not forewarned Rufus, since his friend was bound to squawk.

Shaking himself, suddenly chill to the marrow, Rufus stared at the quiet cabin and the still tepees, vague masses in the night. "Are you insane? You're stealing horses from the Kings? What do you think Nate will do when he finds out?"

"What do you take me for? One of them is helping us. Now, pull on your boots and let's go."

Befuddled, Rufus blindly did as Isaiah requested. Tugging on his battered footwear, he claimed his leather pouch and his long gun. His legs were unsteady as he rose, his blood as sluggish as molasses. Frozen molasses. "Where to?"

"Follow me."

Rufus took a step and nearly tripped over something on the ground. Cautiously skirting it, he bumped his head on the top of the lean-to. "Ouch," he blurted, and rubbed his scalp as he stumbled into the open.

"Damn it! Quit acting the fool!"

Clawed fingers clamped onto Rufus's arm and he was roughly hauled to the left, into the benighted woods that buffered the homestead. Grass clung to his feet. Roots tried to snag his legs. Groping in stark fear, he thrust his other arm out to ward off branches that might gouge his eyes and face.

"Hurry up!" Isaiah hissed. The fool was making enough racket to raise the dead. And Indians and mountain men were notoriously light sleepers. He would not tolerate any interference, not now, not when he was so close. Should anyone presume to intervene, he was fully prepared to shoot them dead.

Rufus winced when a limb scraped his cheek. "Can't we go a little slower?" he protested, and was dragged *faster*. He did not see why they were rushing so. Prudence called for taking it nice and slow.

Isaiah eased counting how many steps he took. At twenty, he abruptly stopped and looked around. This should be it. But there was no sign of the vision of loveliness or the horses. Had he erred? Had he strayed instead of bearing due east? Taking a chance, he whispered loudly, "Where are you?"

"I'm right here," Rufus answered, and chuckled. "You've got my arm, remember?"

Isaiah was beginning to wonder why he had put up with Stern for so many years, why he had saddled himself with a moron for a boon companion. "Not you," he snarled, and stiffened as an hourglass shape materialized.

"This way," Winona said. It had taken a heap of doing, as her husband would say, but she had packed parfleches with everything they would need and prepared the horses without anyone catching on. A note on the table asked Shakespeare to take care of Evelyn until she got back, which shouldn't be later than noon the next day.

"Winona?" Rufus said as he was led deeper into the vegetation. What was she doing there? Oh, God! Isaiah had mentioned someone was helping them. The unthinkable must be happening! Winona King and Isaiah were running off together! Stealing away in the dead of predawn!

"Wait," Rufus said, wanting to talk, but Isaiah yanked so hard he almost lost his footing. They should discuss it. Isaiah must be made to understand the gravity of his mistake. Nate King would hunt them to the ends of the earth, if that was what it took to get his wife back.

Isaiah wasn't waiting for anyone or anything. Jaw muscles clenched, he hustled Rufus along. From out of the stygian veil loomed the horses. Winona was mounting one. Isaiah shoved Rufus at another, then forked a sorrel.

"We will walk them until we reach the lake," Winona directed. That should be long enough. The soft soil along the shore would muffle the hoofbeats. Once they were on the other side they could ride like the wind.

Rufus reluctantly climbed on. He did not want to go, but neither did he care to be left behind. Nate might blame him in some respect. Or the Shoshones might hold him to account. And that giant terrified him. The previous night he'd had an awful dream in which Touch the Clouds tied him to a spit and roasted him over a roaring fire.

Against his better judgment, Rufus trailed the packhorses as Winona threaded through the trees. Twice he came close to being knocked off by low branches she artfully avoided. She must have eyes like a cat, he mused. The woman was wonderfully competent, more so than most men.

Isaiah stayed close to Winona's mare just to catch an occasional whiff of the minty fragrance she favored. An herbal concoction, no doubt, tantalizing just the same. Presently, they were in the open, a brisk wind from the lake stirring his hair. He could see her now, her beautiful profile, her ripe body. As soon as she escorted them safely to the prairie, that body would be his to savor as he desired. And if Rufus objected, well—Isaiah unconsciously fingered his rifle's trigger.

Isaiah had no qualms about the course he had chosen. He had always been one to put his own interests and desires ahead of others'. Why shouldn't he? Everyone else did it—with a few pathetic exceptions like Rufus, yacks who were sheep in human guise. Maybe that was why he had tolerated Rufus for so long. Stern was like a little lost puppy who needed a master to lead him around on a tight leash.

Isaiah glanced at his friend, debating whether to reveal the truth about Rufus's beloved Agnes. The simpleton doted on her, believed she was God's gift to womanhood. Isaiah knew better. He was intimately familiar with every curve of her rather plump figure; he knew the contours of her body better than the man who was pledged to marry her. Isaiah laughed bitterly.

"Is something wrong?" Winona asked. She attributed the strange mirth to bad nerves. People did peculiar things when they were afraid.

"No," Isaiah answered, and laughed again, gaily. Everything was going right for once. Soon they would cross the valley and start their descent. McNair or the old Indian might try to overtake them, but he wasn't worried. Neither would anticipate a lead ball between the eyes.

Rufus was petrified. Continually glancing over a shoulder, he wore his neck sore before they rounded the south shore. It wouldn't be long before someone showed up. Which spelled trouble. Trouble he wanted no part of.

Rufus didn't think it fair for Isaiah to draw him into the brewing conflict. *He* had no interest in the Shoshone. Sweet Agnes Weatherby was the only woman for him, the only one he'd ever wanted, the only one he would ever need. The Good Lord had blessed their union with perfect love, a love as pure as freshly minted gold, as unshakable as the foundations of the earth itself.

A pink tinge to the eastern horizon goaded Winona to greater speed. So long as they were through the gap that linked the valley to the outside world before the sun came up, they would be fine. She scanned the trees without cease, glad they had gotten as far as they had without incident.

Her thoughts strayed to her husband. Winona hoped the hunt had gone well, that before another day had gone by she would hold him in her arms and lavish hot kisses on his lips and face. What was he doing at that exact instant? she wondered. Still sound asleep? Doubtful, since he had always been up before the crack of dawn.

The important thing was that Nate was safe, with two of

his most trusted friends. She couldn't conceive of any harm befalling him, not with Touch the Clouds and Drags the Rope at his side.

At least she had one less worry.

Nate King wiped his sweaty brow with a dirty sleeve and squinted at the rectangle of slightly lighter darkness above. So close, yet so far. So elusive. All night long he had tried to escape the damnable trench, and all he had to show for it were filthy buckskins, more bruises and scrapes than he could shake a stick at, and a partially buckled wall that had filled the cleft as high as his ankles.

Fatigue was taking its toll. Nate was so tired, he couldn't concentrate. Sagging, he mulled his next move. What was there left to do when he had tried everything he could think of? Digging handholds had failed. Propping his arms and feet against the two walls and shimmying higher had been futile. Scrambling out at either end had proved a waste of energy. One idea after another, all rank failures.

He did not know exactly what time it was, but his internal clock hinted daylight was not far off.

Nate was at the end of his rope. Food and rest would invigorate him, but he might as well wish upon a star. Tilting his head back, he hunkered to think. The feeling of being hemmed had grown unbearable. He had to remind himself that the walls were not going to topple, that he wasn't on the verge of being buried alive.

Scooping up a handful of dirt, he randomly dropped it near his left moccasin. The sprinkles raised pale puffs of dust. Deep in thought, he dropped another handful on top of the first. Then a third, and a fourth. Shifting to survey the far end, he placed his hand on the pile and felt how high it had grown.

High? Nate slowly unfurled and palmed his butcher knife. Moving to a point where the earth was especially dry and loose, he tore into it as if he intended to bore clear to China.

With every sweep of his blade more dirt cascaded around his feet. It rose over his toes, his ankles, and climbed up his pants legs.

Until a few moments before Nate had been wary of causing a total collapse. Now he no longer cared. He would escape or he would die in the attempt.

Nate's arm flew. Dust swirled thick, choking his nostrils, making him cough. Covering his mouth and nose with his other hand, he embedded the knife again and again and again. More and more earth was dislodged. The flow became a torrent. The level rose halfway to his knees and still he dug, dug, dug, even while scrambling higher on the ever-rising pile.

It was a long shot at best. Yet it was his only hope of escape before weakness and hunger brought him low.

Somewhere, the stallion nickered. Nate never slackened his pace. When his right arm grew tired, he switched the knife to his left. Swing, twist, tug. Swing, twist, tug. The same movement repeated endlessly. Repeated until his shoulders throbbed. Repeated until his arms were leaden. Repeated until he did not think he could lift the knife anymore.

But lift it he did. Mechanically forcing his body to obey, Nate dug a cavity wide enough and high enough for Evelyn to stand in. It wasn't enough. The dirt was as high as his knees. It had to be a lot higher. Spearing the knife at the right edge, he gouged deep and jerked. When the blade came away, so did a gigantic portion of the wall.

Nate flung both forearms in front of his face as a tidal wave slammed into him. An enormous weight smashed into his chest, ramming him against the other side, pinning him fast. He swatted and kicked and thrashed, but it was like trying to move through rapidly hardening quicksand.

Gradually the flow dwindled. Nate was up to his arms in dirt, unable to move his legs or body. He had held on to the knife, but it would take forever to dig himself out. Wrenching to the right and the left, he fought to gain enough freedom of

155

movement to clamber to safety. But he was encased in an earthen cocoon. His sinews were useless. Now he was worse off than before.

Exhaustion took its toll. Nate's chin slumped. His skin itched terribly and he was caked with perspiration. Beads of it trickled down his ears, across his neck. A low *thump* reminded him he wasn't alone.

Fifteen feet away grazed the stallion. Reins dangling, it cropped sweet grass, its tail swishing although no flies were abroad to pester it. Nate beckoned and urged, "Over here, Nightwind. Come to me."

The horse would rather eat.

"Come," Nate said gently. Setting down the knife, he held out both hands. "Please."

A flip of its tail was like a slap in the face. "Now!" Nate snapped, raising his voice, forgetting what was at stake. Upsetting it, driving it off, would seal his fate. Instantly reverting to a calm, friendly tone, he said, "Please, boy. Walk on over here and bend your head so I can grab the bridle. Come on, Nightwind. You can do it. I know you can."

The stallion did not budge.

Inspiration prompted Nate to cup his right hand and extend it farther. "How would you like some sugar, Nightwind? Your favorite." He wagged his hand as he often did when offering a real treat. "All yours. What do you say?" At last the stallion lifted its head and looked at him. "Sugar. Remember?" Smacking his lips, he pretended to be eating some. Nightwind whinnied softly.

Nate patiently waited, his life hanging in the balance.

Chapter Twelve

A blazing sun crowned the sky, bathing the foothills in its rosy glow, spreading welcome warmth and stirring myriad wild creatures to life. The sunrise was spectacular, but Isaiah Tompkins did not notice. His sole interest was a different example of rare beauty.

From the moment Isaiah could see Winona clearly, he didn't take his gaze off her. He drank in the sight of her raven tresses and her supple figure much as a parched desert wanderer would drink in the sight of an oasis. God, he *wanted* her. He wanted to touch her, feel her, rove his hands and lips all over her. Just thinking about the act spread tingly warmth throughout his whole body.

Rufus Stern noticed, and his anxiety mounted. He had seen that look on his friend many times before, always right before Isaiah indulged in one of his notorious "conquests." Rufus didn't like it one bit. The Kings had treated them decently. This was not how Nate and Winona should be repaid for their kindness.

Isaiah was acting like a crazy man. Like someone gone mad with unchecked passion. Rufus had always known his friend was unduly fond of the opposite sex. But *this* was carrying it to an extreme no sane man ever would.

Rufus conjured an image of his darling Agnes floating before his eyes, and how he would feel if someone presumed to trifle with her. Why, he would be outraged. He wasn't by nature a violent man, but he would gladly pound the offender to a pulp.

Winona was intent on navigating the trail, on leading the packhorses swiftly lower. Eager to get the chore over with and return to her family, she did not pay much attention to the white men. Not until they were a mile below the gap did she rein up on a grassy shelf to give the animals a brief breather. "We'll rest here a bit," she said, facing the greenhorns.

Rufus was staring at Isaiah in apparent annoyance. Isaiah was staring at her. Winona looked into his eyes—and shock ripped through her. The hungry gleam was unmistakable. She had seen it too many times on other men to mistake it for anything other than what it was. But never this intense.

Quickly turning, Winona acted as if she hadn't noticed. Dismounting, she walked to the edge of the shelf to scout the land below—and to think. For now that she reflected on the few times she had been in Isaiah Tompkins's company, she realized there had been subtle clues all along about how he felt toward her.

How could she have been so blind? Why hadn't she seen them sooner? Winona had been much more sensitive to such attention when she was younger. Being married had made her complacent. She took it for granted other men would let her be.

Winona wasn't unduly worried. She had her rifle and two pistols and a knife. Should Tompkins be brash enough to insult her, she would put him in his place readily enough. Then she heard the metallic click of a gun hammer being pulled back.

"Drop your weapons. All of them. And put your hands in the air."

Winona pivoted and froze. The muzzle of Tompkins's rifle was fixed on her midsection. His finger was on the trigger. "Consider what you are doing."

"I have thought about it. It's all I've thought about since I met you." Isaiah licked his dry lips. He'd seen the flash of recognition when she glanced at him. Regrettable, since it forced his hand, but it couldn't be helped. "Do as I told you."

"You won't shoot me," Winona blustered. "You want me alive. You want me whole."

"Yes, I want you," Isaiah admitted, "but a hurt leg won't hamper us too much." He pointed the barrel at her left thigh. "Last warning."

Winona gauged her chances of leaping aside and firing before he could shoot her. At that close range they were slim. Lowering the Hawken, she gingerly drew both pistols and let them fall at her feet. The same with her long knife.

"Excellent," Isaiah commented. His throat was raw, his body hot. Below his belt was a bulge that hurt. His temples began to pound as he advanced a step, openly ogling the swell of her bosom. At that second in time he wanted her more than he had ever wanted any woman. "We're going into the trees," he announced.

"You're not going anywhere."

Isaiah did not turn his head. There was no need. He knew Rufus had trained a gun on him. "So. The mouse squeaks. Stay out of this. It's none of your affair."

"Like hell it isn't!" Rufus Stern declared. His mind was made up. Just as he would not allow anyone to violate Agnes, he could not sit idly by while his friend did the same to this decent woman, either. Rape was a hideous act. Quaking with indignation, he leaned forward. "I mean it, Isaiah! You set down that rifle this minute and you step away from her, or so help me God I'll blow a hole in you!"

159

Isaiah believed it. Slowly rotating, careful to keep Winona covered, he forced a grin and said, "I should have known you wouldn't have the stomach for this. For old times' sake, Rufe, keep going. I'll catch up directly."

"No. It's wrong. It's vile. I won't let you." Rufus looked at Winona. "I'm sorry, Mrs. King. I truly am. I should have done something sooner."

"You have done fine," Winona said, uncomfortably conscious of the muzzle still pointed at her. She knew that if she bent to grab one of her weapons, Tompkins would shoot. "Disarm him, and we will go back. No harm will come to you. I give you my word."

Rufus nodded. "You heard the lady, Isaiah."

That Isaiah had. The moment of decision was upon him. A distraction was called for, and he had just the thing. "All right, Rufus. You win. I appreciate how you're trying to save me from myself." His grin widened. "It's only fair I return the favor."

"How so?"

"Agnes. Your dearest Agnes."

Straightening, Rufus demanded, "What about her?"

"Remember that time a whole bunch of us went to New Jersey? To the shore? We rented cabins for the weekend and spent the days lying in the sun and swimming, our nights strolling along the beach and roasting corn over a fire?"

Sure, Rufus remembered. There had been six guys and seven girls. Agnes's own mother had served as chaperon, but her rheumatism had kept her pretty much confined to her cabin. "It was one of the best weekends I ever had."

"Remember the evening Agnes disappeared for over an hour? How worried her mother was? How worried you were?"

How could Rufus ever forget? Everyone searched and searched, all except Isaiah, who had gone to town. Agnes turned up safe later on, much to his relief, saying she had taken a long walk, lain down, and fallen asleep. The incoming tide had awakened her. They had shared a laugh over the wet sand that clung to the back of her dress, and her disheveled hair. "What about it?" he asked uneasily.

"Did you truly believe she had been asleep all that time?" Isaiah snickered.

The blood drained from Rufus's face. "No. Agnes wouldn't have."

"Come, now. Surely you suspected? And that was just the first time."

Rufus had been suspicious, but he had chalked it up to an overly jealous nature. Now he saw her periodic absences in a whole new light. Sweet Agnes. *His* Agnes. She had betrayed his trust, despoiled their devotion. A groan fluttered from deep within him, and he bowed his head in despair. "Oh, my love, my love," he said forlornly.

"Oh, you dolt, you dolt," Isaiah mimicked, and shot his best friend in the chest. Rufus was lifted clear of the saddle, flung brutally to the ground, and lay with glazing eyes wide in astonishment.

Surprise slowed Winona a second too long. She lunged for a pistol, but Isaiah was already springing. They collided, grappled. The stock of his rifle drove into her stomach, doubling her in half. Tottering backward, she felt her right foot slide over the edge.

Isaiah clutched at her shoulder. In desperation Winona grabbed his wrist. Neither move was sufficient to keep her from going over the side. Down she went, pulling him after her. A bush snared her legs and she cartwheeled, breaking his hold. End over end she fell, losing all sense of up and down, of where the sky and ground should be.

The slope seemed to go on forever. Finally Winona slid to a lurching halt. Covered by welts, scrapes, and bruises, she stiffly rose onto her elbows. If she could get to her feet and up the slope to her guns before the white man recovered, she would—

A muttered curse sounded in her ear. A hand wound into her hair and jerked her to her knees.

"I nearly broke my neck thanks to you."

Winona caught a slap full across the face. Rocked backward, she covered her stinging cheek and glared at the lecher. Evidently, he had lost his rifle in the fall.

"I'll take the fight out of you." Isaiah sneered. "Then we can enjoy ourselves in earnest."

Like an enraged bobcat, Winona came up off the ground in a blur, her nails searing his neck as her other hand sought the knife at his hip.

Isaiah backpedaled in alarm. He was accustomed to tame women. To docile females who tittered coyly and meekly did whatever he wished. The only time a woman had ever resisted his advances had been when a matron used her knee where it would hurt the most and then left him lying in the dust. Which had been just as well. She hadn't really been his type.

No one had ever fought back as furiously as Winona King. Isaiah was momentarily bewildered. He warded off another raking blow while grabbing for his knife hilt. Like someone possessed, she lit into him with a vengeance, tearing open his chin, then going for his eyes. It was all he could do to keep from being blinded.

Anger flared. Resentment that the squaw would not submit—that she dared to resist her better. Balling a fist, Isaiah rammed it into her ribs. "Damn you, you red bitch!" he hissed.

Acute agony spiked through Winona. Gasping for breath, she teetered. As quick and strong as she was, she was no match for Tompkins in a brute clash. She must flee. Living was more important than venting her spite. Whirling, she ran toward a patch of trees, but she had not taken more than four bounds when arms wrapped around her shins and she was brought crashing down.

"No, you don't," Isaiah huffed.

Winona was flipped over, her chest straddled. She landed a couple of punches that had no real effect, then absorbed several of his that did. Senses reeling, she feebly batted at his torso.

Isaiah chortled. The cuts and bumps were of no consequence. Not now. Not when he was on the verge of fulfilling his innermost desire. Pulse-pounding excitement flowed thickly through his veins. He felt more alive than he ever had, more aroused than at any time in his life. To keep her still he slugged her once more, on the jaw.

Winona's consciousness flickered like the light from a dying ember. She almost passed out. Then she felt his hands where they had no business being and indignation sparked new vitality. Bucking upward, she nearly shook him off.

"Damn you!" Isaiah fumed. He was not to be denied. A punch to her stomach left her too weak to resist. Bending, he gripped the front of her dress to rip it from her body. "Now you are mine!"

The pad of rapid footfalls twisted Isaiah around. Rushing toward him was hatred incarnate. Sunlight glimmered on a polished steel blade. He swept both arms up as the figure smashed into him, bowling him over.

"Leave her be!" Zach King screamed, beside himself with wrath. He had spied on the white men the previous afternoon and evening, then gone to sleep in the hollow of a lightning-scarred tree. Faint commotion had alerted him that something was amiss before dawn. It had stunned him when he saw his mother helping the pair.

Saddling his horse without awakening anyone else had taken longer than he reckoned. He would have liked to sneak into the cabin to fetch his bow or rifle, but he did not want his mother to gain too large a lead. Giving chase, but staying well enough back not to be spotted, he had been on a rise above the shelf when Tompkins shot Stern.

Now, incensed by the sight of the vile scum fondling his

163

mother, Zach fought in a bestial frenzy. They were on their knees, facing each other. He stabbed at his foe's heart, missing by a whisker when the man shifted.

Isaiah produced his own blade. "You stinking 'breed!"

Metal flashed. Zach recoiled, parried, countered, doing as his father and Shakespeare had taught him. In a knife fight it was not strength or the size of the weapon that counted, it was skill, plain and simple skill. Blade rang on blade. Zach deflected a vicious thrust at his groin, sheared at Tompkins's eye without scoring.

The white man outweighed him by a good sixty pounds, but that did not deter Zach. He would not rest until the grass was stained red by the ingrate's blood. Meeting a downward arc halfway, he reversed direction and bit the edge of his blade in deep.

Isaiah cried out. A clammy sensation spread across his right side. The wound was shallow, though, and he ignored it as he rained a flurry of blows on the youth's head and shoulders. Or tried to. For each and every one was blocked. The delay was proving costly. Out of the corner of an eye Isaiah saw the woman stir.

So did Zach, and he smiled. His mother would find a gun and end the fight. And at long last maybe she would understand the reason he had behaved as he did.

Suddenly lashing out, Isaiah drove the youth back. Then he spun and leaped, seizing Winona King as she unsteadily began to rise. Clamping his left forearm around her neck, he jabbed the tip of his knife into her shoulder just far enough to draw blood.

Zach checked his rush. Torn between his hankering to turn the white man into a sieve and worry over his ma, he wavered. "Leave her be!"

Isaiah shook Winona, gouging the knife deeper. "Do you take me for a dunce, boy? So long as I have her, you're in my power. Drop your knife and turn around. And don't dally.''

Indecision gave Zach pause. Once unarmed, he would be at the vermin's mercy. And if he were slain, where did that leave his mother? "I'll do no such thing!" he responded. "Harm her and I'll finish you.''

"You're out of your depth, child," Isaiah taunted. To emphasize his point, he dug a little furrow in the Shoshone's flesh.

Winona flinched and had to bite her lip in order not to cry out. Her shoulder was aflame with pain. She was groggy, her legs mush. Weakly, she tried to grasp the white man's wrist, but he shook her again, so hard her vision swam.

"Enough nonsense," Isaiah warned. "Boy, do as I said or I'll run this clear through." He drilled the cold steel inward a fraction, causing Winona to stiffen. More blood flowed.

Zach could not bear to watch his ma suffer. Flinging his knife away, he elevated his arms. "There! There! I've done as you want. Now stop hurting her!''

Mother and son shared heartfelt looks. Love filled Winona, love for this wild offspring of hers who would rather sacrifice himself than see her harmed. She had never doubted he cared. Even when they spatted, she knew that deep down he bore Nate and her a lasting affection. Here was proof. Evidence so potent it brought tears to her eyes. She longed to reach out and hug him, but she had to be content with letting her eyes mirror her sentiments.

For Zach's part, he was choked by feelings he rarely gave rein to. It made him uncomfortable to show his true emotions. He'd rather hide them. Why, exactly, he couldn't rightly say. But now, for a few brief moments, the carefree mask he usually wore was lowered—until he swiveled as the white man had commanded.

"How touching!" Isaiah spat. They sickened him, these two, with their noble attitudes. He scanned the area for his rifle but couldn't find it. Backing up the slope, he growled, "Don't move, 'breed. Not one finger. Because if you do, your mother dies."

Winona knew Tompkins was bluffing. He wouldn't kill her until he had satisfied his perverse hunger. But she dared not shout it out or he just might cut her again. He was close to losing all semblance of self-control. She could sense it.

Zach risked a glance. His innards churned, but he was helpless so long as the man had his mother.

Where was that stinking rifle? Isaiah fumed. It had to be around there somewhere. He kicked at the high grass, throwing a tantrum. All of a sudden, remembering the squaw's weapons, he chuckled and resumed climbing.

Winona's heels dragged. She couldn't help it. Not only had she been severely beaten, but his arm was choking off her breath, making it nearly impossible for her to breathe. Gasping, she pried at his wrist, but he snarled and dug it in farther.

"Enough, you hellcat! I've taken all the nonsense from you I'm going to."

A reddish haze shrouded Isaiah's vision. His blood pounded in his ears and his chest beat to an invisible hammer. Oddly enough, he felt flushed with raw strength. Every sense was alive. He felt as if he could bend metal bars or tear a grizzly to shreds with his bare hands. *Invincible* was the word he wanted. He felt capable of besting anyone or anything.

Twisting to make sure he didn't stumble in a rut or hole, Isaiah forgot about the boy. Ten feet shy of the shelf he thought to check, and his burning wrath became an inferno. Halting, he shifted the knife to the squaw's throat and bellowed, "Where the hell did you get to, brat? I told you what would happen if you didn't listen!"

On his stomach in the high grass, Zach snaked upward. He wasn't the fool the white man believed. Tompkins was going to kill his mother eventually no matter what he did.

"May you rot in hell!" Isaiah roared. Tensing his arm to

transfix Winona, he got a grip on himself just in time. Killing her would be a waste of soft, tempting flesh. He *needed* her. But he could still use her. Hurrying higher, to the rim, he saw her pistols and her knife, and beyond them her Hawken.

Isaiah had won. Shoving Winona to her knees, he darted to the pistols and bent to scoop them up. Between his legs he glimpsed the youth, charging up onto the shelf, thinking to take him by surprise. Isaiah grinned and, whipping around, bashed the half-breed across the forehead with the barrel of a flintlock.

Zach's legs swept out from under him as the world exploded. Torment racked his noggin, rendered worse by waves of dizziness. Flat on his back, he blinked at a fluffy cloud that a second later was blotted out by the distorted features of the madman.

"I've got you now, boy, right where I want you." Fixing a pistol on the 'breed's brow, Isaiah experienced a thrill nearly as intoxicating as the thrill he would soon experience with the savage's mother.

Death stared Zach in the face. An impulse to scream nearly overcame him, but he did not submit to it. He was Stalking Coyote, son of Grizzly Killer. A Shoshone warrior. He had counted coup. He had killed Blackfeet and Bloods. He did not show fear to an enemy. He did not shriek like a terror-stricken child.

Isaiah Tompkins waited for the boy to grovel. To whine. To beg him to be spared. When it was obvious the 'breed was not going to give him the satisfaction, he brought a boot crashing down on the pup's leg. "Come on, upstart. Let me hear you squeal. Plead for mercy."

Gritting his teeth, Zach stifled another outcry. A true warrior would rather die than display weakness.

"I can't hear you," Isaiah mocked, and stomped on the youth's other leg. When that provoked no reaction, he kicked the 'breed's back and arms. Lifting his leg to start in on the head, he transformed into stone at a flinty threat.

"Enough! I will send you straight to your fiery Hell, white man, if you hurt my son again."

Off balance, Isaiah bent his neck. The Shoshone woman had reclaimed her rifle and was pointing it at his shoulder blades. He entertained no doubts whatsoever that she would shoot. The wonder of it was that she hadn't already.

Winona would have. She wanted to kill this human abomination, to rid the earth of his foul presence. But his cocked pistol was pointed at her son, and she had seen men squeeze a trigger in sheer reflex at the moment of death. "Now it is your turn to put down your weapons. Do it very slowly, Mr. Tompkins. Slower than you have ever done anything."

Isaiah was not about to comply. The setbacks were aggravating, but they only delayed the inevitable. He *would* have her. He was not to be denied. Unexpectedly training the other flintlock on her, he barked, "Don't be ridiculous, my dear. What we have here is a stalemate. If you shoot me, I'll shoot the two of you. Are you a gambler? Will you risk your brat's life?"

What else was a parent to do? Winona began to lower the Hawken. Tompkins had beaten her.

"Finally!" Isaiah crowed. The heady spice of triumph filled him with elation. He would shoot the 'breed, have his way with the squaw, and be on his way before any of their family or friends arrived. By riding the horses in relays he would outdistance all pursuers. He had done it!

In that grand and glorious moment Isaiah heard the crash of undergrowth bordering the shelf. He looked up as an apparition burst into the open, a filthy buckskin-clad apparition in an equally filthy beaver hat. Mounted astride a lathered black stallion, the rider bore down on him.

"You!" Isaiah exclaimed.

Winona's hand flew to her throat. "Husband!"

Zach was on an elbow, gawking. "Pa?" he declared.

Nate King had eyes only for the New Yorker. He had reached the cabin an hour and a half before to find an upset Shakespeare and the note his wife had left. Without delay he'd set out again, in his haste neglecting to switch mounts. He'd about ridden the stallion into the ground when he spied the body of Rufus Stern off through the trees—and seen Isaiah threatening his wife and son.

Shooting the greenhorn never entered Nate's mind. Reversing his grip on his Hawken, he held it like a club, controlling the stallion by his legs alone.

Isaiah Tompkins snapped off a hasty shot. And missed. Throwing the spent pistol down, he clasped the other flintlock in both hands. He wouldn't make the same mistake twice. He took deliberate aim at the mountain man's head.

Winona brought her rifle up. The hammer had been cocked. A stroke of her finger would end it. Then her husband hollered—a rumbling "No!"—and she honored his request by not firing.

Zach shoved into a crouch, fearful his pa was about to be slain. "Try me!" he yelled, flinging himself at the lecher.

Too many! Isaiah's mind screamed. The woman had a rifle. The boy was charging. The father was almost on top of him. Which one should he kill first? In that split second of delay he sowed his undoing.

For in a thunder of hooves Nate King was on his quarry. Broad shoulders rippled, cleaving the air with the Hawken's heavy stock—the air and more, for the thick wood splintered Isaiah Tompkins's skull as if his cranium were an overripe melon.

The last sight Isaiah had was of strangely dark blood flowing over his eyes. The last sound he heard was his own rattling wail. The last sensation he felt was of falling into a mysterious void that gaped like the maw of a gigantic nether beast, of falling and falling without end toward a demonic shape lurking below.

David Thompson

In a spray of grass Nate reined up and vaulted down. His wife was in his arms in an instant, her warm lips against his neck. His son paused, but Nate beckoned and held them both close. "You're safe," he whispered in gratitude. "You're alive."

For the longest while sniffling was the only sound. When, at length, Winona stepped back, the three of them moved to the body of Rufus Stern. "He was a decent man," she said.

"We should make sure the scavengers do not get him."

"We will," Nate pledged.

"One other thing, husband, if you please," Winona said, cracking a smile.

"Anything."

"The next time you want to invite company home, check with me first."

WILDERNESS
The epic struggle for survival
in America's untamed West.

#17: Trapper's Blood. In the wild Rockies, any man who dares to challenge the brutal land has to act as judge, jury, and executioner against his enemies. And when trappers start turning up dead, their bodies horribly mutilated, Nate and his friends vow to hunt down the merciless killers. Taking the law into their own hands, they soon find that one hasty decision can make them as guilty as the murderers they want to stop.

__3566-9 $3.50 US/$4.50 CAN

#16: Blood Truce. Under constant threat of Indian attack, a handful of white trappers and traders live short, violent lives, painfully aware that their next breath could be their last. So when a deadly dispute between rival Indian tribes explodes into a bloody war, Nate has to make peace between enemies—or he and his young family will be the first to lose their scalps.

__3525-1 $3.50 US/$4.50 CAN

#15: Winterkill. Any greenhorn unlucky enough to get stranded in a wilderness blizzard faces a brutal death. But when Nate takes in a pair of strangers who have lost their way in the snow, his kindness is repaid with vile treachery. If King isn't careful, he and his young family will not live to see another spring.

__3487-5 $3.50 US/$4.50 CAN

Dorchester Publishing Co., Inc.
P.O. Box 6640
Wayne, PA 19087-8640

Please add $1.75 for shipping and handling for the first book and $.50 for each book thereafter. NY, NYC, and PA residents, please add appropriate sales tax. No cash, stamps, or C.O.D.s. All orders shipped within 6 weeks via postal service book rate. Canadian orders require $2.00 extra postage and must be paid in U.S. dollars through a U.S. banking facility.

Name_____
Address_____
City_____ State_____ Zip_____
I have enclosed $_____ in payment for the checked book(s).
Payment <u>must</u> accompany all orders. ❏ Please send a free catalog.

WILDERNESS

#27
GOLD RAGE

DAVID THOMPSON

Penniless old trapper Ben Frazier is just about ready to pack it all in when an Arapaho warrior takes pity on him and shows him where to find the elusive gold that white men value so greatly. His problems seem to be over, but then another band of trappers finds out about the gold and forces Ben to lead them to it. It's up to Zach King to save the old man, but can he survive a fight against a gang of gold-crazed mountain men?

___4519-2 $3.99 US/$4.99 CAN

Dorchester Publishing Co., Inc.
P.O. Box 6640
Wayne, PA 19087-8640

Please add $1.75 for shipping and handling for the first book and $.50 for each book thereafter. NY, NYC, and PA residents, please add appropriate sales tax. No cash, stamps, or C.O.D.s. All orders shipped within 6 weeks via postal service book rate. Canadian orders require $2.00 extra postage and must be paid in U.S. dollars through a U.S. banking facility.

Name_____
Address_____
City_____State_____Zip_____
I have enclosed $_____ in payment for the checked book(s).
Payment **must** accompany all orders. ❑ Please send a free catalog.
       CHECK OUT OUR WEBSITE! www.dorchesterpub.com

WILDERNESS

#24

Mountain Madness

$\longleftrightarrow$

David Thompson

When Nate King comes upon a pair of green would-be trappers from New York, he is only too glad to risk his life to save them from a Piegan war party. It is only after he takes them into his own cabin that he realizes they will repay his kindness...with betrayal. When the backshooters reveal their true colors, Nate knows he is in for a brutal battle—with the lives of his family hanging in the balance.

___4399-8 $3.99 US/$4.99 CAN

Dorchester Publishing Co., Inc.
P.O. Box 6640
Wayne, PA 19087-8640

Please add $1.75 for shipping and handling for the first book and $.50 for each book thereafter. NY, NYC, and PA residents, please add appropriate sales tax. No cash, stamps, or C.O.D.s. All orders shipped within 6 weeks via postal service book rate. Canadian orders require $2.00 extra postage and must be paid in U.S. dollars through a U.S. banking facility.

Name_____

Address_____

City_____ State_____ Zip_____

I have enclosed $_____ in payment for the checked book(s).

Payment <u>must</u> accompany all orders. ☐ Please send a free catalog.

CHECK OUT OUR WEBSITE! www.dorchesterpub.com

WILDERNESS

#28
The Quest
David Thompson

Life in the brutal wilderness of the Rockies is never easy. Danger can appear from any direction. Whether it's in the form of hostile Indians, fierce animals, or the unforgiving elements, death can surprise any unwary frontiersman. That's why Nate King and his family have mastered the fine art of survival— and learned to provide help to their friends whenever necessary. So when one of Nate's neighbors shows up at his cabin more dead than alive, frantic with worry because his wife and child had been taken by Indians, Nate doesn't hesitate for a second. He knows what he has to do—he'll find his friend's family and bring them back safely. Or die trying.

___4572-9 $3.99 US/$4.99 CAN

The Lightning Warrior

The Indians call the great white wolf the Lightning Warrior because of the swiftness of his attack. But even the giant Colbolt isn't interested in the massive wolf until Sylvia Baird makes the beast's pelt the one condition for her hand in marriage. She thinks she is safe, but when he returns with not only the pelt, but the wolf itself, and demands his prize, Sylvia's only hope is a desperate flight for freedom. Colbolt sets out in determined pursuit, but he's forgotten Sylvia's newest ally. . .the Lightning Warrior.

___4420-X $4.50 US/$5.50 CAN

WARRIOR'S TRACE
Dodge Tyler

The Kentucky River has long been the lifeblood of American settlers near Dan'l Boone's home of Boonesborough. But suddenly it is running red with blood of another kind. The Shawnee and the Fox tribe have joined together in an unprecedented war to drive the white man out of their lands once and for all. And if Dan'l can't whip the desperate settlers into a mighty fighting force soon, he—and all of Boonesborough—might not survive the next attack.

___4421-8 $3.99 US/$4.99 CAN

T. V. OLSEN

LONESOME GUN

In his younger days, Dr. John Fletcher Styles shot men to pieces more often than he stitched them up. Doc swears to put those days behind him, but sometimes intentions aren't enough. Not when you have a reputation. When a letter from an old flame arrives, begging for his help in a savage mining war, Doc turns her down flat. It isn't long, though, before Doc has an innocent man's blood on his conscience—and a smoking gun in his hand. Then there is no turning back.

___4422-6 $3.99 US/$4.99 CAN

Dorchester Publishing Co., Inc.
P.O. Box 6640
Wayne, PA 19087-8640

Please add $1.75 for shipping and handling for the first book and $.50 for each book thereafter. NY, NYC, and PA residents, please add appropriate sales tax. No cash, stamps, or C.O.D.s. All orders shipped within 6 weeks via postal service book rate. Canadian orders require $2.00 extra postage and must be paid in U.S. dollars through a U.S. banking facility.

Name_____
Address_____
City_____ State_____ Zip_____
I have enclosed $_____ in payment for the checked book(s).
Payment <u>must</u> accompany all orders. ❏ Please send a free catalog.
      CHECK OUT OUR WEBSITE! www.dorchesterpub.com